MIND GAME

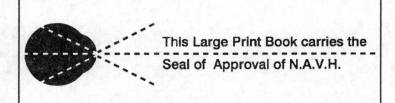

This Large Print Book carries the
Seal of Approval of N.A.V.H.

MIND GAME

IRIS JOHANSEN

THORNDIKE PRESS
A part of Gale, a Cengage Company

Farmington Hills, Mich • San Francisco • New York • Waterville, Maine
Meriden, Conn • Mason, Ohio • Chicago

LIBRARY OF CONGRESS CIP DATA ON FILE.
CATALOGUING IN PUBLICATION FOR THIS BOOK
IS AVAILABLE FROM THE LIBRARY OF CONGRESS.

ISBN-13: 978-1-4328-4448-6 (hardcover)
ISBN-10: 1-4328-4448-2 (hardcover)

Published in 2017 by arrangement with Macmillan Publishing Group, LLC/St. Martin's Press

Printed in the United States of America
1 2 3 4 5 6 7 21 20 19 18 17

MIND GAME

CHAPTER 1

Lake Cottage

The woman's face might be beautiful, but it was also the stuff of nightmares.

And Jane MacGuire just wanted it to go *away*!

She jerked upright in bed, her heart pounding.

She closed her eyes, her hands clenched into fists.

She wouldn't do it again. Not again. There wouldn't be any change from the last time. And if there was a change, what could she do about it?

It was only a nightmare. She sat there in the darkness, every muscle of her body stiff and unyielding. Accept it and go back to sleep, she told herself.

But she found herself reaching for her sketch pad on the nightstand even as she gave herself that very excellent advice.

7

Okay, just *do* it. Get it over with.

She turned on the bedside light and started quickly sketching the woman's face. Same dark flowing hair, high cheekbones, pointed chin, same huge brown eyes, intense, burning eyes, hauntingly familiar eyes, in a face she didn't ever remember seeing before.

Just focus, don't think of anything else but the face you're drawing. Then it would be over and she would be able to go back to sleep.

Maybe.

Because it wasn't quite the same face. The eyes were still intense, but they held despair.

And this time there was blood.

The lower lip of that beautiful mouth was split as if from a hard blow and a trickle of blood was running from it and down her chin.

It was done!

Now leave me alone, dammit.

Jane tossed the sketch pad on the bed and drew a deep, shaky breath.

But there was no question that she wouldn't be going back to sleep anytime soon. She got out of bed and threw on her robe. Okay, get a glass of water and then go out on the porch and get some air.

She padded barefoot to the bathroom and

turned on the light. As she drank the glass of water, she noticed her face in the mirror was as strained as that of the woman in the sketch. Her red-brown hair was rumpled and her jaw was taut.

And her stomach was still churning as she remembered the blood running from the lip of the woman in the sketch.

"I don't *need* this. It isn't fair. Find someone else." She turned on her heel and strode through the house to the front porch.

A moment later, she was standing looking out at the lake. If she'd hoped that staring out at those clear, serene depths would soothe her or give her perspective, it wasn't happening.

All she could think about was the blood.

"Problem?" Eve was standing behind her in the doorway. "You should be sleeping. Your flight leaves at eight in the morning."

"I can sleep on the plane." She turned and smiled at Eve. "You're the one who should be asleep. Michael is the most challenging two-year-old on the planet. Between taking care of him and doing your forensic sculpting work, you need all the rest you can get."

"Nonsense. Michael may be a challenge, but he's pure joy." She came out and stood beside Jane and said quietly, "You didn't answer me. Problem?"

It wouldn't do any good to try to lie to her, Jane knew. From the time Eve Duncan and Joe Quinn had adopted her off the streets when she was ten years old, she and Eve had been so close that anything but total honesty was out of the question. Eve was one of the foremost forensic sculptors in the world, but she was also Jane's best friend. They had been through tragedy and joy together, and now that Eve had given birth to a son, Michael, Jane had been privileged to share that with Eve and Joe, too. "Nothing that I can't handle." She made a face. "Maybe I'm a little sad to be going back to Scotland and leaving you and Joe and the baby. Three weeks wasn't long enough."

"Jane."

"It's the truth." She grinned. "But I was getting to the other." She glanced out at the lake. "I grew up here on this lake and I thought the familiarity would be soothing. It appears not to be happening tonight."

"Why not try me? I'm a hell of a lot better than that lake in the soothing department." Her arm slipped around Jane's waist. "I've been told I have excellent credentials."

"Yes, you do." She felt a rush of love as she looked at her. Eve's face was always intelligent and intriguing, but these days

10

she seemed to glow. "But I'm out in the real world with a career as a budding artist these days. I was trying not to bother you with something that's —" She shrugged. "I just feel helpless. I don't know what I —"

"First, you're not a budding artist; you're totally brilliant," Eve said firmly. "Second, you know there's no such thing as bother when it's family. Talk to me. Or we'll be out here all night."

She meant it, Jane knew. Family was everything to all of them. She drew a deep breath. "Dreams. I've had dreams for the past six nights."

Eve went still. "Cira?"

"No." But it was natural that Eve would jump to that conclusion. At seventeen, Jane had experienced a period when she had dreamed constantly of a young actress from ancient Herculaneum. She had even been so obsessed that she had researched and found evidence that the young woman had actually existed. "Not Cira. But it's a woman." She frowned. "Or girl. At first, I thought she was younger, but now she's different. . . ."

"You're not being clear, Jane."

"*She's* not being clear," Jane said in frustration. "At least when I was dreaming about Cira, I had a story. I knew what was happening in her life. The dreams unraveled, telling me her story. I might have believed I was crazy and it was pure fantasy, but I *knew.* I don't know anything about this woman. All I have is a face. I go to sleep and then her face is there before me. Then I wake up and I have to sketch what I've seen. I *have* to do it." She moistened her lips. "And I think she's scaring me."

"Scaring you? Why?"

"Because I think she's afraid. Oh, she's fierce and angry and bold, but I think she's afraid. And this time there was blood." She swallowed. "And I think I know her. She's . . . familiar."

"You sketched her every time you had the dream?"

She nodded. "I *had* to do it. It was a compulsion."

"May I take a look at them?"

"Why not?" She turned and went back to her bedroom and snatched the sketchbook from the bed. When she got back to the porch, Eve was curled up on the porch swing. Jane turned on the porch light and handed her the sketchbook. "Here she is." She sat down beside Eve. "She. But I feel as if I should know her name."

"She's that familiar to you?" Eve was slowly going through the sketches one by one. "She's lovely. Full of fire and bold-ness . . ." She gazed more intently. "And you're right: The first sketches appear to be of a girl who is younger than in the later sketches. But the background is the same. . . ." She raised her eyes to meet Jane's. "You only mentioned the face, but you sketched in an entire background scene. Snowcapped mountains, garden . . ."

"I didn't pay any attention to the back-ground. I was only concerned with her face. Why can't I remember her? Did I know her when I was a teenager? Is she familiar to you at all?"

Eve's gaze narrowed on the sketch in her hand. "Not really. Perhaps a hint . . ." She shook her head. "Nothing is clicking." She turned to the last sketch and froze. "Blood."

"I told you."

"But you didn't tell me that she thinks she's going to die."

Jane inhaled sharply. "Why do you say that?"

"Because you drew it right here, Jane," Eve said soberly. "I told you that you were a brilliant artist. It's here in front of you. Look at it again. That's why you're so frightened."

Jane lost her breath as she looked down at the sketch. The fear was stark and raw on that face. Boldness, defiance . . . and fear.

Her hands clenched. "I'm afraid because I don't know anything. I'm afraid because I'm helpless to *do* anything. Why do I keep dreaming about her? Why me?" Her voice was shaking. "For all I know, that woman died centuries ago, just as Cira did."

"Or maybe she didn't and is trying to reach you."

"Why me?" she asked again. "I'm not even sure I've ever met her."

"How do I know? Strange things happen. People are chosen. You know that I believe there's a plan for all of us. At times, the plan seems unbearably painful, like when I lost my little daughter, Bonnie. Like the night Trevor, the man you loved, was shot. But sometimes we get lucky and have the chance to make the plan a little brighter for ourselves or someone else." Eve closed the sketchbook. "Maybe you're the only one this woman could reach. You were sensitive to Cira, but she was gone centuries before you were born and there was nothing you could do for her. Perhaps it's your turn to reach out to someone you *can* help."

"You know I've never been entirely sure that I had any actual connection to Cira. Those dreams could have been figments of my imagination."

"Because you're stubborn and a realist

14

who hates to admit to anything that she can't see and touch." Eve smiled. "But those dreams of Cira have dominated you in so many ways. I believe she's as much alive to you as the rest of us in your life. Even when you fight acknowledging that Cira actually existed and reached out to you, you're still drawn to everything connected to her. You spent months on the Internet and in libraries tracking down references to her. When you discovered she might have fled from that erupting volcano in Herculaneum to Scotland, you tracked her down to a connection with the MacDuff clan." She reached out and touched Jane's cheek affectionately. "And you've been at Gaelkar, Scotland, with the MacDuffs for almost two years, trying to find Cira's treasure. Not because you want the treasure itself; you just want proof that your Cira exists."

"But I don't have that proof yet." She looked at the sketchbook. "And if I don't, then maybe I'm just nuts and I need to see a shrink."

"But what if you don't have time to wait for proof?" Eve asked. "Six nights in a row? And each one of these sketches shows an escalation. Something's happening to make her more afraid every time she comes to you."

15

Jane moistened her lips. "Maybe it's already happened. Maybe she's not even alive, Eve."

Eve was silent. "It's possible, I suppose. Do you believe that, Jane?"

"No!" The rejection came instantly. "I don't want to believe it. She wants to *live.* She's out there somewhere. But I could be wrong."

"Or you could be right."

"And what am I supposed to do about that? Look in your crystal ball. All I see is her face."

"And the background. She makes sure that she's giving you the background with every sketch. Study them and see if you can come up with something. Research. Go on the Internet, as you did when you were tracking down Cira."

"It was easier to do research on Cira. That was history."

"And this may be a matter of life and death," Eve said quietly. "Stop being stubborn and do your job, Jane. Isn't that what you were going to do anyway? You're out here fretting and giving yourself arguments pro and con when you know you have to see if you can help her." She paused. "So what's your first move?"

"Eve."

"The Internet?"

Jane sighed. "No, I can start doing that on the plane while heading back to Scotland. I'd like to ask Joe to take one of the sketches to the precinct in the morning and run it through the missing persons database and see if he can come up with anything. She was hurt in that last sketch. Someone struck her. It might be a stranger or a supposed friend or a member of her own family." Her lips twisted. "Who knows? How many times have you run across the murder of a child caused by people who should have been taking care to keep the child safe, Eve?"

"Too many. But this isn't a helpless child; this is a woman who is fighting back." She got to her feet and handed Jane the sketchbook. "And you're fighting back, too. What's the next step?"

"Identify that mountain range in the background. *National Geo* might help."

Eve chuckled. "Listen to you. This has all been simmering in your mind for how long?"

"I told you: I really didn't notice the background." Or did I? Jane wondered. She wasn't even looking at the sketches, and that mountain range was before her, down to the last detail. "Well, maybe I did."

"Maybe you did," Eve said softly. "Choose

the sketch you want to give Joe."

"I will." She made a face. "But he'll probably think it's a waste of time."

"No, you know Joe better than that. He's a realist, too. But he went through that Cira business with you when you were seventeen. And since he's a police detective, he realizes that black and white can sometimes end up gray or even scarlet. He'll get you what you need." Eve leaned forward and kissed her forehead. "And now I'll say good night. If we keep talking, neither of us will be able to function in the morning." She started to turn away and then stopped. "You said you needed to know her name. It's bothering you. So give her one."

"What?"

"Give her a name. Do you remember when I was pregnant with Michael that I felt I had to know his name so that I could be closer to him?"

"I believe this is a little different, Eve," she said drily.

"It doesn't have to be her true name. I give my reconstructions a name before I begin working on them, so that I can form a connection with them."

"I know you do." She had grown up watching Eve work on those pitiful skulls and had known that every one was personal

18

and special to her. "But she may not even exist."

"She'll exist for you if you give her a name. I think she exists for you now anyway." She turned away and headed for the door. "Good night, Jane."

"Good night. Thank you, Eve. I'm sorry to disturb your night. I hope I didn't wake Michael."

"You didn't wake him." Eve turned and smiled at her. "Who do you think sent me out here? He was already restless. I believe Michael was worried about you and sending out vibes. He'll sleep better now that I've done something about you."

"And you'll sleep better," Jane said. The closeness of the bond between Eve and her son was remarkable and far beyond the ordinary. Jane wasn't sure that she knew the full extent of that tie, but she was just grateful that Eve had been given this special child after all the heartache she had gone through after losing seven-year-old Bonnie all those years ago. "Between the two of you, I feel as if I've been railroaded."

Eve's brows rose. "Do you?"

"No, just kidding. As usual, you've managed to cut through all the fog and clarify. You and Michael are a great team."

"With a great deal of help from his father."

Eve blew her a kiss. "See you in the morning."

The next moment, the door closed behind her.

Jane gazed after her for a moment before she looked down again at the sketchbook. She'd been telling the truth. She did feel clearer and more focused now that she'd talked to Eve. Yes, she still had doubts that this dream was anything but pure imagination, but Eve was right: She had to explore before she could take a chance on dismissing those dreams. So research, but don't become obsessed. Look upon it as an interesting exercise.

A name. Eve had wanted her to give the woman a name.

Why not?

She opened the sketchbook and looked down at the first sketch. In this one, the woman looked younger than she did in the later sketches. Maybe only eighteen or nineteen. Still intense, still burning and bold, but somehow more youthful.

A name . . .

Lisa.

The name came out of nowhere.

Not bad.

She looked at the second sketch.

Lisa.

She flipped to the third sketch.

Lisa.

Whatever. She wasn't going to sit here all night and try to think of names when her mind seemed to be stuck on that one. It didn't matter anyway.

"Okay. Lisa it is." She closed the sketchbook and got to her feet. "Now either let me go back to sleep or tell me what I'm supposed to do to help you." She moved across the porch and went inside the house. "I'll take a stab at finding you tomorrow, but I can't promise anything. . . ."

But she could still see that drop of blood trickling from Lisa's cut lip.

And she could see those huge dark eyes staring out at her with fear and a knowledge of her own mortality.

"Well, maybe I'll spend more than just tomorrow," she murmured. "But *help* me, dammit."

Eve was smiling as she passed Michael's nursery. *Satisfied?*

Satisfied.

Jane really can take care of herself, you know. She didn't need us. She would have worked it out for herself.

But you would have gone to her anyway.

More than likely. Now go to sleep, Michael.

21

I will. Only waiting for you . . .

He was gone, slipping away into sleep like the healthy toddler he was.

And thank God he is that healthy, she thought as she opened the bedroom door and glided over to the bed where Joe was sleeping. Though no one could call her son exactly normal, he was healthy and caring and possessed joy, serenity, and an occasional mischievous streak that was wonderful to be around. Okay, so he seemed to sense emotions and disturbance in those around him and could still link with her as he had when she had been pregnant with him. It had been almost as if they were aware of each other's thoughts, as if they were truly one entity. That might fade in time, but for now she cherished that closeness.

She slipped out of her robe and slid into bed beside Joe.

"Everything okay?" He rolled over and took her in his arms. "Michael?"

"In a way." She cuddled closer. "It was really Jane." Her lips brushed his bare shoulder and then she rubbed her cheek on the warmth of it. "She's been dreaming again."

He stiffened. "Cira?"

"That was my first question. No, someone

else. A woman, but Jane doesn't have any idea who she is. She's going to ask you to take her sketch to the precinct in the morning and try to identify her."

"Long shot."

"But you'll do it."

"I'll do it." He made a face. "Maybe we'll get lucky and she'll stop dreaming about her."

"That might not be so lucky for that woman Jane is dreaming about. She may be in trouble." She cuddled closer. "It's not as if this happens that often. Cira has always been the main event, and our practical Jane fought tooth and nail against admitting that dream had any basis in fact. She's fighting this one, too." She paused. "But she's disturbed. She thinks she might know her. I don't want her worrying, Joe. It took Jane a long time to come back after Trevor was killed while trying to save her. She loved him so much, and it scared me that I couldn't seem to help her then. I don't want her spiraling down again."

"You did all you could. Jane just had to have time." He gently stroked the hair at her temple. "And I'll do my best to find this mystery woman as quickly as possible. Definitely no dragging of feet."

"I just wanted to explain. I knew you'd do it."

"Of course, there was no question. Jane is family."

"Family," Eve repeated softly. "I've been thinking a lot about that lately."

"No surprise. It's been less than two years since you gave birth to Michael. You'd be likely to be very family-centric."

"No, that's not it. Or maybe it is. I just feel as if I want to make sure that everything is tight and safe for everyone I love. I want everything that touches them to be just right."

"Not entirely possible." He kissed her. "There's a little thing called fate that we have to look out for. But everything that I can do will be done." He lifted himself on one elbow to look down at her. "And I'll wrestle fate if it comes our way and we don't like it. Anything for you, Eve."

"You're joking. I mean this, Joe."

"I'm not joking. I wouldn't dare." But his face was alight with humor. "I'm just having trouble worrying about the future when I'm so damn happy." He buried his face in her throat. "It's good, isn't it, Eve? Better than ever before," he said thickly. "So don't borrow trouble."

Her arms slid around him. "I'm not borrowing trouble. I feel as if we've been given gifts, and I want to protect them."

"Tell me how."

So that he could go out and battle her dragons as he'd always done since the first day she'd met him. "I'm still thinking about it." She kissed him and whispered, "But I promise you'll be the very first to know when I do."

"It's time for you to leave, Jane." Eve opened the door of Michael's nursery and ruefully shook her head as she saw Jane sitting cross-legged on the floor with her son. "You have a plane to catch. Joe's waiting in the car."

"Just one more minute," Jane said absently as her pencil flew over the sketch she was doing of Michael. "I can finish this once I get to Scotland, but I want to catch . . ." Her voice trailed off as she concentrated on getting the curve of Michael's mouth just right.

"Jane."

"Okay. Okay." She reluctantly closed the sketchbook. "But children change so quickly at this age. I just came in to give him a hug good-bye and I saw the sun coming in the window and his hair looked more red than dark chestnut like it usually does. And then he smiled, and I was lost." She got up and knelt beside Michael and held him close for a moment. "See you next time," she said softly. "You take care of your mother and Joe. Do you hear?"

He cuddled closer to her. "I hear." His small hand touched her cheek. "Jane . . ."

She moved her lips and kissed his palm. "And take care of yourself, too, young man. We can't do without you." She sat back on her heels and looked down at him. So beautiful, with the satin skin that all very young children had. His wide-set eyes were the same tea color as his father's, but his hair was a shade between red and chestnut that seemed to gather light. He was wearing blue jean overalls and a blue shirt this morning. She had to remember how that blue set off his coloring. She'd only had time to draw his face and hair this time.

She gave him another kiss, released him, and stood up. "I'll be thinking about you."

He nodded. "Me, too." His smile lit his face with a special radiance. "See you soon, Jane."

Adorable. She wanted to go back and scoop him up again.

"Jane," Eve said.

"Coming." She turned quickly and left the room, followed by Eve. "It's your fault, you know. You produced that heartbreaker."

"Did I? Joe and I aren't sure how he showed up on the radar. We just thank God for him. When you finish that sketch, I want it."

"If I don't decide to make it a painting instead. Then you'll have to wait until I finish it and put it on exhibition for a few months. I think this one may turn out to be something special. He's looking up at me so inquiringly and yet you'd swear that he had all the wisdom of the ages."

"Maybe he does. Maybe all children do before their vision becomes clouded by life."

"Nah. It's Michael." She grinned at Eve over her shoulder as she reached the porch. "And it's going to make a hell of a portrait. Which will please my agent, since she's not been getting much of anything but landscapes from me for the last year or so. She says that lake in Gaelkar, Scotland, is very picturesque, but she's ready for something different."

"Hasn't she ever heard of Monet's water lilies? I think there're way over two hundred of those. And that lake is mystical. I loved it when I was there."

"I do, too, when I'm not frustrated." She made a face. "I might have given up trying to help MacDuff find the treasure that Cira brought from Herculaneum if that lake itself wasn't such a puzzle. A lake that never loses its mist, that's totally impenetrable?"

"You're the one who had a dream that led MacDuff to think that Cira's gold might be near that lake. You're entirely to blame for MacDuff's being so obsessed."

"MacDuff's been obsessed about finding the treasure for years. He didn't need an excuse. He's been searching all over the world for light systems that could pierce that mist on the north bank, but he hasn't found any yet. The only reason that I was able to come here and spend the last three weeks was that he was going to Perth, Australia, to some lab that's supposed to have had a breakthrough."

"And did it?"

"I'll know when I get back. I figured that it was time that I let you and Joe have Michael to yourselves." She smiled. "I get too comfortable here and I have to remind myself that I have a life and career of my own."

"That's crazy." Eve frowned. "Every moment you spend with us enriches us. We *need* you."

"You also need your space. In a way, you and Joe have started a new life for yourselves. You have Michael and you also took

28

Cara Delaney into your home. I know she's here as often as she can manage to escape from her classes at Juilliard."

"Which isn't that often," Eve said ruefully. "The trouble with bringing a violin prodigy into your life is that everyone wants a piece of her, including her music teachers. We get her for holidays and some weekends when they don't have her doing special concerts. But Cara calls us every other night and that's good."

"Juilliard is in New York. She couldn't study closer to home?"

"She could; she wanted to do that." She shrugged. "But I couldn't let her. It's all about the music with Cara. She had to have the best. You can understand that, Jane. You've heard her play."

"Yes. She's magnificent. I wonder what she'll be like when she's a little older."

"Time flies. She's almost fourteen." Eve made an impatient gesture. "But that has nothing to do with the fact that you've mentally set me up with a family that doesn't include you. Not going to happen. We're all family and that's the way we're going to stay."

"I wouldn't do that. I'm not that much of a masochist. You're stuck with me. But I *will* give you space, whether you like it or not."

She gave Eve a hug and then started down the steps. "I'll call you when I reach Gael-kar. I'll let you know if I have any more dreams about Lisa."

"Lisa?"

"Lisa." Jane glanced over her shoulder. "It seemed right."

"Then it probably is." Changing the subject, Eve said, "You mentioned MacDuff and Jock Gavin several times since you've been here, but not a word about Seth Caleb. Has he dropped by Gaelkar since you went back there after Michael was born?"

"I've seen him once." She tried to make her tone casual. "He and Jock have become good friends. Jock wanted him to look into something for him and he flew in for the day to talk about it." She saw Eve's expression and answered the unspoken question, "Not for me, Eve. He barely spoke to me. Caleb is very cool to me these days."

"Caleb is never cool. Particularly not to you," Eve said drily. "I can see him simmering. I can see him burning. I can see him plotting. I can see him waiting for his chance. Never, never cold. You must have really pissed him off."

Yes, she had, but she didn't want to talk about it with Eve right now. "You might say that."

"And he might have deserved it. But I'm having trouble condemning him for anything these days. Not since the night he saved Michael's life." She added quietly, "I'll always be grateful to him for that, Jane."

"So will I." Her lips twisted. "But you have to be careful about being grateful to Caleb. He's fairly ruthless about collecting on his debts."

"I haven't found that to be true so far. I just thank God that Caleb has that weird ability to control the flow of blood in everyone around him. It saved Michael." She met Jane's eyes. "It even saved you once, Jane. That's two people I love he gave back to me. So until he proves me wrong, I'm going to consider I owe Seth Caleb big-time." She smiled. "Now go get on that plane. I can see Joe is beginning to fret. You'll be lucky if you don't miss it."

"Right." She ran the rest of the way down the steps. "I'll try to get back here for Michael's birthday."

"Oh, I think I might see you before that," Eve said. "You heard Michael. He said he'd see you soon. Michael is usually fairly accurate."

"From the mouths of babes?"

"I've never thought of Michael as a baby except for maybe that first week. He's just . . . Michael." Eve called to Joe as Jane opened the car door. "Stop and bring home Chinese for lunch, Joe."

"Right," Joe said. "And Jane may join us if she doesn't get in the damn car. Stop talking to her, Eve."

"Sorry," Eve said. "She said it was Michael's fault she was late and then I had to ask about —"

"Bye, Eve." Jane was in the car and swinging the door shut. "Love you."

Eve nodded and waved as the car pulled out of the driveway.

Jane watched her as long as she could see her. "She's so happy, Joe. She glows. I've never seen her like this before."

"Neither have I. I believe it's her turn. I just pray it lasts. Because then it's everyone's turn who loves her." He covered her hand with his own and changed the subject. "Dreams, Jane?"

She grimaced. "Yeah, but I'd rather think about Eve. I don't believe that woman I've been dreaming about is anywhere near as happy. I don't even know if she's a real person. Eve thinks I have to treat her as if she is." She handed him the sketch she'd put into a large envelope. "Thanks for the help, Joe."

"What's family for? Now sit back, relax,

and take a deep breath. I'll get you to the airport on time. I just want to take one quick look at the mystery woman." He took the sketch out of the envelope and glanced at it. "Very pretty, but I'm not seeing —" He broke off, his eyes narrowing. "What the hell? Maybe you're right. Familiar. Damn familiar . . ."

Chapter 2

Delta Flight 1037

It was no use.

Jane rubbed her eyes and then impatiently shut down her computer. She'd been combing through search engines and sites for the last four hours since boarding her flight and had come up with zilch. What had she expected? That formal garden could have belonged to any house on the planet. The steepness of the mountains reminded her vaguely of the Alps, but she could be wrong. Even if she was right, the Alps were close to seven hundred miles long and it would be almost impossible to locate a house near them without some kind of clue.

She leaned back in her seat.

I tried, Lisa. I'll keep trying. Maybe Joe will be able to help.

Help me do what? she thought ruefully. She didn't even know why she was having these blasted dreams.

Sometimes people are chosen.

Eve had said that and believed it. It was clear that she thought Jane might have been the one chosen to help this time. Heaven knows how or why. So stop being impatient with yourself and frustrated with Lisa and try to figure it out. Banish the doubts and try to accept that somehow you have a job to do.

Okay, assume that Lisa is trying to get in touch with you for some reason of her own. It would be logical to believe that she is doing it because she can't get help from anyone near her. She has to reach out to a stranger. She is terribly alone.

And both Jane and Eve had received the impression of the danger surrounding her.

Why had Lisa been able to reach out to her? Jane knew psychic power was rare, but she believed it existed. She had known people who possessed it. But why Jane when the only unusual thing about her were the dreams she'd had of Cira? She had told Eve that Lisa was vaguely familiar. Had there been some kind of connection between them that had made it possible for Lisa to contact her?

She opened her sketchbook and studied Lisa's face. It was the eyes, she decided.

Slightly tilted, maybe a little exotic . . . She flipped open the computer again and accessed a search engine that would allow her to check her yearbooks from both high school and the university.

Thirty minutes later, she exited the program and shut down the computer again.

Zero. If she'd ever met Lisa, it hadn't been when she was in school.

Maybe it will come to me, she thought, discouraged. Sometimes if you focused too hard on something, you ended up putting up roadblocks.

But you'll have to do a little more than show me your face, Lisa. You may think I'm a prime candidate because of Cira, but she was a hell of a lot more helpful.

Don't be stupid. She was dead. I'm not dead. It's different.

Jane went rigid. That thought out of nowhere had been defiant and angry and come as a complete shock.

Lisa?

Nothing.

Imagination?

Maybe. Jane knew she might be so tired that she was putting words to the faces in those sketches. She'd been talking to Lisa all day as she'd been working, but she'd certainly not expected an answer.

But it might be that Lisa was becoming desperate and trying to break through to her. So concentrate and try to send a message to her, too.

Which one, Lisa? Imagination or desperation?

Nothing.

But that single bolt of thought had been as if Lisa was monitoring her thoughts and knew all about Cira. And she had expressed one other thing that was filling Jane with profound gratitude.

I'm not dead. It's different.

Somewhere deep inside her the uncertainty that Lisa might possibly be dead had been tormenting Jane.

That was a bit rude, Lisa, but I'm glad you set me straight. Anything else?

Nothing.

Okay, have it your way. She closed her eyes. *I have a couple hours before we land in Edinburgh. I'm going to try to take a nap. You work on it and find a way to let me know what you're trying to tell me. . . .*

San Leandro

"Bitch!"

Lisa's head jerked back at the force of Santara's blow.

37

Pain.

"Did you think you'd get away?" Leon Santara wiped the blood from his wrist, where she'd just bitten him. "You can't last, you know." He hit her again. "You'll have to give in and make the damn call."

She *hated* him.

She shook her head to clear it of the dizziness. "I almost did get away. Next time I will." She glared at him. "And you're wrong: I'll never make that call. I don't care what you do to me."

"You'll make it." He jerked her to her feet and pushed her ahead of him through the hall and up the stairs. "I have my orders, and even if I didn't, do you think I'd let a vicious little snake like you get the best of me? I don't know why they don't let me just cut your throat."

"You know why. You're afraid. You're all afraid."

He muttered a curse as he jammed her hard against the wall while unlocking the door. "You're the one who should be afraid," he said through his teeth. "You're *nothing.* You're just a weak, stupid girl who's going to end up dead if you don't keep your mouth shut. I don't care if you make the call or not. I'll tell them you killed yourself climbing down that cliff."

"No, you won't." Her eyes were blazing. "Because then they won't pay you. Who's stupid, Santara?"

He hit her again.

Darkness.

Lisa was vaguely aware of him pushing her into the room and slamming the door behind her as she fought to remain on her feet.

For an instant she couldn't breathe. Her heart was beating hard.

Stop it. She couldn't let them make her afraid. That would be a victory for them. She was strong and she would only show them strength. So stoke the fierceness and the rage that will keep any fear at bay. Remember every moment of how they have tried to subdue and weaken you since you've been here.

She looked down at her wrists, which were raw and bleeding from the ropes with which Santara had bound her to drag her back up the cliff.

And the healing rage returned in full force.

She would kill them all!

No, she couldn't do it. She'd been forbidden to do it. It was against the rules.

What did she care? He wasn't here. She was alone. She was always alone. He'd made her promise, and then he'd left her. Didn't she have the right to do what she had to do to stay alive?

It would be so easy. . . .

Why should he care if she broke the rule? They wanted to kill him, too. This was all about him. It had always been about him.

But he'd forbidden it. She'd given him her word.

So she couldn't kill them . . . yet, she thought grudgingly. She had to find another way, and that meant trying to reach out again to that Jane MacGuire and make her understand what was important. It was frustrating and she didn't always know what she was doing. The frustration alone made her impatient and angrier.

You listen to me, Jane MacGuire. Hear me! Or I'll have to break my promise.

Done.

Jane drew a deep, shaky breath and dropped her pencil on the drink tray next to her airline seat. She sat there gazing straight ahead. She didn't want to look at the sketch she'd just drawn for a moment. As usual, she needed to catch her breath.

And she was afraid of what she'd see.

When she'd awakened from that short nap, it had been like being caught up in a tornado.

40

Hear me!

The compulsion had been far stronger, more violent, more demanding than the other times.

Oh, I heard you, Lisa.

And now I have to see what I've heard.

She slowly looked down at the sketch.

She flinched.

Darkness.

Anger.

Fierceness.

And the background was no longer a sunlit garden. She was inside a room that was also dark, with only meager light coming from a window across the room. Wooden shelves. Books. It appeared to be a library. Some kind of ebony artifact on the wall. A distressed rough wooden table in the very forefront of the sketch.

She looked back at Lisa's face.

Passion. Fire. Darkness.

And pain.

She had been so shocked by the force and fever of the woman's expression that she had not noticed that there were ugly bruises on her left cheek. First the cut lip, now the bruises.

"What have you gotten yourself into, Lisa?" she murmured.

And then her gaze moved down and she

saw the words written in blood in small block letters on the wooden table in front of Lisa.

He must not come.

Only you.

Fine, nothing like responsibility. Where was she supposed to go? And who the hell was *he*?

Well, she probably wasn't going to be told anything more by Lisa until the next contact. It appeared that Lisa wasn't able to reach her unless she was sleeping, and it wasn't as if Jane could drop off by sheer will alone.

But at least Lisa was trying to be more forthcoming, if that message was any sign. However, she was not being overly diplomatic about it, demanding and angry, not asking, but commanding.

What was she thinking? She was being too hard on a girl who was obviously being abused. And how would she have behaved if she'd been faced with a situation fraught with violence, like Lisa's? She'd always had trouble asking for help, even from the people she loved. What if she'd had to beg a stranger to believe her, perhaps even save her?

Not easy. She might not have been quite so rude, but she could identify with the frustration. Eve had always said don't judge until you walk in someone's shoes.

And maybe this Lisa had never had an Eve or anyone like her. What would Jane have been like if Eve had never come into her life?

She instinctively reached for her phone and started punching in a number. Two minutes later, Joe Quinn picked up the call. "You can't be in Scotland yet, Jane."

"No, about forty minutes out of Edinburgh. I just wondered if you'd been able to access that database yet."

"Give me a break. It takes time. I'm working on it." He paused. "But I keep looking at that sketch and I see what you mean. I feel as if I know her."

"I thought you might. You deal with facial recognition all the time in your job. It's part of your training. But you didn't recognize Lisa?"

"No, and she has a very memorable face. It's beginning to bother me."

"I'm going to e-mail you another photo. It has a different background with a strange-looking wall decoration. Could you maybe add that to your file?"

"Send it," he said, then added, "This is really worrying you, isn't it? Kind of a surprise. I know you'd want to help regardless, but in that sketch, she doesn't come across as being full of sweetness and light. Certainly not someone to touch the heart. But evidently she's managed to touch yours. You have to remember we can only do so much, Jane."

"I know that." She was silent for a moment. "But I was thinking about her and I realized if I hadn't had you and Eve, I might have been as defiant and angry as Lisa is. I was already on my way down that road by the time you took me in."

"No, you weren't. You were always tough, but not belligerent. You survived the streets and would have come out on top regardless of who you had in your corner."

"Bullshit. I was incredibly lucky. Now it seems I have to give back." She added lightly, "Eve thinks I was chosen. So help me find this girl so I can do what I need to do. Okay?"

He chuckled. "It shall be done. Send me the new sketch. Bye, Jane." He hung up.

She took a photo of the sketch and e-mailed it to Joe. Then she sat there looking down at that face. Definitely not sweet or gentle, as Joe had commented. But the more she gazed at it, the more she found herself drawn. All that fire and passion and defiance. Warrior . . . Lisa looked like a warrior who had been attacked, taken down, but never surrendered.

Only you.

Her finger traced the words on the sketch.

Okay, it's a deal. I'll help you out. But you'd better work on an attitude adjustment. Understand?

Edinburgh Airport

Jock Gavin was waiting when Jane walked out of customs. His smile lit his face as he gave her a hug. "The laird asked me to come and pick you up. I think he was afraid that you'd go running back to your gallery in London instead of coming back to Gaelkar. MacDuff is sure that he's found the right lights this time. It's some new space-age technology."

MacDuff had been trying for years, without success, to find a lighting system that would pierce the heavy mist on the north side of the lake, and permit them to explore and hunt for the treasure in that area. "And what do you think?"

He shrugged. "I hope it's true. You know MacDuff needs the money. It takes a fortune every year to keep MacDuff's Run a private residence and not have to turn it over to the National Trust." He picked up her two suitcases and headed for the exit. "We'll set up the lights tomorrow and check them out. But he wants you there in case we can move forward along the north bank."

"I might not be of any use," Jane said. "I've always told him that, Jock."

"Aye, but he thinks you're his lucky rabbit's foot." Jock's face was full of mischief as he turned to her when they reached his car. "Though I've always thought that concept a little unpleasant and certainly unfair to the poor rabbit. Ever since the two of you discovered each other when you were both doing research on Cira, the founder of MacDuff's clan, he's been sure you're kin to one of his ancestors."

"I'm no such thing," she said flatly. "I'm very happy with who I am. And that's not Scottish aristocracy."

"Be who you wish to be," Jock said as he stored her suitcases in the trunk. "As long as it's my friend." He slammed the trunk shut. "I won't give that up, Jane." He opened the car door for her. "Now get in and I'll see if I can find a good place to have tea on the way to Gaelkar. Airplane food is generally ho-hum at best."

He was smiling again, and she found herself smiling back. It was almost impossible not to smile at Jock. He was possibly the most beautiful human being she had ever seen. She had thought that when she had first met him as a young boy, and he was even more riveting now. He was a tall, lithe young man with fair hair and silvery blue eyes and there was a strength to his symmetrical features that doubled their high impact. "I'd like that, if you don't think that MacDuff will be too impatient about showing off his space-age lights."

"He needs to be kept under control," Jock said lightly. "Everyone kowtows to the laird, and I consider it my duty to make him realize that even an earl has his limits." He started the car. "There's a small tearoom on the grounds of a castle on the way. . . ."

Jock was joking. No one loved MacDuff more than Jock Gavin. They had been friends for years. Jock had been the son of the housekeeper at MacDuff's Run and he had grown up running in and out of the castle. And though MacDuff had been older, they had become like brothers. They still were, and there was nothing Jock wouldn't do for MacDuff. "Did you go to Australia with him?"

He shook his head. "I wasn't needed. I decided to go to MacDuff's Run and check it out while MacDuff was gone." He added grimly, "And then I went on to New York to make sure that the investments MacDuff and I have funded there were being handled properly. The broker was being careless and I had to make certain he wasn't also being criminal. I wasn't about to let MacDuff lose money." He shrugged. "But it only took one meeting to straighten him out. There won't be any more problems."

"I'm sure there won't," Jane said drily. He had probably terrified the man. These days, Jock could be everything that was warm and charismatic on the surface. It was only when he was angry or upset that he became the Jock that she had first met all those years ago at MacDuff's Run. He had run away from home to see the world when he was fifteen and the world he'd seen had been a horror story. He'd become the subject of mind-control experiments conducted by Thomas Reilly, a terrorist who was trying to develop the perfect assassin. In Jock he had reached his prime goal, and the body count had been horrifying. By the time MacDuff had found Jock, he was in a sanitarium after trying to commit suicide, and could barely function mentally. It had taken years for him to come back to something close to normalcy, and Jane was aware that buried deadliness might be unearthed at any moment. "And did your broker turn out to be a crook?"

"Marginally." Jock smiled. "But after our discussion, he made restitution to MacDuff and me and seven other clients out of his own accounts."

"Did you fire him?"

"No, he's brilliant. He's going to make us a pot of money. The reason I set up the portfolio was just in case MacDuff doesn't find Cira's treasure. It was insurance. I can't let him lose MacDuff's Run."

"And you'd rather deal with someone who came close to cheating you?"

"*Close* is the key word. It won't happen again." He met her gaze and his silver eyes were ice-cold. "He understood the consequences. I explained that I'm very protective of my friends."

"Did MacDuff know what you were doing?"

"It wasn't necessary. Why bother him with something that I could handle myself? It would only have worried him."

She nodded. "Because MacDuff is protective, too."

His lips twisted. "And he likes to keep me away from temptation. He's never sure if I'm going to break the chains he's hammered to keep me in check."

"He cares about you," she said gently.

"You're worth caring about, Jock."

"Am I? I suppose I do have a few valuable qualities." His smile was suddenly brilliant. "Or you wouldn't waste your time being my friend. I'm glad you're back, Jane. It's time we wound up this search for Cira's gold. MacDuff needs to get on with his life."

"And what about you?"

"I keep myself busy. I have a few degrees behind my name these days. That makes MacDuff happy. He knows where my real talent lies and he's always hoping that it will be submerged by higher learning." He shook his head. "Now stop frowning. We both know that I'm right. I accept it. I am what I am."

"You don't know who you are, yet." She paused. "When you were in New York, did you visit Cara at Juilliard?"

"Of course." He shot her a glance. "I knew you'd tongue-lash me if I didn't. I took her out to lunch and then we went to Central Park and spent the afternoon."

"Good."

"Not so good. I found out when I took her back to school that she'd skipped a full day of classes and was going to be put on detention. She didn't mention any of that when I picked her up in front of the school."

"Oops." She made a face. "But I'm sure

50

she thought it was worth it."

"Maybe. But I shouldn't have done it. I told you that I should let Cara drift away from me now that she has Eve and Joe and a new life."

"And I told you that couldn't happen." The bond of friendship between that eleven-year-old girl and Jock Gavin had been unique. Jane had never seen anything like the closeness that had been born during those few months when Eve had brought Cara to Scotland two years ago. Jock had saved Cara's life, and she was totally devoted to him. "She wouldn't have understood. And she wouldn't have let you go," she added. "All her life she's been on the run and never been able to count on anyone. If you want her to have a normal life, you can't reject her."

"I won't reject her. I just think it's healthier for her not to have me for a friend. I've been trying to distance myself."

"Too late. You should have thought of that before you became so important to her. You're her best friend, you saved her life, and anyone can see that she's not going to let you walk away from her. Now you're stuck with it." She studied his expression. "And you couldn't stand it anyway. You have to know she's well and happy. I bet you've been keeping a close eye on her from that distance you spoke about."

He was silent.

She nodded. "I thought so." She waved her hand as he started to speak. "You'll have to work it out for yourself. But don't hurt Cara because you think that you should fade into the background. She's lost enough. Her entire family murdered, her whole life spent trying to escape the same murderer. She can't lose her best friend, too."

"She won't lose me." He was parking in the lot of a quaint tearoom with mullioned windows. "Though I'd think that you'd realize I'm right about this. She needs a normal life now. There's nothing normal about me."

"Bullshit. Normal is overrated anyway."

He suddenly chuckled. "Now you sound like Seth Caleb. That's something he'd say."

"Caleb?" The sudden mention caused a ripple of shock to go through her. Her glance slid away from him. "Consider the source. No one can call Caleb normal. He doesn't want to be like anyone else. He was born with that weird talent of being able to control the blood flow of the people around him and heaven knows what else. He's arrogant as hell and thinks he rules the world.

Compared to him, you're practically angelic."

He gave a low whistle. "That was a surprise. You're usually more noncommittal about Caleb. It must have been building up." He got out of the car and ran around to open her door. "And Caleb would laugh if he heard you describe me as an angel, unless it was Lucifer." He helped her out of the car and slammed the door. "He's probably all you say, but I'd rather have him in my corner than anyone else I can name. The other doesn't bother me at all."

"It bothers me." She paused. "But he hasn't been around much at Gaelkar in the last months, so I guess it doesn't matter."

"He's been out of the country. But MacDuff may have called him and asked him to come to the lake when we set up the lights. He's never liked strangers on the property, and he trusts Caleb." A smile tugged at his lips. "We all respond to our own needs when it comes to Caleb. He appears to supply whatever makes him invaluable in any given situation."

"Then maybe he's the one who's cloning Lucifer." She grimaced. "Listen to me. I'm overreacting. Caleb has that effect on me."

"I've noticed," he murmured. "Do you want me to talk to MacDuff and ask him not to ask Caleb to come?"

"No." That would have been a defeat in itself and it would probably amuse Caleb when he heard about it. "I don't care." She strode toward the door of the tearoom. "Now let's get a bite to eat and I'll tell you all about Michael. Eve said you hadn't been by to see them since Cara left for school. He's perfectly adorable. I spent half the time I was at the lake house sketching him. I'll show you the last one I did before I left today."

Loch Gaelkar

"It's going to work, Jane." John MacDuff strode up the incline to meet them as she and Jock walked from the road where they'd parked the car. His arresting face was alight with excitement. "Carlisle showed me a demonstration of those lights that knocked me on my ass. He's got contracts with three of the major airlines for his light system, but I persuaded him to let me have the first shipment." He grimaced. "Though it didn't take too much urging after I told him the possibility that I might be able to find Cira's legendary treasure on that north bank. Providing I could pierce that mist that no one has ever been able to do in all of Scottish history. I think he's regarding it as a challenge."

"And that's probably exactly the way you presented it to him. You're no fool, MacDuff." Jane grinned. "There was no way you were going to come back without what you went there to get if you believed there was a chance."

"Aye, I've waited long enough." His blue eyes were suddenly twinkling. "Let those airlines get to the back of the line."

"Not as if that's not your philosophy anyway," Jock said. "Everything has to stop for the pleasure of the laird." He turned to Jane. "See, I told you that we have to keep him under control."

"Jane has no trouble embracing that mantra. She's possibly the most stubborn woman on the planet," MacDuff said drily. "And I'll thank you not to encourage her to defy me, Jock. I've had a hard enough time keeping her here at the lake these past months while I was experimenting."

"I wonder why," Jane said. "I should be absolutely wild about camping out in a tent in the middle of the Highlands, ignoring my career while you try to pull rabbits out of your hat."

"Nonsense. You didn't ignore your career. An artist can work anywhere, and you turned out some damn fine landscapes. And you're just as obsessed as I am about finding Cira's gold. Perhaps not for the same reason, but she called you and you came." He smiled. "True?"

"I guess you might say it's true, in a way." She smiled back at him. "Now you only have to address camping out in the middle of the wilds."

"Who wouldn't want to be surrounded by all this beauty?" He gestured expansively at the lake and the mountains. "And didn't I have a fine shower house built for the camp? What else could you want?"

"I can't imagine," she said gravely. It was true that he had made the tent camp as comfortable as possible for them. Since Gaelkar Castle, the original home established by Cira and her family, was some distance away and in ruins, there had been no real choice. Not that MacDuff would have been inclined to let them go too far away from this lake anyway. "But I'll think about it and let you know."

"You've had a long flight," Jock said. "Go to your tent and rest and I'll bring your cases down." He turned to MacDuff. "Come to the car and help me. Let her get her breath before you start inundating her with all your plans and that overpowering

56

enthusiasm."

"Enthusiasm is contagious," MacDuff said. "And healthy."

"Not when it's mixed with jet lag." He nodded at Jane. "I'll see you at supper."

MacDuff hesitated and then followed Jock. "I'm not doing this because you're right, Jock. I just need the exercise."

"Of course that's the reason," Jock said. "Everyone knows that you're never wrong, MacDuff."

"Bastard," MacDuff muttered.

Jane smiled as she watched the two of them walk back up the incline. It warmed the heart to see a friendship that close. So different and yet forged of experiences and self-sacrifices that had almost melded them into one entity. She had known them both for years and considered them her friends, as well. And she had never lost her appreciation for who they were, both apart and together.

But she was glad that Jock had given her this short time apart from them. It was always a little overwhelming to come back here to Gaelkar after being away.

She turned and started back down toward the camp, her gaze on the deep blue lake. As usual, it took her breath away and drew her toward it. Loch Gaelkar was surrounded by rugged green mountains that plunged down to meet the glittering water on three sides. But the north bank was always blanketed by a heavy mist that swirled and shifted but never revealed what lay beyond.

It was the stuff of which legends were woven. The locals, who had lived with the lake all their lives, said that it was the place where creation either began or would be destroyed. Anyone who saw it found it mysterious and fascinating and even a little frightening. Jane could see why Cira had settled in this part of the Highlands when she had fled from Herculaneum. It had been a wild, challenging country where the strong could carve out an empire. Cira had never hesitated facing any challenge. She had been born a slave and fought her way from poverty to become a successful actress at the theater in Herculaneum. She'd been tough, sometimes ruthless, but honest when she could be. Life had been hard for her, but she'd kept her humanity when everyone around her had tried to use her. It was no surprise that she'd managed to triumph even over the devastation of the exploding volcano. The treasure chest with which she'd escaped after the eruption had been filled with gold and silver coins and one very special coin said to be the payment Judas was given to betray Christ. It would be worth billions in today's market.

But there had been no record of what happened to the treasure chest after Cira had arrived in Scotland.

Jane had reached the bank and dropped to the ground and linked her arms about her knees as she gazed out at the mist.

Is your treasure really out there, Cira? If it's not, why did I have that damn dream that hinted that it was? MacDuff is banking that you were trying to tell me something that could save the family you founded all those centuries ago. I'm not so sure. You were passionate about family, but you saw nothing shameful about struggle.

The sharp wind was blowing over the lake, stirring the mist, as it probably had when Cira had walked these banks. Sometimes Jane felt as if Cira was just beyond that mist and, if she stared hard enough, she would be able to catch a glimpse of her.

Crazy.

But most people would say that her dreams of Cira had been crazy from the beginning and this was no different.

Screw them.

She had her own doubts, but no one had a right to impose their opinions on her. If she didn't find the treasure, then perhaps it would prove that she was a bit off-kilter. If the treasure was somewhere in that mist, then maybe the years of dreams and research had some kind of meaning.

She had to smile as she realized how defiant she was feeling at this moment. It reminded her of the defiance she'd portrayed in Lisa's face in those sketches she'd done of her. It could be Joe was wrong about her not being as belligerent as that girl. Apparently, it only took the right subject to bring it to the forefront.

Two of a kind, Lisa?

She got to her feet and stood there looking out at the lake. "It's good to be back," she murmured. "I've missed you, Cira. Now please be cooperative with MacDuff about his lights. You're driving him crazy with this darned mist." She turned toward the tent area. "But I should tell you I've learned a greater appreciation for you after dealing with this Lisa who's been plaguing me lately. I don't know how she hijacked me, but if you have any influence, you could help her to clarify a bit."

Of course there was no answer but the sound of the water lapping against the bank. She was just lucky Jock or MacDuff hadn't heard that one-sided discourse with Cira, she thought ruefully. Jock would have teased her unmercifully and MacDuff would have used it to convince her that she was even more on board with this treasure hunt than she admitted.

Okay, she'd greeted Cira and this strange world of Gaelkar and now she was ready to go to work. For some reason, she always felt as if Cira was waiting for her to return when she left this place. Maybe MacDuff was right about her having a family connection with Cira. Not that she'd admit that to him. Eve and Joe were the only family she wanted or needed. Even thinking about them gave her a sense that all was right with her world. She turned and headed for her tent. Which reminded her that she had to call Eve after she took a shower and tell her she'd settled in again. . . .

CHAPTER 3

"Joe showed me the photo of that last sketch," Eve said soberly when Jane connected with her a couple hours later. "Not good. He said that you were pretty upset."

"Understatement. I don't like feeling this helpless. Messages written in blood scare me. It's like something from a horror movie." She paused. "And I'm almost afraid of going to sleep and finding out what else Lisa has in store for me. But I'm more afraid of not knowing and then not being able to stop it."

"I can see it. You certainly never had that kind of pressure when you were dreaming about Cira."

"No." She hesitated. "I believe Lisa may be trying to reach me in a way outside the sketches. When I was on the plane, I was thinking something akin to that comment you just made. I received a bolt of very impatient and uncomplimentary feedback regarding my comparing her to Cira."

"Really? Intriguing."

"Bizarre," Jane substituted. "But I'll take it if it means that I can get to the bottom of this any faster. I need to get her safe and take my life back."

"Or at least your nights."

It felt like more than that to Jane. She was noticing that every subject that came to her mind seemed to drift, swirl, like that mist on the lake, until it had some connection to Lisa. "Whatever. She's definitely a distraction." She changed the subject. "And speaking of distractions, how is Michael? After supper, I'm going to try to finish his sketch. It will be a relief to concentrate on something that has nothing to do with anything but hope and youth."

"He's fine. Are you going to give me that sketch?"

"I think you've lost out. I'm going to do it in oil. This time next year, you'll get it."

"Okay. You'll probably do a dozen sketches of him between now and then anyway." Eve paused. "I've been thinking I'd like to have one of him beside Cira's lake."

"What?"

"Just a thought. I spent so much time beside that lake when I was pregnant with Michael, and you were helping me to hide

Cara away from the people who were hunting her down. I feel as if that lake is part of both of us." She added quickly, "Never mind. As I said, just a thought. You said you're going to start putting up those lights tomorrow?"

"So MacDuff said. It's kind of a complicated installation and may take a while. He can hardly wait to dive into that mist again."

"He's had so many trial and errors that he should have it down to a science by now. I can remember MacDuff, Jock, and Caleb working to put in those light poles on that north bank. MacDuff was so disappointed when the infrared lights didn't work." She paused. "Is Caleb going to be there to help?"

"Probably. I believe MacDuff called and asked him to come." She kept her tone casual. "You know how MacDuff dislikes any strangers around when they're working on the north bank. He doesn't mind his sentries guarding the perimeter of the property, but he doesn't want any of them near the actual hunt area."

"But he trusts Caleb," Eve murmured. "I'm sure you have trouble understanding that."

"So did you for a long time," she said. "For God's sake, you saw him kill a man before your eyes."

"That man was a serial killer. And Caleb was never charged. He didn't touch him."

"He didn't have to touch him. You told me Caleb was able to send a rush of blood to his organs that caused him to bleed to death and finished off with a massive heart attack." Jane added impatiently, "At the time, you didn't want me anywhere near him."

"But Caleb wanted to be near you," Eve said ruefully. "And he's a law unto himself. We couldn't seem to stop it, so we had to trust you to use your own judgment. You seemed to be able to hold your own with him."

And sometimes it had been like dancing on hot coals. For years he had moved in and out of her life, and every encounter had been disturbing and electric and filled with an overpowering sexual tension. "Of course I held my own. I'm an adult. I didn't expect you to treat me like a child who needed to be protected. I was always wary of him." She paused. "It's just that everything got complicated when I realized I was in love with Trevor. He was everything that I wanted in a man, loving, gentle, intelligent. . . ." She swallowed. "Everything that I wanted, Eve."

"I know," Eve said gently. "And Caleb

wasn't the white knight; he was the black prince. Anyone could see that he was about to explode whenever he was around the two of you."

"Trevor actually liked Caleb, or maybe he just understood him. Caleb can be . . . persuasive. It's one of his talents." She took a deep breath. "But there's no use talking about Caleb. He is what he is. And I told you I barely talked to him the last time he was here."

"But you didn't tell me why he's pissed off with you," Eve said. "And since it's obvious you don't want to do it, let's drop it. Hey, it's time I gave Michael his dinner. Let me know how MacDuff's lights work out."

"I will. Give Michael a hug for me. Bye." She hit the disconnect button.

She sat there for a moment. As usual, she felt a reluctance to break the tie with Eve and Joe. Even when the conversation was charged or conflicted, it was a comfort to share it with the people she loved.

And talking about Seth Caleb was always charged and disturbing. Put the thought of him behind her. She'd face him when she had to do it.

She rose to her feet and headed toward MacDuff's tent, where they usually gathered for their meals.

■ ■ ■ ■

"So you enjoyed your time with Eve and Joe Quinn?" MacDuff asked as he was walking her back to her tent after supper. "I'm always afraid that you're going to insist on staying with them when you head for Lake Cottage. Eve is a magnet for you."

"Can't deny it." She smiled. "But that's love, MacDuff. You ought to try it sometime."

"Someday. Too busy right now." His gaze went to the lake. "We're going to find Cira's gold this time, Jane. I feel it."

"And that's why you were so anxious about my coming back here? Why? I'm not really that important to this hunt now."

"The hell you're not. I've been looking for Cira's treasure for most of my life, but I never really had much hope until you came on the scene."

"With my crazy dreams about her? Or was it my passion to prove to myself that I wasn't as crazy as I suspected I was?" she asked wryly. "You must have been pretty desperate to believe that I could be of any help at all. No proof, MacDuff."

"But there may be such a thing as racial or ancestral memory. The portrait in my gallery of my ancestor Fiona could be your double."

"Coincidence."

"Really? And yet that last dream you had about Cira led us to this lake."

"And if I've led you here, you don't need me any longer."

"Yes, I do. Cira must have wanted you here. I'm just an invited guest. I'm not going to risk that you might wander off and spoil everything." He added lightly, "All the stars must be aligned."

She chuckled. "When we get deep into the mists, we won't even be able to see our hands before us, much less the stars."

"But my new lights are going to take care of that." He stopped in front of her tent. "Have faith, Jane."

"You have faith. I have hope." She looked up at him. "And that dream was far from specific, MacDuff. It just seems logical Cira would choose to hide the treasure in one of the caves in that mist."

"Then we'll go with that unspecific but entirely hopeful dream." He gazed at her inquiringly. "Unless you've had a more recent one to update us?"

She shook her head. "No dreams of Cira."

His gaze narrowed on her face. "You hesitated."

She had no intention of telling MacDuff about Lisa. He wouldn't be able to help and he was totally focused on Cira anyway. She repeated, "No dreams of Cira. You know I can't dream on demand. Sorry, MacDuff."

"Oh well, maybe once we get through the mist."

"Maybe." She impulsively took a step closer and kissed his cheek. "I want this for you, MacDuff. And I'll keep coming back here until we find out if we're right or wrong about the mists." She grinned. "Though I may have to take an occasional break to go back and see Eve's baby, Michael, now and then. They change too quickly at this age and I want to catch every phase."

"Deal," he said gruffly, and gave her a quick hug. "But you may not have to take any breaks after this week. The lights are going to work and we're going find that treasure chest." He turned on his heel. "Now get to sleep. I'll see you at breakfast."

Jane watched him walk away. MacDuff was always so full of vitality that it was impossible not to be caught up in whatever project he was embracing. And when it came to his obsession for finding Cira's treasure, there was no question that she would be swept in the center of the torrent.

She started to turn to go into her tent.

Then she stopped. It was all very well for MacDuff to tell her to get to sleep, but that wasn't going to happen for a while. She was on edge about what was going to happen in those mists tomorrow.

And she was dreading going to sleep and facing what might have been happening to Lisa over these past hours.

And admittedly, she didn't want to lie there and think about seeing Caleb again.

So she decided to give herself time to relax and unwind. She turned and moved down along the bank toward the point where the mist started to form on the lake. She stopped as everything around her began to disappear and shift into the mists. Better not go any farther. She was not afraid. Somehow she had always felt comfortable here in the midst of the fog. But one false step and she could end up in the lake and have a cold swim back to shore.

She dropped down under a tree a few yards from the lake.

Dampness.

Darkness.

Mist.

You could become disoriented in only a short time in conditions like this.

That was all right. She liked the sensation of being in another world.

Cira's world.

Only it hadn't really been Cira's world. This had been the domain of her young son, Marcus, who had played here all his young life. Cira's world had been the castle some ten miles from here. But Jane's dream had not been of the castle; it had been of these mists. . . .

"Are you sure you want to do this, Cira?" Antonio moved to stand behind her. He put his hands gently on her shoulders, and whispered in her ear. "You don't have to say farewell to him here. We can go back to the castle and have the priest give the gods' blessings and bury him near us."

"No." She looked down at the small casket she'd had the carpenters craft with such care. "I want it to be here by the lake. Marcus liked it here." She could feel the tears sting her eyes. "He told me someday he was going to go into that mist and bring me gifts of gold and jewels fit for a queen. I told him not to be foolish, that I had all the riches I could possibly want already." She looked over her shoulder at Antonio. "It's true, you know. This is a hard, wild land, but we've made it our own. I have everything I ever dreamed about in those days when I was a slave in Herculaneum. I have a husband I love who gave me

five strong sons and two daughters who may be even stronger."

"You would think that." He kissed her temple. "You did not feel love for me when you were going through those birth pains."

"It just seemed unfair that a woman has to bear all that pain. But I can see why the gods didn't entrust having children to men. We do it so much better."

"Whatever you say, love."

She could feel his tears on her temple and knew he would not argue with her at this moment. He was feeling her pain at the loss of Marcus as well as his own. Marcus, eight years old, beautiful as the sun, who had been ravaged by the fever and fallen into darkness.

She couldn't stand here looking down at that small casket any longer. It was time to say farewell and send her son to take his final journey.

She stepped away from Antonio and gazed into the mist. "We're lucky, you know. To have had him this long, to have him the only one of our children whom the gods wanted with them."

"It doesn't seem lucky to me."

"No. At first, I wanted to rage and beat my head on the stones. But then I started to think of Marcus and I was still angry, but there's a kind of comfort in knowing that he'll be here

72

*where he wanted to be. I can ride down here
and imagine him running out of the mist and
telling me how he'd just been hiding and playing in the caves and had great adventures to
tell me." The tears were running down her
cheeks. "And now I believe we'd better go
take him into that mist so that he can begin
those adventures. Then we can go back to
the castle and tell our other children that they
must stop grieving and start living. Does that
not sound like a good plan?"*

*"A fine plan," Antonio said thickly as he
touched her damp cheek. "A magnificent plan,
my own Cira. . . ."*

Jane felt her throat tighten and tears sting
her eyes. The memory was as fresh and
poignant as it had been the night she'd had
that painful dream.

She looked out into the mist. She could
imagine that sad journey that Cira and
Antonio had taken to Marcus's final resting
place.

Is that where you put the treasure that
was to protect your family? Did you give it
to your Marcus to guard until it was needed?

No one could know. It was what Jane had
thought was likely. It was what she thought
Cira would have done. Cira had been part
of her life, part of her youth; there had to

be some reason why Cira had let Jane get to know her so well. Why else would Cira have given her that final dream?

Jane could only guess and follow MacDuff when he went deep into the mist.

She took a deep, shaky breath and straightened against the tree. Time to get out of this mist and away from that heart-breaking memory of Cira and her Marcus. She had come seeking isolation and another world, but that world had been too painful tonight. Go back to the real world and face —

Her cell phone rang and she glanced down at the ID.

Seth Caleb.

Shit.

He was more reality than she wanted to face right now.

But she wasn't going to avoid him. As she'd told Eve, she was an adult. She just didn't feel like it all the time when she confronted Caleb. He managed to dominate effortlessly if she wasn't on guard. Even now, when she hadn't even answered the phone, she could see him before her. Olive skin, high cheekbones, dark eyes, dark hair with that thread of white, the faint indentation in his chin, that beautifully sensual mouth.

And that aura of fire and power that always seemed to surround him even in his most casual moments.

Answer the damn call and get it over with.

She punched the access button. "Hello, Caleb. Jock tells me that you're coming to help MacDuff tomorrow."

"That's why I'm calling you." His deep voice was faintly mocking. "I want you to have a good night. I didn't want you to be tense or on edge when it wasn't necessary."

"How kind. But I doubt if your intentions were entirely without another agenda."

"Of course not. We both know how self-serving I can be." He paused. "How are Eve and the baby?"

She could feel the muscles of her shoulders stiffen. "Fine. Wonderful. Michael is totally exceptional." She waited, but he didn't speak. She forced herself to go on. "She was just mentioning before I left how grateful she was that you were able to save him when all the doctors didn't think he'd survive that poison in her system when he was in the womb."

"Really?" He added mockingly, "Then you must not have discussed the arrangement you offered to get me to do it."

She didn't answer.

"No, of course you didn't. You wouldn't

want to tarnish anything to do with Eve and her child. Everything has to be perfect for Eve."

"Yes, it does. I love her."

"And I like her." The mockery was gone from his tone. "She's a unique human being. I was very happy for her when I heard she was pregnant."

"You never said anything."

"Would you have believed me? I'm always under your microscope. You're never sure if I have an agenda. Just as you aren't sure tonight. Deny it?"

She couldn't deny it. Caleb was too volatile and he had too much power and magnetism. She'd never been able to discover what lay beneath that mystique that surrounded him, and she was too wary to explore it. "I never know what you're thinking. I don't believe that you actually want me to know. Maybe you don't want anyone close enough to find out what you care about."

"Very perceptive." The mockery was back. "So I rely on being a challenge to you. That should be enough, right? Understanding is so tame compared to sex." There was the faintest edge to his tone as he added, "That's why you came to me and offered to let me screw you if I'd just try to save Eve and her child."

"I was upset; I was desperate." She moistened her lips. "I shouldn't have done it. I should have just asked you to help her."

"Oh, you mean as you would have asked anyone else who knew and liked Eve? But I'm not like anyone else, am I? I'm not one of the good guys. God knows, I accept that. You couldn't trust me to give her that gift, to give *you* that gift. That's not how you think of me."

"It was a mistake. I know it made you angry."

"Why should it? I took you up on it, didn't I? When you offered me a deal, I said yes. It wasn't the way I wanted it to happen, but the opportunity was too good to miss. It's what I've wanted since the moment I met you. But it did sting. That's why I decided not to call in the debt until I had time to get over it. I wasn't certain what I'd do to you. We both know I'm not altogether civilized." His voice became silky soft. "It's what you've wanted, too, if you'd admit it. But you've been too afraid of me to take that step."

"I'm *not* afraid of you," she said fiercely. "Look, I admitted I made a mistake. But I'm not the only one to blame. What do you expect? You're not like anyone else. You can do that thing with controlling blood flow.

You can save lives, but you can kill, too. And, dammit, sometimes you can use that blood flow to the brain to alter perception and persuade people that black is white," she added.

"People? You mean you. And you enjoyed it, Jane."

"And, yes, I've seen you . . . wild. Damn right it makes me uneasy."

"Have I ever hurt you or anyone you cared about?"

"No."

"Even when it came to your wonderful Trevor, who should have been very high on my list. I actually tried to save him after he was shot."

"I know you did," she said wearily. "None of that changes the fact that you're not what I want in my life. You'd turn it upside down."

"Probably. But you'll never know until you let me in." He added recklessly, "Or I break down the doors, which is what you expect."

"I never know what to expect from you. That's why I made that mistake. I'm going to say good-bye now and go back to camp. This conversation isn't going to make me sleep any better, if that was really your intention."

"It wasn't. I like the idea of your lying

there thinking about me. I just wanted you to know that I'm not going to ask you to meet your obligations while I'm at Loch Gaelkar this time. I intend to take my time with you, and I may have to leave right after we finish setting up those lights. I have a commitment I can't put off. Relieved?" He paused. "Or disappointed?" He didn't wait for a reply. "Never mind. I can't expect an honest answer in your present mood. Where are you? You said 'back to camp.' "

"I'm on the north bank. I needed a walk after supper."

"And you needed to go into the mist and touch base with Cira again."

"Perhaps."

He was silent. "But it made you sad."

How did he know that? "She lived a full life, and sadness was part of it."

"Oh, I approve of everything about Cira. I think she approves of me, too. She'd have no objection to a little wildness, would she?"

The words brought back the memory of Caleb over her on this bank, his hands on her, his mind building erotic fantasies in the mist. She could feel her heart start to pound.

Heat.

Back away.

"I'm going to say good-bye now," she

79

repeated.

"Be careful going back. I wouldn't want my upsetting you to cause you to take a dip in the lake. I'll see you tomorrow, Jane." He hung up.

As usual, he took the initiative away from me, she thought with annoyance as she shoved her phone into her pocket and started to walk down the bank.

But what did it matter? She was probably just on the defensive, as she usually was around Caleb. Actually, she was glad that he'd called tonight. Now everything was out in the open. What she'd done that night at the hospital had hung over her like a dark cloud for many months. She'd wanted to blame Caleb for striding away from her and not letting her say anything more after that terse and sardonic acceptance, but how could she have when she'd been in the wrong? She'd realized it almost at once.

Because she'd thought she'd actually seen hurt, when Caleb never showed hurt. But he'd armored himself so quickly that she hadn't been certain.

Forget it. For heaven's sake, she was worrying about hurting his feelings when he'd taken advantage of what she'd done and still expected her to jump into his bed the minute he snapped his fingers?

Nothing was ever completely as it should be between Caleb and her. If Caleb had his way, there would be plenty of other opportunities for both of them to heal or hurt each other.

And she wouldn't give him the satisfaction of being right about her lying awake in her bedroll and thinking about him. She'd been doing more than enough of that on this walk back to the campgrounds.

She stopped and took one last look at the lake before she went inside her tent.

The mist . . . and Cira.

That's all she should be thinking about tonight.

But Caleb had intruded and, as always, had disturbed any tranquility she might have experienced. Oh well, Cira had never liked tranquility anyway. She had wanted to live every minute.

Jane ducked into the tent and lit her lantern, then started to undress.

She saw her sketchbook on the canvas table and continued to gaze at it as she put on her nightshirt.

It seemed to be waiting for her.

Lisa?

Or not.

But Jane knew that she wouldn't be able to forget that sketchbook even after she turned off the lantern.

Nor should she.

She got into her bedroll, pulled up the blanket. Then she turned off the lantern and plunged the tent into darkness. She closed her eyes.

The mist.

Cira.

The sketchbook.

Lisa.

Sorry, Caleb, you'll have to stand in line. They're way ahead of you tonight. . . .

"Hurry!"

I'm trying, Lisa. Jane was fumbling desperately with lighting the lantern even as she reached for the sketchbook on the table. *Stop nagging and let me work.*

She had the lantern lit now and was flipping through the pages of the sketchbook.

You should have had it ready.

I wouldn't have been able to sleep with it staring at me. . . . She was drawing now, closing everything out but the pencil and the paper before her. Her pencil was moving at top speed.

Don't think.

Let it flow.

Let *her* flow.

Lisa.

Don't try to tell the story. You don't know it.

Let it come.

Fifteen minutes later, she threw the pencil down, breathing hard.

Done.

The sketch is different this time, Jane thought immediately when she pulled herself together enough to gaze down at it.

Lisa was standing at a tall, narrow window, looking down at the cliff below, which towered above a crashing surf. No view of her face at all, just her dark hair tied back, her slim body dressed in pants and a peasant blouse. One hand resting on the windowsill, which appeared to be smeared with a few drops of dried blood.

It appeared to be the same dark room, its dimness lightened only by the single window.

"You wanted me to see the cliff?" she murmured.

What else? Impatience. *And that island in the distance. Pay attention to it. It's a way out. I almost made it.*

Jane went still. The thought had been clear and unmistakable. She tried to gather her thoughts together and send a message back to her. *You're answering me. And now that I think of it, you were nagging me and trying to wake me. Why didn't you do that before?*

I do what I can. I'm not good at this. I've never been taught. I'm having to learn every-thing by myself. You're certainly no help.

Did you happen to get my message about attitude adjustment?

Yes, but you'd help me anyway.

But far more enthusiastically with a little politeness thrown in.

I don't have time for it. I can only get through to you for a short time after you do the sketches. You're not strong enough to hold me.

Jane could sense the desperation behind the words, and it frightened her. *Then con-nect with someone else who is strong enough. I'll do everything I can, but you're obviously in danger. I don't know anything about this kind of thing. Don't fool around with trying to reach me, Lisa.*

I can't do it. You have the connection. It has to be you. Now pay attention. The shore at the bottom of the cliff is rocky, but maybe a boat . . . Silence. Then she said desperately, *I can feel you fading away from me.*

Jane quickly tried another way. *Then tell me where you are. Tell me how I can get to you.*

Not yet. Not until I know I can trust you to keep your word. Not him. Only you. It has to

84

be only you.

Then tell me your name. If it's some kind of kidnapping or something like that, maybe I can reach your family.

You're not listening to me. Only you. And I told you my name. Lisa . . .

Big help. Please, your full name?

No answer.

Lisa!

Nothing.

Evidently, Lisa's time had run out.

Crazy. The entire thing was bizarre and beginning to be terrifying.

The bruises.

The message written in blood.

The smear of blood on that windowsill that Lisa had probably been clutching before she climbed down to the cliff below.

The desperation, the frustration . . .

The vulnerability that Lisa was trying so hard to hide.

Just the fact that she was trying to hide both that desperation and vulnerability touched Jane.

What would she see in the next sketch?

She swallowed and reached for the bottle of water on the canvas table beside her bedroll.

If you're still around, I hope you know you scared the hell out of me. I don't know why, but like it or not, I'm beginning to care about you. Now help me to help you.

Nothing.

She drank half her bottle of water and then gave herself a moment before she took a photo of the latest sketch and texted it to Joe. Then she got up and went outside the tent and took a deep breath of the chilly night air. She gazed down at the lake and watched the mist move over the water. Tomorrow the lights would arrive and she would be down there helping to unpack them, getting ready to explore Cira's world.

So different from Lisa's bewildering, terrifying world.

"But you'd probably understand Lisa, Cira," she murmured. "She might be a little like you. Not as seasoned, not as savvy, but she's a fighter. You'd appreciate that in her." She turned to go back into her tent. "I do. . . ."

The truck with the Australian lights and transformers arrived at noon the next day. The boxes were carried down from the road by four of MacDuff's sentries and deposited on the shore leading to the north bank. Then MacDuff sent them away, and for the next four hours Jane, MacDuff, and Jock unpacked the contents, which resembled

86

the light assembly on a high-tech movie set.

Complicated. Very complicated, Jane thought as she paused to wipe her forehead. "I hope these came with instructions, MacDuff."

"A few." MacDuff grinned. "We're lucky they're in English. Since I refused to let Carlisle come and set it up himself, he felt no qualms about making it hard for me. He did agree to accept my phone calls."

"Thank heaven for small favors," Jock murmured. He began to load the first of the lights on a dolly. "I'll take these back to the north bank, to that rock formation where we set up the poles."

"For those other super-duper infrared lights that failed miserably," Jane said drily.

"But look on the bright side," MacDuff said. "We already have the heavy work done. All we have to do is set up Carlisle's power source and attach it."

"After you figure out how to do it," Jock said.

"There is that small hurdle," MacDuff admitted. "But it's going to work."

"If you say so," Caleb said as he came down the bank toward them. "But I hoped you'd have a little more accomplished by the time I got here."

Jane went still and then forced herself to

turn and look at him. The same. All force. All power. The same mocking smile and riveting charisma. "We might have accomplished more if you'd been here to help. As usual, you managed to bow out of the manual work, Caleb."

"Hello, Jane. That dew of perspiration on you is very attractive. Sort of a glow." He smiled. "And you know my expertise lies in other areas. Anyone can do common labor." He turned to MacDuff and shook his hand. "Though I did mean to get here a bit sooner. I was out of the country." He looked at the dolly Jock was loading and sighed. "But it appears that I'm still going to be forced to do my part. The poles by the boulders?"

Jock nodded. "You take the dolly and I'll finish unpacking that final crate."

"I'll do it," Jane said. "Take another dolly and both of you go, Jock. You'll be able to unpack them faster and get back for another load. It's starting to get dark, and we'll want to get the rest of this stuff off the bank and where it's supposed to go." She glanced slyly at MacDuff. "We wouldn't want a random crow flying around to grab one of MacDuff's miracle lights to line her nest."

MacDuff flinched. "Sacrilege."

"I'll make amends by going back to camp

88

and putting on the coffee while you're all bustling around in the mist."

Caleb looked over his shoulder as he reached the trees. "That might not be an intelligent division of labor. You're so good in the mist, Jane."

The mist surrounding them, the cool dampness beneath her body. Caleb over her, his hands on her breasts, no breath in her lungs, wild eroticism everywhere.

She met his eyes. "Yes, I am. But it's my choice if I want to go there." She bent over the crate. "I'll see you all back at camp."

"Pity . . ."

MacDuff glanced at her as Jock and Caleb disappeared into the woods. "I'll finish unpacking that crate. You can go back to camp now. You've worked hard today. That's not why I want you here."

"No, you want my invaluable vibes to soothe Cira." She smiled. "But I don't mind pitching in. You may not get much work out of Caleb."

"You'd be surprised. He works hard when he chooses. That pose just amuses him. And he's right: His talent lies in other areas. I just needed another man I trust to help with these lights. And Jock and he work well together." His lips twisted. "They're on the same wavelength."

"It's a wavelength you've been trying to keep away from Jock since you found him in that sanitarium." She shivered. "He was an assassin, MacDuff. I would have thought you'd try to discourage him from being around a man like Caleb."

"Jock runs his own life now. And there're no other men like Caleb. They're both deadly. I just have to hope that they're not too explosive together." He shrugged. "Hell, I'm only asking them to help me with those damn lights. It will be fine. Caleb shouldn't be here too long. He warned me he couldn't give me that much time."

"Then all the more reason I should finish here before I go back to camp." Jane pulled out another lamp from the box. "Now hush while I work up some more of that 'glow' Caleb was so sarcastic about."

It was nearly ten that night when Jane saw MacDuff and Jock come out of the forest and walk toward the campfire.

She tried to make her tone casual as she hurried toward them. "It's late. I was beginning to worry. What happened?"

"Nothing." MacDuff smiled. "We just got caught up in the moment. Or should I say hours?"

"We got caught up in Caleb," Jock interjected drily. "He was in a fever, and we became infected." He went to the fire and picked up the coffeepot. "We only meant to start the job, but then we thought, Why not? So we went at it full speed." He poured coffee in his cup. "As full speed as possible in that mist and dark."

"We got a lot done," MacDuff said. "We finished the attachment on the first pole and Caleb almost finished the second himself."

"And where is Caleb?" She handed MacDuff a cup of coffee.

"He said he only had a little to finish on the second pole and for us to go back without him." Jock finished his coffee. "Now I'm going to grab a sandwich and then hit the shower."

"Should you have left him alone?"

"What's going to hurt him? We've never run across any wildcats or any other large animals." MacDuff grinned. "And if Caleb did, I'd bet on him. He's one of the most nimble men in the forest I've ever seen, almost like an animal himself. And if he fell in the lake, we'd just laugh at him. No, he'll be fine."

He's undoubtedly right, Jane thought. She was being foolish to worry about Caleb. She had seen him on the hunt in a forest in the Alps years ago and she knew what MacDuff meant about him resembling an animal. Wild . . .

But things could still happen. That mist remained a complete mystery to them. There could be sinkholes and underground currents in that lake. Agile or not, he could fall and break his stupid head open.

"He'll be fine," MacDuff repeated as he munched on a bacon sandwich. "Trust me. I wouldn't have left him if I'd thought there was a danger." His eyes were twinkling. "I might need him too much in the next couple days. He truly swept us along with him tonight." He finished his coffee. "Now I think I'll follow Jock and try to get this mud off me. It was a good first day, Jane." He was moving away from the campfire. "If you and Cira have a nocturnal get-together, you might tell her about it. . . ."

But the day wasn't over for Caleb.

She stared at the mist rising from the forest. Good God, she actually wanted to go after him. How dumb that would be. Caleb was no child and could take care of himself. He would only be amused if he knew she was worried about him.

And she would want to slap him.

She should go to bed and forget about him, as MacDuff and Jock were doing.

But she would only lie there and not sleep.

That would amuse Caleb even more. Okay, she told herself, stay here by the fire and wait until you're sure he is safe. He'd told MacDuff he wouldn't be long out there in the mist. It wouldn't look weird for her to stay up a little longer and enjoy the fire.

She got another cup of coffee and settled down to wait.

Caleb didn't come out of the woods for another two hours.

She smothered her relief as she jumped to her feet and started to leave the campfire and head for her tent. "The coffee's hot," she called. "You should have come earlier if you wanted anything to eat."

"Stop right there." He was running along the bank and barred her way. "I'm damp and I'm cold and evidently I'm going to starve, but I'm not going to do it alone. You're coming back to the fire and keeping me company while I dry out."

"We said what needed to be said last night."

"You don't have to talk. I might prefer that you don't. But I always like to look at you. Come on." He turned and headed back toward the campfire.

She hesitated. Then she slowly followed him and dropped down on the ground before the fire while he poured a cup of coffee. "There might be some rolls and cheese in that metal saver over there."

"That you weren't going to offer me. So I don't have to starve?" He shook his head as he sat down and crossed his legs Indian-fashion. "I'm not hungry. The adrenaline is still pumping. I find it interesting that you're annoyed with me but that you still waited up until I came back."

"I wasn't sleepy. I wasn't waiting for you."

He tilted his head and gazed at her appraisingly. "I think you were. Tell me, were you afraid Cira would strike me down out there in the mist? She wouldn't do that. I told you: She likes me."

"Why should I be afraid for you? As MacDuff said, he'd bet on you against anything you might run into."

"But you still stayed up and waited." He nodded. "I'd do the same. Only I'd probably go after you."

"Finish your coffee. I'm not going to sit here and chat. You should have been back hours ago."

"I told you: I don't have much of a window to do what MacDuff needs me to do. He and Jock have time to play with those lights. I've got to help set them up and get out of here."

"Why?" She shook her head. "Never mind. One of your commitments. It doesn't matter. I never know what you're doing. It's none of my business."

"And you like it like that." He took another sip of coffee. "So do I, most of the time. But I liked it that you made it your business to sit here worrying about me · tonight. It made me feel . . . warm. I think it might have erased that lingering bit of anger I was feeling toward you."

"And that's supposed to make me feel all soft and fuzzy?"

He chuckled. "Heaven forbid. There's nothing soft and fuzzy about you, Jane. But it should make you feel a good deal more secure. I really did want to punish you."

"Bullshit."

"But it's gone now. Do you want to know what's in its place?"

Lust. Heat. Erotic fantasy.

"No, I don't." She got quickly to her feet. "I'm going to my tent. Will you still be here in the morning? Or did you finish tonight?"

"I have a few more things to do, but I'll be out by noon."

She started toward the tents. "Have a good trip."

"I'll walk you to your tent." He rose to his feet. "You're in escape mode and you might be conveniently busy tomorrow morning. I consider that I deserve a prize for interrupting my business to help MacDuff. We've already discussed the fact that I'm not one of the good guys."

"And I'm the prize? No way, Caleb."

"Not the grand prize. Though I do think I deserve it. I just want to see you smile at me. I didn't realize how much I'd missed seeing it during these last months." He grimaced. "Though you were never very generous with me in that regard. You were always too wary."

She stopped outside her tent. "And I'm supposed to grin at you like a Siamese cat to please you?"

"That would be nice, but not expected." He smiled. "So I'll smile at you and set the example. Good night, Jane."

"Good night." She stared up at him. The moonlight was dim, but the glow of the fire in the distance outlined his features: the curve of his lips, the indentation in his chin, the slash of dark brows over his eyes. Everything was sharp and defined in this light. Usually, she was so aware of the power and personality behind those features that she didn't notice the details. But every feature was intriguing. "And I don't need examples. And I wasn't worried about Cira.

I thought you might fall off that damn pole and bust your head. That happens even to men like you."

He laughed. "It certainly does. And if I was that clumsy, I'd deserve it."

"And it doesn't change anything."

"Then I'll have to work on it." He turned away. "I'll be back as soon as I finish up my business. Sleep well, Jane."

"I will. I won't have anyone to keep me awake by doing —" She inhaled sharply, staring at him. Profile. Sharp silhouette. Black and white.

He looked back over his shoulder. "What?"

"Nothing."

She turned and bolted into the tent. Her heart was jumping out of her chest.

She stood there in the dark for a moment, trying to get control.

It couldn't be, could it?

Of course it could.

Okay, give yourself a little time to check and then try to make sense of it.

She should have been happy and relieved.

But she couldn't imagine a worse scenario for her.

CHAPTER 4

An hour later, she was walking quickly up the hill toward the tent MacDuff always allotted Caleb when he was here.

"I'm coming in, Caleb," she called sharply when she was a few yards away. "I thought I'd warn you. I'd appreciate it if you don't cause me to have a heart attack or use one of your other methods of ridding yourself of people." She pushed through the canvas opening. "Because I sure as hell don't want to be here."

"You're angry." In the darkness, she could see him raise himself up in his bedroll across the tent. "I told you that we don't have to deal with this right now. It's probably best that we don't. Go away, Jane."

"I *can't* go away." She was in the tent and fumbling with his lantern. "Oh my God, you think this is about sex? I'm not here to pay any debts, Caleb." She finally got the lantern lit and turned to face him. "You're

98

naked." She took his blanket and tossed it over him. "Get some clothes on."

"Presently." He was studying her. "I don't feel the need of any barriers against you as I did two minutes ago. It may be better that I find out the problem first."

"Suit yourself." She came a step closer, reached down, lifted his chin, and glared down at him. "*You're* the problem."

"I gathered that. In what way?"

"Here." She rimmed his left eye with her forefinger. "And here." She touched the faint slant at the corner. "I thought I should remember her. But it was *you.*" She dropped his chin and stepped back. "It was always you, dammit."

He stiffened. "I don't like this. I believe you'd better be a little clearer, Jane."

"Do you think *I* like it?"

"What is this about?"

"Not what. Who." She tossed the sketchbook she was carrying under her arm onto his lap. "Lisa."

His face remained impassive, but she saw the ripple of shock that went through his body. "What do you know about Lisa?"

"Not enough. All I know is that I have to sketch her every time when I wake up after going to sleep." She dropped down on the floor next to him. "But I'm going to know

99

more. Look at the sketches."

"Oh, I intend to." He took the sketchbook and opened it to the first sketch. He gazed at it for a moment. "She's . . . changed."

"Has she? I wouldn't know. But you would. You're related to her in some way, aren't you? The shape of your eyes is so similar. Nothing else jumped out at me when she started making me draw these sketches. But that was very familiar. I thought I must have known her sometime in the past. Why else would I be drawing those damn sketches?"

"Why else indeed?" He turned to the next sketches. He went still as he reached the one that showed the blood pouring from Lisa's cut lip. "When was this one?"

"The night before I left Lake Cottage. Who is she to you?"

He didn't answer. He was going slowly through the last sketches, scanning every detail. "This is the last one? When?"

"Last night." She repeated, "Who is she to you?"

"Every time you go to sleep? She reaches out to you then?"

"She says that's practically the only time she can. She's very angry about it."

"She would be. Lisa's never patient about anything."

"I found that out. I should have known she was related to you. You want things all your own way, too."

"But I've learned sometimes I have to wait. You should have seen me when I was her age."

"What is her age? She looks younger in those first few sketches, but I can't tell now from the most recent ones."

"Lisa is nineteen now." He looked back at the last sketches. "And she's evidently maturing rapidly with what's going on with her. That's not good." He glanced up at Jane. "You mentioned she said it was the only way she could communicate. Then she *is* reaching you in other ways than through the sketches?"

"Briefly. She's angry about that, too. She says she's having to teach herself." Jane looked him directly in the eye. "And I'm not answering one more question until I get answers myself. I have an idea I was pulled into this because of you, and I don't like it, Caleb."

"Neither do I." His lips twisted. "Or maybe I do. I didn't mean to do it, but it could be a way to get what I want. You know what a selfish bastard I am."

"Yes. Now tell me who she is to you."

"My sister. Lisa Ridondo is my sister." He

flipped back to the last sketch, in which Lisa was gazing down at the cliff. "Did she tell you where this cliff is located?"

"No, and that's not enough information. Why did you say she's changed? How long has it been since you've seen her?"

"Five years."

"Not exactly a close family relationship."

"It was better for her."

"Not if it ended with her being beaten up and forced to climb down cliffs."

"It was better at the time."

"Why?"

"I was a threat to her."

"Evidently you let someone else take over that threat. She's scared, dammit. She won't show it, but she's scared."

"I'll take care of it."

"Not likely. Not if you couldn't even stand being around her for the past five years."

"Shut up." He was suddenly on his knees beside her, his dark eyes blazing in his taut face. He grasped her shoulders and his fingers dug into her flesh. "Not now, Jane. I can't take it now."

Fury.

Wildness.

And something else that made the response she intended to make die unspoken on Jane's lips.

She was silent a moment. "Let me go, Caleb. You're hurting me. I'm not the enemy."

He slowly released her. "Of course you're not." He was totally in control again. "But you have a tongue that tends to sting on occasion. Sorry, I'll make it up to you."

"And so you should. But perhaps not right now." She scooted away from him. "Because I need to know what's happening. I made Lisa a promise and I have to know why she made me give it."

"What are you talking about?"

"You saw what she wrote in blood on that table. 'He must not come. Only you.' I didn't know what she was talking about. But it was clear that any help had to come from me. The mysterious 'he' wasn't to be involved. Tonight when I was going over everything I remembered about her and the sketches, that was very clear. And I realized that it was you she was talking about." She paused. "I thought you might be an enemy she didn't trust. I still wasn't sure when I broke in here."

"Why should you be?" His lips twisted. "I've always been the enemy."

"Not always. But you've always been the unknown quotient." She added impatiently, "Because you won't let anyone close enough to know what you're thinking. Look at you right now. You're still mocking and arrogant, and yet I know you're hurting."

"Do you?"

"Stop it," she said. "Or maybe you can't stop. Maybe it's gone on too long. But I have to know what's happening so that I can help that girl."

His faint smile vanished. "She trusts me, Jane," he said quietly. "She knows I'm not the enemy. I'd sense it if there was any change in that. But I don't know why she doesn't want me to go and help her."

"Then we'll have to figure it out," she said. "I take it you don't recognize any of the background features. Not the mountains, garden, cliffs?"

He shook his head. "I've never seen them."

"I have Joe trying to identify them. He's also doing facial recognition on Lisa. I'll tell him to stop that now. Lisa Ridondo, not Lisa Caleb?"

"No, I took my uncle's name when I left my home in Italy and moved to Scotland." He shrugged. "It seemed best under the circumstances. I was persona non grata among my dear family." He handed her the sketchbook. "I believe it's going to be a long night. Why don't you make us some coffee down at the campfire while I get some clothes on?"

"That's right, you're still naked. I'd forgotten."

"That would have been a terrible blow if I believed you." He got to his feet. "But since my ego won't permit it, I'll survive." He turned away and reached for his clothes. "The coffee, Jane."

The coffee was hot by the time Caleb joined Jane at the campfire. "That smells good." He sat down. "I had to make a couple calls, or I would have been down here sooner."

"I wasn't timing you." Jane handed him a cup of coffee. "Though I wasn't thinking about telephone calls. I was considering the possibility that you might need a little time to pull yourself together like a normal person. Silly me."

"Normal? Yes, silly you."

She took a sip of her coffee. "Not so silly. Not about Lisa. I think you feel something for her." She frowned. "And I think she feels something for you. She wasn't afraid of you; it was *for* you. She's trying to protect you, isn't she?"

"I don't know. It's a possibility. At any rate, I can't let her do it."

"It may be difficult to stop it." She tapped her chest. "Only me."

"Bullshit. She belongs to me."

"She belongs to herself. And I made her a promise. I may let you help, but I can't involve you."

His dark eyes were glittering. "You'll have no choice."

"I always have a choice. That's what I've been trying to tell you." She met his eyes. "And I won't know how to make it until I know everything surrounding this, Caleb. I want the whole story, not just a glimpse at the outline."

He didn't speak.

"I mean it, Caleb. Lisa said that she couldn't reach anyone else but me because I was the only one who had the connection. I think she was talking about my connection to you and her connection to you. Somehow it enabled her to reach me. But she didn't try to contact you. She was desperate not to involve you. So if she decides I've betrayed her by bringing you into this, she might break her contact with me. She'd be alone then, Caleb. I won't permit that to happen." Her voice was shaking with intensity. "She tries to be strong, but she's scared and vulnerable. She's *not* going to be alone."

Another moment of silence.

"I can see that." He looked away from her and down into the coffee in his cup. "Okay.

No outlines. But it goes back a long time. You might wish you'd opted for the abbreviated version."

"No way. Any more than I'd want my work to be reviewed as a sketch when I'd done a full oil painting."

He shrugged. "You know some of it. I felt bound to give you and Eve some of my background the first time we all met." He grimaced. "It was kind of a necessity, since I'd just caused a killer to have a massive heart attack in front of her. The only thing that saved me in your eyes was that he was going to kill Joe Quinn, too. That weighed pretty heavy in the balance."

"Extremely heavy. But we didn't understand how the hell you could do it, or why it didn't make you as much a murderer as that monster you'd killed."

"And sometimes you still have doubts." His lips twisted. "Because of my inimitable talent with blood? It scares most people. I joke about all those vampire myths, but it still lingers in the mind. Tell me, did you ever have a nightmare about me sucking your blood?"

"No, I have not," she said in disgust. "I know your talent has nothing to do with that nonsense. Though it's probably more dangerous. And I remember you said that through the centuries it encouraged those imaginary myths about your family."

"Yes, and since you want the complete story, let me refresh your memory a little." He took a sip of coffee. "I come from a very old Spanish family, the Devanezes, who were known to have a number of psychic talents that made them very unpopular with their neighbors. Particularly during the fifteenth century, when they were turned in to the Spanish Inquisition for witchcraft. The entire family had to flee the country or be burned at the stake. The Ridondo brothers, my particular ancestors, chose to settle in the village of Fiero in Italy. They decided the only way they could protect themselves from informers to the church was to keep the villagers terrified of retribution." His lips twisted. "It worked. They became the scourge of Fiero, the purveyors of the black arts, holding the villagers in thrall for decades. They used the blood talent and their other gifts to make themselves seem to be demons of darkness." He shrugged. "And perhaps they were. But how much blackness can a soul take? When they decided to leave the village and break free, it was almost too late. They settled a good distance from Fiero. They had children, grand-children. Time passed." He grimaced. "With only a few minor incidents that could be called truly wicked. But the call of the blood never entirely goes away, and neither does the knowledge that it's there ready to be tapped at will. Most of the Ridondo descendants decided it was safer to become hunters, where they could indulge innate violence without falling back into the pit. Our family's talents were very much in demand with governments and armies and heads of states. Of course we had to pick and choose, but there's a whole world of monsters out there. It's not too difficult to find them."

"As you did?"

"As I did. But I was spurred on by a particularly savage prey that had to be destroyed, as you know."

"Jelak." She nodded. "He was a serial killer who devoured the blood of his victims. He had the crazy idea that by drinking the right kinds of blood he could become a kind of vampire God and have supernatural powers. He was connected to a cult that actually sacrificed people whose blood they thought would be of prime value." Jane shuddered. "Horrible."

"Yes, and naturally they'd targeted my family. Why not? There were all kinds of stories floating around in the underground about our wicked past." He paused. "And certain other powers they found very desirable. But they didn't want to tackle any of the males in the family. They had a certain respect for us." His expression hardened. "So they went after my half sister, Maria. Jelak kept her alive for a long time, taking her blood, and trying to see if he experienced any surge of power when he drank it. But he was disappointed. She had no power and was weak and died too soon."

Jane could see the pain as well as the dark fury in his expression. "You don't have to go into this, Caleb," she said gently. "You told Eve and I most of this after you destroyed the cult and killed Jelak." She suddenly went rigid. "Unless you think that Lisa's situation has anything to do with that same cult?"

He shook his head. "I've been monitoring a resurgence possibility ever since that happened. I would have known. It has to be something else."

"Then why did you bring all this up?"

"Because you have to get the whole picture so that you'll know I'm the one who has to go find Lisa."

"Why? I don't see any connection, then." She added, "Unless you're feeling guilty about not visiting her all these years? But you didn't even mention you had another sister when you told us about Maria."

"I didn't tell you about a lot of things then. And I lied about many others."

"Why?"

"I wanted a place in your lives," he said simply. "I found you and your family filled . . . something. So I made myself acceptable. You might have had trouble if you'd known everything about me."

"Then how do I know you're not lying now?"

"You don't. I'm very good at twisting and manipulating the truth. It's one of my talents. It's known as the *Persuasion*. You were very bitter about that particular gift." He met her eyes. "But I've tried not to lie to you since that day. It was at great cost, because I often had to let you see me as I really am. I'm not lying now, Jane."

And she believed him. Crazy. "And what did you lie about then that has any bearing on what's happening to Lisa?"

"Eve asked me if I was close to anyone. I told her of course I was close to my family. It was only partially true. Most of my family hated me from the time I was a small child."

Her eyes widened. "What?"

He smiled crookedly. "I realize it's hard to

believe when I'm such a charming soul. But I had a few faults that my parents found unforgivable. Imagine that."

"No small child has unforgivable faults."

"They do if they exhibit signs that they're a throwback to family members who are considered completely unacceptable." He took another swallow of coffee. "Over the last century, the blood talent as well as the other psychic skills had gradually been fading away, and when they did occur, they were weak and almost unnoticeable. My family had the hunt instinct, but no children born in the last fifty years had inherited the talent itself. The family was both relieved and grateful. They'd become very wealthy and liked the social status that went with it. They enjoyed the normalcy and the lack of threat to their lifestyle." He tapped his chest. "Until me. When I started to display troublesome signs of having certain talents that they regarded in the monster category, I was whisked away to the country house and taken care of by tutors for most of the year. I didn't see either of my sisters except for a few months in the summer. They were both younger than I was and had been told not to become too close to me, but children often don't pay attention to adults." He met her eyes. "And I wanted them to like me. I *needed* them. So I made it happen."

"Or maybe it was a case of three children thrown together and nature taking its course."

His brows rose. "I wasn't brought up to think in those terms."

"Maybe if you had been, you wouldn't have turned out so damn weird."

His lips turned up at the corners. "And maybe that was why I wanted you and your family in my life. There's nothing usual about any of you, and yet you accepted me under conditions that would have scared off anyone else."

"Maria and Lisa," she prompted.

"You know what happened to Maria. I'd left Italy by then and we'd lost touch. When I was a teenager, I was tossed to my uncle who lived in Scotland to handle when I became too unmanageable for my parents. My parents died shortly afterward, and before they died, they set up a trust fund for Maria and Lisa that was administered by Gino Romano and his wife, Teresa. They were my parents' closest friends and neighbors. One of the provisions of the trust was that I not be permitted access to either of my sisters."

"That must have hurt."

"It's not as if it wasn't expected. I was the

pariah. Any more than it was a surprise that the Romanos were chosen to keep me at bay." His lips twisted. "Because I knew them both very well indeed before my parents sent me away. Gino was an investment banker with old money, and his wife, Teresa, was high in social circles in Rome. They'd become very close to my parents since the time Teresa had decided that it would benefit them to do so. They had no children of their own and appeared to be at least tolerant of Maria and Lisa."

"Tolerant is never good enough."

"Not everyone has someone like Eve Duncan in their lives," he said drily. "Tolerance has to suffice sometimes. But I was resentful because Maria and Lisa belonged to me, so I spent a month near the Romano estate, watching and seeing how the girls were being treated. Neither of the girls liked the Romanos very much, and they found their lifestyle pretty boring. But they were away at school most of the time and hardly saw them. And it was far more normal than the life I could have given them at that point. I thought they'd be safe and have a decent life." He smiled crookedly. "So I didn't do anything to cause the Romanos to wish to terminate their guardianship. Not violence. Not a hint of Persuasion."

"I don't believe you'd give up that easily," Jane said.

"I didn't. I'd fade in and out of the Romano estate and see them whenever I was in the area. Maria and Lisa both thought it was a great adventure to keep our meetings secret from their guardians."

"Because you made them think of it like that. I've seen how that Persuasion talent of yours works. It's almost like hypnosis."

"They were *mine*. I had to make sure they were safe and happy." He nodded. "And, yes, I needed them, too. Satisfied?"

She didn't answer. She wasn't satisfied. She was finding out new and different things about Caleb that were disturbing. "How long did it go on?"

"Not that long for Maria. She was older and went away to school in Paris. Lisa was different. She was just a kid and always in trouble and I had to stay close enough to help."

"I can see why she'd be constantly in hot water," Jane said drily. "And why did you break off seeing her?"

"Maria," he said. "After Maria's murder, the Romanos made their estate an armed camp. I didn't know whether they were more afraid the same thing might happen to Lisa or that they might be on the receiving end of the backlash." He paused. "I didn't give a damn about them, but I couldn't handle the idea of Lisa's being in danger. All it would take would be one monster that I'd missed when I went after that cult that had murdered her sister. If I'd destroyed the security around Lisa, then I might have let in the monsters. If I'd taken her away, she would have been even more vulnerable. She was only fourteen, Jane. She wasn't ready to take care of herself, and I've made myself a target over the years. I'm a magnet that would draw those monsters to her."

"Evidently one might have managed to find her anyway." She paused. "And I don't believe you would have just walked away from her. You don't let go of anything you want."

He was silent. "I haven't seen her."

"But you didn't let her go."

He smiled. "Okay, as you noticed, Lisa and I have a connection. I taught her how to refine and strengthen it. I was there when she needed someone to be there."

"A link between the two of you that was stronger than any other element in her life."

His smiled faded. "I had to be there for her sake. It wasn't to dominate her life. She was sent to a private school in Switzerland after her guardians felt safer about letting her leave the estate. I had to know she was safe and could contact me."

"Which she's refusing to do now. Why would she do that?"

"I don't *know* why. I'm trying to find out from you."

"She won't tell me. I told you: She won't trust me. She's afraid I'm going to rope you into going to get her out of the fix she's in. Whatever little clique you formed between you with that damn connection you developed is messing up everything."

"It was necessary."

"Why, dammit?"

"To keep her safe. I had to monitor her."

" 'Monitor,' " she repeated distastefully. "You make her sound like a science experiment. She's a young girl with her whole life before her and has a fixation on keeping you —" She stopped, her gaze narrowing on his face. "Monitor. Why, Caleb?"

He didn't speak. Waiting.

"My God, she's like *you*. That so-called connection is just the tip of the iceberg."

"Very good. What else, Jane?"

"I don't know what else. You tell me. You said that Maria had no power, that she was too weak for Jelak's purposes. But Lisa is different. You even said it. 'Lisa was different.' She's a throwback, just like you. She did have the power. You needed to be there for her."

"And I was, during the crucial period. I knew what it was like to stumble through it alone, with no one who understood. But she was in the same prison I was and she had to learn to pretend that she was like our parents and not like me. She had to know she wasn't a freak but that she would be treated as one. Then I had to teach her to smother the impulses and not let the fire inside out at anyone." He added, "And, finally, to love me and to keep any promise I demanded of her. That was essential."

"I think she just broke training," Jane said flatly. "And you should have known that if you'd been in touch with her lately."

"I've been trying to contact her, dammit. She hasn't been linking with me for the last two weeks. I went to the Romanos' estate in Italy and it was closed up. The bank shows Romano on an extended leave of absence. I've been trying to track them down by accessing computer and credit card records. Nothing. I hired several agents whom I've used in the past to extend the search to Switzerland and France." He paused. "I was afraid that perhaps Lisa had exploded and done something that had caused the Romanos to know about her potential. They might have decided to totally isolate her from me and the rest of their social set." He added bitterly, "Just as my parents did me."

"Could they have forced her not to link with you?" she asked skeptically. "You brainwashed the poor girl."

"I did *not* brainwash. I suggested. And she is not poor in any sense of the word." He shook his head. "But, no, she wouldn't have reacted to force."

"Then we're back to her protecting you." She frowned. "And us finding and protecting Lisa." She remembered something else he'd said. "How much protection is she going to need? Just what is her potential?"

"Considerable. I was careful not to let her explore the boundaries. It's certain that she has the blood talent. I sense that all the time. She's had no training, so she can't control it. I wanted it entirely subdued while she was a child and a young adult. It could make her life hell."

She tilted her head, her gaze searching his expression. "Did it make your life hell?"

He didn't answer. "I was going to teach her how to handle it later, after she reached maturity. As for the Persuasive skills, she hasn't shown them to me."

"Nor to me," she said drily.

"But I understand they sometimes go along with the power to link. They could come later, when I start opening the layers."

"Actually, she could use a few layers of persuasiveness. She's definitely a diamond in the rough."

He nodded. "But you don't appreciate that talent in me."

"You have a tendency to misuse it. You enter my space. Hell, you violate my space. While you're training Lisa, you might teach her not to do that."

"I won't get the opportunity to train her if she ends up dead," he said bluntly. "I have to know where she is."

"So do I. You're this great hunter. You spent years tracking down every member of that cult who murdered your sister Maria. Why can't you find Lisa?"

"I'll find her." He threw the rest of his coffee into the fire and the wood hissed and sputtered. "But you're going to help me. I can't wait. I have to know."

"By using force? I told you: I can't let her break her contact with me."

"I'll handle it." His eyes were cool. "She's mine. Back off, Jane."

"Go to hell. She chose me. Do you think I like any of this? But she needs someone and she chose me. Now she's my responsibility."

"No way. I saw those sketches. She's afraid and I have to take that away. You have to help me take it away." He got to his feet. "I can make you want to do it." He was suddenly kneeling beside her, his eyes holding her own. "Just a shift in perception," he said softly. "You know I've done it before. You'll just suddenly realize how right I am. How much you want to do what I want you to do."

She could feel the waves of power and persuasion he was emitting. She could sense her subtle shifting of will, the heat, the yielding. She glared up at him. "You son of a bitch. This isn't about seduction or one of your sex games. Don't you dare try to do that to me. I'll fight you. You'd have to hurt me. And if you managed to do it, then you'd risk destroying me. Do you really want to do that?"

He stared at her for a long moment.

"Hell no." He was on his feet in one smooth movement and sat down again across the fire from her. "I can't hurt you. Okay, I'm a bit upset. It just seemed a tool I could use that would give me what I needed. As you say, I'm a son of a bitch."

More than a bit upset, Jane thought as

121

relief rushed through her. That persuasiveness was almost more powerful than his more deadly talent. She knew he had no compunction about using it to get his way with other people if necessary, but he was very careful about stepping over that line with her. It only showed how serious he was about finding Lisa.

"You care about her," she said quietly. "It's not about possessiveness or duty to someone who is going through the same thing as you did as a child. You do love her, Caleb."

"You find that so strange?" His smile was bitter. "My parents would have agreed with you. I was supposed to represent everything dark in their own lives. I should be incapable of affection, right?" He shrugged. "Somehow it managed to slip in over the threshold like one of those vampires they thought I might become."

"I don't find it strange. How could I? You don't let me know enough about you to judge. But I think I might be learning a little tonight." She shook her head. "But I'm frustrated because when I realized that you had a resemblance to her, I was hoping you'd know where I could find her."

"Did you get the impression that she knew her location?"

"I didn't get much of an impression at all. She wanted me to see where she was being kept and that she was a prisoner, but our link was only with the sketches until recently. She seemed to be trying to teach herself to extend the contacts for a longer period, but it was slow going. She said she'd never been taught and she had to teach herself." She grimaced. "And that I was no help at all. I couldn't keep her with me."

"But I could."

She looked at him. "Are you back to square one?"

"No, you're too stubborn to let me try to go to her right now. But I can go into your mind and insert a stay that will allow Lisa not to spin away from you."

She gazed at him warily. "I don't like the sound of that."

"Because you're finding it hard to trust me after I tried to adjust your perception. You can trust me in this. If I can't do what I need myself, I'll try to facilitate your doing it. Anything to get what I want. You know that's my mantra."

She nibbled at her lower lip as she studied him. Coolness. Mockery. The mask was firmly back in place. But she'd seen something behind it that might give her a chance to help Lisa.

"Why couldn't she do it herself?"

"She told you: She's not been taught. You saw what kind of temperament Lisa possesses. She's impulsive, a little volatile, passionate. And she's had no one around her to temper those characteristics. Certainly not Teresa Romano. No gentling influence there." His lips twisted. "And I wouldn't teach Lisa anything to do with mind games until she's capable of a little more restraint." He paused. "But you said she's teaching herself. That could be a formula for disaster."

"Who taught you?"

"No one. I learned everything on my own. That's why I know the dangers. I didn't want that for Lisa."

"Well, it seems to be heading toward her like a runaway train." She was silent a moment. "If I let you put that 'stay' thing in my mind, will Lisa know you had something to do with putting it there?"

"Really, Jane."

"None of your damn arrogance. Would she know?"

He shook his head. "She'd just realize that she has control. If she's teaching herself, she might believe she's doing it."

"And then she could be there long enough for me to question her." She frowned. "If she'll answer me. She doesn't trust me."

"She *wants* to trust you. As you said, Lisa came to you, not me."

"I think I was the only one she could reach. I don't know why."

"I do." He held her eyes. "My link with you is very strong. It's always there. She used it as a springboard."

She pulled her gaze away and looked at the fire. "And that's why she's afraid I'll pull you into helping her."

"Probably. She knows I usually have a certain influence over people around me."

"Understatement." She was silent again. "Okay, you can do it. But I still won't have unlimited time to question or influence her. My time with her is triggered by those sketches I do after I wake."

"That may change. As she gets stronger, she may be able to reach out to you at any time. As she could do with me, if she chose." He picked up the sketchbook and flipped it open to the first page. "Now let's go over these sketches again to see if we've missed anything." His gaze was raking Lisa's face and expression. "This is where she must have realized that she was in trouble and she might be going to have to have help to deal with it. There's stress but not desperation. It's always difficult for Lisa to imagine that she can't handle situations herself." He pointed to the mountains and flowering garden in the background. "Calm, beautiful surroundings. Whoever is holding her here is going very slowly, probably trying to use persuasion." He flipped through a few more sketches. "Same background, but her expression is changing; it's becoming more tense, her jaw harder, her eyes alert and fierce."

"I just thought she looked a little older."

"She does. But it's because whatever is happening to her is causing her to mature more rapidly."

"What?"

"I deliberately did everything I could to extend that peaceful period in her life and keep her body and mind from jump-starting." He grimaced. "And becoming like mine. But she's feeling a threat and she's instinctively becoming what she feels she has to be to combat it." He flipped a few more pictures and found the one in which Lisa's lip was bleeding. He paused a moment, as if he had to control himself. "You see the expression is becoming more intense. She's in fight mode." He went to the sketch with the bloody message. "And it increases and increases. She's being hurt and she knows exactly what she's facing now. It's causing her to change. Childhood's end." He pointed to the letters written in blood. "And she's learning to control her blood flow. Those abrasions on her wrists shouldn't have bled that freely. She needed enough blood for her message and caused it to come to the surface." He flipped to the sketch where Lisa was looking down at the cliff with her hand resting on the windowsill. "You see her wrist here? It's been only a little over twenty-four hours and it's nearly healed. She might not even know it's happening, but her blood is doing what it needs to do to protect her."

"Let's hope that we find her right away and don't have to worry about her making any more progress." She glanced at him. "She's being hurt. All the signs are there that she has to be doing this to protect you. Why? Do you have any idea?"

"Not a clue," he said grimly. "As I said, it's not a cult. I've been on guard against that possibility since they killed Maria. Why would anyone try to take me down? I'm a hunter. I've killed for armies, police, personal vendettas, and the Devanez family, who's the core of my own heritage. There are always people left behind who could turn hunter, too. Whoever they are, they brought Lisa into the middle of it." His lips tightened to iron hardness. "That's not permitted. I'll have to demonstrate that to them."

Jane was suddenly chilled. She knew what Caleb was capable of doing and she had never seen him more lethal. "Could it have anything to do with the Romanos? They don't seem to be on the scene. Do they have some kind of vendetta against you? You said that they wouldn't permit you to see Maria or Lisa."

He was silent. "It's possible. I have a way of attracting that kind of feeling, don't I? Sometimes I encourage it. But they had years to try to plan some way to get rid of me and they didn't do it. The most that they did was to keep my sisters away from me." He added, "Though I'm certain that they felt the same horror and distaste for me that my parents did. I can remember when they first visited my mother and father and the way they looked at me whenever I was around. Granted, I behaved atrociously. Gino was always nervous and impatient that I was allowed in his august presence. Teresa was more subtle, but she was all sympathy toward my mother. That was somehow . . . worse." He paused, thinking back. "Yes, Teresa was far more subtle. I didn't realize until later how much more clever her approach was than Gino's. No wonder they were given custody of Maria and Lisa."

What must that have been like for him? Jane could feel the anger begin to stir at the sheer unfairness of it.

"Good God, you're beginning to feel indignant for me," Caleb said roughly as he caught her expression. "Next it will be pity. Stop right there. That's not an emotion I ever want you to feel for me. I didn't need it then, and I don't need it now."

"Heaven forbid. I'm just trying to understand those people. If they're that callous, I can see them not caring if something bad happened to you. You apparently didn't exist for them as a person."

"You're right there." The violence was gone from his voice. "And it's something I've begun to consider. They might not be involved in any plan to rid the world of me, but they might not be moved to keep it from happening. You might ask Lisa a question or two about that when you have the opportunity." He rose to his feet. "And now it's time for you to try to go to sleep and see if Lisa will give you a chance to do that." He pulled her to her feet. "I'll see you in the morning. Or whenever you choose to share with me. I think you know that I want to be told what's happening as soon as possible."

"I'm being sent to bed on a mission?" she asked wryly.

"Not the mission I'd choose for you." He picked up the sketchbook and handed it to her. "But the one that's necessary at the moment."

She started to turn away and then stopped. "What about that 'stay' thing you said you had to do?"

"Oh, that." He took a step closer to her and his hands were suddenly moving on her temples with deep, mesmerizing strokes that caused her to inhale sharply at the touch. Then his hands dropped away from her. "That should do it."

Jane frowned. "That's all?"

He nodded. "No big deal. I actually didn't have to touch you to insert the stay. I'd already done it the minute you said I had permission to do it."

"Then what was that about?"

"I wanted to touch you," he said simply. "I'm not entirely pleased about having to give in to you about this, so I thought I'd take whatever I could from the situation."

"Impossible." She turned on her heel and strode up the hill toward her tent. He is more than impossible, she thought. Caleb was accustomed to winning and manipulating everything around him, and when he couldn't, there was no telling what action he would take to get his own back.

Get his own back. Those words suddenly struck home to her. That was what Caleb was attempting to do in a very real sense. He considered Lisa as belonging to him and he was going to try desperately to get her back. His relationship with Jane might make it easier or harder for him, but she was aware that she would be tied to him until that occurred. It was what she had dreaded when she had realized it was Caleb who had a relationship to Lisa.

She was still wary, but she felt a little better that she had faced him down once tonight. How many other times she would be able to hold her own with him, she had no idea. But she had to do it. Because they both wanted the same thing and had to find a way to get it.

To have Lisa come out of this alive.

CHAPTER 5

The cliff.

Lisa wanted her to pay special attention to it.

Why?

It didn't matter. Just do it.

Jane's pencil flew over the page, documenting detail after detail. The cliff . . . a path . . . Was that an island in the distance?

She finished the sketch.

Then she drew a deep breath and, as usual, tried to pull herself together.

Lisa, still in that dim room, her gaze on that cliff and path . . .

Dear God, more bruises.

Deep bruises on her throat and shoulders. Her peasant blouse torn at the shoulder, revealing a long, livid scratch.

For God's sake, what's been happening to you, Lisa?

The answer came swiftly and with impatience. *What do you think? It's pretty obvious, isn't it? Sometimes I wonder why it has to be you.*

It has to be me because somebody up there probably knows no one else would put up with you. I don't deserve this, so now answer me politely.

Lisa was silent and then said, *Santara is getting impatient. He's afraid to do too much. But he has pressure, and I don't make it easy for him.* She paused and then the next thought was hurled with sudden ferocity. *As if I would do what he wants. As if anyone could make me.*

Santara? That's who did this to you?

Yes, Santara. I think he said his first name is Leon.

Is there anyone else there on the island?

I've seen three more men, but I don't know their names. I think there are others. Santara is the only one who deals with me. She paused. *I feel the link . . . is stronger with you. This time yesterday you were slipping away from me by this time.*

Maybe you are stronger. You told me you were working on it.

Yes. Another pause. *But I didn't expect it would happen this soon.*

I'm just glad it did, Jane said quickly. *If you want my help, I need answers. Do you have*

*any idea where you are? You seemed uncer-
tain before.*

*I don't know. I had a blindfold when they
brought me here. You saw the mountains and
then the cliff on this side of the house. When I
was trying to get down the cliff, I saw that
island in the distance.*

*Did you notice anything else? Something
that struck you as different about the place?*

No. Silence. *Except it felt . . . kind of golden.*

What?

I don't know. Just an impression. She went
on quickly, *But I thought that island might be
important. It was pretty far away. I wasn't sure
if I could swim that far. But I might try it
anyway the next time.*

Don't do it.

*I'll do what I please. You don't seem to be
helping.*

Lisa.

She was silent for a moment. *I have to
leave here. Santara's hurting me. He'll make
me break my promise.*

*Because you'll have to do what this Santara
is trying to force you to do?*

*No, don't you know anything? I'd never do
that.*

Then what are you saying?

*I promised. But I get so angry and I think
that I have to do it. And they'll hurt him if I*

don't do it.

Do what, Lisa?

Kill them. Kill them all.

What the hell was she supposed to say to that? Lisa might just be capable of doing what she wanted to do if Jane believed Caleb. But it brought up a host of questions. Would Lisa's fledging talent be enough to take down the people she was facing? Caleb had kept it smothered and she was only now aware of its power. If she tried and didn't succeed, it could get her killed. And Caleb had said that the people who held her mustn't be made aware of her capabilities. Added to the fact that there were all the psychological and moral ramifications. But there were all sorts of complications in communicating with Lisa.

And are you going to tell me to whom you made that promise?

Why? You have to know already. I feel him whenever I reach out to you. It's Seth Caleb.

Okay, but you haven't been very forthcoming about anyone or anything concerned in all this.

I didn't have time. I didn't trust you to protect him. But I may have to trust you. Things are . . . changing.

I can see that by the bruises, she said drily. *How badly are you being hurt, Lisa?*

Silence, then: *Not bad. I'm fine. I just need to get out of here.*

I'm not sure I believe you.

Believe what you like. I'm fine. And I might be able to stop them without you.

I don't think that's wise. I believe you have to do what Caleb wanted you to do. We'll work out something else.

What? The question was passionate. *It's all about him. They want me to call Seth and tell him to come here. And not to warn him that anything is wrong. I'll never do that. I'll never let anything bad happen to him. Not ever. No matter what they do to me.*

Love and passionate dedication and the willingness to sacrifice. It was all there in those few sentences. Jane was unbearably touched and she could feel her throat tighten.

As I said, we'll find a way to get around it. Just don't do anything that could get you killed until we figure it out. You may not have any respect for me, but I'm going to make sure that I get you out of this.

Silence, then: *I suppose I might have respect for you. Seth must think you're okay, to have such a strong link with you. You were the only one I could reach when I was trying to get help.*

And avoid reaching out to him.

He mustn't come here. You promised me it would be only you.

I'll keep my word, unless you give me permission to break it. She added, *But you know Caleb will be looking for you. He cares about you as much as you care about him. Don't you think that it would be safer not to let him go at it blind?*

Not if you get me away from here right away. She was silent; then she suddenly burst out: *He knows, doesn't he? That's why I'm not having any trouble keeping you with me. That's why you're trying to persuade me to let Seth help me.*

Jane felt an instant of pure panic. So much for Caleb's assertion that Lisa wouldn't guess that he was involved. Now she didn't know which way Lisa would jump.

Look, I kept my promise. I just had to know more than you were telling me. I didn't even know he was your brother until I pinpointed the resemblance. And Caleb already knew something was wrong. You must have known he would when you cut off your link to him. He's been searching for you.

Only you!

I told you I'd keep my promise. I won't let him come near you. But he's not going to stop until he knows what's happening.

Listen to you. You're asking me to trust you.

I don't like having to trust anyone.

I know that, but you don't have many options. Neither do I. I can't let you be alone in this.

There was no answer, and Jane was holding her breath.

I don't want to be alone. Then Lisa went on quickly: *Not that I'm afraid, but I might need someone else to take care of Seth if something happens.*

Then I'll volunteer for that, too. Just don't think you have to face this by yourself. Okay?

Okay. The word was definitely grudging.

Then I need to ask a few more questions and then we have to work out a strategy. Agreed? She didn't wait for an answer. *Where were you when you were taken?*

At the Romano estate. I went to bed one night, and when I woke up, I was on a helicopter and had a bad headache. And my hands were tied behind my back.

Drugs?

I don't know about that. Maybe.

Were your guardians taken with you?

No, I was alone at the estate except for a couple servants. Teresa and Gino went to Rome two days before that. The only one on the helicopter was the pilot and a man who said his name was Leon Santara. He said that I wouldn't be hurt as long as I did what he said. Then a couple hours later he blindfolded me and later we landed here. That's how it started.

And how did it go on?

They treated me okay for the first few days. Gave me a bedroom, fed me. But Santara kept bringing me into this tower room upstairs and threatening me, telling me what I had to do.

And what was that?

Seth. I told you: He kept saying I had to call Seth Caleb and tell him I needed him to come here. It was all about Seth. They didn't want me; they wanted Seth. He kept saying that they didn't want to hurt him. That they only needed him to do something for them. But they think I'm just a stupid girl and will believe any lies they tell me. Why should I let him get hold of Seth? she added fiercely, *And that's why it has to be only you. I won't give him Seth.*

Shh. Jane could sense the anger and force that was electrifying the girl. *You don't have to keep repeating that. But I think you know that Caleb can take care of himself.*

No one will use me to hurt him. I won't let that happen. Even if I break my promise to him.

What promise?

Ask him. He's the one who made me give it.

But he's wrong, he's wrong.

Then I'm sure that the best thing would be to let —

Santara! Panic. *He's coming! I have to go. I hear him in the hall.*

At this time of night? Are you sure?

Of course I'm sure. He hasn't let me sleep much the last few days. He's opening the door. He's coming into the room and he —

Lisa was gone.

Jane drew a deep breath and slowly closed the sketchbook. A disturbing and revealing episode and she still didn't know enough to have a clue about finding Lisa. She would have to wait and see if she could learn more the next time.

She glanced at the clock. It was 4:35 in the morning.

He hasn't let me sleep much . . .

Bruises. Sleep deprivation. What else was in store for Lisa?

And it was clear she wasn't going to be able to give them what they wanted. Not a promising picture.

Promise.

Ask him. He's the one who made me give it.

And she would, but she wasn't going to jump up and run down to Caleb's tent again tonight. It was close enough to morning to lie here and try to get her thoughts together

140

before she exposed herself to the disturbing force that was Caleb.

She reached out and turned off her lantern. She lay staring into the darkness while her mind skidded at top speed from thought to thought. Lisa. Caleb. What they were together and apart. How she was involved with both of them and was somehow caught in the middle.

But it was that last fact that was the only important thing. Caught in the middle and she had to ignore everything else and concentrate on extricating herself and Lisa from the center of this mess.

Okay, she thought. Go over everything and see what you can come up with before you talk to Caleb.

But she was too on edge to wait any longer than six before she left her tent and walked down to the campfire.

Caleb was already there, fully dressed, his hair wet from the shower. "Fresh coffee." He handed her a cup. "But I wasn't about to cook you breakfast. You can eat later. I wanted to talk to you before Jock and MacDuff surface. You've kept me waiting long enough, dammit. I saw your light go on at four." He took the sketchbook from her and flipped it open to the new sketch.

"Punishment escalating," he said grimly. "They're getting impatient. She's probably not only refusing to do what they want but giving them a bit of verbal abuse. Lisa is never shy about making her thoughts known."

"So I've noticed." Her lips tightened. "And it makes me sick to see her like this. Is there any chance I can convince her to keep her mouth shut until I can find a way to help her escape?"

"Probably not." He lifted his eyes from the sketch to meet her own. "But I could do it. If you give me the chance."

"Don't be too confident. Your influence might be waning. She's not at all certain that your advice is either smart or desirable."

"Indeed?" He shrugged. "I'm sure you're going to elaborate."

"You bet I am." She quickly and concisely went over her recent communication with Lisa and ended by saying, "And the word *wrong* was used very emphatically when connected with you, Caleb."

"And you enjoyed it enormously."

"I enjoyed the chance to prick your ego, but I'm not enjoying anything else about this," she said wearily. "And if I could turn you loose on Lisa to work your magic, I'd do it. But I could tell I was skating on very thin ice when she found out that you'd already become involved on even this limited basis."

"I could convince her."

"I won't take the risk." She paused. "What promise did she make you, Caleb?"

"You probably have a good idea. I worked with her on initiating her talents when she was a youngster. But I made her promise she would never free them until I judged the time was right and gave her permission."

"And reinforced it with that mojo you use on occasion."

"It was necessary," he said through set teeth. "Look, as long as no one knew she wasn't normal, she wouldn't be treated as a freak by anyone in her circle. She had a chance of what they call 'living a happy life.' What was more important as she grew older and the talent grew, is that it protected everyone around her from a minor temper tantrum that could prove deadly." He paused. "And Lisa from being victimized or used by anyone who might want to employ that talent."

"Like her sister, Maria?"

He nodded. "And Maria had no talent."

"And you, Caleb. Did anyone try to make a victim out of you?"

"Of course. But thanks to my dear parents, who made me suspicious of who and what I was, I grew up to be wary of everyone around me." His lips twisted. "I assure you, I was such a son of a bitch that no one ever had the slightest chance of victimizing me."

"But according to what Lisa said, this Santara told her that the reason they wanted to reach you was because they needed you to do something for them."

"Which could have been a complete lie. I have a lot of enemies."

"That's what Lisa thought. But why go to all the bother of kidnapping her just to get hold of you? Why not go for you directly if they want to kill you?"

"And your point?"

"I don't know. Only that they've asked for no ransom. They want Lisa to get you in a position where you see how helpless she is. That's very persuasive if you want to barter something. Perhaps Santara wasn't lying."

"Possibly," he said. "Or maybe he was." He finished his coffee. "Either way, we have to find out where they're keeping her. I'm starting with the Romanos, who conveniently left Lisa alone on the estate for two days before Santara went after her. They supposedly went to Rome, but I couldn't find any trace of them when I was looking

144

for Lisa. If the estate was closed up within a couple days of the time when Lisa was taken, they would have had to sign contracts or give verbal orders to get it done. I'll track it down." He added grimly, "Or track them down."

"You think they may be involved?"

"It's looking that way. I told you that the Romanos had no liking for me. If they're using Lisa to get to me, then they certainly know what they'd get for their money. Maybe they're earning a little extra cash setting me up for one of my more than plentiful enemies." His smile was reckless. "Or perhaps they found a use for the freak that they considered so disgusting. We do have uses, don't we, Jane?"

He was no longer talking about Lisa, and Jane wasn't going to let him go there. "Back off. I made a mistake. But this isn't about anyone but your sister. You saved Eve and Michael and I'm going to do my damnedest to help Lisa. Neither has anything to do with the other." She turned away. "I'm going to make breakfast for everyone and then I'm going to call Eve and Joe and tell them what's happening. Are you going to help Jock and MacDuff today?"

"Until noon. Then I'll be on the phone checking out Santara." He was silent. "And

I really need to link with Lisa. It sounds as if she's ready to —"

"No. I think she's stronger than you think, stronger than she thinks. But we do have to get her away from that bastard who's abusing her." She paused. "I don't want to have to wait for her to use those sketches to bond with me. Can you find another way to make it happen? Can I go to her?"

He raised his brows. "If you let me come along."

"No."

"It's the only way. You'd be satisfied because it would be visual, as well. Actually, you'd be coming along with me." He smiled. "You've been down that road before with me, but it would be a little different. No mind games. Just a clean link with Lisa."

"And risk her breaking with both of us."

"Trust me."

She shook her head. "I'd have to be desperate."

His smile faded. "It may come to that. Don't wait too long. I'm trying to go along with you on this, but there are ways that I can —" He stopped as he saw Jock coming toward them. "Don't wait too long. . . ."

"Caleb . . ." Eve said thoughtfully when Jane had finished. "Yes, I can see the resem-

146

blance there, now that you bring it to my attention. It was just that none of us was expecting it."

"I'll second that," Jane said curtly. "We didn't know Lisa existed. He lied to us."

"Yes, he did. But I imagine that Caleb has had to lie a lot in his life just to survive."

"You're defending him."

"No, but I'm trying to understand him. I think you're getting a new view on Caleb, too."

Jane couldn't deny it. "But it doesn't alter the fact that all of us still have to find ways to survive Caleb. And he doesn't allow anyone close enough to understand what drives him. Certainly not me."

"He let you know that he cares about Lisa. That may be a breakthrough for him."

"Look, Eve, this isn't about Caleb. It's about Lisa. Caleb is only important because he can help us to help her."

"But from what you said, getting her away may depend on giving Caleb to this Santara."

"I didn't say that." The idea sent panic through her. "Not that Caleb wouldn't be able to take care — But we'll find some other way to —"

"Shh, I know that's not on the agenda. I'm just trying to clarify the problem."

"I didn't phone to dump all this on you. I just wanted to let you know what was happening and update Joe on what we have to be on the lookout for." She changed the subject. "How's Michael doing?"

"Magnificently. Right now he's discovering the intricacies of building a skyscraper from his blocks. Nothing simple for Michael. But he's missing you."

"I miss him." She added lightly, "And his parents. I have to go now and see if I can lend a hand with those lights down in the mist. I'll keep you informed."

"Do that." She paused. "Be careful, Jane. I know this situation is driving you crazy, that you have to stand by and not be able to help that girl. Just don't make a move without letting us help."

"Right now, I can't make any move. I don't know where she is, dammit." She added grimly, "But I'll find out. Bye, Eve." She hit the button to end the call.

Try not to think about Lisa for the next few hours, she told herself.

She was terribly frustrated and there was a cold feeling in the pit of her stomach. She wanted desperately to reach out and find a way to do more for Lisa.

Before it was too late.

She got to her feet and headed down the

148

bank toward the mist.

I'm coming to see you, Cira. I need to think of someone who has already lived their life and solved all their problems. I wish you could give me a hint how I can do that. . . .

Lake Cottage

"Stop worrying." Joe slipped his arm around Eve and drew her closer on the couch. "I sent out a message to Interpol to be on the alert for anything connected to the Romanos or this Leon Santara. It's all we can do right now." His lips brushed her temple as he added wryly, "And I don't imagine that Caleb is going to stop at Interpol to find Lisa. His contacts aren't nearly as law-abiding, but I'd bet they're so afraid of Caleb that they'll come through for him."

"That doesn't mean they'll find her in time," Eve said. "Or that Jane's going to wait if she's given even a hint about where Lisa is. She's terribly frightened about her."

"And you're terribly concerned about our Jane," Joe said. "You hate the idea that she's so far away and you can't swoop to the rescue if she gets in trouble."

"And you don't?" Eve glanced up at him. "Bullshit."

"Watch your language in front of my son."

Eve glanced at Michael, who was still building some kind of colorful, complicated structure with his blocks across the room. "Yes, everything changes because of Michael, doesn't it? I've been feeling that more and more lately."

"I've noticed. Very contemplative."

"And grateful. In the end, this isn't only about Lisa; it's about Caleb, too. He saved Michael. We owe him, Joe."

"Do you think I don't know that?" he said thickly. "He saved you, too, that night when he blocked that poison from your bloodstream. You never mention that unimportant fact, but it's not unimportant to me. It's my whole life." He paused. "Yeah, I owe Caleb. Suppose I take a trip across the big pond and see what I can do about locating Lisa and giving her to Caleb as a gift." He grinned. "Lord, that would annoy him if I got there ahead of him."

She chuckled. "He might surprise you in this case. He might even be grateful."

"Now that *would* surprise me." He kissed her on the forehead. "I don't know how I'd respond."

"By rubbing his nose in it." She shook her head. "And I don't think that I can allow you to be so ungracious. I think we'll have to handle it differently."

His brows rose. "What are you talking about?"

She gazed thoughtfully at Michael across the room. "Just something I've been thinking about for quite a while . . ."

Good idea, Michael?

Michael lifted his eyes from his blocks and smiled at her.

San Leandro

He'd broken her thumb.

Santara looked down at the girl crumpled on the floor. Lisa was panting, her dark eyes blazing up at him, as she cradled her hand. "I should have broken your neck instead," he said. "I might still do it. Make that call."

"No." Lisa's voice was shaking. "It only hurt for a minute. Do you think I'll do anything you tell me to do? Do whatever you want, but I'm counting it all up. I'm remembering, Santara."

For an instant, the passion in her voice caused a ripple of uneasiness to go through him. Then he dismissed it and chuckled. "Is that supposed to scare me? You're just a weak little girl who's going to break anytime now."

"And what does that make you? Do you

151

only dare beat up on weak little girls?"

Santara could feel the rage sear through him. "I think I'll do the other thumb next."

"Whatever. But I don't think they want me too damaged, do they? They're afraid of what my brother will do. Why don't you ask them?" She licked the blood from her lip. "You should be afraid, too."

"Then call him and bring him here."

She didn't answer. She just stared at him with eyes that glittered with hatred in her white face.

Bitch. He wanted to put an end to her right now. Usually he enjoyed the torment, the fear, the weakening, but he wasn't getting any of that from this girl.

And he'd better make that call the little bitch had taunted him about. He pulled out his phone and dialed Teresa Romano. "How long is this supposed to go on? You tie my hands and still expect me to get results?"

"I take it from that explosion that you've done something stupid and are about to make excuses. What is it, Santara?"

"The girl won't make the call." He added, "Okay, I broke her thumb. But just beating her up wasn't doing any good. We have to move on with it."

"I can see how you'd be frustrated, but you'll have to rein it in. Gino and I value your opinion, but we have a plan and I won't permit you to ruin it. I told him that you liked that part of the job a little too much." She said slowly and clearly, "No permanent damage. Breaking a bone was a little too close to that. We want Caleb to see a *token* example of what can be expected if he doesn't do what we wish. We don't want him to become angry enough to unleash that ugly temper. It might be counterproductive."

"I can handle this Caleb. I don't know why you're worrying about his temper. He's only one man. I can crush him like a cockroach."

"I realize that you don't know why we're concerned about Caleb. You don't have to know. I only pay you to obey orders," she said coldly. "Let's just say that Caleb possesses a certain talent that's going to make Gino and me a fortune if we can manage to turn it loose on Haroun. A very valuable talent that's absolutely foolproof." She added impatiently, "But Caleb can be very difficult and he has to be handled correctly. Lisa is the best way to do that. He has a fondness for his sister that we can manipulate to permit me to guide him in the way I need him to go." Her voice hardened. "Now, if you can't find a way to get what I need, in the way that I need it, I'll cut you loose and hire someone who can. Do you understand?"

Santara could almost see her, every shining strand of blond hair in place in that chignon, blue eyes stone-cold, no expression on that mature, beautiful face. Gino Romano might control the finances, but Teresa controlled Gino and everything else around her. But not me, Santara thought. I wouldn't let her control me. This young girl lying on the floor in front of him wasn't the only female Santara was tempted to butcher whenever he talked to this frigid bitch. "I understand. But I'll expect a list of acceptable methods you will approve. Evidently you had no better luck than I did with her in the past."

"It didn't enter into our relationship. If it had, luck would have had nothing to do with it." She hung up.

Santara's hand tightened on his phone, trying to get control. He wanted to *kill* the bitch.

"I told you that they wouldn't like it." Lisa was looking up at him, still cradling her hand. "You don't understand anything, do you? I can tell from listening to your side of the conversations that you're just a tool."

"Am I? Well, this tool can cut deep." He

kicked her viciously in the ribs. "She doesn't want permanent, but she doesn't mind pain."

Lisa gasped in agony and couldn't speak for a moment. " 'She,' " she repeated finally. "You were talking to Teresa Romano, weren't you? I thought it might be them." She lifted a shaking hand to her head. "You never tried to hide the fact that you were taking orders from someone else. You even talked to them in front of me."

"I didn't mention names."

"No, you didn't. But Teresa and Gino left for Rome right before you scooped me up. Someone in that house drugged me. And you had to have had access to the house in some way to get me out of there." She added unsteadily, "And not many people know that Seth might come after me if he thought I was in trouble. I haven't seen him for a long time, but Teresa and Gino knew what he'd done when my sister was killed." She shuddered as another wave of pain struck her, and she tried to get her breath. "But I don't know why they'd *do* this. Why they'd let you do it. They didn't care anything for me or Maria, but I didn't think they hated us. It annoyed Teresa when I didn't do what she wanted me to do, but she just ignored me and saw that I was away at school all year. I wasn't worth her effort unless I got in her way. And Gino was always just a shadow figure. I hardly saw him at all." She shook her head. "But that's all changed, hasn't it? Now Seth *is* worth her effort . . . so I guess I am, too. But why now? When they've ignored him all these years?"

"Profit. The name of the game. She tells me it's a big score."

She was silent, her gaze searching his face. "I notice you're not denying that it's Teresa and Gino. You wanted me to know it was them, didn't you?" She moistened her lips. "Because you don't want them to argue about your killing me later. Otherwise, I'd be a witness against them."

"Very smart. Too bad you can't keep your mouth shut. I decided after the second day with you that you weren't going to last any longer than I had to put up with you."

"Second day? I thought it was after the first day. I could see it whenever you looked at me."

"I might change my mind if you make the call to Caleb."

"No, you wouldn't. It won't happen." She closed her eyes. "Now either keep on hurting me or go away and let me sleep. I don't want to look at you any longer. It makes me want to break my promise, and I'm trying to hold on for a little longer. . . ."

"He broke Lisa's thumb." Teresa grimaced as she turned back to Gino. "He wanted me to say that he had carte blanche to do what he wanted with her. We may have to replace him. He doesn't understand that Lisa has to be handled with great skill. She can be almost as stubborn as her brother. I never dreamed she'd be this protective of Caleb after being separated from him for this long." She smiled as she poured tea into her cup. "He actually asked for a list of approved methods. Isn't that amusing?"

"I don't find it amusing." Gino scowled. "I heard what Caleb did to some of those cult members who killed Maria. I'm not certain we should be using Lisa."

"Of course we should. We had no choice." She lifted her cup to her lips. "She was the perfect solution. Everyone knows that he doesn't give a damn about anyone or anything. Except perhaps Lisa. If Caleb was to be used, we had to have a key."

"Then we shouldn't try to use Caleb." Gino was hyper, too edgy, and she could tell he'd started using the coke earlier than usual today. "You should have listened to me. I told you that from the beginning."

Teresa tried to hide her contempt with a smile. "And I told you from the time that his dear parents told me what a monster Caleb was that I could find a way to make that monster an asset to us. I've put in a good deal of effort to make that possible. I *know* Seth Caleb. True, there are certain risks, but I can use him." She took another sip of her tea. "And if you hadn't been so careless as to almost bankrupt us, I might never have seen fit to put that plan into action. Just two more years and we would have been able to find a way to tap into Lisa's trust fund and none of this would have been necessary. But now I've tossed all my eggs into the golden basket and I have to see that I get everything that you've lost back in triplicate."

He glowered at her. "It wasn't my fault."

"Of course not." She added maliciously, "Did I say that? Oh, I did, didn't I? Forgive me. I know how sensitive you are. Now, why don't you get on the phone and check and see how Haroun is doing? It may affect how much more time I give Santara before I take over persuading Lisa myself."

"I'm leaving," Caleb said as he strode toward Jane that afternoon. "I'm heading for Rome to check out what's been happening with the Romanos. They have to have something to do with this. It's all too pat. I'll call later to find out if Lisa's managed any other contact with you."

Jane hesitated. "Maybe I should go with you."

"You're not invited." He stared her in the eye. "Not until I get that invitation you've been denying me to pay a visit with you to link with Lisa. You've forced me to go out on my own to try to find her. You can't have it all your own way."

"I'm trying to have it *her* way," she said curtly. "You were on the phone most of the afternoon. Did you get any leads on Leon Santara?"

"Not yet. But it might be an alias. I'm looking into it."

"Will you let me know if you do hear anything about him while you're gone?"

He didn't answer.

"Don't you *do* this to me, Caleb. I know you're angry, but I have to know about Santara. He's *hurting* Lisa." Her hands closed into fists at her sides. "I think he's doing more to her than she's telling me. I have to know if he's crazy or vicious enough to kill her. I may not have your influence with her, but maybe I can talk her into toning down the rhetoric."

"But you won't let me step in and do it."
He didn't speak for a moment. "I'd like to
refuse, but I can't do it. I'll let you know
what I find out about Santara. But I'm not
going to forgive you if you make a mistake
that causes me to lose her."

"I wouldn't forgive myself," she said
quietly. "Don't you think that's a possibility
that's haunting me? But I can *feel* how willful she is. I think she must be like you before
you managed to become a little civilized.
She could explode at any moment. I'm just
trying to strike a balance between the two
of you that will give her a chance."

"Then change your mind, dammit. Let
me do what I do best." He turned on his
heel and strode up toward the road where
his car was parked.

She watched him leave. He was difficult
as hell, but she couldn't blame him for being angry. Lisa meant something to him that
perhaps no one else on Earth did. Jane realized she was probably lucky he'd been as
restrained as he had been with her. But that
didn't mean it made the situation any easier.

"He's gone again?" Jock Gavin was strolling up the bank toward her. "I guess we
were lucky to have Caleb as long as we did.
He did a good job while he was here. He
said he was off to Rome?"

"That's what he told me." She smiled at him. "Are you two done for the day?"

"Just breaking for lunch." His gaze was still on Caleb. "He's tense. Very tense. You wouldn't care to tell me what's between the two of you at the moment? Besides the obvious, I mean."

She went still. "Obvious?"

He shrugged. "You want me to be blind, I'm blind. It's between the two of you. But there's something else stirring. . . ." His narrowed gaze shifted back to her face. "Isn't there?"

He was too good a friend to lie to. "Yes."

"And it's bad?"

"Very bad."

"May I help?"

"No." She reached out, her hand closing affectionately on his forearm. "No one can help right now until we get a handle on this. I might ask for help later. So keep on helping MacDuff with his darned lights and I'll yell if I need you."

He grinned. "By that time, I'll probably be ready for a long break. You may like communing with the spirits of the mists, but it gets a bit boring for me. If it wasn't MacDuff's passion, I'd be off to something a little more entertaining."

"Do you need my help this afternoon, now

161

that you've lost Caleb?"

He shook his head. "Caleb was here long enough to get us to the point where we start installing the transformers. That's going to be a long and tedious job. And since those Australian components are so damn complicated, it's better if we take our time with them." He waved at MacDuff, who was coming out of the mist. "And you don't have to worry about MacDuff grilling you about Caleb. He's so absorbed right now in the hunt for Cira's treasure, that's all he's seeing. He got what he needed from Caleb and that's all that was important to him." He turned and moved toward the campfire. "We don't actually need you right now, either, Jane." He glanced back over his shoulder and grinned. "I'll let you know when MacDuff feels like you should be around to invoke Cira to bless his treasure hunt."

It was like Jock to analyze the situation, accept it, and then try to smooth out all the bumps along the way. "Are you trying to get rid of me?"

"Just giving you an opening. I know you'll be here for MacDuff when the time comes."

"I wouldn't think of doing anything else." It was nice of Jock to set up a scenario where she was free to leave the camp, but he didn't realize that she had nowhere to go now that Caleb had refused to let her go with him to Rome.

Nowhere to go? She was suddenly filled with self-disgust. *Let* her go? Caleb couldn't stop her from doing anything she wanted to do. Yes, he might be able to get more information on his own, but that didn't mean he controlled what she did. And who the hell knew if Rome was the right place to track down the Romanos or Santara or anyone else? She had her own resources in the sketchbook and the conversations she'd had with Lisa. Now was obviously the time to analyze and try to come up with something of value.

"I'll keep that in mind, Jock." She turned and strode toward her tent. "In the meantime, I have to do a little research and a lot of thinking. Have a good afternoon. I'll see both of you at supper."

CHAPTER 6

For the next few hours she studied every one of the sketches down to the last detail. Since she was seeing what Lisa was seeing, everything about the natural surroundings and the rooms in the house should be totally accurate.

She hoped.

Don't hope. Assume that Lisa is being allowed to reach you for a reason. Eve had said Jane was chosen. Okay, then there had to be something here she could use.

If the mountains were the Alps, where were they located?

Question mark.

The island?

Not a large island, but it seemed to have a long, curving road up the side that Lisa was facing. The lower side to the east jutted out in a flat, triangular fashion. Lots of trees.

The cliff was steep, but not completely impassable if Lisa had made it down to the rocks and beach. Definitely sea. Not a river.

What sea?

Lisa had been kidnapped at her guardian's estate in northern Italy. She'd been taken on a helicopter to her destination. She hadn't mentioned any stops to refuel.

What direction?

The sea . . .

Try south.

She pulled up the map on her computer.

"Okay, Lisa," she murmured. "If I've been chosen, tell me where the hell I'm going. . . ."

A few hours after Lisa regained consciousness, she'd reached her destination. But who knew if she'd been unconscious for hours before that time. She might have had time to reach Morocco, on the African coast.

Then again, the helicopter would probably not have been chosen for a long-distance journey. Wouldn't Santara have switched to another plane?

Okay, time to go back to the sketches and conversations. She was becoming blurry from looking at maps and computer screens.

But she needed a breath of air and a few minutes outside the confines of this tent. She was getting claustrophobic.

She dropped down outside on the bank

and looked out at the lake. She tried to relax and just absorb all that information she'd gathered about helicopters and the Mediterranean and the Aegean and the distances from the Romanos' estate, and a hundred other details she'd crammed into her mind.

Let it go. Just take this moment.

Her gaze shifted to the north bank, where Jock and MacDuff were probably moving, working, somewhere in that eternal fog. Looking for the treasure, searching for the end of the rainbow, searching for the end of the story.

Searching for Cira . . .

The lake was as beautiful as always and the late-afternoon sunlight was casting a luminous golden glow over the mist. Jane always loved it at this time of day, when it was almost like —

She stiffened, her breath leaving her body. "Oh my God!"

She jumped to her feet and ran into the tent to get her computer.

8:40 P.M.

Her hand was shaking as she punched in Caleb's number. "You come and get me. I'm heading for the Edinburgh Airport. Don't argue with me. Just get in that fancy jet of yours and come and pick me up."

"Something's wrong? I told you that —"

"Something's right. And I don't care what you told me. You come and get me. I'm not going to go through another night wondering what's happening to Lisa." She hung up.

Then she turned and went to Jock, who was back now and sitting at the campfire. "I need your car. Will you give me the keys?"

He immediately took them out of his pocket and tossed them to her. "Am I allowed to know when I get it back?"

"It will be at Edinburgh Airport. Thanks, Jock."

"No problem. I offered. If you need anything else, let me know."

"I will." She headed up the incline. "I hope it will all be over soon."

"I think you should know that Eve was on the phone with MacDuff earlier this evening. He didn't tell me why. Is she concerned about this?"

"Eve is always concerned about everything if it has to do with family." But Jane was surprised that Eve had thought she had reason to contact MacDuff. "But if he mentions anything, tell him we're taking care of it."

"You and Caleb?" He was smiling that

warm, radiant smile. "That makes me feel better. I didn't like the idea of your bolting out of here by yourself. Even though I can see you're full of vim and vigor and ready to conquer the world."

"Only a small part of it," she called back to him. "But I'm praying that may be enough."

Three hours later, Jane was standing at the private terminal when Caleb's Gulfstream 650 pulled up at the hangar. The moment the stairs were lowered, she was climbing them, and she met Caleb as the aircraft door opened. "Turn around," she said curtly. "I don't want to waste any time. Get back in the air."

"A good many orders seem to be being hurled around," he said silkily. "Am I going to be allowed to pilot my own plane?"

"Yes, I told you to get back in the air, didn't I? You know I don't fly." She went past him into the plane. "It seemed like a long time for you to get here, but it really wasn't. You must have started right after I called."

"I'd hardly dawdle when you were so adamant." His lips tightened. "I was afraid something had happened to you." He went ahead of her to the cockpit. "Though you were obviously not prepared at the time to confide in me."

"I had to get you here in a hurry. You have a tendency to play games or argue with me." She took out the bottle of water she'd bought at the airport and took a long drink. It tasted good going down, though she probably should have brought coffee. The adrenaline was fading and she might need a stimulant. She dropped down in the copilot's seat. "Could we please leave now, Caleb?"

His lips quirked. "Shouldn't I file a flight plan?"

"Why? You've been known to change them en route."

"True." He smiled mockingly. He was taxiing down the runway. "What's this about? Did you by any chance get a hint from Lisa about where we can find her?"

"Nothing new from Lisa. No dreams. No sketches. Did you find anything out in Rome about the Romanos?"

"Only that Gino was on the verge of bankruptcy and their estate was mortgaged to the hilt. He resigned from his position at the bank three weeks ago and the bank is trying to keep it from the investors. Lisa's trust fund seems to be intact, because it can't be touched until she is twenty-one.

But I can see how the Romanos could be frustrated about having all that money just out of reach and be bitter toward Lisa."

"And do they have any connection to this Santara?"

"Not that I've been able to establish yet," he said, then added, "And now that you've squeezed everything I know about the Romanos out of me, it's time that you —"

"I haven't squeezed everything out of you, only what's happening now with them. If they've had anything to do with hurting Lisa, I want to know them like you know them."

"That would be a difficult feat to accomplish." He made an impatient gesture as she opened her lips. "Okay, I'll try to give you what you want. Gino is old money, inherited his estate and partnership in the bank from his father. Likes the good life, was a playboy when he was younger, spent money like water, never married until he was in his fifties. Then he met Teresa Matalo, good family, but impoverished. They couldn't keep up with the rest of their set. All her life, Teresa was subject to slights from the society that she'd been taught was all-important. When she was twenty-five, she met and apparently seduced and then married Gino, almost thirty years her senior.

She took over everything in his life and made him like it. Most of the time. She was always trying to find ways to move up and secure her position in society. She's beautiful, totally self-serving, perhaps the most ambitious woman I've ever met." He reached for his phone and brought up a photo. "And she has the equipment to make most of those ambitions bear fruit." He handed her the phone. "Gino and Teresa."

It was a photo of a man and woman sitting at a table beneath an umbrella. The man was in his fifties or sixties, handsome, a little overweight, with black hair threaded with silver and wearing a gray business suit. The woman was much younger, sleek, blond, blue-eyed, with almost perfect features, and wore a navy blue dress that had to be by a designer. "You're right, she's stunning."

"I'm right about the rest, too," he said tersely as he took the phone back. "Now stop cross-examining me and tell me what the hell I'm doing here. I believe I told you that you weren't invited, and yet here you are."

"Because I'm more generous than you," she said curtly. "And since I may not have a choice, I might be forced to issue you an invitation of my own."

171

He went still. "If that means what I think it means, I believe you'd better let me get this plane on course before you make any explanation."

"Whatever." She looked out the window at the ground below gradually disappearing from view. "The quicker the better." Now that the decision was made and the action taken, she was being bombarded by doubts. She was working mostly on guesswork, wasn't she?

No, dammit, it felt *right*.

Ten minutes later, Caleb turned to her. "You've changed your mind? You're going to let me link with you and Lisa and question her?"

"No, I didn't say that." She moistened her lips. "In Lisa's eyes, it's probably much worse than that."

"What the hell are you talking about?"

"I'm going to do the one thing she's been fighting against from the beginning. I'm going to let you take me to Lisa and try to get her away from Santara."

His body became even more rigid. "You lied to me? She did manage to communicate something to you?"

"I didn't lie. But I suppose you could say that Lisa did manage to tell me what I needed to know. She's been trying to do that all along. Today I just concentrated and tried to put everything together. I believe I know where she's being held, Caleb."

"Talk."

"She was taken to that gray stone house in a helicopter and that meant probably no really long distances or high mountains. The time factor she told me about indicated that, too." She held up her hand as he started to speak. "I know, that's not much. I was getting frustrated, too. But when I asked her if she'd noticed anything else about the place where she'd been taken, she said she'd gotten an impression it was sort of golden. Very casually, she just threw it into the mix and moved on."

"And?"

"There's only one place on earth that I've ever been that would have that kind of strong impression on someone who was in the emotional state Lisa was at the time. I spent six months there as an art student because I was drunk with the sheer headiness of waking up to that golden light." She paused. "The Greek Isles, Caleb. If those sketches hadn't been black and white, I would probably have shown how it cast that wonderful glow on everything that —" She shrugged. "The light pervades everything. You've been there, haven't you? Do you see what I mean?"

He slowly nodded. "I never noticed it from an artist's point of view. But I've heard people talk about its effect on them. I guess I don't tend to embrace the light as much as you do." His lips twisted. "Maybe I'm more fire and brimstone."

"Anyway, the moment I realized the possibility, I started to try to pull it all together. I spent hours on the computer, calling real estate companies and tourist bureaus to track down the exact location. A large gray stone house on the coast with a tower that overlooked the ocean and an island some distance away. Mountains to the north, a garden . . . The island helped. The curving road leading to the top and that flat, triangular area to the east that was fairly unusual. But there are so many islands. . . . Over six thousand, but not nearly that many are inhabited. And that road leading to the top of the island indicated it was inhabited. Still, I nearly went blind Googling them all. I found two that were similar and I did a scan of the areas on the coasts within view of them. One in the Aegean Sea had no mountains anywhere near it. The other one had mountains. That was in the Ionian Sea, fairly close to the boot of Italy." She met his eyes. "And it also had a gray stone house with a tower."

"Show me," he snapped.

She pulled out her computer and found the page. "The stretch of coastline is called San Leandro. It's hard to tell anything much from this overhead satellite view, but it's —"

"Close enough," he said, interrupting, not taking his eyes off the computer page. "Because I'd bet that square near the house is a helicopter pad."

"I wondered about that. But I didn't see a helicopter."

"Which only means that they were dropped off." His gaze was raking the rest of the screen. "But this isn't good enough to show us any details of where Santara's men would be located. It would take extensive reconnoitering to make it a safe hit."

"Then you believe me?"

"I believe you believe it. Show me that sketch you did of Lisa looking at the island again."

She dug into her bag and pulled out her sketchbook. She flipped it open to the correct page. "It's the island of Zakyos. You see the triangular shape on the lower east side? The island is small and it has only fishing and a small inn in the hills open to tourists during the summer."

His brows rose. "You did some research."

"As much as I could on the computer. I need to do more, but that may have to be on the phone. But I had a three-hour wait for you at the airport and I didn't want to waste it."

"Heaven forbid."

"Time's important. I can't stand the thought of her being there any longer than she has to be," she said. "I thought it was probably safe to ask questions about the island on the Net. I didn't want to risk making any inquiries about San Leandro or that house with the tower. The last thing I wanted was to have Santara know we might have found out where he's keeping Lisa. He might have whisked her away somewhere." She added deliberately, "Or he might have set the trap for you that appeared to be his intention from the start."

"We might just oblige him," Caleb murmured. "I believe he might deserve to meet me."

"No." Jane had seen that flickering, lethal recklessness before and she had no intention of dealing with it now. "I know you're tempted to indulge yourself, but back off, Caleb. I didn't bring you here to turn you loose on this Santara. I want Lisa out of that house in as safe a manner as possible."

"Providing that's where she is," Caleb drawled. "No proof. I might have to go in and determine it for myself. We wouldn't want to disturb the neighborhood for nothing, would we?"

"Back off," she repeated. "As you say, no proof." Then she added fiercely, "But it's where she is, dammit. Everything fits together. And you think so, too, or you wouldn't be so eager to go in and cause your particular brand of mayhem. Admit it."

He glanced away from her. "Perhaps." Then he looked back at her. "I humbly admit it. You did well, Jane."

Her eyes widened. "Humble? You?"

He smiled. "I only threw that in to catch you off guard." He added quietly, "Very smart, Jane. My small contribution about the Romanos pales in comparison. Yes, I'll have to check it out, but I'll bet you're right." His smile faded. "And my particular brand of mayhem is going to be necessary from now on. So step down, Jane."

"The hell I will. Do you think I didn't know that you'd react like this as soon as you were convinced?" She glared at him. "I even thought about not calling you. Jock would have been willing to help me."

"That would not have been a good move," he said softly. "I like Jock."

"But that wouldn't have stopped you from doing exactly what you wanted to do. Mayhem or not."

"It might have. But I would have had to think about it."

"But now you don't, because Jock isn't involved. But that isn't why I didn't ask him. Lisa is your sister and you share something that no one else does. You have the right to help her. She's wrong about keeping you away from it."

"I believe I've made my agreement known on that score," he said drily.

"And you have a greater stake in this than anyone else . . . except maybe me." She wearily shook her head. "No, more than me. Except that Lisa pulled me into this and made me responsible. You say that she belongs to you? I believe she belongs to me, too, now. I think about her all the time. I worry about what's happening to her. I don't think she's been telling me everything. Every time I see one of those damn bruises, it nearly kills me. That's why I called you and told you to come and pick me up. I can't bear to see her hurt any more than she has been and know that I had a chance of stopping it."

"You have stopped it. Turn it over to me now."

"No, I promised her that I wouldn't let you come after her. I lied to her and she's not going to forgive me. But there's no way that I'll let you go into that house. She'd fight you; she might not even go with you. Her first impulse will be to push you away. She might even run from you. I've had a demonstration of how stubborn she can be."

"Then I'll take care of it."

"No, you won't. You'll stay outside that house. I'll go in and get her and bring her to you. I'll keep that much of my promise."

"No," he said sharply.

"Yes," she said fiercely. "You plan something clever and foolproof to get us away from Santara and keep Lisa alive. But if she thinks there's a chance of your being hurt because of her, she's not going to budge from that place. And she'll be so upset that there's no telling what reaction it will trigger. She might go after Santara herself. Possible?"

"Possible," he said slowly. "You've gotten to know her very well."

"I've never even seen her in person. But, yes, I know her," Jane said. "Now, can we get any help? Santara is supposed to have three men on the island."

"I'll check it out. It could be more dangerous to Lisa if we call in the local gendarmes.

Santara's been paid to do a job. If threatened, he may decide to cut his losses and get rid of her and go on the run."

"You're saying he might kill her."

"I'm saying we have to think about it. We don't know anything about him yet."

She didn't want to think about it. It frightened her too much. "Three men, plus Santara," she repeated. "And Lisa thought he might have more men in the north sector, where she wouldn't see them."

"I'll make a decision once we've reached Greece. The only thing that seems clear is that we should probably use that island as a place to launch any action. You were right: We need to find out more about it on the flight down there."

"I told you that I'd do it."

"Okay." Caleb glanced at her. "But you still haven't convinced me that I should let you do this."

"I don't have to convince you. I'm the one who invited you. If you don't go along with the rules I make, we part ways once I get off this plane in Greece."

"Unless I decide to tie you up and leave you in the plane."

"You won't do that. You're not Santara."

"There are people who believe I'm much worse."

"I'm not one of those people." She paused. "Neither is Lisa. Don't prove either of us wrong."

He chuckled. "That sounded almost like a threat." He held out his hand. "Pull up that Google map on your computer again and let me study it. I can at least memorize the outbuildings and natural features while I'm winging my way toward Lisa."

She handed him the computer. "I'm right, you know. If you walk into that house, she'll go ballistic. It has to be me."

"So she's been saying." His lips tightened as he glanced down at the computer screen. "But just because she's willing to sacrifice you on my altar, I find I'm not inclined to do it. She doesn't realize that you have a certain value to me that would be made totally invalid if you ended up dead. . . ."

5:40 A.M.

"Go get cleaned up and grab something to eat," Caleb said as he opened the door of the aircraft after he'd landed at a private airport near Athens. "I have details to arrange and a few calls to make before we head for the island."

"Are you going to try to slip away from me?"

"So suspicious." He smiled. "I wouldn't stand a chance. I may be a hunter, but you have a determination that's beyond belief. I was merely being considerate. You look completely exhausted and I don't want you fading away on me."

"I'm fine."

He shook his head. "Go in the terminal and eat." He was going down the stairs to the tarmac. "I'll come and get you at the restaurant when I'm ready to move."

"How far are we from Zakyos Island?"

"About an hour and forty minutes by speedboat."

"I knew you couldn't take the jet, but I thought that you'd choose a helicopter."

"Too noisy. I have to take a look at the coastline of San Leandro, and a speedboat will probably be more efficient and definitely less suspicious." He turned and looked up at her. "You did your job. You gave us a chance to get to her." His lips tightened. "Now take a break and let me do what I have to do if I'm going to let you go into that house without me. Okay?"

It wasn't okay. Her nerves were stretched taut and she wanted to move at warp speed now that she could almost see a way to free Lisa.

"I know." Caleb's gaze was on her face. "I

want it, too. Just give it a few hours, Jane."
He turned and strode into the terminal.

Jane stared after him and then slowly followed him down the steps. Follow. That was the last thing she wanted to do. She wanted to take the initiative and move forward. But it wasn't what she wanted; it was what was good for Lisa. Caleb was a hunter, and the lethalness of his talent had been proven over the years. She had brought him into this not only because of his love and connection to his sister but for that very skill. She knew the fundamentals of self-defense because Joe had taught her from childhood, but she was an artist, not a warrior. She was very much afraid that it was a warrior who would be needed before this was over.

So she decided to accept that she would have to follow for a while and grit her teeth until the situation changed.

"Come on." Caleb strode up to her table at the restaurant two hours later and threw down some bills. "We need to get on the road. I want to lease the fastest speedboat in the harbor and be at that island by late afternoon." He turned and headed back toward the door.

Jane jumped to her feet. "It's not as if I was holding you up." But she didn't like this sudden urgency. Caleb appeared both grim and electrified. She caught up with him at the door. "What's wrong?"

"Leon Santara." He showed her a photo on his phone of a tall, fortyish, sandy-haired man in a khaki jacket and army boots. "Or Gilbert Monlagi, as he's known in half a dozen countries in Europe and the Middle East. According to my contact, he was getting a little too notorious, so he's been using the name Santara for the last two years and trying to stay under the radar." He held the door open for her. "He's what's wrong. Very, very wrong."

"Bad?" she whispered.

He followed her toward the taxi waiting at the curb. "Born in Naples. Grew up on the streets and became a thief and drug runner, then later a mercenary in Africa, where he combined both careers. He was with the death squads in Angola and took money from the Iranians and the Taliban. These days, he sells his services to the highest bidder, usually works with his own team, all of whom are very competent." His voice was harsh and he wasn't looking at her. "He likes what he does. He likes the money and he likes the power. Santara won't hesitate to kill, but he prefers to make sure that his victim suffers enough to be aware who holds that power. He may be hurting Lisa to get what he wants from her, but he's enjoying it." He paused. "And he's been known to lose control on occasion."

"You're afraid he'll kill her."

He didn't answer directly. "I think we'd better get her out of there fast. He's no longer an unknown element, and what we know isn't good. Considering that Lisa is probably constantly provoking him, it's the only way we'll keep her alive." He opened the taxi door for her. "It's just as well, I don't believe either one of us could wait around and take the thought of the punishment he may be inflicting." He got into the cab. "So we head for the harbor and get to Zakyos Island as soon as possible."

Zakyos Island
Ionian Sea

The sun was low on the horizon when Caleb and Jane anchored the blue-and-white speedboat in a bay on the far side of the island. He jumped onto the beach and lifted her out of the boat. "You know what to do?"

She nodded. "For heaven's sake, of course I do. You went over it with me in detail. I go to the inn up on the hill and ask if we can have a room for the night. I say you're an accountant who's also a fanatical fisherman and you heard that the fishing was particularly good here. I tell the reception clerk that you're talking to the fishermen down here at the beach and sent me ahead. Then I sit down in the pub and ask casual questions of any guests or employees about whether there are any strangers or other interesting tourists on the island. Just to make sure that there aren't more men who were sent here besides the three that Lisa knew about on San Leandro." She made a face. "But all that sounds fairly unimportant and like you're trying to get rid of me." She stared him in the eye. "Are you?"

"Yes, for a little while. I'm going to go over this island so that I'll know it like the back of my hand myself. I'll try to recruit a couple men from here to help us. But everything I asked you to do was absolutely of value. It just might not be absolutely necessary. But then again, it might."

"But you're not going to get back in that speedboat and go get Lisa without me?"

"Tempting."

"Caleb."

He shook his head. "I've been thinking about Lisa, and you could be right about her reactions," he said grimly. "And if I force it, I could damage her. So I'll have to figure out a way to make it as safe as possible for you. You just have to do exactly what I say or I won't be able to keep myself from doing what I want and not what you want. Understood?"

She nodded. "I know how to obey orders. I grew up with Joe Quinn, a police detective, remember? The orders just have to make sense to me."

"That's what I'm afraid of. Sometimes I have problems communicating that concept." He handed her sketchbook to her. "I promise I'll be only a few hours. Go up to the inn and play artist."

"I don't play artist. I am an artist." She started up the twisting road that led to the inn. "But I'll do a sketch or two to lend authenticity when I'm in that pub." She stopped and looked around her. Zakyos was incredibly beautiful. Set like a jewel in that deep azure blue sea, it was green and flowering, with that golden Greek ambience that was like a heady wine. "Be careful. This place is like something from that movie *Mamma Mia!* When something is too good, it sometimes hides a rotten core."

"Now that sounds entirely too cynical coming from you. Who have you been hanging around with?"

"I won't answer that."

She heard him chuckle, but when she looked back, he was gone.

This island might be as balmy, golden, and breathtakingly wonderful as she'd told Caleb, but she was as uneasy as she'd said. It seemed impossible that this magical small island could be the place that Lisa had seen from that tower window. Had she made a mistake? There were so many islands, so many —

A gray stone house looming over the cliff, dominating everything around it.

San Leandro.

Jane had turned a corner in the road and was suddenly facing the gray stone house with the tower across the expanse of blue sea. She could see the white-capped mountains in the background. It was as if she'd been given an answer to all those doubts.

She stood there staring, her heart beating hard. Was Lisa in that tower room now? If she looked out that window, could she see Jane standing here only miles from where she stood?

No, it wasn't likely that she'd be able to make out a figure on this road from that far away. But the thought gave Jane a feeling of closeness to Lisa that was banishing the uneasiness and uncertainty that had been plaguing her.

"We're here, Lisa," she whispered. "We're coming for you. You're not alone anymore."

9:40 P.M.

"Paid in full." Jane smiled as she tore off the sketch she'd done of Risto, the young teenage boy who worked in the kitchen. "Save it. Once I'm famous, you'll be able to sell it for a small fortune."

He shook his head and grinned. "No, I'll keep it forever and tell everyone that I won it playing darts with a beautiful woman who was foolish enough to bet against the great Risto. That's a much better story." He looked critically at the sketch. "Yes, you've made me as handsome as I really am. It's clear you wish to do more with me than just draw my face."

"Oh, does she?" Caleb had appeared in the doorway of the pub. "But I might have a few objections to her doing that."

Risto stiffened as soon as he saw Caleb.

Jane couldn't blame him. Caleb's tone was casual, but there was seldom anything casual about Caleb. Power. Electricity. Force. Possessiveness.

Risto said quickly, "I meant no offense. She is —"

Jane interrupted. "He knows you didn't,

189

Risto. He's obviously a little bad-tempered at the moment. And no one has the right to make objections but me." She smiled at him. "Take your sketch and go back to the kitchen. Maybe tomorrow you can play against my friend here and beat him, too."

Risto nodded quickly, grabbed his sketch, and vanished in the direction of the kitchen.

She turned to face Caleb. "That wasn't necessary. You didn't need to intimidate him. He's only a boy."

"Who kept you entertained." He shrugged. "You're right: I'm a little bad-tempered at the moment. The sight of you spinning your web and drawing him to you annoyed me."

"Spinning my web?" She gazed at him incredulously. "I'm no vamp and you know it. I was being me and trying to do exactly what we agreed I'd do." She drew a deep breath. "Okay, why are you so bad-tempered? What went wrong?"

"Nothing. I accomplished everything I set out to do." He paused. "And perhaps a little more. I just knew that you were going to fight me on a couple things."

"What things?" She stiffened. "We're still going after her tonight?"

"Yes." He turned on his heel. "But not

right away. You got a room for us? What floor?"

"There are only two floors." She headed for the stairs, which curved upward on the left side of the reception desk. "No elevator. It reminded me of the hotel I stayed at when I was a student." She unlocked the door and preceded him into the room.

He glanced around the room at the simple white wrought-iron bed with its blue-and-white embroidered spread, the rocking chair, the mirror over the sink in the corner, the white-framed French doors leading to a balcony against the far wall. "Nice. I can almost see you sitting there on the balcony drawing. I would have liked to have known you then."

"Are you stalling?" She turned to face him as he closed the door. "What aren't I going to like?"

"I have to know everything about that tower room and where Santara is in the house and his schedule. And I can't rely on waiting for Lisa to reach you using those sketches anymore. I'm going to need the information fast and clear so that I can act."

"What are you saying?"

"You're going to go visiting. Visual. Auditory. The works."

"No," she said flatly. "You said that could

happen only if you were there to link us. Tonight's going to be difficult enough. I told you what her reaction would be to you."

"Yes, you did."

"So I won't do it."

"Yes, you will." He paused. "Because I lied."

Her eyes widened. "What?"

"I lied. I thought it was important that I be there to influence Lisa, so I lied to you."

"You son of a bitch."

He nodded. "I thought it was worth a try. I was going to give it a day or so and then give in on the link if I didn't get what I wanted. Or sooner if I saw an urgent reason for it."

"But it was going to be your decision. You were tying my hands and anchoring me to those sketches."

"For a little while."

She was struggling to smother the anger tearing through her. "Damn you, I don't know if I can forgive you for this, Caleb."

"That was the chance I took," he said simply. "But I should point out that it was important to me or I would never have done it. I knew it might take me a long time to regain what little trust you have in me."

"That goes without saying."

"But I said it anyway because you have to

realize that I knew exactly what I was doing. I have to get Lisa out of there no matter what I have to give up."

He meant every word. No mockery. No mask. Jane could see that for once Caleb's emotions were raw and visible for her to see. She stared at him for a long moment and then turned and walked toward the French doors that led to the tiny balcony. "A very long time, Caleb." She looked out at the moonlight shimmering on the dark sea. Get a grip. She couldn't afford this anger. "But there's no way that I'd punish Lisa because I'm furious with you. I believe you were aware of that. So tell me what's going to happen tonight."

"In about two hours, we take the speedboat to an inlet on the beach at the foot of the cliff. It's about a mile and a half from the house. I located the three men Lisa mentioned. Actually, there were four more. Four on sentry duty on the path leading to the mountains, one patrolling along the cliff, the other two in the back garden."

"You went over there to San Leandro already? You said you wouldn't do that."

"I said I wouldn't go after Lisa without you. I had to see what we were up against. Now I know."

She kept her gaze fixed on the sea. "Only

half a lie this time?"

"Yes." He went on quietly, "You wait in the boat while I take care of Santara's men. Hopefully, you will already have found out where Santara is in the house, so then you go in and bring Lisa out to me while I take care of him."

"All by yourself?" she asked. "What the hell do you mean? I thought you intended to try to recruit a couple men on the island to help."

"I did. But that's for later. They'd get in my way during this initial bit." He added soberly, "And if they made a mistake, they could get Lisa killed."

" 'Initial bit'? It doesn't seem like a 'bit' to me."

"I can handle this, Jane. It's not as if I'm going to have to defend myself from an assault by those men. It's just a matter of picking them off one by one."

"That's right, you're a hunter," she said bitterly. "You know all about things like that."

"Yes, I do. I'm an expert. And we're both going to be grateful that I am." He was silent. "Are you ever going to turn around and look at me?"

"I don't want to look at you."

"But I want to look at you." He was close

behind her now. "It's going to be a rough, hard night and looking at you makes me remember all the good things and not the ugly ones. Do you know, I actually feel as if you fill me and complete me. Isn't it bizarre you would have that effect on a man like me?"

"I have no idea, since I don't know if you're telling me the truth."

"Ah, there's the rub." He turned her around to face him. "But let's pretend that I'm telling you the truth this time." His dark eyes were holding her own and she thought she could see a reflection of the sea in them. "Yes, that's what I wanted. . . ."

"Let me go, Caleb."

"I'm only indulging myself a little," he whispered. "I wouldn't be fool enough to take more than you'd permit at a time like this." He was pulling her across the room, toward the bed. "But you might as well be comfortable when I link you with Lisa."

"Now?" She couldn't look away from him. That overpowering persuasiveness and charisma were in full force. He was smiling and she felt as if he were wrapping her in dark velvet. "It's time to do it?"

"Yes." He was pulling her down on the bed and holding her with the most exquisite gentleness. "It's time." His fingers were moving with mesmerizing tenderness on her throat and then up to stroke her temples. "Find out everything I need to know. Prepare Lisa."

"And how . . . do I do it?"

"I have no idea. That's up to you." The velvet surrounding her was no longer dark, but glittering and swirling around her. "You don't trust me, but I trust you, Jane. . . ."

CHAPTER 7

The tower room was darker than Jane had drawn it in her sketch.

That was the first thing she noticed when she opened her eyes. She drew a deep breath and tried to get her bearings. It was like Caleb to throw her into this situation where she had no experience and no way to judge what was real and what was not.

Okay, it wasn't as if she hadn't been down this road before. Except that then, the entire scenario had been orchestrated by Caleb as a sexual fantasy. This time, that wasn't the case. But she still felt everything about her was absolutely real, nothing dreamlike about it. So assume that and accept it, she told herself.

And get the job done.

She looked around her again. Yes, there was the narrow window overlooking the cliff. The room was also more cluttered and there were also books on the far wall, which Lisa had not been facing.

But where was Lisa?

Jane felt an instant of panic as her gaze wildly searched the room. Was she still here? Had she been moved? Had Santara taken her from the house and put her on a helicopter and sent her —

"What are you doing here?" Lisa asked harshly. "I couldn't get to you all last night, and now you just appear? I thought you'd left me." She came out of the shadows beside the door. "And I don't like this."

"Neither do I." Jane's gaze was raking the girl's face and body. Dear God, more bruises, a black eye, and she was favoring her right side as she came toward her. "That's why I'm here. You look terrible. I knew you were lying to me."

"I didn't lie. I just didn't tell you everything. I could tell how soft you are. I knew I had to be careful, or you'd do something dumb." Her eyes were glaring at Jane. "And you did it, didn't you? There's no way you could link this way with me. I can't even do it. Only Seth. It was Seth, wasn't it?"

"It was Seth Caleb." Jane glared back at her. "And you're not dumb; you're absolutely crazy. Look at you. How long were you going to take that kind of punishment? I didn't want him involved, either, but you're his family and he does have a right."

"Not unless I choose to give him the right," Lisa said fiercely. "And I won't let them touch him."

"Bullshit. You're going to get him killed just trying to protect him. You came to me because you want to live and you didn't want him to die. Then you put all kinds of restrictions on me, and I'm sick of it. We're going to get you out of here and you're not going to give orders; you'll take them." Her voice was steel-hard as she added, "Because I broke my word and brought Caleb into this and I'm not going to be responsible for either one of you getting killed. I won't have that on my shoulders. Do you understand?"

"If you'd done what I wanted, it would have been fine and everything —" Lisa stopped and closed her eyes. "Or maybe not. I'm confused right now," she said wearily. "I've been confused since this all began. I knew I had to protect him, but I didn't know how to do it. I didn't know how you could do it." Her eyes opened, and Jane could see they were glittering with tears she refused to shed. "But you seem to know, so I have to believe you. I don't want to do that. I'm scared to let go and do that. I've never believed anyone but Seth."

"Then heaven help you," Jane said drily. "Better you than me. However, I do think you

199

can trust him to help us get out of here. He cares about you."

"Of course he does. That's why I'm the bait." The fierceness was suddenly back. "And you shouldn't talk like that about him. You don't know anything. I thought you were close, linked, or I would have never tried to get you to help."

"Caleb's relationship with me is complicated." And this was no time to go into the nuances. Lisa was clearly passionately defensive of him and once again Jane was feeling that urge to reach past that wall of anger and hostility to touch her. Lisa seemed so terribly alone, and the fact that she wasn't battling to save herself, but the brother she loved, made her appear even more appealing. She said gently, "But the only thing that's important is that we're both here tonight to get you out."

Lisa froze. "Here? What do you mean?" Her gaze flew to Jane's face. "This is just a link, right? I'd know the difference."

"And I know practically nothing about these damn links." She paused. "But I do know that Caleb wanted to use this one to prepare the way for us. You're leaving here tonight."

"No," she whispered. "You're scaring me. I can't do this."

"Yes, you can. We've found you and we're going to take you."

"Seth is here? How could you do that? That's what I didn't want. This place is a trap."

"Then we'll spring it on that bastard who's been beating you up," she said roughly. "Get used to the idea, Lisa."

"I can't get used to it," she said through her teeth. "Not Seth. Tell him to leave here."

"I made him promise not to come into the house after you. I'll be the one coming here to get you. He'll be waiting down on the beach with the boat." She grimaced. "That should please you. That way, you and I are the only ones running the risk of Santara."

"It doesn't please me." She moistened her lips and then said stiltedly, "I never wanted Santara to get hold of you or hurt you. I just didn't know what else to do."

"And you had priorities. I understand."

"Do you? I don't know how." She lifted her chin. "But they can't have Seth. Maybe I could just run down to the beach by myself. I don't need you to come here."

"But I need to do it. I made a promise. And you look as if you're barely able to stand, much less run anywhere." Then as Lisa opened her lips to protest, Jane said quickly, "It's going to happen. Stop arguing. But I have to have information from you to help it along." She looked around the room. "Two doors. Where do they lead?"

"One is to a small bathroom; the other leads to the hall and down the stairs to the foyer and front door."

"And this door is locked? You mentioned one time that Santara was unlocking the door."

"It's always locked. I stole the key once and that's how I got out and down the cliff."

"And the front door?"

"I don't think so. It wasn't locked that time. He might be even more careless now. Santara may not be afraid I'll get out anymore." She paused. "I think he'd like it if I did. It might give him an excuse to kill me. He wants to do that now."

She made the last statement almost without expression, Jane realized. It just underscored all that Lisa had gone through during these last days. "Then we'll see if we can't please the bastard by getting you out of this damn house. Does Santara have his quarters in the house?"

"Yes, he has a room at the far end of the hall." Her lips twisted. "He likes the idea of having me at his disposal at all times of the day and night."

"Does he leave the house to check on his men at regular periods?"

"I think so. I know he phones them a lot. And I hear him going down the stairs two or three times during the evening. But not at all later at night."

Then he would still be in the house when she and Caleb came to get Lisa tonight. That was not good.

"You weren't expecting that." Lisa's gaze was on her face. "You don't have to come for me tonight. It can be anytime. Whatever's best for Seth and you."

And any delay would mean that Lisa would face more pain and abuse. Jane couldn't stand the thought of it.

"We didn't know what to expect," Jane said. "But we'll make adjustments. It does have to be tonight. It will be okay." She added, "I do have to know what kind of shape you're in. As I said, you don't look like you could make it down that cliff. That could be bad for all of us. No stoic bullshit; I need details."

Lisa was silent a moment. "I have a few burns on my arm, but that's nothing. My wrists are completely healed now. You see the bruises. I have two more on my back that you can't see. I think he may have either bruised or cracked my ribs when he kicked me. It's kind of hard to breathe. I have a broken thumb on my left hand. I tried to bandage it and didn't do such a good job. But I don't think it will bother me. None of it will be a problem. That's all, Jane."

That was all? Jane tried to stifle the pity and

rage she was feeling. She had to steady her voice. "No, we'll make certain that none of that will be a problem for you. I'll get you down that cliff. Be ready."

"I will." Lisa hesitated. "You'll keep him safe?"

Not herself. Caleb. "I'll keep him safe. He'd laugh at that, you know."

She smiled shakily. "Yes, but that doesn't matter, does it?" She paused and then said awkwardly, "I . . . thank you, Jane MacGuire."

"Say that when we get you out."

"Don't tell me what to do. I wanted to say it now. . . ."

Darkness.

Velvet.

Caleb's dark eyes were looking down at her, she realized vaguely. His eyes were so like Lisa's. She should have realized that sooner. . . .

"You didn't even know I had a sister." He was stroking her hair back from her face with that gossamer gentle touch. "You did well. Ever since this started you've done everything you could do. I'm proud of you. You should be proud of yourself."

Why did it mean so much to her that he said that? She had thought she had been wandering around in a daze, getting nowhere. Even with Lisa tonight, it had —

But she wasn't with Lisa any longer, she realized suddenly. She was lying on that white wrought-iron bed with Caleb holding her.

She stiffened and pushed him away. "There's nothing to be proud of until we get Lisa out of there." She sat up in bed and ran her hand through her rumpled hair. "I suppose you did a little eavesdropping?"

"I thought it would save time." He raised himself on his elbow to watch her as she got off the bed. "And I didn't hear anything that you wouldn't want me to hear."

"Well, I heard a few things I didn't want to hear," she said jerkily. "Though I think I knew it all along. That's why I wanted so desperately to get her out of there. I knew she was going through more than she was telling me. Dear God, she has courage."

"Yes. She always did." His voice was without expression. "From the time she was a little girl."

But there was something in his tone that caused Jane to turn to look at him. His face was as hard and without expression as his voice had been. "You had an idea Santara was putting her through this."

"Operatives like Santara can be very determined. Yes, I thought there was a possibility. I deliberately kept myself from dwelling on it. The confirmation tonight wasn't pleasant for me." He met her eyes. "That was why I'd lie and cheat and kill to get her away from him. That's why I'd even lie to you if I had to do it. Without either hesitation or question."

And the cold mask he was wearing wasn't hiding either his hurt or the terrible rage. He might be able to hold everything inside, but she had known him too long not to see it. Well, she shared that rage and she wasn't going to pretend otherwise. "Then let's stop talking about it and go do it." She went to her suitcase, which was tucked in one corner of the room, and pulled out her Beretta pistol and tucked it into her jacket pocket. Then she turned toward the door. "But you'd better start worrying about that locked door and the fact that Santara will still be in the house. . . ."

San Leandro
11:35 P.M.

"No one will be able to see the boat unless they're on the beach itself," Caleb said as he pulled the speedboat onto the sand. "The overhang on the wall of the cliff will hide it from anyone above." He reached in his pocket, brought out a key, and handed it to her. "Skeleton key. It's specially crafted and it's very good. You should have no trouble. I've used it many times before."

As the hunter stalking prey. How many houses? How many kills? "I'm sure you have." Her hand closed tightly on it. "No wonder you weren't worried about the lock. I hope you have an answer for all the other problems."

"All it would take is one for which I don't have the answer. But I don't believe that will come up." He was out of the boat. "It will probably take at least forty minutes to an hour for me to take care of securing the perimeter and then get back here." He handed her a slim silver cylinder. "Press the button on this if you see anything that worries you, and I'll be back in a heartbeat. Otherwise, don't get impatient if I'm a little late. I'm going to have to do a little rigging. . . ."

With that, he was gone.

She could see only a shadow as he moved up the twisting path toward the top of the cliff. Sleek and lithe and purposeful, and he was probably enjoying himself.

No, that wasn't fair. Caleb was dead serious and driven tonight. It was just that she had watched him before on the hunt and knew the instincts and barbaric pleasure that took over when it drove him.

Seven men. Three guarding the house, four guarding the path to the mountains.

He might not be worried, but for her this hour would be excruciatingly long.

Try not to think of what Caleb was doing right now, she told herself.

Think about Lisa.

Her hand closed on the gun in her jacket pocket.

Think about what you have to do to that monster Santara if he gets in your way.

12:58 A.M.

He was back!

She hadn't heard Caleb come down the cliff, but he was suddenly there. His dark eyes were glittering and his face held that same wild exhilaration she had been expecting to see. "Come on." He swung her out of the boat and was pulling her toward the path leading up the cliff. "I want you in position in the next few minutes."

" 'Position'?" She was running to keep up with him. "What do you mean? I'm supposed to go inside that house. Lisa is expecting me."

"And she'll get you. I just don't want

208

either of you to get anyone else there as company."

"Did you manage to take out those sentries?"

"The ones I wanted to take out." He'd reached a shelf in the cliff wall twenty yards from the top. "Now we do the cleanup." He pulled Jane onto the shelf and pushed her against the cliff. He reached in his pocket and pulled out a small graphite device. "And a slight deterrence for Santara to keep him busy. I don't want him phoning and checking on his men and not getting an answer." He leaned against her as his finger went to the black button on the device. "Hold on to me. We're going to rock."

She instinctively grabbed hold of him. "What are you —"

Kaboom.

The earth shook and boulders and earth rained down over the sheer face of the cliff.

Caleb held her steady as the shock waves rippled through the ground above them.

"What — did you do?" she gasped.

"C-4. A present for the sentries closest to the mountains."

"So that's what you meant by rigging."

The rumbling had lasted only a couple minutes and then he was nudging her back on the path.

"Why?" she asked as he pulled her up toward the top of the cliff.

"Why not? I believe that should catch Santara's attention and get him out of the house, don't you?" He was smiling recklessly as he moved up the final twenty feet to reach the top of the cliff. He put out his arm to keep her behind him and stop her from joining him as his gaze zeroed in on the house. "Front door wide open and ajar." His eyes shifted to the burning inferno of fire in the trees leading to the mountains and the tall sandy-haired man disappearing into the smoke. "Oh, yes. That did it. He'd have to go see who was attacking that sentry outpost." He turned and pulled Jane the rest of the way up the path. "Go get Lisa. I'll stay down here on guard. Just in case Santara changes his mind and turns back."

Jane was already flying toward that open front door. Until this moment, she had not been certain that Caleb wouldn't go himself at this last moment in spite of what she had told him. No time to try to analyze anything Caleb would do or not do. Just get Lisa out of here.

She was inside the house, running up the stairs.

An oak door at the top of the steps.

She twisted the knob.

Locked.

Her hands were shaking as she pulled the skeleton key out of her pocket and inserted it in the lock.

It didn't work!

Don't panic. Caleb said it would work.

She inserted it again and slowly, carefully turned the key.

It clicked!

She threw open the door.

"It took you long enough." Lisa was standing there with a faint smile on her face. "But then, I didn't expect you to blow the place up, either." She was hobbling out of the room and heading toward the stairs. "Seth?"

"Yes." Jane was on the other side of the girl, supporting her weight as she started down the stairs. "I didn't expect it, either."

"Get out of my way," Lisa said impatiently. "I can do this by myself. You're being too careful. We have to hurry."

"And falling down the steps won't help anything." They had reached the bottom and Jane pulled her across the foyer. "Okay, we don't have time to be careful now. We have to go at top speed." They were out the front door and she pushed Lisa toward Caleb, who was standing at the top of the path. "I kept my promise to her, Caleb. Now get

211

her down that damn path."

Lisa stopped in her tracks, her gaze on Caleb. "She told me you were coming. I didn't think you'd be waiting practically on the doorstep. You might just as well have come knocking on my door upstairs." Her hands clenched at her sides. "You were stupid to come at all. I didn't want you here. I would have handled it."

"You weren't doing too well."

"That was your fault."

He smiled. "Yes, it was." He held out his arms to her and his next words were softly coaxing. "Now come here and help me make it right."

Lisa didn't move, her gaze on his face.

Jane inhaled sharply as she saw the expression on the young girl's face. Total love. Total devotion. Total bonding.

Lisa took one step toward him, then another.

Then she was running toward him and he was enveloping her in his arms. He held her close for just a second and then he was lifting her in his arms. "And you're the one who's behaving stupidly," he said lightly as he started down the path to the beach. "You should have walked, instead of run, to me. And you got yourself entirely too damaged, and I know it was because you couldn't let

Santara have the last word. Now I'll have to spend some time healing those damn ribs."

She clung closer, but said gruffly, "Serves you right."

"I may drop you over the cliff. Jane, go down ahead and start the damn boat."

"Absolutely." Jane moved around them and down the trail. "I can handle only one of you at a time. And neither of you seems worried enough that we're not out of this yet."

"I'm worried." His gaze went to the baleful glare lighting the mountains in the distance. "And a little regretful . . ."

"Regrets? That's not like you. About the explosion?" She was frowning, puzzled as she ran down the twisting path ahead of them. "I suppose those guards didn't actually hurt Lisa."

"But they didn't help her, either," he said coldly. "No regrets there. I just wish I'd been able to set it up so that Santara had been caught in the blast. It would have been more efficient than having to go after him later."

"You don't do that," Lisa said sharply. "Do you hear me, Seth. You don't *do* it."

"Hush . . ." His gaze was lifted toward the top of the cliff. "I thought I heard something." He increased his pace and was close behind Jane when she untied the boat and started the engine. He set Lisa down on one of the rear seats and pushed the boat off the beach. Then he jumped in the boat beside Lisa. "Gun it, Jane."

Jane pressed the accelerator and the speedboat leaped forward with magnum force.

And a bullet exploded on the teak console next to her!

She could hear Caleb cursing behind her. She glanced up at the top of the cliff as she started zigzagging over the water. A tall figure was silhouetted in the moonlight and he was aiming an automatic rifle.

Santara? She couldn't tell for certain in the darkness, though he looked as if he fit the description of the man in the photo Caleb had shown her. She shouted back at Caleb, "Is, it Santara?"

"That's my bet."

Another bullet seared by her ear and ricocheted off the windshield!

It didn't matter who he was; that shot had been too close. He was very, very good. Even in the darkness he knew his target and was accounting for all the evading maneuvers she was making.

And, as the one driving the speedboat, Jane was the target.

"Move over." Caleb had slid over the top of the seat from the rear and was pushing her down on the floor. "Keep down and let me —"

Another bullet hit the console!

"You can't do anything more than I was doing," Jane said fiercely. "Keep zigzagging and keep down yourself. Or let me do it and just stop him from shooting. I'm sure you're better with guns than I am."

"I don't like guns."

"Oh, shit."

"I didn't say I didn't know how to use them." He had his gun out. "Grab the wheel. Give me a minute." He turned and carefully aimed at the figure on the cliff. "But this gun won't have near the range of that automatic rifle he's using. The shot would have to be just right to take him down. And he knows it. Arrogant bastard. He thinks he's in control. Let's show him he needs to reassess. . . ."

He took the shot.

Santara fell to the ground.

"Yes!"

But Santara was rolling over, aiming, and the next moment another bullet tore through the windshield only inches from Caleb's head.

"Seth!" Lisa was suddenly on her feet and

215

launching herself at Caleb from behind, trying to cover him with her body. Her face
was white, her eyes frantic. *"No!"*

"Get down, Lisa." Jane reached back and
tried to jerk her away from Caleb. "For
God's sake, get away from —"

Another shot.

Lisa jerked. She gasped, her back arching.
Then she collapsed and fell forward against
Caleb.

Dear God.

Jane could see the blood seeping from the
wound in Lisa's upper back, staining her
white peasant blouse. Her eyes closed. . . .
Limp, so terribly limp.

Another shot. Close, again.

"Take care of her," Caleb said hoarsely.
He pushed Lisa gently toward Jane. "I've
got to get us out of here." He aimed once
more. "But first I have to make sure the son
of a bitch stays down."

Jane was already crawling into the rear
seat and cradling Lisa in her arms. Blood.
And still. So still.

Caleb fired several times in succession and
then lowered the gun. "I saw him jerk once.
I might not have killed him, but he won't
be getting up anytime soon." He turned
back and started zigzagging once more over
the water. He was looking straight ahead,

his face even paler than Lisa's. "Was I too late, Jane?" he asked jerkily. "Did he kill her? Is she dead?"

"I don't know." But she was terribly afraid. . . . Her fingers were probing the pulse point in Lisa's throat.

Nothing.

She frantically pressed harder.

Her own heart skipped a beat. "I think I feel something. I think she's alive, Caleb."

"Then keep her that way." Caleb said, his eyes on the island just ahead. "Just keep her alive until I can stop and get to her."

And how am I supposed to do that? Jane wondered desperately.

Try to stop the blood.

It looked as if the bullet had entered from the back and gone straight through. Close to the shoulder. She could only pray it hadn't struck anything vital. She took off her blouse and tore it into strips and tried to bind the wound. Then she applied pressure, but it only lessened the bleeding, not stopped it. What am I doing? she thought in frustration. This was Caleb's area of expertise. "She's bleeding. I'm putting pressure, but it's not doing much good. *Do* something."

"I can't do much right now. Maybe I can lessen it, but I can't heal it. And I can't sense what's happening inside her while I'm driving the damn boat. Give me another few minutes. Keep the pressure steady."

Give him another few minutes? She wasn't the being who could dispense either time or mercy. All she could do was pray and keep up the damn pressure. Lisa was young and vital and had everything to live for and she had tried to give her own life for Caleb's. Surely that would count in her favor?

Keep the pressure steady.

But whatever Caleb was doing must be working, because the bleeding seemed to be lessening.

Relief rushed through her. She didn't know what else was happening with Lisa, but she'd take any good sign she could get. "The bleeding isn't as heavy."

"No, but that may not be enough." Caleb was pulling into the dock at Zakyos Island. He jumped out of the boat and took Lisa from Jane and laid her gently on the beach. Then he was kneeling beside her, holding both her hands, his thumbs on the pulse points of her wrists.

Jane got out of the boat and dropped to her knees beside them. She didn't speak. Caleb's expression was intense, and whatever he was doing, she didn't want to risk disturbing that concentration. She had no idea of the intricacies of how he adjusted blood flow and kept damaged arteries and veins from interrupting vital life-force functions, but she had been present before when he had done it.

But, dammit, Lisa was so still. . . .

"O . . . kay?" It was only a breath of sound. Lisa's eyes were open, Jane realized thankfully. She was looking up at Caleb and that word had definitely come from her.

"Hush," Caleb said. His hands tightened on her wrists. "I'm trying to repair some of this damage you did to yourself. Now be quiet and let me work."

"You're . . . okay?" she repeated.

"Why shouldn't I be okay? You saw fit to take that bullet for me. Now relax and let me see what you've done. I don't suppose it occurred to you that you could have been killed?"

"No . . ." Her eyes were closing. "Didn't . . . think. But you wouldn't . . . let anything bad . . . happen to me. . . ." She was unconscious again.

He knelt there, looking down at her. Then he reached out and gently touched her cheek with his forefinger. "No, I'll never let anything bad happen to you. Never again."

Jane could feel her eyes sting as she gazed at the two of them. She wasn't certain what she was seeing, but it was both moving and bewildering. "How is she?"

"Not good." He turned to her. "But it's mostly blood issues, thank God. She's going to need surgery, but I don't detect any serious damage to her lungs or heart."

"You're sure?"

"Could I be mistaken? Yes. But the blood is everywhere in the body and I know how it behaves around any injury." His gaze went to San Leandro, which was still aflame. "Santara may have been able to call for reinforcements and might have that helicopter on top of us at any minute. We've got to get Lisa out of here."

"Should we move her again?"

"Yes. No choice." He picked her up in his arms and was carrying her down the beach.

"Wait." Jane was running after him. "Where are you going? We're not taking the speedboat?"

"Not that one." He'd stopped by an orange-and-beige speedboat down the line. "I told you I'd hired some help from a couple of the islanders. I traded our speedboat for this one and a small service from Pieros Naxon, one of the fishermen who was hanging around the beach admiring it."

"What service?"

"When they see activity on San Leandro

and any boats heading in this direction, they just jump in our blue-and-white beauty and lead them a merry chase."

"A distraction."

He nodded. "And they know these waters so well that they'll be able to lose them with no trouble and give us the time we need to get back to Athens. I'll call him once we've started." He nodded at the wheel. "You drive. I have to be in back to work on Lisa."

She nodded and jumped into the driver's seat. "Right. Do we take her to a hospital?"

"Not here. I'll call and have a doctor meet us at the plane in Athens with X-ray and other equipment and fly with us to Glasgow. I know those doctors at that university hospital from the time when I worked with them to remove the poison from Eve's bloodstream. I have a better chance of being in control."

"Not that you wouldn't be anyway." She watched him settle carefully with Lisa in his arms and then started the speedboat. "It would just be more difficult for you."

"If you'll notice, I haven't had any real degree of control since all this started." He was looking down at Lisa, his thumbs once more on her wrists. He whispered, "Yes, that's definitely going to change. . . ."

"Stay here," Caleb said over his shoulder to Jane as he hurried down the hall, following Lisa's stretcher toward the emergency room. "I'll be out and give you details as soon as I can. I think we're okay. The X-rays the doctor took on the plane didn't show too much damage."

Then he was gone.

Jane stood there in the hall, looking after him. It had been a breathless, frantic journey from Athens to Glasgow and Lisa had only stirred one time when the doctor's assistant had positioned her for the X-rays once they were in flight.

She had opened her eyes, frowned at the doctor, and then looked up at Jane. "Don't . . . like this. Can't you . . . stop them?"

"I could, but I won't." She'd taken Lisa's hand. "Because we have to know how to get you well." She'd smiled. "And you're probably thinking, If you can't give me what I want, then what good are you, Jane MacGuire?"

"No . . ." Lisa's eyes had begun closing again. "I . . . know . . . what good you are. . . ." Her hand had tightened on Jane's.

"Stay. . . ."

"You couldn't pry me away."

Jane hadn't known if Lisa heard her or if she was unconscious again. It didn't matter; she'd made a promise. She'd sat down on the floor beside Lisa's stretcher and held her hand throughout the flight.

Now that Caleb had whisked her away from Jane down that corridor, she was feeling strangely empty and without purpose.

Foolishness. Lisa was in the best possible hands and Jane's role had been played and was over. Caleb would see that she was no longer needed, and Lisa had appeared to be more annoyed with their interaction than pleased. It was probably healthy that she was free to walk away now.

Not now, but soon. Not until she was sure her responsibility for Lisa was completely over.

After all, she'd been chosen.

She smiled as she remembered Eve's words that night on the porch, which seemed so long ago now. The opportunity to make things brighter, to help them go right, instead of wrong. It had been a very close call, and she was still uncertain what the outcome would be. The fact that Lisa was in that ER was a testament to that narrow escape.

Did I do okay, Eve?

She'd have to call her and ask her — as soon as Caleb came out and gave her a definitive answer.

She dropped down on the bench and leaned back against the wall, waiting for him to come out of the ER.

"I just called Jock and told him to come pick you up and take you back to the camp," Caleb said as he strode back toward her over an hour later. "He should be here within the hour." He held up his hand as she opened her mouth to speak. "Lisa is going to be fine. They're keeping her a couple days longer for observation, but then she'll be released."

"What are they going to *observe*?" Jane asked as she got to her feet. "She was shot, for God's sake."

"The arterial damage." He shrugged. "Everything else is fairly clean. But they're always doubting Thomases when it comes to repairing veins and arteries in a patient whose status is critical."

"But not so critical that you can't help her?"

"Two days," he said. "And I'd need those two days anyway."

Her gaze narrowed on his face. "Why?"

"I think you know."

"Tell me."

"Let's just say I have to rebuild more than those arteries." His lips twisted. "It's been five years."

"From the expression on her face when she saw you, it could have been yesterday for her. She loves you."

"Then she has to learn not to love me quite so much. I don't want her ever to be put in that position again."

"I don't believe you're going to be able to convince her," Jane said. "If a five-year desertion didn't do it, it's not going to happen. She's very stubborn."

"I'll find a way."

"You usually do." She looked down the hall. "May I see her before I leave?"

He shook his head. "The next twenty-four hours are all mine. But she said she wanted to see you before they wheeled her out of the ER. I'll call you day after tomorrow and you can come."

"She wanted to see me?" Jane shook her head. "She's a constant surprise. I thought once she had you again, I'd be history."

"Because she's difficult and self-centered and sometimes completely rude?" He smiled. "That's another thing I have to take up with her. But it's hard to do, when all of this was about her trying to give her life to save mine. Just accept that you'll have to put up with a good deal from both of us if you're going to permit us to hang around."

"I haven't noticed the concept of permission being brought up very often with either of you," she said drily.

"I'll have her work on it."

She raised her brows.

"Too late for me." He shrugged. "Too late for most things. She's young enough to be molded. My molding took place when I was very young, and most of it was negative."

She wondered what form that molding had taken. She wanted to ask him, but she knew he wouldn't answer. "I want you to call me and tell me how Lisa is doing." She paused. "And I've been worrying about Santara. From what you said about him, I wouldn't think this would be the end. We still don't know what was behind his taking Lisa."

"No, but I'll find out," he said grimly. "Stop worrying. On the way here, I phoned Palik, one of the agents I use, and told him to get to San Leandro and keep an eye on Santara and the situation there. I told him not to let Santara out of his sight. I don't want to lose him while I'm dealing with Lisa."

"And then you're going to do exactly what Lisa didn't want you to do."

He shook his head. "She didn't want to be bait. I'm sure Lisa's enough like me to have no qualms about removing Santara in the most painful way possible." His expression hardened. "After all, he inflicted enough pain during their time together."

"She wouldn't want you to endanger yourself because of something that happened to her."

"I disagree. It didn't 'happen'; it was planned. We'll see. At any rate, I won't address it for another forty-eight hours." He turned away. "I need to get back to Lisa." He looked back over his shoulder. "By the way, did I say thank you?"

"I don't believe you did. Nor should you. I didn't do anything for you; it was all for Lisa."

"What a relief. Gratitude is so boring and interferes with my basic egocentric philosophy."

Jane watched him walk down the hall before she turned and headed for the elevator. She never knew when to take him seriously, and this time was no different. But if there was one thing she had learned from this time with him, it was that he was dead serious about Lisa. With the emphasis on *dead,* she thought ruefully. There was not going to be any stopping him from going after Santara as soon as it was possible.

And maybe that was good. Both Caleb and Lisa could be in danger if he wasn't eliminated. Oh, she just didn't know. She couldn't think straight. She was tired, and the events of the rescue and the stress of Lisa's injury had taken their toll.

So she'd have to forget about Caleb and Lisa until she could do something about them. In a short time, she'd be seeing Jock and be on her way back to Loch Gaelkar. Back to MacDuff and Cira and her own life and not being drawn into that passionate, dark torrent orchestrated by Caleb.

It would be a relief. Once she was certain Lisa was safe and out of all danger, life would return to normal.

And it was only the aftereffects of the crackling high energy of the last twenty-four hours that made that normal seem flat by comparison. The last thing she needed was to walk down that path where Caleb stood beckoning.

CHAPTER 8

The hospital room was dark, but Lisa knew that Seth was sitting there in the darkness as soon as she opened her eyes. She could *feel* him; his force was always too dominant to ignore. Even when it was a mere link with her, it was powerful, but also soothing. Yet there was an underlying vibrancy in him that was like no one else's in the world.

"Go back to sleep, Lisa," he said. "The minute you open your eyes, your mind lights up and blows everything I'm trying to do with you." She could hear the humor in his voice. "Can't you do anything right?"

"You should talk." Her throat was painfully dry and she was hoarse. "I saved your life, didn't I? If you were going to rescue me, you should have done it better. I shouldn't have been put in that situation."

"There's a possibility you may be right." He came toward the bed, and she felt a straw slipped between her lips. Cold water slid down her throat, easing the dryness. "So I'll refrain from giving you a scathing retort that would completely devastate you."

"It wouldn't devastate me." But she knew it would. She could accept disapproval from anyone else, but never from Seth. "How long have I been here?"

"In this hospital? About twelve hours." He sat down on the edge of the bed. "You were obliging enough during that period to sleep and let me have time to heal you. But I'm not finished. So go back to sleep."

"I will." She took another sip of water. "So I'm not going to die or anything?"

He chuckled. "No, though I'm not sure what you mean by 'anything.' You know I wouldn't let that happen to you. Though you made it very difficult for me."

"I had to do it. They wanted to hurt you in some way. I don't know how, but I knew I couldn't let you come."

"So you called Jane instead." His voice was suddenly steely. "Not a good idea, Lisa. It can't happen again."

"That made you angry? I didn't want to hurt her. I like her. But it was either her or you. It couldn't be you."

"And it can't be her. Understood?"

"Maybe. She didn't fight it; she just came."

"Because that's Jane. Not again."

She knew that tone and she couldn't bear for him to be angry with her. "Not again." She reached out and touched his hand in the darkness. He felt warm and hard and alive. "Turn on the light. I want to see you."

"And I want you to go back to sleep."

"I'll turn it on," she said, then added deliberately, "Though it might hurt me to do it."

"Brat." He reached over to the bedside table and flipped on the lamp. "Five minutes."

"Maybe. If you're so good at this blood stuff, you might be able to spare a few more minutes." Her eyes hungrily raked his features. "Though I don't know why I should want to look at you anyway. You didn't come to see me for all those years."

"It was for the best. It wasn't as if I neglected you."

No, the link had always been there when she needed him. But it wasn't like seeing him, being able to reach out and touch him. "But you left me with those . . . people. Teresa and Gino didn't like you any more than our mother and father did. You shouldn't have done that."

"It was safer for you." He smiled crookedly. "And I knew that you wouldn't be

231

exposed to them too much. Gino and Teresa were always completely self-involved. You had the best tutors; you went to the best schools and had the safety of a normal household when you weren't at school." He paused. "And there wasn't anything normal about me. I was trying to save you from that."

"I never asked you to do it," she said fiercely. "I don't want to be saved from you. You're my brother. You're the only one in the world I love. I don't care about normal." Her hand tightened on his. "And you told me a long time ago that I wasn't normal, either. I'm like you. So stop shutting me out."

"I also told you that pretense could save you," he said quietly. "And it did for a long time."

"But it didn't save me from Santara."

He slowly shook his head. "No, it didn't." He reached down and gently touched the bruise on her cheek. "And that's when I realized that it was time for the pretense to be over."

She felt a rush of relief. "Thank heaven. I don't think I could have kept my promise much longer. You were wrong, Seth."

"So Jane told me." He tilted his head. "But not entirely. I'll release you from your promise, but I'll ask another one. That you don't volunteer the fact that you're a freak like me. Use the talent if it becomes necessary, but I don't want you to become a target. A talent is always weakened if an enemy knows you have it."

She grinned at him. "No other rules?"

"In the end, you'll make your own rules." He grimaced. "And mistakes. And I'd be a hypocrite if I gave you rules when I don't obey them myself."

"I think you do have rules." She gazed at him, trying to put it into words. "They're just . . . different." She paused. "And I've never wanted to use the blood talent on anyone but Santara. Then I *really* wanted to do it."

"It will probably come again. Maybe you'll have a perspective on it by that time." He smiled recklessly. "Or maybe not. If you make mistakes, come to me and I'll try to get you out of them."

She shook her head. "That would mean getting you into trouble to save myself. I couldn't do that."

"You see, you're already far ahead of me on that scale. I must have been right to keep you to that promise all these years."

"You weren't right to keep me away from you." She lifted his hand to her cheek. "I don't care what anyone thinks of me. Do you know how angry I got whenever our parents called you a freak? They had no right to hurt you like that. I wanted to *hit* them. If you hadn't stopped me, I would have."

"You came close enough. I was far beyond being hurt by them by the time you were trying to come to my defense." He smiled. "But I remembered it later and it gave me a certain warmth."

"Good."

"And it also drove home the fact that you were extremely emotional and could be hurt." He took his hand from her grasp. "And that I had to make certain no one would ever call you that until you were old enough to have developed a tough skin."

She grinned. "So it comes back to your always being right?"

He grinned back at her. "Of course. What else?" He reached over and turned out the lamp. "You're only nineteen. You have many lessons to learn and many rivers to cross. I'll start teaching you how to control the blood talent tomorrow. It won't take that long. Your body is instinctively teaching you on its own. We'll let the Persuasive talent go for the time being. It takes a lot more time and study, and you may not have the knack for it." He chuckled. "Though Jane believes it might do you a world of good."

She giggled. "Attitude adjustment."

"I believe that might help you." He got to his feet and moved back to his chair across the room. "Now go back to sleep and let me finish that arterial healing. We've got a busy schedule ahead."

"I don't want to go to sleep. I want to talk to you."

"Do it anyway. I don't want to have to help it along." His voice was suddenly coaxing. "Consider it a first lesson assignment."

"Okay." She was quiet for a while. "But I'm never going to let you send me away again. Not ever. Not unless you just don't want me. Then I'd go. Could that ever happen, Seth?"

He was silent. "Not in this lifetime, Lisa."

Relief. Joy. Hope.

"Then I'll go to sleep." She closed her eyes. "First lesson?" She concentrated and felt the blood in her body slow and her mind blur. "Easy, Seth. . . ."

"You fool." Teresa Romano could barely control her voice. She wanted to reach through the phone and strangle the stupid son of a bitch. "You said you had the perfect setup, Santara. That there was no way anyone could find you on San Leandro. Well, someone did, didn't they? You're sure it was Caleb?"

"I'm sure. I showed his photo on my phone to the people on Zakyos Island and they identified him. He was with a woman who registered at the inn as Jane MacGuire. She was here, too. I caught a glimpse of her on the boat. You never mentioned her."

"I don't know her. But I will soon." She added icily, "And you will, too. You'll know everything about Caleb and MacGuire and anyone else who is protecting Lisa."

"You want me to go after her again? I told you that I shot her. I'm not sure she's still alive."

"And you may have eliminated her use to me." Her rage was rising by the moment. "But perhaps not. I'll have to see. Caleb wanted Lisa badly enough to come after her this time. If you're not too much of an ass, you might be able to gather him up if you can get hold of her again." She was trying to think. "I didn't want to handle it that way, but I may have to make a change. We have to use every bit of everything we've got to make this come out right."

"It would be simpler for me just to go after Caleb now."

" 'Simpler'?" Her voice was shaking. "He

made a *fool* of you, and he didn't even do half of what he's capable of doing."

"He didn't make a fool of me," Santara said harshly. "I don't know how he found us. The girl didn't contact anyone, and she sure didn't call him. But it doesn't matter now how he found her. I'm going to find her and find him and serve them up to you. Okay, Caleb is good, or he wouldn't have been able to do what he did to my men. But I've known men in the field who are probably just as good. *I'm* just as good. He just caught me by surprise."

"He made a fool of you."

"Don't *say* that. I won't take that from anyone."

Teresa knew she'd better back away for the moment. Santara was obviously angry and humiliated, and that might serve her well. Also, he was a bird in the hand and she didn't have time to go looking for another man with his qualifications. "Then prove to me that you're the man I hired. Give me what I want and there will be a bonus for you. Maybe you won't underestimate Caleb from now on. Just realize that he's lethal and we need to keep him under control until we get him in a position where I can force him to finish Haroun. Find his Achilles' heel, dammit."

"No doubt about it," Santara said roughly. "How much time do I have?"

"Haroun is still not critical, but it could change at any minute. Keep that in mind." She hung up.

Teresa sat there trying to compose herself. It was going to be difficult to go back to Gino and face him with Santara's failure. She was gradually easing all power away from Gino, but she was not there yet. And he was always ready to blame her when things went wrong. He never took into account that almost every positive thing in their lives was there because she had stepped forward and made it happen. He had always dragged his feet in the mud, and she had made their life a glowing success.

And in this disaster she would do the same thing. She stood up and lifted her chin and strode from the room to tell Gino that son of a bitch Seth Caleb had managed to spoil her plans.

But only for the moment.

"I'm relieved," Eve said. "Lisa is going to be all right?"

"So Caleb said, and you know no one argues with Caleb," Jane replied.

"Except you."

"I didn't want to argue about that. I was

too scared. I haven't heard from him since yesterday, but I think he would have told me if she'd gotten worse. I'm just grateful we were able to get her away from Santara without getting her killed."

"I'm grateful, too." Eve chuckled. "But I think that Joe will be a little disappointed that you managed to wrap it up in just these last couple days. He was all set to fly over to help you find her."

"Was he?" Jane found herself smiling. "That's like him. But I'm glad that it wasn't necessary. You need a backup team with Michael."

"True. But we had it all worked out. In fact, it was Michael-approved." She changed the subject. "How are the lights working out?"

"Still installing. MacDuff is wildly enthusiastic. I was down in the mist this morning helping out."

"I imagine he was glad to have the help. We ought to do something about that."

"Caleb's still at the hospital, working with Lisa. MacDuff will survive until he's able to get back here." She paused. "Providing Caleb doesn't find something else he wants to do."

"Santara?"

"He hurt Lisa. Caleb loves her. Do the math."

"I already have. I remember what Caleb did to Jelak after he killed his sister Maria." Eve was silent. "MacDuff might have to do without Caleb."

"So be it. He's not irreplaceable."

"He only thinks so." Eve was laughing. "I believe we'll have to show him he's wrong. In fact, it's already in the works."

"What?"

"Nothing. I have go now. Joe is on the other line. I'll have to break the news to him that you don't need him to find Lisa. But I believe I can substitute something that will mollify him. Love you. Bye." She hung up.

Jane was smiling bemusedly as she put down her phone. Those last few sentences had been a bit cryptic, and Eve was seldom cryptic. She was always honest and aboveboard. Oh, well, not to worry. Eve had sounded cheerful enough. She would ask her what she meant when they next talked.

She got to her feet and moved down the hill to the campfire. She'd grab a cup of coffee and go back to the north bank and see if she could help again. As usual, the mist was calling her.

Cira was calling her.

We got Lisa back, Cira. Maybe you already know that. Do you care? She's just as contrary and difficult as I thought. But she knows about love and sacrifice, and that might even the balance. I think it would for you.

The late-afternoon breeze was ruffling the surface of the lake and turning the mist into shifting phantom figures. Jane cradled her cup of coffee in her two hands and gazed into the mist, trying to see if one of them was Cira.

Her phone rang and she looked away from the lake to the ID.

Caleb.

She accessed the call. "Is she okay?"

"Fine. Healing fast and becoming more difficult with every passing minute," he said. "She wants to see you. Can you come right away? If not, I'll put up with her until you can. But I really need to get away from her before she —" He laughed. "She threw her pillow at me. I don't believe she's supposed to be able to do that in her condition. Perhaps she's even better than I thought. Except for her foul temper."

"But you want me to put up with it?"

"Fresh blood."

"That's between the two of you. I prefer to keep mine intact."

"Are you coming?"

"Yes. You knew I would."

"Yes, I did." He chuckled. "I promise I'll give her a lecture on how to treat guests."

"Which will only antagonize her."

"Exactly. But she has to learn how to handle it. She's clearly not been properly taught by all those schools and tutors. Which she blames solely on me."

"And probably rightly."

"Possibly. I'll see you when you get here." He hung up.

She threw the remains of her coffee into the flames after pocketing her phone. Then she started up the hill to her tent to clean up. It appeared she wasn't going to be spending the rest of the day with Cira, but with an equally challenging female. She was actually looking forward to it.

After all, anyone who would throw a pillow at Caleb couldn't be all bad.

"At last," Caleb drawled mockingly. "You took your time. Have you no sense of my suffering?"

"I thought you'd survive," she said as she walked into the hospital room. "I had to clean up. I spent the morning down in the mist with Jock and MacDuff."

"And Cira."

"Yes, and Cira." She looked at Lisa. "You

look much better than when I left yesterday." It was an understatement. Lisa's eyes were bright and alert and she was only a little pale. "How do you feel?"

"I want to leave here." She looked challengingly at Caleb. "I should know when I'm ready, shouldn't I?"

"No," he said. "*I* should know. And you're not and you'll leave here tomorrow after I find a safe place for you. Right now, I need to go and shower and change and make a few phone calls." He turned to Jane. "I expect Lisa to be here when I come back." He glanced at Lisa. "And I expect Jane to be happy with you and not telling me that you misbehaved."

"Children misbehave." Lisa met his eyes. "I'm not a child. She'll have to take her chances."

"No, you'll have to take yours," Jane said with a smile as she dropped down in a chair beside the bed. "Run along, Caleb. We can get along fine without you."

"That's what I'm afraid of," he murmured. "Enjoy. . . ."

The next moment, he was gone.

"I really do need to get out of here, Jane," Lisa said immediately. "You can see I'm doing well and I —"

"Don't test the waters. I agree with Caleb.

If I didn't, we could talk about it." Jane leaned back in her chair. "But what we could talk about is the real reason you want to leave here."

"Because it's sensible for me to do it when I don't need to be here any longer. I'm a little weak, but I can take care of myself."

"Caleb doesn't think so. What does one more day matter?"

She grinned. "I get impatient. It's my nature. So convince him to spring me from this place."

Jane tilted her head and gazed at her. "Is that why you couldn't do without my company, and I had to run, not walk, here? I thought it was a little strange. Caleb seemed to be all you needed or wanted."

Lisa's smile faded. "I did want to see you. I wanted to thank you. Seth wasn't pleased with me that I used you and put you in danger. I told him I didn't want to do it. I like you."

"But you love your brother."

"Yes," she said jerkily. "I love Seth. I had to save him, no matter what." She lifted her chin. "I can see why you wouldn't understand."

"I can understand. I just regret being in the middle of your problem." She met Lisa's eyes. "And I believe that if I'd been hurt or killed because I was trying to help you, you'd regret it, too. You try to be very tough, but you couldn't feel as strongly as you do about Caleb if you didn't have some empathy for people around you. Though you do try to hide it. I think if you made the wrong choices, it could devastate you."

"It couldn't be a wrong choice to save Seth," she said flatly. "Who else will do it? Everyone else has someone to reach out to when they're about to fall into a pit. Not Seth. There's never been anyone there for him. Not even me. I was too young. He wouldn't let me fight for him." She gazed at Jane defiantly. "But I'm here now and he's promised he's not going to send me away. I'll try never to involve you again, but you have to know that he has to come first."

"I'm not arguing that point." How could she? The passion and intensity of the girl was overwhelming. "Hopefully, you won't need me again and the question will be moot."

"No, that's not what I mean. What if *you* need me?"

Jane blinked. "What?"

"Well, you helped me, didn't you? I couldn't *not* help you if you got in trouble." She frowned. "Though I hope you don't. It could be very inconvenient."

Jane's lips twitched. "Sorry. I'll keep that in mind. But I usually can take care of myself."

Lisa nodded. "And when you can't, Seth would be there for you. His link with you is very strong." She tilted her head curiously. "Do you sleep with him?"

"That's not a question you should be asking. Very rude, Lisa."

"Is that a yes?"

"No," she said. "Our relationship is complicated. Caleb and I have known each for a long time and that's probably the reason you could link with me."

"I don't think so." She shrugged. "It would have to be stronger than that. I just thought that sex might be it. Seth probably sleeps with lots of women, and you're beautiful." She gazed at Jane appraisingly. "More. You have character. Seth would like that."

"I hate to break it to you, but the decision wouldn't rest solely with Caleb," she said drily.

"Most of the time, it would. After all, he has the Persuasion." She chuckled. "Which he's refusing to teach me right now. Even though you think that he should."

"I'd be content with politeness and diplomacy. That abrasiveness must be a problem for you . . . and anyone with whom you interact. Tell me, how did you get along at school?"

"Fine. I was there to study, not socialize." She made a face. "Though that's what Teresa wanted me to do. She wanted me to make contacts to spread her influence among all those billionaires and minor royalty who sent their kids to my schools. All the more reason why I shouldn't be either polite or diplomatic. Why should I give her anything she wanted when she wouldn't let me see Seth?"

"Maybe because it might be lonely without a friend or two?"

"I was fine. I didn't need anyone." She smiled. "But it wasn't as if I didn't have company when I wanted it. I made super grades, so they couldn't kick me out, but I did pretty much what I pleased."

"You broke all the rules." Jane nodded slowly. "And there's something very alluring about that to teenagers. I don't doubt that you became a kind of rebel rock star to them." And not only to the young. Caleb was an outlaw, too, and no one could deny his fascination. "No real friends, though?"

"I didn't need them." She added impatiently, "Why do you keep going on about it?"

247

"Just trying to understand you. You're nineteen; are you going to the university this year?"

"Maybe. I don't know what I want to study. Maybe I'll travel a little until I decide." She looked at Jane. "You're an artist. Did you always want to be one?"

"Most of the time. It was always there in the background. I became distracted now and then. Life does that to you."

"Cira."

She went still. "Yes, Cira. What do you know about Cira?"

"Only what I picked up while being linked with you. It's not as if I could read your mind or anything. I don't even know if Seth could do that."

"I sincerely hope not."

"But then, I don't have any idea what he can do. He doesn't share it. I think he learned not to do that when he was a kid." Her face became shadowed. "They punished him, you know. All the time. My parents never treated him like they did me and Maria. Any little infraction and they'd bring out the whip. They said that he shouldn't be permitted any lapse or he might fall deeper. He couldn't do anything to please them. All they saw was the bad in him." She moistened her lips. "He was wild, but why wouldn't he be? They *hurt* him."

"But he had you," Jane said gently. "That had to be a comfort to him."

"I don't know. I was much younger. All I could do was love him. I was almost glad when they sent him away to Scotland to his uncle. At least he wasn't being punished." She drew a deep breath. "No, I'm lying. I hated it when he left me. I thought together we might be able to do something about it."

"And now you are together. Time to put the past aside." Jane wanted to pull Lisa away from those bitter memories. They had shocked and appalled her and she could see how those experiences had tied the brother and sister together in an unbreakable bond. "That sounds a little saccharine. I guess I mean that new starts are good. I know memories are forever, but we can build on them."

"And I'll make a new start." She paused. "As soon as I'm certain that Seth is safe."

Jane was silent, gazing thoughtfully at her. "And we've made a full circle back to why you frantically wanted me to visit you."

"Not frantically. *Frantic* sounds very weak. I'm not weak."

"No, you're not weak." She smiled faintly. "So tell me why I'm here."

"I need to leave here. I need to find a

place to hide until I can heal a little more."

"Hide?"

"Santara will be coming after me. Teresa and Gino will make him do it." She added bitterly, "And even if they didn't, he'd still come after me. He hates me. I *made* him hate me." She looked down at her bandaged thumb. "I wouldn't give in to him."

"You heard Caleb. He's looking for a place where you'll be safe."

"But then he'll stay with me and protect me. I don't want him to do that."

"It's going to happen, Lisa."

"And that will make me the bait that they wanted to make me. Can't you see? If they can't get their hands on me, maybe they'll threaten to just shoot me, or poison me, or whatever. Anything to get him to do what they want. I'll be playing the same role as at San Leandro, only with a different location."

"You said he'd promised to let you stay with him. You know what that means. You can't have it both ways."

"Yes, I can. I've got to," she said. Her eyes were bright with eagerness and determination. "Look, everything's different now. I can take care of myself." She made an impatient motion with her hand. "Or I'll be able to do it soon. Seth released me from

250

my promise." She wrinkled her nose. "Well, he actually modified it. Anyway, I'm not helpless any longer. I can fight back."

"I don't want you to have to fight. Haven't you gone through enough?"

"Yes, and so has Seth. I won't go looking for trouble, but he might decide to do it. I don't want to be a pawn. You get me out of here and find me an apartment or condo to stay at. I don't have money right now, but I'll owe you. I'm good for it. I've got all kinds of money in my trust."

"So I've heard. It's not a question of money, Lisa. It's a question of either Santara finding you and killing you or Caleb finding out that I did this and killing me."

"He won't kill you. It's too strong a link. He was angry with me for putting you in danger."

"Did I forget to mention that I'd be worried to death to have you out on your own? Protection is not a bad thing."

"Then protect Caleb," she said harshly. "Keep me away from him. It's what I wanted from the beginning anyway. Look, I'll just disappear. Find me an apartment. You'll probably want to get me a nurse to check on me now and then, and that's okay. Then just leave me alone until I'm a little stronger."

Jane shook her head. "Too dangerous."

Lisa gave a sigh of exasperation. "Okay, then I'll find another way to do it. It's not as if I'm asking very much, Jane. It's only until I'm strong enough. Then I'll go back to Seth. When I can help him, not hurt him."

Jane went still. "Strong enough for what?"

"To protect him," she said simply. "My blood talent is getting stronger and stronger all the time. Seth said it was really teaching itself. Though with this wound, it's slowing me down a little. But soon enough I'll be able to do what I need to do."

"For God's sake," Jane said. "I take it you're not speaking of the healing aspect of it. And you're not working toward defending yourself, either. You're going the Caped Crusader route."

She looked away from her. "Don't be silly."

"You weren't able to protect Caleb when you were a child, so you're going to do it now. He won't put up with it, Lisa."

"Don't lecture me."

"I'll do what I please. I'm just telling you that you don't know what you're doing."

"I know. I thought about it. I told Seth that I've never wanted to use it to do any harm. Except for Santara." Her hand clenched on the coverlet. "But if I had to do it to protect Seth or anyone else I cared about, I could do it." She added, "Of course, I don't care about anyone but him, so that leaves me a narrow field, doesn't it?" She frowned. "But I'd do it to protect you, too, Jane. So I guess that means I do care about you."

"I appreciate the sentiment, but I'm not pleased that you came to that conclusion by deciding that you'd cause some slimeball to have a heart attack to protect me. There's something basically wrong in your reasoning."

"I'm trying to do the best I can," Lisa said fiercely. "I'm what I am, and I won't apologize for it. Seth fought to make sure I wouldn't have to do that. He might not have always been right, but I won't have him lose what he gave up for me."

"But you're not your brother. You might not be able to do . . ." She paused. "I just don't want you to do anything that would cause you to be hurt. Sometimes the things that Caleb does are the stuff of nightmares."

"And the people he gives them to probably deserve them. And sometimes he saves lives, instead of taking them," she said defiantly. Then her belligerence faded. "You're trying to be kind to me." There was a touch of wonder in her voice. "And it's not phony. Genuine. You really care, don't you?"

"I really do. Somehow or other, you managed to make that happen." She took Lisa's hand. "And you didn't even have to use that Persuasion talent. Imagine that."

Lisa gave Jane's hand an awkward squeeze. "How do you know? Maybe I'm using it right now." She released her hand and her smile widened. "Okay, how can I use this to get what I want?"

Jane chuckled. "You can't. Nice try." She was silent. "But let me think about it. Maybe we can come up with something. . . ."

South Glasgow University Hospital
Twenty-Four Hours Later

"Good afternoon." Jane moved brusquely into Lisa's room with a young black nurse in tow behind her. "This is Beth, Lisa. She's going to help you dress and pack. Be nice to her."

"Why?" she asked blankly.

"Because she's a nice person and is going to help you get what you want." She turned to Caleb. "Come out in the hall with me. You aren't going to get exactly what you

254

want and I don't want you to set a bad example for Lisa."

"Indeed?" He got to his feet and strolled behind her into the hall. "What are you up to, Jane?"

"Trying to save myself time and trouble." She turned to face him. "And the possible prospect of having to start drawing any more sketches of Lisa. I can't let that nightmare happen again, Caleb."

"The situation has changed. I have her safe."

"Do you? I don't think so. You have her safe as long as she wants to stay safe. That's going to last only while she thinks that her presence doesn't make you unsafe."

"What are you talking about?" he asked impatiently.

"She has this thing about wanting to protect you. You saw it at San Leandro. It shouldn't surprise you. It seems to run in the family." She met his eyes. "And it's been ingrained in her since childhood. Did you know how bitter she is that she wasn't able to help you then?"

"I know," he said without expression.

"Well, I didn't. It's no wonder she was so fanatical about not letting you help her with Santara. It would be her worst nightmare to cause you any hurt."

"That's all in the past. What is this about?"

"The fact that she's not going to let you take her some place and stand guard over her. Not when she thinks she could be thrown into the same position she was in at San Leandro."

"I'll convince her it's best."

She shook her head. "And she'll run from you. Just as she would have that night at San Leandro if we hadn't handled it right." Her lips twisted. "Only now she might decide to come back when you least expect it and stand guard over *you*. Since you obligingly lifted restrictions so that she could go out and make people bleed to death or have massive coronaries."

"It wasn't like that." He was scowling. "I was actually fairly moderate . . . for me."

"I can imagine."

"No, you can't." He was suddenly smiling. "You would have to have been there. But don't worry, she'll understand me."

"I do worry. That's why I'm here. You have a major disadvantage in caring for Lisa. She loves you. That could be fatal. She's afraid of being used to hurt you. But if you force her to run, that has a greater chance of happening." She looked him in the eye. "And you know it."

Silence. "Perhaps."

256

"No perhaps," she said. "So I decided to take matters into my own hands."

"What?"

"I'm taking her to the camp with me. I talked to MacDuff and got permission to let her stay at Loch Gaelkar. He's going to put on more guards and bring them closer to the camp. Lisa will be more than safe. I'm not even mentioning Jock and MacDuff. You couldn't ask for a more lethal escort, could you?"

Caleb thought about it. "I guess we could go —"

"Not *we*. You're not invited."

He stiffened. "Bullshit."

"You can come and visit her occasionally, but you can't hover over her. That's what she's trying to avoid."

"And that's what I intend to do," he said coldly. "Back off, Jane."

"No way. Do you think Lisa and I don't know that you'll be going after Santara? Only you'll be forced to stay close to Lisa while you're doing it if you insist on guarding her. Dangerous for her. Let me take care of Lisa. You go do whatever you have to do."

"She's not your responsibility."

"I can't get out of the habit of thinking that she is. So that must make it true." She grimaced. "And I believe that she's fast moving to a place where she won't allow that to be a factor much longer." Jane tried to see if she was getting through to him. He was always hard to read. But his eyes were narrowed and they were flickering with intensity. "Let me have her, Caleb. I promise you that I won't let anything happen to her."

He didn't speak for a long time, and she thought she might have lost him. Then he smiled. "Heaven help you, Jane. She's difficult for me to handle. She'll put you through hell."

She felt a rush of relief. "No, she won't. I actually think she's mellowing a bit. Just keep in touch with her so that she won't think she has to go and rescue you."

"I'll do that. And you're not going to get rid of me so quickly. I intend to be the one to take her to the camp and check to make sure that everything is as it should be." He turned and headed down the hall. "I'll go to the administration office and sign her out of the hospital. Have her ready to go when I get back."

Chapter 9

"It's beautiful." Lisa stood on the road, her gaze taking in the mist wreathing the lake. "I saw lots of cool lakes when I was in Switzerland, but this is . . . different."

"Yes, it is," Jane said. "No other like it." She started down the incline. "I wanted to invite you to meet Jock and MacDuff, but that will have to wait for evening, when they come out of the mist."

"That sounds like some kind of horror movie." Lisa chuckled as she started down the incline. "I think I like it —" She broke off as Caleb picked her up and began the trek down toward the encampment. "I can make it, Seth. Stop treating me as if I'm a baby."

"You need a couple more days. You could make it and then have to stay in your bedroll tomorrow and rest. Moderation in all things."

She laughed. "That from you?"

"Do as I say, not as I do." He was looking around the camp as he spoke. "Four of MacDuff's guards in plain view. Two more in the trees over there."

"I told you that I'd take care of her," Jane said. "MacDuff was very agreeable when I asked him for extra security. He said that he'd been planning on putting more guards on anyway."

"The treasure?"

"I don't know. He just said it was going to be necessary right away." Jane looked over her shoulder. "So does the situation meet with your approval?"

He nodded. "Probably. I'll still go over numbers and check-in procedures with Jock. I thought it would. I just had to be certain." He smiled faintly. "It was my responsibility. You're making me give up control and it doesn't please me."

"No one makes you do anything, Seth," Lisa said. "You only realized that Jane is right and you were wrong."

"And you had nothing to do with it?"

"I had everything to do with it." She caught Jane's look and amended her statement. "But she made it happen, and that's good, too."

"I'm glad that you think my small part is worthy of your master plan," Jane said drily.

"You can drop her now, Caleb. Preferably on her head."

"Not yet." He put her carefully on her feet beside the campfire. Then he held her close for a moment before releasing her. "Next time." He turned and headed down the bank. "I'll see you before I leave, Lisa. I'm heading down to the mist to thank MacDuff for taking on a headache like you. I'm going to owe him."

"I won't be a headache," Lisa called after him. "Jane said I've got to make myself useful and not be a bother."

"Excellent idea." He looked at Jane. "I'll be curious as to how you implement it."

"So will I," Jane said. "We can but hope."

Lisa watched him until he disappeared into the woods. "I will do what you want," she said quietly. "I don't cheat. You gave me my chance to keep Seth away from me and safe. I'm not going to cause you any trouble."

"Yes, you will," Jane said. "But perhaps not intentionally. You're Caleb's sister and you're very like him in many ways. So trouble goes with the territory."

"Maybe." Her tone was abstracted as she looked out at the lake. "This is Cira's lake? The one where the treasure is supposed to be hidden?"

"Yes. But right now, *supposed* is the key word. We're not certain of anything."

"How could you be?" Lisa murmured as she took a step toward the lake. "It's not a place that reveals its secrets. It's kind of . . . wonderful."

Oh, Cira, have you captured another one in your spell? "Yes, totally wonderful." Jane moved to stand beside her. "And secrets can be wonderful, too."

She frowned. "But you're trying to find out her secrets."

"Only if she wants to whisper them to us. She's held them close to her for centuries. Maybe she'll find it's time to let us share them."

"Maybe." She was still looking out at the mist. "But you know some of her secrets now, don't you? Seth said that you had dreams about her."

"Yes, I did. But that could be fantasy, not secrets."

"Do you think it's fantasy?"

"For a long time I thought I was having delusions. It became an obsession to me."

"You didn't answer me. Do you think it's fantasy?"

"Sometimes. Her story has become my story, and that makes it true to me. But I'm a realist. I have trouble with anything that's not grounded in reality." She smiled. "But then I started having to draw sketches of you. So if I believe in you, I have to believe in Cira, don't I?"

"I guess you do." Her gaze shifted back to Jane. "I want to know about her. Will you tell me?"

"What do you want to know?"

"Everything."

Jane laughed. "I don't know everything."

"Well, almost everything." She looked back at the mist. "I think she's there, don't you? I can feel . . . something."

She hadn't expected that from Lisa. It was clear the girl was caught and held by the mystique. "Sometimes I've thought her spirit may be there."

"Tell me."

Jane gazed thoughtfully at her. It was probably only curiosity and Lisa's usual intensity about everything in her immediate world. Yet hadn't Jane had that same intensity when she had started to dream about Cira all those years ago? Who was she to judge or question?

She turned away from the lake. "Why not? Providing you sit down by the fire and rest. I have a sketch I have to complete of my brother, Michael. I'll work on it while I tell you about Cira and her husband, Antonio, and her son Marcus." She headed for the campfire. "Would you like coffee or tea?"

Caleb didn't come back from the north bank for over four hours. When he did appear, his shoes were covered with mud and his shirt was open.

"Don't ask," he said as he came toward them. "MacDuff needed some temporary help and he drafted me. The man is totally ruthless."

"And you just couldn't say no?" Jane asked. "Poor Caleb."

"He's taking care of Lisa." He looked at his sister curled up asleep on a blanket in front of the fire. "Is she okay?"

"Fine. She just overdid it a little today. The nap will be good for her." She smiled. "Or maybe I bored her into a coma. She wanted me to tell her all about Cira."

"And did you?"

She nodded. "Anyone who is in Cira's world should know her. Lisa seemed to have an empathy for her."

"Of course she did. It's a family thing. I keep trying to convince you that Cira likes me." His gaze was still on Lisa. "I'm too dirty to carry her up to her tent now. I'll go and clean up and come back for her."

"She can walk up to the tent area. That

hill is only a slight incline. You don't need to help her."

"And she'd probably be indignant." He gave Lisa a last glance. "Okay, maybe I'm overcompensating. I wasn't there for her for a long time. And I'm leaving her again within the hour."

Her brows rose. "Guilt?"

"Perish the thought. When did I ever feel guilty about anything?" He turned and strode up the hill toward his tent.

She watched him until he disappeared into his tent.

When did you feel guilt, Caleb? What do you feel about anyone or anything? The more she learned about him, the more mystery she found surrounding him.

Like Cira's mist, she thought suddenly. Like Cira herself. But she knew most of that story. She wasn't sure that she'd ever know Caleb's.

And she wasn't going to stand down here and let herself worry and puzzle about him. The only part of her life that was connected to Caleb right now was this girl sleeping by the fire. She'd taken responsibility for Lisa and she had to be made aware of anything that might concern her.

She drew a deep breath and quickly moved up the hill after him.

265

"I need to talk to you, Caleb," she called as she reached the tent.

"By all means, come in. This is very reminiscent. Only the last time, I was naked." He came to the entrance. "This time, I'm only half naked." He'd stripped off his shirt, and his body and hair gleamed with drops of water. "But if you're disappointed, I'd be happy to re-create."

"In your dreams." She entered the tent.

His lips twitched. "No, that's your category." He tilted his head. "And I thought we'd already been talking."

"Not about what I need to know. And I didn't want to discuss it in front of Lisa. She has a tendency to become involved and try to run things."

"I've noticed." He took a towel and began drying his hair. "A passion for control. I wonder where she gets it."

She ignored that and said, "I know you've been on the phone and tapping every source you have since you took Lisa to the hospital."

"I've not made a secret of it."

"But you haven't told me what you learned." She paused. "Or where you're going when you leave here. I know that you'd have fought much harder to keep Lisa close to you if you hadn't had an agenda already in mind. Do you know where Santara is now?"

"No."

She took a step closer to him. "Don't lie to me, Caleb. I have to take care of Lisa. I don't want to be dancing around your half-truths."

"It's not a lie." He shrugged. "But I knew I'd be fighting this battle for a long while."

"Because you admitted you lied to me before."

"Then you have to take your chances, don't you? However, I'd be foolish not to ration my untruths a bit. After all, I've already demonstrated that I have a vested interest in maintaining our relationship. Lies seriously damage that goal." He nodded. "I do have an agenda. I'm very angry with Santara, as you know. I've become certain that Gino and Teresa are involved, too." His voice dropped to lethal softness. "So the agenda is to kill them all in the most painful way possible. I don't believe that comes as a surprise to you." He added, "But you want a progress report, don't you? Like Lisa, you have to be involved."

"I am involved."

"Yes, you are," he said gravely. "And I only hope that involvement remains long-distance. I admit that was one of the reasons that was most persuasive when you ambushed me about bringing Lisa here with you."

"Progress report," she prompted.

"I've had Dimek Palik, my info agent, investigating both the Romanos and Santara while I've been tied up here. He was to concentrate on both their actions during the last six months. Also time and depth of any interaction between them."

"And?"

"Santara was working as an enforcer with a drug dealer in Morocco until three months ago. Very violent, very lucrative. But then he suddenly parted ways with his employer and left the country." He paused. "He went directly to Rome and rented a villa on the edge of town. He stayed there for a week and then flew to Dubai."

Jane frowned. "Dubai?"

He nodded. "He stayed there for five days and then returned to Rome. But this time, he checked into a palatial hotel on the river, until he disappeared about the time when Lisa was kidnapped."

"And what was his interaction with the Romanos?"

"Palik didn't find any interaction. They were never seen together. None of his cohorts knew what Santara was doing in

Rome. They did think it was odd he rented the bungalow. Santara likes the high life when he's not on a job." He tilted his head. "But the Romanos had an apartment in Rome. And they were in the city at the same time as Santara. It would have been easier for them not to be seen with Santara if he wasn't in the center of the city."

"What about Dubai?"

"The Romanos weren't in Dubai at the same time as Santara." He smiled faintly. "But they happened to be vacationing in the ancient city of Petra, which is three hours away. It appears that they've been visiting the area frequently over the last three years. Gino had many clients among the royal family and the important business-men who are the power figures in Dubai. Teresa has given parties for them and entertained extensively when she visited in Dubai."

"If they're that familiar with the country, it would be easy for them to move around and meet with Santara and make plans," Jane said.

"Very easy."

"But why in Dubai?"

"I have no idea. That's why I'm going to meet Palik there and find out. Rome is a natural choice for a meeting if you want to hire scum like Santara. But there must have been a purpose about going to Dubai."

"Palik can't find out for you?"

"He might, given enough time. He's most efficient at gathering information and seems to have 'cousins' and 'uncles' all over Europe and the Middle East who do him favors. But I'm in a hurry. And I have certain advantages."

"Yes, you have," she said drily. "And you don't hesitate to use them."

"Oh, I hesitate . . . sometimes." He reached out and tucked a stray hair behind her ear. "You have no idea, Jane. Do you want to know anything else?"

"Is there anything else to know?"

"Not that I can think of at the moment."

"Will you call me if you find out anything?"

"I could do that."

"But *will* you do that?"

He smiled. "Trust. I'm not playing word games with you. Haven't I been good today?"

She was silent and then nodded. "I think you have."

"See, I'm trying to regain that trust."

"And you know I'm like Lisa and will go after the answers myself if I'm not satisfied."

He laughed. "That, too. I wasn't joking

that I was glad to have the two of you here under heavily armed guards." His smile faded. "And I'll call and keep you informed because I want to be certain everything is safe here. I've already promised to call Lisa every night. We still haven't located Santara."

"I'll keep her safe. I promised both of you."

"You did, didn't you?" He tossed his towel aside. "And I believe you. But we've discussed how I have this thing about control. Now suppose you go down and see if Lisa is awake so that I can say good-bye. I think I should go very, very soon." His eyes were suddenly twinkling. "Unless you want to change your mind about my shedding the rest of these clothes? It would be awkward with Lisa so close, but I'm sure she'd be understanding."

Heat.

Her breasts were suddenly swelling, pressing against her shirt.

She was achingly aware of his being only inches away. The tight muscles of his abdomen, the drop of water still caught in the thatch of dark hair on his chest. The *scent* of him.

Totally sexual. Totally Caleb.

And he wasn't smiling any longer.

She had to get out of here.

She whirled and headed for the tent opening.

"It wasn't me, Jane," he said quietly. "It . . . just happened. Believe me, I'd pick a more convenient time and place."

She didn't look at him. She knew he had been joking and he wouldn't do anything to endanger her relationship with Lisa. She wasn't about to blame him. "I know that." She steadied her voice. "You're right. It just happened. After all, it's only sex."

"Only?"

It was the last word she heard as she started running back down the hill toward the campfire.

"Only . . ."

"I don't want him to go." Lisa's hands were clenched as she watched Caleb walk up the steep incline toward the road. "Maybe this wasn't such a good idea."

"Lisa."

"Okay. Okay." Lisa turned to Jane. "It's a good idea. I just don't like it right now. I want to be with Seth." She glanced back at Caleb, who had reached the road and was heading for his car. "He told me he was going to Dubai. What's he going to do there?"

"I have no idea. I don't believe he does

right now. Why didn't you ask him?"

"I did." She grimaced. "I didn't like his answer. So I thought I'd see if he'd told you anything more."

"You're as manipulative as he is." Jane shook her head. "Look, you wanted to keep him away from you for a reason. Now you're trying to insinuate yourself into his life long-distance? That's not why I arranged for you to come here. I took you at your word, Lisa. Now back off from this."

"It was only a minor slip." Lisa sighed. Then she grinned. "And I'm glad he didn't tell you anything more. When I woke up, I could tell your link with him was stronger than I've ever sensed it. I didn't want to be left out."

Jane looked away from her. "No one is leaving you out. We're all just trying to survive you."

"That's easy. Just keep me busy. I usually get into trouble only when I get bored."

"Then I'll definitely keep you busy. That's what I was thinking anyway. What can you do?"

"Well, I can't draw wonderful pictures like you. But I'm not stupid. I'm a whiz at a computer. I can usually make people do what I want when I make the effort." She held up her hand. "No, I don't have the

Persuasion like Seth. But I can make people see my point of view."

Jane cocked her head. "That seems remarkably like the beginning of that particular talent."

"Does it?" She shrugged. "I thought it was just showing them that my way is more intelligent."

"Because it is *your* point of view?"

"Maybe."

"What else can you do?"

"I'm a wonderful swimmer. I'm good at most sports. Exceptional at climbing. None of that would help here, since I have to be careful because of the wound."

"I'm glad you realize that."

"I'm a fantastic cook. I took a course at the Cordon Bleu in Paris one summer on a break from school." She glanced at the grate on the campfire. "But that would be a challenge."

"French sauces would be more than a challenge," Jane said drily.

"And I speak seven languages fluently and I can pick up others in a very short time."

"How short?" Jane asked curiously.

"On a visit to Beijing, I was able to learn enough Chinese in a day and a half to get around comfortably."

"Impressive."

"Seth speaks a lot more of them than I do. And it's not helpful out here in the Highlands." She paused. "I thought . . . perhaps I could go out on that north bank and help with those lights you told me about." She added quickly, "Not climbing poles or lifting anything. But maybe I could hand people stuff or be a kind of gofer."

"No," she said firmly. "You're not in shape to do even that kind of work yet."

Lisa opened her lips to speak and then closed them again. "Probably not. But maybe in a few days I will be. I'd be very careful, Jane."

"I'm sure you would be. But there's no way that MacDuff would want to have to worry about taking care of you while he's caught up with the hunt. He'd probably drown you if you got in his way."

Her grin deepened. "No, he wouldn't. I told you: I'm a very good swimmer."

"You'd have to be." She tried to read her expression. "Is this about Cira?"

"Of course. This entire place is about Cira. Can you blame me for wanting to go and see if I can help them find her treasure?"

"No, but I'll be the one blamed if you injure yourself."

She frowned. "I wouldn't want that to

happen. I'm not going to let you be hurt. Don't worry, I'll handle this myself. I can make it work."

"Oh dear." Jane shook her head. "I'm afraid to see exactly how that's going to take place." Her gaze went to the north bank. "But evidently I'm going to find out soon. There's MacDuff and Jock coming in for the day."

Lisa's gaze flew to the two men coming toward them. "Good heavens. The Highlander and a Greek god." Her eyes went to Jock. "Why isn't he in Hollywood? He's spectacular." Her gaze shifted to MacDuff. "He's the one who might throw me in the lake?"

"That's the laird," Jane said. "But neither of them are easy, Lisa."

"Sharp . . ." she murmured. Her eyes never left the men as they approached. "They're important to you, Jane?"

"Yes."

"Do you sleep with the Greek god?"

"No, I do not sleep with Jock. Nor MacDuff. I told you that we're not discussing my sex life."

"I just thought that might be the reason you don't sleep with Seth."

Jane had a sudden thought. Lisa was both vibrant and beautiful, and it wasn't unusual in this day and age for girls her age to have sex. "And I don't believe Caleb would like it if you decided that you should sleep with either Jock or MacDuff to get what you want."

"I wouldn't like it, either. Sex . . . confuses me."

Confuses?

But she dismissed the thought because Lisa was taking a few steps forward and holding out her hand to Jock. "I'm Lisa Ridondo. You're perfectly wonderful-looking, but I'm sure you're much more than that if Jane is your friend." She shook his hand. "I just want you to know I won't get in your way and I'll do anything you need me to do."

Jock's brows rose as he gazed at her curiously. "Thank you, Lisa."

But she was already turning to MacDuff. "And you allowed me to come here, and I'm grateful. You've probably been told that I can be difficult, but you'll never see it. I can keep it hidden." She smiled. "And Jane says that you might throw me into the lake, and that's okay if it makes you feel better. I can handle it."

"I'll keep that in mind," he said drily. "Welcome to my Gaelkar." His gaze raked her from head to toe. "Should you be wandering around? I hear you were wounded."

"I'm fine. You'll be surprised how quickly I'll heal." She turned and moved away from them. "But you're tired and hungry and don't need someone like me getting in your way. I'll go to my tent and rest if Jane will show me the way. I just wanted you to know that anything you want done, I'll be glad to do. Phone calls, computer work. I could probably translate, if you needed it. Anything. I know you want to be freed from that kind of drudgery. You have something more important to do."

Jock chuckled. "What an offer. Maybe a little too generous?"

"You think I'm conning you?" She gave him a level look. "I'm absolutely sincere. Cira is important to all of you. I think she's important to me, too. I'll have to see. But until I have the opportunity to find out, I'll do whatever I have to do to get you to accept me." She turned away. "But I'm tired and hurting a little, so I'll have to start tomorrow."

"Or maybe the next day." Jane was right beside her, helping her up the slight hill leading to the tents. She glanced behind her and saw Jock and MacDuff still looking after them. "Well, I do believe you made an impression."

"That doesn't matter. I don't think either of them is going to believe words. I'll have to show them that I meant what I said." She looked at Jane as they stopped beside a tent. "Just as I'll have to show you."

Lisa was standing very straight, but Jane could see the paleness of her face and the tightness of her mouth. Not only was she obviously struggling with pain but she was alone here with strangers and she had temporarily lost even Caleb, who was the only person she loved.

"Right now you don't have to show me anything." Jane whisked her inside the tent and lit the lantern. "We'll get you to bed and then we'll start new tomorrow."

Lisa nodded. "Tomorrow." She started to unbutton her shirt. "It's been kind of a long day." She was fumbling with the buttons due to the bandage on her thumb. "But a night's rest and I'll be ready again."

Jane brushed Lisa's hand away and unbuttoned her shirt. "That's right." She finished helping her undress and tucked her in the bedroll. "There you are. I'm in the tent next door. If you need me, call."

Lisa bit her lower lip as she gazed up at Jane. "I *hate* to be this helpless."

"I know you do." She headed for the tent

door. "So get well so you can tell me to go to hell."

Lisa shook her head. "I couldn't ever . . . do that. Too late." She closed her eyes. "Not you, Jane. . . ."

5:50 A.M.

What on earth?

Jane stood outside her tent, her stunned gaze on the scene at the campfire below. MacDuff and Jock were sitting eating before the fire and Lisa was sitting across from them, drinking a cup of coffee. She was smiling and talking and her demeanor was a world away from the fragile girl Jane had tucked into bed last night. The scent of bacon and coffee drifted to Jane and she heard MacDuff laugh at something Lisa had just said.

Jane slowly started down the hill, her eyes still on the three at the campfire. She had gotten up, prepared to go in Lisa's tent and help her again before she went down and made the coffee. But it appeared that Lisa didn't need help, or if she did, she was hiding it with amazing efficiency.

"Good morning, Jane." Jock had seen her and rose to his feet. "Let me get you a cup of coffee." His eyes were twinkling. "Other-

280

wise, our Lisa will be jumping up and waiting on you, too. MacDuff and I are feeling quite guilty enough as it is."

Our Lisa?

Jane took the cup of coffee and sat down beside Lisa. "Really? We wouldn't want that." She looked at the remains of food on the men's plates. Something that looked like eggs, bacon, pancakes, and a delicious hash brown casserole. "I take it you're feeling better this morning, Lisa?"

She grinned. "I felt better before the hash brown casserole. That took a surprising amount of arm movement. I didn't think it would."

"You must have gotten up early to prepare a feast like this," Jane murmured.

"Not too early. It's all in the prep." She smiled at MacDuff and Jock. "I wanted them to get a good start on the day."

"Aye," Jock said. "And so you did." He finished his breakfast. "What else could a man need?"

"I'm certain you can think of any number of things," Lisa said. "And I'll guarantee to try to supply them. Dinner will be much better than this once I can send someone for the ingredients I need and pick up a camp oven." Her gaze shifted to MacDuff. "And I'll get those Munich contracts you mentioned translated and ready for your signature by the end of the day. You say they're in the briefcase in your tent?"

MacDuff nodded wryly. "Where they've been sitting for the last two months. I've been preoccupied."

"With Cira." Lisa nodded. "But I'll try to make certain you're not disturbed by things like this again. You'll have to make decisions, but I can do the donkey work."

MacDuff studied her for a moment and then smiled. "We'll see how it goes. You don't remind me of any donkey with whom I've made an acquaintance."

"But she does remind me a little of her brother," Jock said quietly. He lifted his cup in a mock toast to Lisa. "Drive and determination. Long may it reign."

"It will," Lisa said. "You know Seth. Are you friends?"

"Sometimes. We have a good deal in common." He finished his coffee and set his cup aside. "We understand each other as much as either one of us can bear being understood."

"What is that supposed to mean?" Lisa was frowning as her gaze searched his face. "I *want* Seth to have friends. He's always been alone. If you understand him, then you should realize that he'd be a good friend."

"And if you understood him, you'd realize that he'd still be alone even if I called him my friend." His smile was suddenly gentle and lit his face with a warm radiance. "But it's good that he has you, Lisa. You give him a gift beyond compare. That's one thing that we've both learned to appreciate." He got to his feet in one lithe movement. "And now it's time we got to the task of giving MacDuff a gift beyond compare." He turned to MacDuff. "Come on, you've indulged yourself too long. We have to get to work. Do you believe that treasure is just going to emerge like Venus from her shell?" He grabbed his backpack and headed toward the north bank.

"I wasn't the one who had seconds on those pancakes," MacDuff called after him as he got to his feet. He gave a half bow to Lisa. "My compliments to the chef." He glanced at Jane. "Keep an eye on her. She's one of those who will go until they drop."

"I know," Jane said. "But it didn't stop you from taking advantage of that gourmet breakfast."

"She wanted to be tested." He grinned. "So we tested her." He headed down the bank after Jock.

She turned away from watching them to look at Lisa. "And how did you survive the test? You look . . . normal."

"Pretty normal. A little rouge on the cheeks helped quite a bit." She was watching Jock and MacDuff. Her back was ramrod-straight and there was a smile fixed on her lips. "And I believe I came out of the test with flying colors. I gave them something wonderful to eat, we got to know each other a little better, and they know that I won't stop until I'm part of Gaelkar." She watched the two men disappear into the mist. Then she gave a deep sigh, her smile vanished, and she slumped over. "But the test is done now." Her hand was shaking as she put her coffee cup down. "They're very, very smart. Both of them. Did they see through me?"

"Probably. But they liked what they saw," she said. "Did you eat anything yet?"

"No. I was onstage. Besides, I was afraid I'd get sick." She swallowed and said wryly, "I wouldn't tell anybody else that. Aren't you lucky?"

"I think I am." She put bacon and a small bit of egg on a plate. "Eat this. Do you need that wound rebandaged?"

"No. I told the truth. I'm getting better. I'm healing." She was eating the bacon. "And I spent time last night concentrating

284

on repairing. Seth taught me how to do that."

"Well, good for him. Now all he has to do is teach you how to avoid exhaustion." She took two slices of bacon herself and then one of the pancakes. The pancakes really were excellent. "What's this about Munich contracts?"

"It's something of value for me to give. Food is good. But I had to go a step further." She finished the eggs. "And it was easier for me to get MacDuff to talk about it after he'd eaten his breakfast."

Jane chuckled. "Lisa, I believe you may have the makings of a temptress. I'd never have believed it, from where we began."

She made a face. "That kind of thing is easy. It's more like business negotiations than seduction. And you only saw me when I was fighting for Seth's life. You couldn't expect me to act reasonably around Santara."

"Which you certainly didn't." She sat back on her heels. "Are you planning on doing this every morning?"

"Yes. It's a gift I can give. I'd judge people like MacDuff and Jock like to return gifts." She smiled. "Even though MacDuff's already given me one in this safe haven here."

"But you want something else," Jane said. "Cira?"

"Cira. It's something to look forward to, something to work for," she said simply. "It's going to drive me crazy worrying about Seth until I'm well enough to go to him. I have to keep busy. Nothing about Cira is easy."

"You're right. Not one thing." Obviously, Lisa had been captured like the rest of them. "So by all means wriggle your way into working with MacDuff and Jock in the mist if you can."

"You won't mind?" She hesitated. "I won't try if you do. After all, Cira does belong to you."

Jane laughed. "Cira belongs to herself. If anything, she sees that we belong to her. By all means, if she welcomes you, then who am I to put obstacles in your path?" She looked out at the lake. "Eve told me that I might have been chosen to find and save you. That sometimes we're given those choices. It's strange that all this happened at the same time I was planning on going into the mist to find Cira's treasure." She smiled. "Maybe you were chosen, too, Lisa."

"That's all a little too mystical for me," Lisa said as she unfolded one of the blankets beside the fire. "All I want is to keep busy until I'm ready to go help Seth. Cira will do that." She lay down and pulled the blanket over her. "But one step at a time. First, I have to prove myself so that when I'm ready, MacDuff will be ready for me. I got too tired today and I have to take a nap. It's only smart to ration my strength. When I wake up, I'll make out a grocery list. Can you send one of those guards to a town close by and fill it for me?"

"If you don't get too fancy with ingredients."

"I won't. But I think I'm going to need some kind of portable oven, too. It was kind of hard today. I'll have to think about it." Her eyes closed. "And while he's gone, I'll tackle those Munich contracts."

"You do that." Jane got another cup of coffee and sat back down, her eyes on Lisa. She could see that the girl was drifting off. She'd planned to go down into the mist herself today, and she might later. But right now it seemed to be more important to get Lisa settled at the camp. Or maybe just to do what MacDuff had said and keep an eye on her. She was settling in herself at lightning speed and probably doing too much. She might not be able to stop Lisa, but she might be able to modify her behavior. Lisa was being more thoughtful and accommodating toward her than she had dreamed possible. Astonishing in a girl as willful as Lisa. At moments she had touched her and amused her and frustrated her, but she had not bored her. Of course, she might be lulling her into a false sense of security, but somehow she didn't think so. She thought perhaps Lisa was beginning to reveal facets of her personality that were as complex and changing as the sketches she had made during that last week.

So she'd sit here and have her coffee. Then she'd work on Michael's sketch.

And when Lisa woke, she'd set herself to doing what was necessary to keep her promise to Caleb to take care of his sister.

And explore what new facet Lisa was going to show her next.

There was no way I'd be able to make the shot, Santara thought with frustration as he sighted his rifle carefully on Lisa Ridondo lying by the fire. The distance was much too far and MacDuff's men would be on him the minute he fired. He had reconnoitered the entire area and the damn place was an armed camp, he thought sourly. And besides, Teresa Romano didn't want a dead girl; she wanted something to trade.

But *he* wanted the bitch dead. Lisa was

proof of his failure, and he did not fail. He shifted the sight to Jane MacGuire, who was sitting sketching now. No, not her yet, either. All his work and he couldn't touch either of them until he got Teresa's okay.

His finger caressed the trigger, his gaze on a point in the center of Jane MacGuire's temple. She had been there on San Leandro with Caleb and been part of his humiliation in front of his men. He had decided that night that no one who had witnessed that degradation was going to live to tell about it. "I'll have you, too," he murmured. "Just not right now."

He took out his phone and punched in Teresa Romano's number.

"I've found your Lisa," Santara said as Teresa picked up the phone. "I located the little bitch today. I traced her through Jane MacGuire, who had to show her passport at the inn on Zakyos when she checked in. She's some kind of artist, and I went to her gallery in London and questioned the receptionist and found out she'd been submitting paintings of a lake in the Highlands of Scotland for the last two years. That's where I am now, and lo and behold, who would I find but MacGuire and Lisa Ridondo."

"But not Seth Caleb?"

"I haven't caught sight of him yet. But I can't move around too freely. This place is too well guarded."

"Of course it is," Teresa said with disgust. "Caleb wouldn't leave her anyplace that wasn't safe. I'd bet that he stashed her away and then took off looking for you." She added harshly, "And me. He'll have put most of it together by now and he'll be on the hunt."

"He won't be able to find out anything about Haroun. We were too careful."

"You'd better hope you didn't make a slip. Because if you did, he'll find it. I won't have all my plans ruined by your incompetence."

His hand tightened on his phone. "No slip. All the people I put in place are beyond reproach. No one will talk. Now what do you want me to do? I've told you that I've found Lisa and the MacGuire woman. It would be really difficult, but I might possibly be able to pick off one of them to send a message. Or I could get some guys from Liverpool and try to go in and get Lisa. The only problem with that is MacDuff, who owns this property, is some kind of bigwig and it might bring the local magistrates down on us."

"That's all we need," she said sarcastically.

"And that would mean Interpol and publicity."

"What do you want me to do?" he said through set teeth.

"What do you expect me to say? What did I hire you for? Find a way. Find out everything you can about how to get to Lisa."

"I'd rather go after Caleb."

"Ask me if I care. You're so angry that you might try to damage him. That's the last thing I want. He's the key to Haroun."

"You could use me instead. I could do what you want if I'm given enough time."

"And you had so much success with Lisa?" She paused. "Haroun is scheduled for two weeks from tomorrow. If you don't manage to find me a tool to get Caleb here and cooperative by two days before that time, I'll put all the money I've agreed to pay you for this job as a bounty on your head. How long do you think you'll last among your very greedy and bloodthirsty cronies?"

"Longer than you will, if I decide to go after you."

"We'll see. It would be more sensible not to put either of us to the test. I'm going to concentrate on finding a way to correct this catastrophe. Do your job, Santara." She hung up.

The bitch would do as she threatened, he thought savagely. He struggled to smother the anger and the bloodlust. Later.

Now he would work and give the cobra what she wanted and decide later how to make it bite her in the heart.

He put his rifle down and punched in a number on his cell phone. "Jacob, I need you here in Scotland. Bring your equipment."

CHAPTER 10

"They're coming back early." Lisa was frowning as she watched MacDuff and Jock walk out of the heavy mist. "It's not even sundown. Yesterday they didn't show up until almost nine. Do you think that something went wrong with the lights?"

"It wouldn't surprise me. Something always appears to go wrong with the lights." Jane looked up from her canvas with a mischievous grin. "Admit it, you're not really worried about the lights. You're frantically doing math and ingredient adjustments in your head to make certain your dinner won't take a hit because you thought you had more time."

"It would have helped if they'd called and let me know." She grimaced. "Dear God, did that come from me? Only three days and I sound like the nagging wife in a sitcom. It's good that I'm almost well."

Not so good, Jane thought. It was true that

Lisa had made tremendous strides in the last three days, but she wasn't as well as she claimed. She was just impatient and had conquered every challenge she had set herself. She knew that Caleb had kept his word and called Lisa every evening, but when she got off the phone, she was always restless and brooding. For heaven's sake, she was only nineteen. What could she expect? But she wasn't about to argue with her right now. Tackle it later, when she knew what problems MacDuff was facing.

"Well, neither of them appear to be too depressed." Jane put her brush down and watched them come around the bank. "Maybe it's just a little glitch."

Lisa brightened. "And maybe it's something that I can turn into a new job opportunity. What do you think?"

"I think that you're optimistic. You hit MacDuff with that yesterday."

"But today, something changed." She gave Jane a sly glance. "Maybe Cira told him she'd chosen me to be his primary gofer out in the mist. You said yourself that your Eve told you that —"

"And you only believe what you want to believe. You're very cynical for a youngster."

"But you told me you were a realist, too." She was cocking her head and looking at

Jane's canvas. "But that's not true. That picture of your little brother is like a love song. Very soppy. No kid looks like that."

Jane's lips twitched. "No?"

"No, some of them are cute. But they don't —"

"I yield to your vast expertise on the subject," she said, interrupting Lisa. "You're right: I'm merely a sister who sees qualities in him because I'm besotted."

"You're making fun of me," Lisa said. "Okay, my mother used to tell me I saw things in Seth that weren't there, either. She was wrong. It doesn't matter. It's going to be a wonderful portrait anyway."

"Thank you. Then you won't mind if I continue to see him from the heart and not the mind?"

She shook her head. "It's kind of . . . nice." She turned to Jock, who was now only several yards away. "Is something wrong? You said the transformers were going in well."

"They are, but MacDuff got a call while we were in the middle of installing them and said we had to get back to camp." Jock smiled. "I made no objection. I think you promised us some exotic delight of a Calcutta dish tonight, didn't you?"

"Which takes time. I might have to put it

off until tomorrow."

"I think you'll have time," MacDuff said as he came up behind Jock and unslung his backpack. "As long as you keep the coffee coming for a while. Or maybe I'll break out the wine."

"Wine?" Jane's gaze narrowed on his face. "Is this a celebration?" Her eyes widened. "Did you find something in the mist today?"

He chuckled. "Aye, this is a celebration. And, no, I found nothing but that constant damnable cold and dampness today." He turned to Lisa. "But don't the meals you've been serving deserve fine wines?"

"Of course. I was going to suggest it. But wines should breathe, and you're usually hungry when you come back from the mist," Lisa said. "And that's not the celebration, is it?"

"No." He looked at his watch. "It's more of a surprise for Jane. The call I got was from Darren, one of the perimeter guards."

"A surprise?" Jane was frowning. She looked at Jock. "What's this about?"

Jock held up his hands. "It's MacDuff's surprise. Let him tell you. The bastard just saw fit to tell me today."

"Well, actually, I was merely an instrument." MacDuff was grinning. "As you'll agree, we all are on occasion." He glanced up the slope toward the road. "But the wielder of that instrument should be getting out of the car now, so I believe you should go to meet and greet, Jane."

"What?" Jane's gaze followed MacDuff's to the road. She saw nothing and had no idea what MacDuff was —

Then she heard a car door slam.

The next moment, she saw the sunlight shining on red-brown hair.

"Eve?" she whispered.

"Come help me, Jane," Eve called as she moved from the road toward the slope. "I have to stay up here to keep an eye on Michael in the car. And I don't want him being introduced to Gaelkar by rolling down this steep slope." She laughed. "Though he'd probably love it."

"You brought Michael?" Jane was tearing up the slope. "Why? What are you doing —" She reached Eve and enfolded her in a bear hug. "Is something wrong? Where's Joe? Why didn't you —"

"Hush." Eve was chuckling as she returned the hug. "Give me a chance. Though I know I let myself in for this when I didn't tell you what I intended to do."

"MacDuff said a surprise." Jane took a step back. "That's an understatement. Why, Eve?" She had a sudden thought. "It wasn't because of Lisa? I told you that we have her safe."

She shook her head. "Well, I told you that Joe would be disappointed, but these particular plans had nothing to do with Lisa."

"Michael?" She had a vague memory of Eve's saying something about how she'd like to have a painting of Michael at the lake. But she hadn't thought that Eve had been that serious.

"Oh, yes. Michael was a huge part of it. I'll explain everything if you give me a chance." Eve smiled. "Now stop guessing and help me to get down this slope with both Michael and my dignity intact. I left him in the car until I could flag down some help."

Jane followed her toward the black Toyota rental car. "You left him with Joe?"

"No, Joe had something else to take care of, so we decided I should bring him on my own." She opened the passenger door. "Michael didn't mind. Everything is an adventure to him. We're just his guides on the path."

"I'll take him." Jane was already unfastening his car seat. "Hi, Michael," she said softly. "I've missed you. I think you're going to like it here."

He was smiling, his tea-colored eyes bright

and shining as they looked up at her. He reached out and gently touched her cheek. "Jane."

"Right." She turned her face and kissed his palm. "You'd better remember me. I've spent a heck of a lot of time living with that last sketch of you I did."

"I always remember." He touched her hair. "Jane . . . and mist."

Her eyes widened and they flew to Eve. "Mist? That's weird. Did you —"

"No," she said quickly. "But who knows what he might have picked up. I always think of that song 'Children Will Listen.' We're lucky he doesn't repeat anything obscene . . . yet." She grabbed a brown duffel out of the backseat. "Let's go. I'll come back later for the rest."

"No, you won't." Jock was suddenly beside them and taking Michael from Jane. "Grab that other suitcase and I'll take the lad. We've got to get down there fast or we'll have Lisa climbing that slope to help you. Jane would not be pleased. She's been tactfully trying to keep Lisa from doing damage to herself for the last three days." He held Michael up above his head. "Good day to you," he said to him. "You've grown since I last saw you. I'm Jock."

Michael nodded and a brilliant smile lit

his face. "Cara's Jock."

An indefinable emotion flickered across Jock's face. "Aye, something like that. Clever of you to make the connection." He brought him down and then lifted him on his shoulders. "Hold tight. We're going fast and hard."

Michael was squealing and laughing uncontrollably as he rode Jock's shoulders while he ran down the steep slope.

Jane and Eve stood at the top and watched them. So much joy and beauty in this moment, Jane thought. The sun shining on the child's chestnut hair and Jock, who was as beautiful in his way as Michael.

"Come on." Eve took her arm. "Michael's body clock must be out of kilter, but he should still eat something. He didn't want to have anything on the plane." Her gaze was searching the people below. "And that must be Lisa." She smiled. "Restless, lovely, and she's coming toward us, looking determined." She hurried forward down the slope. "Lisa, I'm Eve Duncan." She extended her hand. "I'm very happy to meet you. I guess Jane has told you that I feel I have a connection with you."

"She told me," Lisa said. Her voice was polite but reserved. "I know she's happy you're here. If there's anything I can do to help you, let me know."

Eve's gaze searched her face. "I certainly will. Did she also tell you how grateful I am to your brother? I consider him my good friend, and I can never pay him back for all he's done for me."

"No." She was still reserved, but the ice was melting. "You should be grateful. He's wonderful. I'm glad he could help you."

"So am I." She looked at Michael, whom Jock was still holding. "With all my heart. And I hope we can be friends, too."

Lisa nodded. "That might be . . . nice." She turned away. "If there's nothing I can do for you, will you excuse me? I have to start dinner. Is there anything I should make for your son?"

"I'll come and look everything over after I say hello to MacDuff. I brought some food with me, but Michael usually likes every-thing."

"Fine." Lisa moved toward the campfire. "I'll see you then."

"Not easy," Eve murmured, looking after her. "But then, you told me she wasn't."

"You hit the right note. She adores Ca-leb."

"And she likes you," Eve said. "It was obvious. It was you she wanted to help, not me."

301

"Well, I like her," Jane said. "I think you will, too." She chuckled. "Though she couldn't believe that Michael could ever be as wonderful in real life as in my painting. I know you'll hold that against her."

"Not at all. She's ignorant and misguided. Michael will straighten her out."

"While I straighten you out." She took the duffel Eve was carrying. "I'll take these up to your tent while you chat with MacDuff. I can't believe you were able to con him into letting you come and surprise me."

"Believe it. And more. I'm going to owe MacDuff a great deal before this is over." Her eyes were suddenly twinkling. "But I think the laird will enjoy being able to tap on that gratitude if he gets the chance. It's his nature. After all, he's descended from Highlanders and border bandits."

"And Cira."

Eve looked out at the mist on the lake and said softly, "Yes, we mustn't forget Cira."

"And we mustn't forget that you haven't told me what you're doing here," Jane said pointedly.

"You wouldn't let me, my dear. But this isn't the time." She turned and headed for MacDuff. "Later, Jane . . ."

"That meal was incredible." Eve took a sip

of her merlot and gazed out at the moonlight glinting on the lake. "Is Lisa always that good?"

"Often better. And in three days she's whipped MacDuff's executive affairs back into shape so that he can at least deal with them in his spare time while he's on the hunt." She reached over and tucked the throw higher over Michael, who was curled up asleep on the grass a few feet away. "She's remarkable, and I don't believe that we have any idea of the depths of how remarkable. Every time I turn around, she shows me something new. It's as if she's been learning and gathering little nuggets all her life and hid all that skill and knowledge beneath that facade of defiance and rebellion." She shrugged. "And maybe she did. Caleb wanted her to hide her psychic talents while she was growing up; perhaps she closed herself off in other ways."

"Possibly. But she's beginning to open those doors now. Interesting."

"Fascinating. I'm enjoying her tremendously . . . sometimes." She sipped her wine. "When I don't have to be on guard that she'll do something that will hurt her. The salvation for both of us has been that she's kept herself busy. Now she wants to help MacDuff in the mist. We'll see if he gives in on it."

"Well, maybe we'll be able to give her something else to do instead." She smiled. "If she'd be willing to help. She did offer, didn't she?"

"Eve." Jane's eyes were suddenly narrowed on her face. "What are you up to?"

"You sound like a mother suspicious of a mischievous child." Eve's smile widened. "Don't worry, I think you'll like this. Though it may surprise you. It surprised me."

Her eyes widened. "Good God, you're pregnant again."

Eve's jaw dropped and then she threw back her head and laughed uproariously. When she could finally speak, she said, "In my wildest dreams I never thought you'd go in that direction. No, Michael is quite enough for me at present." She looked at the sleeping child and her face softened with love. "More than enough. I've just come to believe that we should try to be more than enough for him. Take all the extra steps to keep him safe and secure."

"With you and Joe as parents, there's no question that Michael will be both," Jane said. "And you know I'll be here for him forever."

"Yes, I know that's true." Eve reached out

and covered Jane's hand with her own. "And I couldn't be happier to trust him to you if it became necessary. You're everything he would need." She shook her head. "But Joe and I have no intention of giving you our son anytime soon. Forget it. Life's too good with him around."

"That goes without saying," Jane said. "Then what the hell extra steps are you talking about? You're driving me crazy."

"Sorry. It's just one extra step that's going to happen here at Gaelkar." Her smile was gone and her hand tightened on Jane's. "I asked MacDuff's permission to arrange for Joe and I to be married here."

"What?" Jane stared at her, stunned. "Married?"

Eve chuckled. "That was my reaction when I made the decision. And Joe's was even more extreme. He practically went into shock."

"You've been living together for years and you've never seen fit to get married. I just assumed that it was the choice you'd made. I didn't know if you'd even discussed it."

"We discussed it. For years after I lost Bonnie, our relationship was very rocky. I was obsessed, and he couldn't stand the pain I was going through. We weren't even sure it would survive while we were trying to find her killer. Then, later, it was so solid and secure that saying words in a registry or chapel didn't seem necessary." She added softly, "We knew what we had and that love was the only thing that was important."

"But that's changed now?"

"No, that's still the only thing that's important." She smiled. "But we're ready to let the world in to see what they're missing." She made a face. "In exchange for making Michael's life easier by letting bureaucracy take him under its wing."

"Easier?"

"Entrance into medical facilities, schools, anything that requires the system to work. The world runs on the concept of certain rules of behavior and family order. I want everything to go smoothly for him. We adopted you when you were ten, and thank heaven you were healthy and didn't require hospitalization at any time. But when we entered you in college, it was a nightmare of paperwork."

"I remember. I was a street kid who'd lived in dozens of foster homes. There weren't any good records of who my real parents were."

"And Joe and I had to sign medical permission slips for each other because we weren't married. Bureaucracy, again. Times are changing, but bureaucracy keeps growing."

"And you want to eliminate that hurdle for Michael."

"All the hurdles. Of course, I'm not going to be able to do that. But maybe I can help get rid of this one."

"Maybe you can. How do you feel about it?" She gazed at Eve searchingly. "It's not only Michael. It's you and Joe."

"How do I feel about it?" She was silent, thinking. "I don't have any experience with the conventional happy home. I'm illegitimate; Bonnie was born out of wedlock, too. Joe's parents were married, but it didn't make for a happy home or family. You came into our lives when you were ten and those years with you couldn't have been happier, but they weren't ordinary, either. In the end, I believe the only important things are love and family. Joe and I are fantastically blessed in that department, and I can't imagine an official document making it any better. But if that document makes it a little easier for Michael to negotiate a few of the pitfalls of this world, then it will make me happy." She looked at Jane. "Is that enough of an answer?"

Jane nodded. "Anything that makes you happy is the right answer." She could feel her eyes sting with tears. "But why here? Why now?"

"Michael is almost two. You said yourself that he's changing all the time. He'll have to face the world sooner than we think. I figured it was time to start putting preparations in motion." She looked out at the lake. "Why here? I kept thinking about Cira and her son Marcus and the mist. I kept thinking how close I felt to Joe when we were here when I was pregnant with Michael. It's totally private and there won't be any question of publicity of any sort. It just seemed the right place." She smiled. "And you were here. I couldn't tell how long you'd be tied up with MacDuff's treasure hunt, so I arranged to come to you."

"I'm glad you did." She grinned. "But I would have dropped MacDuff to come running to you."

"I think he knew that, and it may be why he's been so cooperative," Eve said. "He said anything I wanted would be provided."

Jane had a sudden thought that put a damper on the euphoria she was feeling. "That's why he was putting on the extra guards. He wanted to make sure that I'd feel you had full protection." Her gaze flew to Eve's face. "I'm not sure you should have come. Lisa is here, and she might still be a draw for Santara. I don't want you and Michael exposed to any threat."

Eve tilted her head. "And do you feel Lisa is in danger here?"

"No. I wouldn't let her stay here if I did. I made certain she'd be safe. MacDuff is supercareful and so is Jock. And Caleb looked over the security and approved it."

"But you still aren't sure it's safe enough for us?"

"You're Eve." Jane looked at the sleeping boy. "And Michael. I want to wrap you both in cotton wool."

"And you've done it. Do you think MacDuff didn't tell me all this? That Joe didn't call him and talk to him? Do you think I'd put Michael in danger?" She reached out and covered Jane's hand with her own. "Do you know that MacDuff's guard Darren searched my car before he let me cross the perimeter, even though he'd been told to expect me? This may be the safest place on the planet right now for Michael."

Jane still gazed at her uncertainly.

"I *feel* this is the right place." Her hand tightened on Jane's. "And so does Michael. I'd know if he was in danger."

Jane believed her. She drew a deep breath. The decision had been made. All she could do was embrace it.

"When? What day?"

"I haven't decided. It depends on Joe. Within a week or so." She chuckled. "But it's not as if MacDuff is going to have to go to elaborate lengths to help me out. This is going to be a very simple ceremony."

"Most weddings start out that way, I understand. Why does the date depend on Joe? Why did he stay behind?"

"He's bringing a few guests, and he may have trouble locating them."

"So much for privacy." Jane laughed. "And this wedding must mean more to you than you've said if you're bringing friends hopping over the Atlantic to attend."

"Perhaps. But friends are family, too, if they're close enough. I admit this is a sort of landmark event in our lives. I don't want to leave anyone out who might want to come." She looked down at her sleeping child. "And Michael might want to remember their being here."

Jane lifted a brow. "At two years?"

"Michael remembers more than you'd think." She got to her feet. "And that young man needs to be put to bed." She leaned down and carefully picked him up and cuddled him close. "Before dinner, I caught a glimpse of the portrait you're doing of him. You're right: It should be in oils."

Jane nodded. "But I'll do a sketch of him here at the lake, and you might decide you prefer that one." She watched Eve tuck the throw around him. "I'll carry him for you. You've had a long, hard day."

Eve shook her head. "I love these moments. But he's already getting a little heavy for me. Soon they'll be gone. Life with children is constantly giving up moments we never get back."

"Mama . . ." Michael's drowsy murmur drifted up to them as he cuddled nearer to Eve. "Always . . ."

"Yes, always." Eve pressed her lips to his forehead. "But never the same." She carried him up the hill toward her tent. "Good night, Jane."

"Good night." She watched until Eve disappeared into her tent. She was still stunned about Eve's announcement, but she supposed she shouldn't be. In spite of all the practicality Eve had voiced, this marriage was also a gesture of completion for Eve and Joe's relationship. Jane had watched their love grow through the years, had been part of it and them since she was ten. How lucky she had been to have them with her. Their life together had always been interesting and full of love, but with a multitude of changes waiting just around the next corner. And now there was going to be still another change.

She lifted her wineglass in a half salute to that change as the lantern in Eve's tent went on. "Good luck, Eve. Be happy." She whispered Eve's last words, "Always . . . but never the same."

Jane's phone rang two hours later, waking her from a sound sleep.

Caleb!

Sleep vanished.

She sat upright in bed as she reached for the phone. "You always call Lisa. What's wrong, Caleb?"

"Maybe nothing. That's why I'm calling you. I just talked to Lisa and she told me that you've had an influx of visitors tonight. What's Eve doing there? Did you call her and tell her to come?"

"Hell no." Her heart was steadying, but her temper was not. "Why would I do that? She brought Michael, for God's sake. I believe Lisa's safe here, but I wouldn't deliberately bring anyone else here if there was even a minute chance of a problem. It was Eve's idea entirely."

"Why? Was she worried about you?"

"No, why would she be? It's Lisa who's

the target."

"Is it? Why is Eve there? Did Joe hear something from Interpol?"

"No." Just tell him and get it over with, she decided. "She and Joe have decided to get married here at Gaelkar. Eve just told me before she went to bed tonight."

Silence. "What the hell?"

She was immediately on the defensive. "If she wants to do it, then we'll make it work."

"Whatever Eve wants . . ." Caleb said drily. "That's your mantra, isn't it?"

"Yes, and it's a good one. All through our years together, Eve never thought twice about making certain I had what I wanted or needed. This is important to her. I'll make certain she gets it. You're not going to be able to —"

"Do you need me there?"

"What?"

"I know that I'm not going to be able to dissuade you. But I'm not going to let Eve or her child be threatened. She's a new element in the mix and I don't like it. But I'll deal with it. I need to know if I should break off what I'm doing here in Dubai and fly back to Gaelkar. Do you need me?"

She was taken off guard. She had expected an argument but not commitment.

"Jane."

She thought for a moment. "I don't need you. The security situation here hasn't changed appreciably just because Eve is here. It's not as if they're going to be running around the countryside. I'll see to that. MacDuff's already increased his security forces since they arrived. You know how lethal Jock can be. Joe's not here right now, but when he arrives, I believe you'll agree that he's capable of being a megaforce in that area."

"No doubt about it." Caleb paused. "Have you seen any sign of strangers about?"

"Santara? No strangers. Jock questions all the security people every evening, and no one has seen anything suspicious since we got here. He keeps them on constant alert."

"That's good, but Santara is very good. You might not be able to see anything suspicious if he doesn't want you to."

"Comforting."

"I don't want to be comforting, I want you to be worried and scared. Because I am. I hate like hell not being there."

"What are you doing in Dubai? Lisa said you hadn't found out anything yet about the meeting between Santara and the Romanos."

"Moving forward. Palik has located a local contact Santara uses when he needs information about jobs he's planning. The word is that he definitely met with Santara during that time period. Palik should know by later tonight."

"Call me."

"Really?" His voice was mocking. "But you have a wedding to plan."

"Caleb," she said slowly and precisely. "I might have a funeral to plan instead. Call me."

"Very well. I'd actually prefer to call you instead of Lisa at this point. I've noticed that she's beginning to be a little too eager."

"You haven't seen her after you've hung up," she said drily. "She's on the edge. Having Eve here to keep her busy may be a godsend."

"I hope you're right," Caleb said. "It was your call, but I find myself very grateful that you saw fit to take care of her when you cast me into the outer darkness."

"As you said, it was my call." She added, "But if you're so grateful, you can take the trouble to call me if Palik comes through for you."

"I'll think about it. But you've never been certain any of my softer emotions were really authentic, have you? Good night, Jane." He hung up.

Leaving me disturbed and troubled and

315

bewildered as usual, she thought as she lay back down. Palik might be pointing the way, but Caleb was the hunter and he'd be the one who would go after the prey and get answers. He would be the one to face one of Santara's accomplices, who could be just as dangerous as Santara was.

But whoever it was couldn't be as lethal as Caleb. Why was she worried?

Close your eyes, she told herself.

Go to sleep.

He probably wouldn't bother to call her anyway.

She was right: He didn't call her.

But a text came in two hours later.

I HAVE A NAME. SAID BEN KEMAL. YOU SEE, YOU WERE WRONG. I DO OC-CASIONALLY LET MYSELF COME IN OUT OF THE DARKNESS.

Nothing else.

No indication what he was going to do or had done after he found out that name.

Damn him.

CHAPTER 11

Dubai

"You're sure he's here?" Caleb asked, his gaze on the balcony overlooking the spectacular man-made lagoon that added to the lush oasis setting of the apartment building. "I've no desire to climb up to that balcony and disarm the alarm if there's no payoff."

"He's there. I told you what he was planning for tonight. But your payoff may be a dagger in the gullet," Palik said sourly. "Ben Kemal's very good with a knife. If he kills you, word may get around and my contacts here in Dubai may dry up like that desert out there."

"But Dubai specializes in turning deserts into lagoons like this apartment's. You'll be fine," he said, then added softly, "As long as you didn't tell Ben Kemal I was coming in exchange for favors. Then you won't be fine at all, Palik."

317

"I'm not a fool. You're a good customer. Besides, though I'm not above a little betrayal now and then, I've seen the remains of a few people who have displeased you." His white teeth flashed in his olive face. "I don't intend to be one of them. I'm going to get rich on people like you, buy a palace in Morocco and live a long life."

"I applaud your ambition." Caleb moved across the garden and started to climb the trellis at the side of the building. He hadn't really thought Palik would betray him, but it never hurt to send a ripple of uncertainty through people with whom you worked. Palik was smart and his contacts infallible, but, as he'd said, he'd seen Caleb at work. Fear could do strange things to twist a man's thinking in ways other than the desired direction.

He reached the balcony and jumped silently down and glided toward the French doors. The alarms in this apartment building were top of the mark, as was everything else here. Sometimes that assurance bred a false confidence in the people who rented the luxury spaces. It took Caleb only ten minutes to disable the outside alarm and five to take care of the motion detectors inside.

The hunt was on.

He could feel his blood start to sing in his veins as he moved across the huge living room toward the bedroom area in the north side of the apartment.

He stopped and listened.

Yes, Ben Kemal was in the apartment. He could hear sounds from the bedroom just ahead — the sounds he should have expected from what Palik had told him of Ben Kemal's sexual preferences. Perhaps he should have trusted Palik.

As if that was going to happen.

He moved toward the bedroom door.

Sobbing.

And that sharp leather crack. . . .

He silently opened the bedroom door.

It was what he'd expected. A handsome young boy of twelve or thirteen was tied naked to a huge bed with a carved headboard. His thin body was crisscrossed with livid whip marks, and as Caleb opened the door, another cutting stripe was added on his lower body.

The boy arched upward with an agonized moan.

The dark-haired man standing above him wielding the whip laughed. "Louder," he said mockingly in Arabic. "Tell me who owns you." His face was flushed and he was fully aroused. "Tell me who is your master."

He hadn't even noticed the door opening, Caleb realized. He was too involved with the sobbing boy on the bed.

He did hope that Ben Kemal wasn't going to prove to be easy prey. He found he was very annoyed at the sight of that young boy.

"Stop moaning and give me the words." Ben Kemal raised the whip again. "Do you want me to tell Mohamed that you didn't please me?"

"No, please. He will —" The tears were pouring down the boy's cheeks and he couldn't speak. "Anything but that —"

"Not fast enough, Ahmed." The whip was coming down.

But Caleb was there before it reached the boy, and he jerked it away and out of Ben Kemal's hand. "I thought his answer was quite adequate, Ben Kemal. You're much too picky."

There was an instant of shock on Ben Kemal's face. "Who —" He broke off and dived for the drawer of the nightstand a few feet away. The next instant, he had a gun in his hand and was rolling on the floor behind a chair.

A bullet tore past Caleb's ear and buried itself in the carved headboard!

Not too easy, Caleb thought with satisfaction.

"That bullet almost hit the boy." He was zigzagging across the room. "Of course, you wouldn't care about that. But I really don't like bullies, and your particular preference is a prime example." He was over the top of the chair and landing on Ben Kemal like an attacking jaguar. "So you'd better be very cooperative and not displease me."

"Son of a *bitch.*" He was struggling to get his gun up to aim at Caleb. "I'll blow your brains out. Who the hell are you?"

"Someone who needs information. That's what you sell, isn't it?" Get it over with quickly, he told himself. No matter how much time he'd like to spend on the bastard, he needed to get in and out of here before anyone else showed up. Palik had said Ben Kemal sometimes invited friends to these parties. He liked to watch, as well. The edge of his hand came down on Ben Kemal's forearm, causing the pistol to fly out of his hand and sail halfway across the room. "So you're going to talk to me, but first I need to get rid of the boy. You'll be going to sleep for the next few minutes. Take advantage of it. You'll need the rest." His hand reached down and clamped Ben Kemal's carotid artery, and the man slumped sidewise, unconscious.

Caleb jumped to his feet and went over to

the bed. He quickly cut the ropes binding the boy. "Get dressed and get out of here, Ahmed. Go down to the garden and you'll see a man in a brown suit and beige vest. I'll call ahead and tell him to take care of you."

The boy was looking at the slumped body of Ben Kemal. "He'll kill me," he whispered. "He'll blame me and hurt me."

"No, he won't. That's over. This may be your lucky day. I'll see that Palik will give you a chance. After that, it's up to you." He saw that Ben Kemal was beginning to stir, and he reached for his phone to dial Palik. "Out!"

By the time he'd finished talking to Palik, the boy had dressed and scampered out of the apartment.

Ben Kemal was glaring at him as he came fully awake. "Who are you? Why did you take the boy? None of this was necessary." Then he was trying to make his tone ingratiating. "We could make a deal. I would have sold my time with Ahmed to you. I had him for the whole weekend."

"Did you? Then I'm afraid that you've lost your money. You weren't listening. I got rid of Ahmed because he was in the way." He paused. "And I thought that he'd been traumatized enough without witnessing what I'll do to you if you don't tell me what I want to know."

"Are you threatening to torture me?" he asked scornfully. "Don't waste your time. I grew up in Afghanistan and I was trained by the Taliban to resist torture."

"Yes, I was told that you might prove difficult." He knelt beside Ben Kemal. "But there is torture, and then there is torture. You'll find it completely different to have your own body betray you and eventually kill you. It's bewildering and exquisitely painful. You *will* break, Ben Kemal."

"Screw you."

"Just the response I wanted from you, but I feel bound to give you the opportunity to tell me the information I need." He paused. "Santara contacted you when he was last here. He spent at least two days here at your apartment. Another day, you drove to the house he'd rented out of the city. I think that might have been the day that he'd arranged to have you meet with the Romanos. Is that right?"

"I don't know any of those people."

"You'll remember them soon. All I want to know is what information Santara and the Romanos wanted from you. Or was it more than information? Did they pay for services, too?"

"I'm not stupid. How do you think I've survived as long as I have?" he asked. "I sell only information and leave the rest to bastards like Santara and you."

"And then go back to pretty boys like Ahmed to expend all your money and venom." He put his hand on Ben Kemal's wrist. "This is your whip hand, isn't it? Yes, I remember. . . . In one minute it's going to swell to twice its size and blood is going to start pouring from beneath your finger-nails." His hand tightened. "Just a small harbinger of things to come."

"You're crazy."

"Tell me what information Santara paid you to get."

"Nothing," he said defiantly. "I gave him —" He stopped as he saw the blood gushing from beneath his thumb. His eyes widened in horror. "What?"

Caleb's hand moved to the bridge of his nose. "Thirty seconds and the blood will start pouring out your nostrils and down your throat as the vein ruptures. If I don't stop it, the blood could choke you. What information?"

Ben Kemal was looking down at his swollen hand, which was now gushing blood from every finger. "Get away from me!"

"No. Next we'll go to your lungs. In fact,

I'll start the pain there now."

Ben Kemal was suddenly frantically clutching at his chest. "What's happening to me?" he gasped.

"Only what I told you. Ah, there comes the blood from your nostrils." He moved his hand. "I need to know what Santara wanted from you."

"No!" It was almost a scream.

"Very well. It may take a little longer than I thought. Bad for you, good for me." Caleb sat with legs crossed, gazing down at him with a smile. "I'll wager about fifteen minutes. . . ."

Chapter 12

It took twelve minutes.

"Interesting." Caleb rose to his feet and headed for the bathroom, where he washed and dried his hands. He came out and gazed down at Ben Kemal. "I'm tempted to spend a little more time with you, but I think I know everything you know. Do I?" He studied the panic twisting Ben Kemal's features. "Oh, yes. Then there's only the final instructions. I'm leaving now and you'll lie there for the next twenty minutes. I was never here. You never talked to anyone about your time with Santara or the Romanos. The moment you open your lips to do it, your heart will start to pound and the pain will begin again." He smiled. "You might experiment to make sure. I admit I like to think of you suffering because of your own ugliness and stubbornness."

"Monster." Ben Kemal's eyes were glaring up at him with rage and horror. "Devil."

"I've been called both. I wonder what you're called at that whorehouse where you get your playmates." He headed for the door. "By the way, I think you should obey your Koran and leave those little boys alone from now on. And you do want to please me, don't you?" He heard Ben Kemal cursing behind him, but he wasn't moving or making any effort to come after Caleb. A minute later, Caleb was on the balcony and climbing down the trellis.

Palik appeared out of the shrubbery. "It took you long enough." His gaze went to the balcony. "Quiet. You got what you wanted?"

"As much as he knew." Caleb moved down the path toward the parking lot. "But I'll find out more once I trace Santara's steps and go over the info Ben Kemal turned over to him." He shrugged. "It offered a few surprises."

"I assume some that you're going to have me explore?"

"Of course. I'd never think of giving my business to anyone else. There are so many unscrupulous people in your line of expertise. It's such a waste of time weeding them out."

Palik gave another glance at the balcony. "But I believe you may have enjoyed the 'weeding' this time. Is he going to cause you any trouble?"

"No." They had reached the car. "Where did you send the boy?"

"To my cousin's village near Petros. There's construction work there, as there is all over Dubai. She'll see that he gets some schooling on the side. He can live with her until he can find a place for himself. And I'll add his rent to my increasingly hefty fee from you."

"I didn't think anything else. I never rely on generosity from anyone." He got in the passenger seat. "But there's something I want you to get on right away. You haven't been able to find a trace of the Romanos anywhere. I thought perhaps Italy or Greece, but you came up with nothing. Ben Kemal said that the Romanos weren't only vacationing when they were here; they were looking for a temporary residence. He thought that they're probably still here in Dubai or at least close by."

"So you want me to find them," Palik said. "Top priority?"

"They control Santara. Or rather, Teresa does. After talking to Said Ben Kemal, there's absolutely no doubt that he thought Teresa Romano was pulling all the strings. Her loving spouse, Gino, appears to be fading fast into oblivion," he said grimly. "Hell yes, top priority."

Loch Gaelkar

By five-thirty in the morning, Jane was tired of tossing and turning and mentally heaping curses on Caleb's infuriating head. Just forget him and get on with your life, she thought as she jumped out of her bedroll and started dressing. Then she was striding out of her tent and into Eve's tent next door.

"Come on, Michael." Jane scooped up the little boy and snatched the clothes that Eve had set out for him the night before. "We're going to leave your mama alone to sleep in and go help Lisa cook breakfast."

"I don't need to sleep in." Eve yawned. "It's just a little jet lag, or I would have been up sooner." She smiled. "And I don't think Lisa needs help, either, judging by that meal last night."

"You're right. But it won't hurt you to have a little time to yourself." She headed for the door. "One hour and I'll call you for breakfast." She balanced Michael on her hip as she left the tent and started down the hill.

"Down, Jane," Michael said firmly.

"That sounds like a command you'd give

a puppy." She put him on the grass and just held his hand. "Though you've never had one yet. I have to introduce you to my dog, Toby. But right now, he's going to school on Summer Island. Just like you'll be going to school in a couple years." She saw Lisa preparing breakfast by the fire and started to increase her pace. Then she slowed as she realized Michael couldn't keep up with her.

Adjustments. So many adjustments with a child. And Eve had made all of them beautifully. Amazing, since she had been able to keep up with her forensic sculpting, as well.

"Hi, Lisa," she said as she came into the glowing circle of the fire. "I'm trying to give Eve a break with Michael, but I'm realizing I'm not great at this."

Lisa glanced up from the dough she was kneading on a cutting board a few yards from the fire. "You seem to be doing okay. What's the problem?"

"Adjustment." She was quickly changing Michael from pajamas to his jeans and green plaid shirt. "Mind-set. All of the above." She wiped his face with a cloth dipped in a pail of water from the lake. He giggled and grabbed for the cloth. "Oh, you like that?"

"It's cold." Michael was laughing up at

her and reached a hand in the pail to splash her face with water. He laughed harder as she splashed back at him. "Swim?"

"No, not now. That's going to be up to your mama. This lake is different from the one you're used to at home."

"Different." Michael repeated the word as he gazed out at the mist hovering over the lake. "But still . . . home, Jane."

"You think so?" Jane asked gently as she wiped his face and then her own. "You'll have to discuss that with your mama."

"But in the meantime, would you like a cup of orange juice?" asked Lisa, who was suddenly beside them with one of the child's cups that Eve had given her the evening before. "Is that okay, Jane?" She was frowning. "I don't know anything about the care and feeding of children."

"I'm surprised. You've seemed to pick up a little of everything in your nineteen years. I'm sure you're annoyed with yourself that you missed out on this." She handed Michael the cup. "Okay, Michael?"

"Okay." He was smiling at Lisa. "Thank you."

Lisa's brows rose as she watched him drink the orange juice. "Manners? Isn't that unusual in a kid his age?"

"It depends on the kid. But then, Michael

is unusual. As Eve says, he picks up everything that comes his way. I tried to tell you, Lisa."

"Yes, you did. But he's still not what I was expecting." She paused. "Neither is Eve Duncan. She played me well yesterday. I knew she had to be clever, but I didn't believe she could do that."

"She was sincere," Jane said. "Eve's always honest."

"I could tell that. But that doesn't mean she can't be clever enough to get her own way when she chooses." Lisa smiled faintly. "And I think she loves you. She didn't want anyone around you to be uncomfortable, because it might make you unhappy. That's . . . extraordinary."

"No it isn't. It's just Eve."

"And it's you, too. I watched the two of you together. Was it like that all the time you were growing up?"

Jane nodded. "From the time we came together." She glanced at Lisa's face. There had been nothing in Lisa's barren life that resembled the strength and tightness of the family bond Jane had known. "And perhaps you're right. But I know how lucky I am."

Lisa shook her head. "No, you don't. You just think you do. But I can see why Caleb wanted to save her. *He* knew."

"Eve was only interested in saving Michael. You must have seen how she adores him. He's pretty extraordinary himself."

Lisa's eyes were narrowed on Michael's face. "He said 'swim.' "

"He lives on a lake. He's been in the water all his life. Eve wanted to make certain he knew what he was doing, so she had an instructor out from the local YMCA who specializes in teaching toddlers to give him lessons."

"Jody." Michael lowered his cup. He'd evidently been listening. "She likes to float. Nice. But boring."

"And lifesaving for most small children," Jane said sternly. "She did a good job, Michael."

He nodded. "Nice."

Lisa suddenly chuckled. "Diplomatic, but noncommittal. And he already understands the concept of boring." She turned to Jane. "I think I like him."

"I'm sure he'll be grateful." Jane got to her feet. "And I'll be grateful for a cup of coffee. But first, I have to run up to the tent to get his set of building blocks to keep him amused. He's into construction right now. Will you keep an eye on him?" She'd already turned and was hurrying back up the hill. "Don't look so wary. He's completely nonthreatening."

"So you say," Lisa called after her as she watched Jane disappear into the darkness. Nonthreatening? He was a beautiful child and appeared to be good-tempered, but being responsible for any child is frightening, Lisa thought. That was why she had avoided them through the years. They had a tendency to slip beyond the barriers, and she didn't allow anyone to do that. It hurt too much when they went away. But this is only for a short time, she told herself. It will be fine. She turned to Michael. "Okay, what do we do?"

He smiled at her. Dear God, that was an enchanting smile.

"Don't give me that. Save it for all your fans." She went back to kneading the biscuits. "I have to finish these biscuits, or I'll lose my credibility with MacDuff. You have to give something to get something in this world."

"Mist."

She stiffened and looked at him. He was still smiling radiantly at her. Well, what had she expected? "Yes, exactly." Though that had to be an accidental reference. "Want some more juice?"

He was on his feet and coming toward her. "No juice. Biscuits." He plopped down on the ground beside her and watched her hands move on the board. His face was intent, his eyes fastened with fascination on the formation of the dough. "Me?"

"You want some dough?" She gave him some. "Okay, but don't eat it raw. I don't think that's on a healthy kid's diet."

He shook his head impatiently. "Not eat. Build it." His hands were separating, kneading, copying her movements. But he got the dough too thin and it fell apart as he tried to form the circle of the biscuit. He looked baffled and then he gazed up at Lisa again. "More?"

"Whatever." She gave him some more dough and then stood up and took her completed biscuits and put them on the cookie sheet. "But you're on the right track. That's how I learned a lot of things. You just do it, and then make it better and better." She straightened the biscuits. "Pretty soon, you're the best. It's important to be best. People can't argue with best. It's the —" She stopped. She had turned back to Michael and he was giving her that smile again.

And the biscuit in front of him was fully formed and round, a tiny bit off-kilter, but acceptable by even Lisa's standards.

"Not best." His smile widened eagerly.

"Next time?"

She stared at that radiant, sunny expression and slowly nodded her head. "Maybe. I wouldn't put it past you. But give yourself a little time. I get impatient, too, and sometimes I don't let myself enjoy things." She was sure this wasn't how she should be talking to a two-year-old. Too bad. It felt right and she'd go with it. She held out her hand to him. "Come over to the fire and we'll sit and smell the biscuits and watch them bake. Good idea?"

He took her hand but said firmly, "*My* biscuit, Lisa."

She laughed and carefully picked up his biscuit. "By all means, *your* biscuit, Michael."

"I just got off the phone with Joe," Eve said as she came down from her tent an hour later, when they were all gathered for breakfast. "It seems we may get the first guest arriving for the ceremony today," she wryly. "Rather unexpected. She won't wait to come with Joe when he brings the others. The minute she heard what was happening, she told him she had to be with me right away."

"I guess we don't have to guess who that is," Jane said ruefully. "And it's not unexpected. You know how protective Cara is about you and Michael. It was barely okay as long as you were safely ensconced with Joe only hundreds of miles away from her school. An ocean is a different matter."

Jock stiffened. "Cara's coming?"

Eve nodded. "Joe wanted her to stay another week and finish her semester. She wasn't having any of it. She told Joe to put her on the first plane out today."

"Cara," Lisa repeated trying to dredge down to make the connection. "Cara Delaney? She lives with you, Eve?"

"When she's not at Juilliard. She's sort of our ward. Family." She made a face. "But she sometimes thinks Michael and I are *her* wards."

"Today?" Jock's body was tense as he leaned forward, ignoring everything but what was important to him. "When?"

"Four today," Eve said. "Joe's putting her on a flight to Edinburgh in a few minutes. He asked me to send one of MacDuff's men to pick her up." She glanced at MacDuff. "I thought maybe Robbie Madonald would be —"

"Not bloody likely," Jock said sharply. "I'm going to go get her."

"MacDuff needs you at the north bank," Eve said quietly. "I don't want to be here one day and start disrupting routines."

"You're not doing it. It's Cara," he said curtly. "She should have stayed with Joe, where she'd be safe."

"Joe wouldn't have sent her if he hadn't thought it would be safe for her."

"Then we don't agree." He smiled recklessly. "And I'm on the spot, so I win."

"I can go after her, Jock," Jane said.

"With all due respect, I don't regard your capabilities in the same league as Joe's." He turned to MacDuff. "I can give you until two today and then I have to go get her."

MacDuff shrugged. "I don't like it. You're sure it's necessary?"

"I'm sure. She's a target. She's the granddaughter of the most influential mob boss in Russia. He has enemies who might love to hand Cara's head to him on a platter."

"But the fact that she's Koskov's granddaughter also offers her protection. Nothing's happened to Cara since Eve took her under her wing. Wouldn't they hesitate to go after her if it meant facing him?"

"Hesitate? Screw hesitate. It's not going to happen. I won't have it. And how do you know they wouldn't have gone after her?" He got to his feet. "I'm going down to the mists and get started. Don't worry, I'll bring her to you, Eve."

"I know you will." She was gazing at him thoughtfully. "And you said 'wouldn't have gone after her,' Jock. Curious sentence. It makes me wonder if you put some insurance in place to keep her safe during these last months. Did you?"

He didn't answer.

"Jock?"

"Aye." He shrugged. "She was alone in New York at that school. Perhaps I had a contact keep an eye on her."

" 'Perhaps'?" Eve shook her head. "And no one can take care of her but you? We *love* her, Jock."

"I know. But she almost died before you and Joe took her into your home, and it was my fault. I'm not going to let it happen again. Learn to live with it, Eve." He turned and headed for the north bank.

"Well, that appears to be that." MacDuff shook his head and took a last swallow of coffee before he got to his feet. "It appears that there's a chance I'm going to be short-handed for at least today." He glanced at Lisa. "Are you in any shape to come help? I promise I'll be easy on you."

Lisa's head lifted, her eyes bright and alert. "Right now?"

"No, let's limit it to half a day to start out. You can stay here and make preparations for dinner." He grimaced. "I don't intend to do without that luxury. I've begun to look forward to it. Come around two, when I'm being deserted." He looked at Eve. "I'd forgotten what a distraction Cara could be when I invited you to treat my lands as your own. Her only saving grace is her entertainment value."

"Wrong. That's only her most obvious one," Eve said. "And you know it, MacDuff. Want me to pack up and go somewhere else?"

"I didn't say that," he said gruffly. "I like the lass." He turned away. "Besides, I'd lose Jock if he had to go chasing after Cara to make certain that she was safe." He glanced at Lisa. "We'll work it out."

Lisa smiled. "You won't be sorry, MacDuff. I learn fast."

"I believe you. Don't disappoint me." He followed Jock down the bank.

Lisa immediately turned back to Jane. Her cheeks were flushed and her eyes shining. "I've *got* it."

Jane nodded. "Cold, damp, invisible work in the mist. Lucky you."

"But it's different and interesting. . . ." Her eyes were on the mist. "And Cira."

"Then you'll have to thank Cara when she gets here," Jane said. "I think Jock's tempo-

340

rary desertion was the straw that broke MacDuff's will."

"I would have gotten him anyway. It just would have taken longer," Lisa said. "And I don't think I should thank her. If she knew Jock had hired someone to keep an eye on her, it might annoy her. It would me."

"Cara is the furthest thing from you in the universe," Jane said drily. "But it probably would annoy her in this case. For a youngster, she's very independent."

"Youngster? How old is she?"

"Fourteen."

"The same age I was when Seth left me." She shook off the memory. "Then she's old enough to get through anything. It's rough for a while. But I got along fine, and so will she."

"She doesn't doubt that," Eve said quietly. "And Cara has had it rough all her life and survived it. When I found her, she'd been on the run from a murderer from one of the Mexican cartels since she was three years old. Her older sister and her best friend had already been murdered by that time."

Lisa gave a low whistle. "If she went through all of that, I definitely don't think that she needs Jock to take care of her."

"You won't be able to convince him of

that," Jane said. "You heard him."

"I heard him." She was frowning, puzzled. "But I didn't understand it. What is she to him?"

Jane and Eve exchanged a glance. How to explain that bond that linked Jock and Cara? "Best friend? Sister? Soul mate?" Eve shrugged. "When I brought Cara here two years ago and she met Jock, it was as if they made an immediate connection. I'd never seen anything like it. They'd both had backgrounds that were tortured and left them feeling terribly alone. They seemed to . . . fulfill each other. They became very close. He was the perfect big brother. She adored him. She still does."

"He said he almost got her killed."

"The hit men who were after Cara almost took out MacDuff, and Jock went after them. She followed him and walked right into their hands."

"But she got away from them?"

"Eventually. But it was a total nightmare. Jock went after her and saved her life." Eve added, "So you can see why he's a bit protective of her. He's not going to let that happen again."

Lisa nodded slowly. "You have to take care of the people you love. You shouldn't let them be alone."

Jane didn't like the direction this was heading. "But you can also be a handicap if you're not capable of contributing and they have to end up helping you."

Lisa smiled. "And of course you're not talking about me? You're talking about Cara, who was only a twelve-year-old child at the time?"

Jane smiled back at her. "Of course."

"I thought so." She turned away. "But I'm getting very close to not being a handicap any longer. A few days of gentle exercise working with MacDuff in the mist might just put me over the finish line. I can probably afford those days. Seth hasn't told me anything that would hint at something different."

But Caleb had told Jane about Said Ben Kemal, and that was the first break he'd had. He might be trying to keep the knowledge from Lisa, but she was his sister and possessed that link with him. Jane didn't know if Lisa might somehow sense he was keeping something from her. "Well, at least you'll get those few days in the mist after all your hard work paving the way." She turned away. "Now, I think I'll take Michael for a walk along the bank and then get one of those tents ready for Cara."

■ ■ ■ ■

Cara Delaney saw Jock as soon as she arrived at customs.

Lord, she had been hoping he would be here to meet her. And there he was, standing outside the barrier and wearing a white shirt and black jeans, and he was as wonderful-looking as always. But then he never changes, Cara thought as the joy and excitement poured through her. The first time she had met him, she had thought he looked like the prince in a fairy tale. But then she had learned there was so much more to him inside than out that she hardly noticed it anymore except at moments like this.

"I'll be right there, Jock," Cara called to him. "No checked luggage. Just my carry-on and my violin."

He nodded. "I'm surprised you brought a carry-on. After all, the violin is the only thing that's important to you." He smiled. "Take your time. I'll wait."

"You'd better." She nodded and turned back to the crowded desk. Ten minutes later, she was grabbing the duffel and her violin and almost running behind the barrier. She dropped both and flew into his arms. "Jock," she whispered as she hugged him as tightly as she could. She wanted to stay there, but she let him go and stepped back. "I was afraid they'd send someone else," she said unsteadily. "I know how busy you are."

"True." He smiled down at her. "And why would I want to drive all this way to pick up a brat like you?" He brushed his lips on her forehead. "But I happened to have a few spare hours, so I thought that I'd save anyone else the bother." He looked down at the duffel and violin she'd dropped. He clucked his tongue. "Careless. Very careless. I imagine that's the first time that violin was dropped so rudely since it was crafted in the eighteenth century."

"It's very well padded." She picked up the case. "Too bad your skull isn't. Because I'm going to crack it if you don't tell me you're glad to see me."

"It's possible." He grabbed her duffel. "No, probable." He was guiding her toward the door. "But I would have preferred that you hadn't traveled by yourself. I'm not fond of impulsive moves on your part. I believe we discussed that when I saw you in New York."

"You mean lectured." She smiled at him. "Probable. Why is it so difficult for you to say? I'll say it again. I miss you all the time and I'm glad to see you. You're my best friend and I don't see enough of you. Now you say it."

He was silent. "Cara, you're just a kid," he said gruffly. "You have a good home with Eve and Joe now. You have your music and friends at school; it's time to step away from me. How many times do I have to tell you? I get in your way."

"You keep telling me that. Stop it." She shook her head. "I'll never step away from you. You're my best friend. You saved my life. You *know* me, the way no one else does." She looked at him. "And I'm not going to let you spoil these couple weeks by pushing me away. You're always doing that anyway. I came here early because I wanted to be here for Eve and Michael, but you're a plus and I'm going to enjoy it." She grinned. "So you say it, Jock. I'm listening."

He was silent, gazing down at her. "The older you get, the more stubborn."

"You once told me I owned my soul and my choices. It meant a lot to me and I've been trying to live by it. Say it."

He gave her that radiant smile that lit his whole face with warmth. "I've missed you and I'm glad to see you." He reached out and touched her hair. "And you *are* my best friend."

"Thank you." She cleared her throat. "But you could have been more generous about it."

"That's what I'm trying to be." He opened the car door for her. "You have a chance to have a good life after the hell you've been through. I just have to see that you take advantage of it." He shut the door and ran around to the driver's seat. "Now tell me about that new music teacher at your school that you e-mailed me about. Is he really that good?"

"Taldoff?" She nodded. "He was with the Sydney Symphony, and he's wonderful. I'm lucky to have him as a teacher."

"He's lucky to have you. Someday he'll brag that he taught Cara Delaney."

"No he won't. With him, it's all about the music."

"Like you."

She nodded. "In the end, there's nothing else. And there doesn't have to be."

"Not for anyone who listens to you, either. You give gifts." He was gazing straight ahead as he pulled out of the parking lot. "You should be a little chary with those gifts. Have you heard from your grandfather lately?"

She had known this was coming. "No. But I probably will soon. He's been very patient."

"The hell he has. You don't owe him anything. Koskov is head of one of the most notorious Mafia groups in Moscow. He can just keep the hell away from you. You don't have any business being anywhere near him."

"But I do," she said quietly. "I asked him to help save Eve's life when she was pregnant with Michael, and he did it. But I realized at the time that he didn't believe anything was free. We both knew that I'd have to pay."

"No, you won't. It just means that I make a visit to Moscow." He smiled recklessly. "Or you just tell him no. Make a choice."

"It's not as if he's asking so much. He just wants me to spend one month a year with him, and I choose the place."

"And you think he'd keep his word? He's a criminal who's made murder a way of life since the time he was a young man. You spent only a few weeks with him and yet you believe you know him?"

She shook her head. "Sometimes I do. Sometimes I don't. I don't know why he wants to spend that time with me. I think it has something to do with the music." Her lips curved in the ghost of a smile. "And in spite of what you think, he was patient. He gave me time to settle in with Eve and Joe, and then these last months to get used to being at Juilliard."

"It probably pleased his vanity that you'd been accepted there," he said bitterly. "Just being in his circle is a danger to you. If he doesn't get bored and decide you're expendable, one of the heads of a rival crime syndicate might decide to punish him by killing you."

"You told me that in New York. I won't live in a cage, Jock. I spent my life running, but a cage is just as bad. I'll be careful, because I want to live, but I can't be afraid all the time."

"A little more fear would be in order. Tell your grandfather you've changed your mind about this damn deal."

"Eve would have died and so would Michael if he hadn't helped," she said. "How could I change my mind?" She forced herself to smile. "Don't talk about it anymore, Jock. I haven't heard from him yet. Who knows? Maybe I won't."

"And maybe you will. Will you tell me if you do?"

She didn't want to promise him that. It was bad enough that he still thought himself the assassin who had been created when he was a boy not much older than she was now. If he believed he was protecting her, he could become very close to reverting back to that time. "No."

He was silent a moment and she could see a subtle hardening in his face, a coldness that was frightening her. She had seen that expression before and it terrified her. "I'll find out anyway," he said softly. "I've been trained in all the paths that lead to a kill. I'm good at it. That's why you should take that step away from me. If you tell me, we can at least talk about it. You can try to persuade me."

And that was the only way to stop him. That hardness was knife-sharp, and he'd almost reached the point where she couldn't reach him. But she *had* to reach him. "I'll tell you." She looked him in the eye. "And I *will* persuade you. You won't do it."

"And why not?"

"Because it would break my heart," she said simply.

His expression flickered, changed. "Oh shit. How am I supposed to fight that?"

"You can't. So let's not talk about it any longer. You've already spoiled a perfectly beautiful drive," she said jerkily. "Tell me, did you come to pick me up because you were as eager to see me as I was you? Or did you just want to make certain no one was going to shoot me?"

He was silent for a moment. "Well, I wouldn't be honest with you if I didn't tell you that I told them all that I had to go because it was my job to keep you from getting killed."

She wished she hadn't asked that question. "And that was why you came?"

"Absolutely." He was silent for a moment. "What I didn't tell them was that I couldn't bear the thought of anyone but me being there to watch over you. Do want to know why?"

"Yes." He was smiling, and she knew it was going to be okay. That terrible keen edge was gone and there was no way he was going to say anything that would hurt her. He was the Jock she knew now. "But it better be something good. I deserve it after all that stuff you just put me through."

"It had to be me, because who wouldn't want to be the one to watch over their very best friend in the world?" His voice lowered to honey gentleness. "And it had to be me because I didn't know how I'd survive without her. That will always be the reason, Cara."

She cleared her throat. "That was pretty

good. And you wanted to see me as much as I wanted to see you. Right?" she prompted.

"Without question."

She breathed a sigh of relief. "Okay, then that's over. Sometimes it's like pulling teeth with you." She leaned back in the seat. "Now, tell me all about the new lights you've been putting in the mist and what Jane's been doing. And how does Michael like the lake? And all about that Lisa Ridondo that Joe was telling about. . . ."

CHAPTER 13

"Eve!"

Eve turned and saw Cara running down the slope toward her. She barely had time to hold out her arms before the girl reached her. She was enveloped in a huge embrace, which she returned with equal enthusiasm. Then she pushed Cara away and smiled down at her. "You could have waited for Joe. It's not as if I was having an emergency. It's just a wedding, Cara."

"You might need me. I don't know anything about weddings, but I thought I should be here."

Cara always thought she should take care of her, Eve thought with rueful affection. From the moment she had come into their lives, she had wanted to repay Eve and Joe for taking her under their wings and protecting her from the cartel enforcer who had killed her sister. That devotion could be both touching and exasperating. "I always need you." She kissed her on the cheek. "But that's because I love you. No service required. Where's Jock?"

"Coming. He told me he'd bring down the luggage. I think he wanted to give me time to say hello." She smiled as she looked out at the lake. "It's just as I remembered it. I don't wonder you wanted to have the wedding here. Not everything that happened at Gaelkar was good, but I think you and Joe were happy here." She gazed at the mist. "And it wasn't because of the place. There's music here, Eve."

"Is there?" And who would know better than Cara, who was filled with music herself? "I believe you. I don't hear it, but sometimes I think I can feel it."

"It's there. Sometimes sad, sometimes joyous, always strong."

"Like life?"

She nodded and pulled her gaze away from the mist. "Where are Jane and Michael?"

"I think she needed a break from having Michael watch her painting that portrait of him. He's fascinated, but he wanted to do it himself. She decided that she'd take him for a walk along the bank to meet Lisa and MacDuff when they came back for supper."

"Maybe I'd better go after them and help

her with —"

"No." Jock was suddenly beside them. "You go to your tent and change and catch a few minutes of rest." He set her violin case and duffel down. "Trust me. I'll go make sure that they don't disappear into the mist."

"I didn't think that Jane would —"

But Cara was talking to air as Jock strode away from them down the bank. She made a face. "Bossy. I just wanted to help."

"You always do." Eve's lips were twitching as she picked up Cara's duffel. That moment she had witnessed between them was so very familiar. Jock, the strong, charismatic young man; Cara, no longer a child but not yet a woman. But the strength of the bond almost visible between them. "I'll help you get settled. You started traveling early this morning. You've got to be tired."

"A little." Cara started up the hill toward the tent area. "But the trip here from the airport wore me out more than the jet across the ocean." She was frowning as she looked back at Jock. "He's always so . . . difficult these days. Why can't he just be happy?"

"Because he's Jock," Eve said. "Because of the life he's led. Because he never expected that anyone like you would come into his life, someone for whom he'd suddenly feel responsible." She paused. "Of course, if you don't want to deal with that difficulty, you could just let him go."

"No." Cara's eyes widened with alarm. "I couldn't do that," she whispered. "Never. I just want him to be happier. He *should* be happy. He has that wonderful shining inside." She stopped at the tent. "I have you. I have my music. I'm happier than I've ever been. Except for Jock."

Eve nodded. "And that's probably not going to go away anytime soon. It's a long-range problem that you'll probably have to deal with yourself."

"And I'll do it." She gave Eve a hug. "I'm sorry. I didn't mean to complain. Slap me if I do that again."

"I'll take that under consideration. At the moment, I'm too glad to see you to inflict violence." She set Cara's bag down inside the tent. "So just do what that 'bossy' Jock told you to do and get a little rest. I'll call you when it's time for supper." She stopped as she was going to leave. "What kind of delay was Joe having that you didn't opt to wait for him to bring you?"

"Margaret Douglas," Cara said. "He couldn't find her and he knew she would want to be here."

"I should have guessed," Eve said. "Margaret is as close to a Gypsy as anyone I've ever met."

"I know. I like her. You told me that she had a wonderful talent with animals."

Eve nodded. "She has friends at a special veterinary clinic on Summer Island, in the Caribbean. I'll tell Joe to put out feelers there." She smiled. "He's not had an easy job. My friends appear liable to be in the four corners of the earth at any given moment."

"He'll find them," Cara said. "And you're not the only one. He had his own list. He was also looking for someone named Venable and a Sean Galen."

"Then it's good that you didn't wait," Eve said. "Venable is CIA and can be very elusive."

"I'm glad that you're not upset with me," Cara said. "I know that I can be annoying when I push too hard. It's just so important that I take care of you and Michael. You sent me away to school, so I can't do it all the time. But let me do it during the next week or so, okay?"

"Okay," Eve said gently. "But you'll find plenty of other things to do here, Cara. MacDuff is close to finding his treasure. And Caleb's sister, Lisa, is always trying to do too much." She tilted her head. "I wonder how the two of you will get along. She's not at all like you."

"I'll just do what you tell me. I won't cause you any trouble."

Eve laughed. "Not at all like you," she repeated. She gave Cara another kiss on the forehead. "I'll see you in an hour."

The sun was low on the horizon and casting a golden glow on the mist as Eve left the tent. She could see MacDuff, Lisa, and Jock coming toward the camp with Jane and Michael, who were following them at a slower pace. Lisa was walking stiffly, holding her shoulders very straight.

She's hurting, Eve thought. She had done too much. She was supposed to have had a light day, but she'd probably pushed herself and not let MacDuff see how tired she was getting.

Then she saw Jock grab Lisa's backpack, ignoring her protest, and then fall back to where Jane and Michael were walking. He was smiling as he said something to Michael and then lifted him on his shoulders.

She saw Michael laughing as Jock trotted ahead of the others in the group coming down the bank. The sunlight fell on Jock's shock of fair hair and burnished it as he moved.

He has that wonderful shining inside.

Cara's words came back to her as she watched him. That beautiful exterior and the scars that sometimes hid that shining that Cara could see so well and that Jock refused to believe was there.

Eve could see it now. She could see the strength and beauty in all of them. MacDuff, with his humor and tough drive, which hid a heart that made his people love him. Lisa, who was emerging from pain and struggle and yet would give her life for Caleb. Jane, her wonderful Jane, who had been through so much and was still battling.

Eve suddenly had a sense of infinite rightness as she looked down at them with the lake of golden mist behind them. Her friends, her family, this place, this time.

Did you ever feel like that, Cira?

Somehow she thought that she might have.

She kept her gaze fixed on those very special people enveloped in that golden haze as she slowly started down the hill to join them.

Jumaira, Dubai

It was here!

Teresa Romano quickly took the document from the FedEx envelope and turned and went back inside the villa.

Gino was sitting by the indoor Moroccan pool and looked up with a scowl. "Only seven more days, Teresa. You promised me Santara would come through for us. I never should have believed you."

More complaints. She was sick to death of putting up with him. She'd increased the drugs she made available to him. She'd furnished him with different whores every day to distract him, but he still managed to get in her way. She had been nervous enough herself during these last days without having to soothe Gino.

Just a little longer. Then she would be on that plane to Moscow and wouldn't have to serve anyone but herself.

"Santara will come through. He's not clever, but he's efficient. I can still work with him. He just had to be guided in the right direction."

"And if you can't, we'll lose everything we've invested in this crazy plan of yours. We'll be paupers." He added maliciously, "You're not going to like living on the crumbs of all the people here in Dubai you so carefully cultivated. You think that those people who snubbed you when you were growing up were bad? It's nothing like it is here in Dubai. Here the rich are rich and the rest are nothing."

He was enjoying this too much. When things had gone sour for them, he had begun to fling her background at her. She had never liked him, but that's when she had begun to hate him. She held on to her temper. Don't strike out, she thought. It isn't going to be that long. "That's not going to happen. Caleb is still the key. I refuse to give him up when he's so perfect. The plan is still the same. I just had to readjust it a little. I admit I was overconfident because I felt I knew Caleb so well. I started out with too little information." She held up the envelope she'd just received. "No longer. Even a man as private as Caleb leaves footprints. What do you think I've been waiting for? I contacted Alex Nalari, one of the investigators you hired when you needed to use leverage on someone." She opened the envelope and was scanning the report. "All I need is a weapon. . . ."

His smirk vanished. "And you think that Nalari's going to give you one?"

Teresa was going quickly over the contents on the first page, then the second, then the third. Could it be? She went back to the first page and checked. Yes, she'd found what she needed. She felt excitement start to climb as she realized what she had in her hands.

I've got you, Caleb.

"Oh, yes." She went to the desk and underlined a name on the second sheet. "I just have to tell Santara to look for an opportunity. Nalari has definitely given me the weapon I need."

Loch Gaelkar
12:40 A.M.

Beautiful, Lisa thought drowsily as she roused from sleep.

The wind . . .

The mist . . .

No, both of them . . .

Surrounding her, becoming her . . .

She shook her head to clear it. No, it was just music. . . .

Just music?

She sat up in bed and threw her blanket aside. It was a violin, so it must be Cara Delaney playing somewhere out there in the darkness. She hadn't met her yet because Jane and Eve had ganged up on her after she'd arrived back at camp and made her go immediately to her tent after eating a light meal. She hated to admit it, but they'd probably been right, because she'd collapsed and been lost to the world five minutes after she'd reached her tent.

Until the music.

And it was still playing, luring her as the mist had lured her.

Why not? She had to know what she had to deal with in terms of Cara Delaney. Just as she always took the measure of everyone else who came into her life.

She put on her shoes but didn't bother changing out of her nightshirt. Then she was out of her tent, listening, her gaze searching.

The far bank, just before the woods that led into the mist . . .

She could see the bright moonlight outlining the girl, gleaming on the violin she was holding as she sat there on the bank.

Lisa was down the hill and moving swiftly around the campfire to the bank.

The girl doesn't even know I'm coming toward her, she thought impatiently. She's so absorbed in the music that there's no one else on her radar. Not smart. She'd been told that Cara Delaney had been on the run for most of her life. It was a wonder that she hadn't been caught and killed before this. Someone should tell her that she shouldn't be out here by herself and —

The music stopped and Cara was looking

at her. She lowered her bow and then the violin to her lap. "Hello, you must be Lisa Ridondo. I'm sorry, did I wake you?"

"Yes," Lisa said curtly. "No big deal. It was fine once I figured out where the music was coming from. It was kind of pretty."

Cara smiled. "I promised I'd practice every day. It was the only way I was able to leave school before finals. There was a big furor, and the principal was threatening to kick me out."

"That's happened to me a few times." Lisa dropped to the grass a few yards away. "But you held your ground and called their bluff?"

"No, I think they meant it. Juilliard's rules are very strict. I told them that they had to do what they had to do." She added simply, "And that I had to go to Eve."

"Then it *was* a bluff," Lisa said adamantly.

She shrugged. "It didn't matter, did it? I like the teachers at Juilliard, but it's the music that's important. And they only asked me to promise to practice every day, so it was cool. I would have played every day anyway, so it's easy to keep that promise."

Lisa's gaze was narrowed on her face. "But you would have kept it anyway."

"Promises are important, even when they're difficult to keep." She changed the subject. "Are you all right now? Eve said that you'd been hurt."

"I'm fine. I was just a little tired today." She added testily, "Eve can be very determined. I didn't need to go right to bed."

"Yes, you did. Or Eve wouldn't have told you to do it." Cara smiled. "And you're stubborn, so you wouldn't have done it if you hadn't known she was right. It just gave you a reason."

"What do you know? I don't need reasons."

Cara was silent.

Lisa suddenly chuckled. "Okay, sometimes you have to build on what people expect you to be. You wouldn't want to disappoint them."

Cara smiled back at her. "That seems to take a lot of effort." She tilted her head. "And it sounds like something Caleb would say. I can tell that he's your brother."

"You should," she said fiercely. "I'm *proud* that he's my brother. He's wonderful."

"You don't have to be defensive about him around me. He did me a big favor a couple years ago. I don't know quite why he did it, but I'm grateful that he did."

"What did he do?"

"He took me to see my grandfather when everyone else was telling me I couldn't go."

She grinned. "It got him in trouble with everyone."

"The grandfather who's some kind of mob boss?" Lisa shrugged. "Well, if Seth wanted to do it, why not?"

"I think you'd say that no matter what he did. I'm just saying that he's different. I've learned that people have the right to make their own choices. He made one that helped me and caused him a headache."

"Jock," Lisa murmured. "He mentioned something about your grandfather's being a danger to you."

"Jock wasn't pleased. But he and Caleb are okay now."

"I'm certain that Seth wouldn't have been worried about that."

"Then you'd be wrong," Cara said quietly. "Caleb would be worried about anything that affects Jane, and she considers Jock family. It's best that you know that."

Lisa looked at Cara in disbelief. "Is that a threat?"

"No, I just want you to understand. I think you must love Caleb very much. I don't want you to make a mistake."

Lisa was silent. "And you don't want there to be any chance of Seth or me or anyone else hurting Jock. You're trying to protect him."

Cara repeated gently, "I don't want you to make a mistake."

Strength. Beneath Cara's almost fragile gentleness was iron-hard strength. "I seldom make mistakes. Ever since I was a little girl, I've studied and learned so that won't happen."

"Good." Cara picked up the violin off her lap, her hand caressing the exquisite wood. "I did, too. But I had my friend, Elena, to help and keep me safe, until I lost her." She tucked the violin beneath her chin. "I'm going to play now. I'll try to make it soothing if you want to go back to bed."

She was being dismissed in favor of that violin, Lisa realized in amusement. She had an idea that Cara would have done the same to anyone unless it was Jock. None of them was important at this moment in comparison to the music.

The music. The wind. The mist.

Just the thought of that wisp of melody was beckoning, luring Lisa again. "But you shouldn't be out here alone at this time of night, you know."

"Then neither should you."

"You're just a kid. I can take care of myself."

"That's how you got shot?"

"Things are different with me now."

"Eve said there are all kinds of guards around the property, and Jock and MacDuff. All I'd have to do is call out. And Joe is beginning to teach me karate. I'm getting fairly good."

But Lisa had been older and stronger than Cara, and Santara had managed to take her.

She looked down at her bandaged thumb. What would a broken thumb mean to Cara Delaney? What would it mean to her life and her music?

She found her stomach clenching at the thought. Cara was probably right about her being safe. But bad things happened, and they both knew it. They had different ways of looking at how to face and handle things. Of course, Lisa's was the intelligent way to do it. So she should just get up and go back to her tent.

She didn't move.

Even though she was right, she had an idea that it would not help this worry go away. So why not give in to it? After all, it was purely selfish and had nothing to do with actually protecting Cara. If it made Lisa feel better, it wouldn't hurt to stay and form a barrier against some of those bad things that might possibly be waiting for the kid.

"Okay, okay." Lisa waved an impatient

hand. "Have it your way. But I might as well stick around until you finish. I liked that music you were playing when I came down here." She stretched out and cradled her head on one arm. "But don't be offended if I fall asleep."

"I won't." Cara smiled into her eyes. "But you won't fall asleep, Lisa."

She started to play.

Music.

Cara was playing, Jane realized drowsily. How good it was to have her here. What a beautiful way to wake . . .

The strains of music streaming through the night, touching everything around it. Rippling over the lake, caressing the mist, creating a fragile rhythm on the path as she walked along the bank.

Soon she'd be there. Soon she'd be with him. . . .

"You're certain about this?" Antonio asked. "It will be difficult to retrieve the chest if we ever have to flee here as we did Herculaneum."

"Then the solution is never to have to flee," Cira said. "I'm done with running away. We've built our home and we'll fight to keep it. Here is where we stay." She looked at Antonio. "Where I stay. I hope you'll stay with me."

"How good of you to include me, since I've given you a number of fine sons and daughters to start your dynasty." He reached over and gently kissed her cheek. "I'm content in this land. I'm just trying to be sensible in case I have to defend my family in the best way I can."

"You will do it very well right here," she said unsteadily. "And I'm glad that you don't choose to leave me. I would feel very much alone without you."

"And I would feel as lost in the world as I do in this damnable mist. The torch helps a little, but not nearly enough." His gaze left her to strain to see through the thick mist ahead. "I can't understand how Marcus ever found his way through it. It's a wonder he didn't end up in the lake. I'm surprised you let him play down here without you."

"He was full of dreams and he felt at home here. Me? I was just glad he had his dog, Galo. I could call Galo's name and he'd come running." She felt the tears sting her eyes. "And then Marcus would come running. So happy. So eager . . ."

"He's still here, Cira." Antonio's hand closed on her own. "You've told me that you feel him sometimes."

"Yes. But it's hard for me not to be able to see him." She wiped her cheeks with the back of her hand. "I think perhaps Galo sees him. Every now and then I see him cock his head and stare at . . ." She paused and shrugged. "Nothing. It doesn't seem fair that a dog should be able to see my son and not me."

"Imagination, love?"

"Maybe. How do I know? Perhaps Marcus needed his playmate and I couldn't go where he goes. Galo didn't want to leave him when we brought him to his final home here. And he's always eager to run back to the cave whenever I bring him with me to visit Marcus." She swallowed. "And I may think it unfair, but I pray that Marcus does still have his friend."

"As do I," Antonio said gently. "But may I suggest that you call Galo to come and get us and take us the rest of the way? Because we've reached the point where I can't see a thing now."

Cira laughed. "Nor I. But that means we're very close. Galo!"

Barking.

Then the lean tan hound was dashing through the mist toward them.

He stopped short, his gaze on Cira.

Then he turned and moved slowly ahead of them, looking back to make sure they were following.

A few minutes later, the cave loomed ahead of them.

Antonio went forward and rolled the boulder aside.

Darkness.

It took Cira a moment to light the torch affixed to the wall.

Marcus's beautifully carved wood and bronze casket with its polished granite inlay rested on a rock shelf directly ahead.

Cira closed her eyes for a moment.

"Hello, my dear love, I hope all is well with you."

She opened her eyes and saw Galo lying contentedly beneath the stone shelf, his head on his paws. "You think it is? Then I will, too." She said over her shoulder to Antonio, "Bring it in. I think over there in the cavity in the cave wall, don't you?"

"As good as anywhere." Antonio lifted the chest of the crude wagon they had been wheeling down the bank. He paused a moment, gazing at the casket. He blinked rapidly and then carried the chest over to the wall that Cira had indicated. "We have a duty for you, my boy. Duty is good. Not always enjoyable, but good." He slid the chest deep in the cavity and then started to pile rocks up against it. "But I think you might want to help us in this way."

"I'm sure of it," Cira said unevenly. "You always liked the idea of playing that you were

372

bringing me jewels out of the mist, Marcus. This is very close. Keep it safe to protect the family you love and who love you."

She stood there looking at the casket, remembering all the vitality, the laughter, the joy of him. It seemed impossible that she had to turn away and leave him again.

A whimper, not of sorrow, but of joy.

Her eyes flew to Galo lying on the floor below the casket. But his gaze was not looking up at the casket as he was whimpering. His tail was wagging in welcome, but he was looking at her. No, not at her, she realized suddenly, something to her right . . .

Or someone?

She inhaled sharply as she felt the wave of overpowering certainty sweep over her.

Standing beside her in comfort and love? Trying to tell her that he had not really left her?

"Cira?" Antonio was beside her. "Are you ready to go?"

He didn't understand and she couldn't tell him right now. She was too filled with the closeness and the completeness of what Marcus was trying to convey to her. She would tell Antonio later, when she understood more herself.

She nodded jerkily and reached up to take the torch from the wall. "Come on, Galo. Lead us out of here. It's time to go."

Because now Cira knew what Galo knew, that there was no reason to stay.

She knew that she would never really go away from Marcus because he would always be with her. . . .

Jane realized tears were pouring down her cheeks even before she opened her eyes.

Darkness.

Dawn.

Sadness that was no sadness.

Love that never went away.

Cira.

She sat upright in bed and tried to stop sobbing. Stupid. There was nothing to cry about. That was what Cira had been trying to tell her, what she had discovered that night in the mist.

She took a long, shaky breath.

I'm okay now, Cira. I guess I'm not as strong as you are. You kind of blew me away.

She tossed her blanket aside and got to her feet. Then she was out of her tent and going down the hill toward the bank.

No music, she realized vaguely. No Cara. The camp was quiet. Everyone must be asleep. She had no idea how much time had passed since she'd become aware of the sound of Cara's violin when she'd been on the edge of slumber.

The edge of Cira's world.

It wasn't important how much time had passed; it was only important that she stay here by the lake until she made sense of what had happened tonight.

She stood on the edge of the bank and looked out at the mist. The moonlight was shading it with pale silver, but it was as mysterious and inexplicable as ever.

As enigmatic as Cira had always been to Jane since that first dream when she was seventeen. No, that wasn't true. She had always understood Cira; she just didn't know why Cira had wanted her to understand. All the years that had passed, Cira's life and story gradually unfolding to Jane even as she grew in spirit and experienced her own tragedies and struggles. Through it all, Jane had never known the reason.

And she didn't know why Cira had brought her here to this place tonight and shown her the depths of her sorrow and her soul.

And her triumph.

Why, Cira? Why now? Wasn't I ready before?

No answer.

But the answer would come, Jane knew suddenly. If she stayed here on the bank, if she let the wind and the mist tell her what she needed to know.

Your move, Cira . . .

"Eve," Jane whispered. She shook her gently. "Wake up."

Eve tensed, even as she opened her eyes. "Jane? What's wrong?"

"Nothing. At least I don't think there is."

"The hell there's not." Her hand was on Jane's arm. "You're cold."

"Cool," she said, correcting her. "I've been outside by the lake for a few hours. I'm fine."

Eve sat up and brushed the hair away from her face. "Something about Lisa?"

"No. Something about me." Her hand reached out to grasp Eve's. "Something about Cira. I've been out there trying to figure it out. I believe I may have done it." She smiled. "But, as usual, I had to run to you for confirmation and help. That goes on forever."

"Wrong. You don't come running to me nearly often enough."

"Well, I'm here now." Her hand tightened on Eve's. "And I need you to do me a favor, Eve. . . ."

"You're not painting today?" Lisa asked Jane as she glanced at the covered easel. "I thought it was going well."

"It is," Jane said. "But I didn't come here to paint. I thought I'd go to the bank this morning and see if I can help."

"I tried." Lisa made a face. "It's all your fault for sending me to bed as soon as I got back yesterday. MacDuff didn't like it that I got so tired. He said that he'd give it a couple more days before he'd let me help again. I couldn't talk him out of it."

"That must have been disappointing."

"Well, he has Jock back today. It wasn't that I didn't do a good job."

"I'm sure it wasn't." She was looking out at the mist. "And there's not much that I can do today, either. I just want to be there."

"Why?" Lisa's gaze was fixed on her face. "Are you okay? You look a little weird."

"Do I? I had trouble sleeping last night."

"Well, it wasn't Cara's fault," she said quickly. "She didn't play that long, and it was all quiet stuff. So don't blame her."

"I wouldn't think of it." Jane smiled. "Since you evidently don't."

"She promised the people at her school that she'd practice. She had to keep her

377

promise."

Jane chuckled. "Lisa, you don't have to defend her. We all love her music. A little less sleep is okay when weighed in the balance. I guess you found that out."

Lisa nodded. "But I'll try to get her to practice in the daytime today. I don't care what she says; it's not smart for her to be sitting around in the dark playing that violin."

"You do that." Jane grabbed her backpack. "What else do you plan to do today besides trying to run Cara's life?"

"Cook. Make myself invaluable to your Eve and the kid." She grinned. "Maybe look up a few recipes for wedding hors d'oeuvres on the Internet. Do some of MacDuff's paperwork to show him how generous and forgiving I am." She paused. "And think about how quiet you are today and why you want to go to the north bank."

Jane wasn't really surprised that Lisa had sensed something in her demeanor that had sent up flares. Lisa might not have been linked to Jane, but she was Caleb's sister, and they were evidently close enough for her to pick up vibes. "I'm never permitted to be quiet around you because you have entirely too many questions." She met Lisa's eyes. "And you once asked me if I minded your working in Cira's world because she belonged to me. The answer is still no, but that doesn't mean that the time won't come that I'll have to be the one to do what she's always wanted me to do."

Lisa's smile faded. "What's happening, Jane?"

"I'm not sure, but I think that it's what's supposed to happen." She started down the trail leading toward the bank. "We'll have to see, won't we?"

1:25 P.M.

"When do you think you'll be able to turn on the lights?" Jane asked MacDuff in the middle of the day as she stopped to wipe her brow. "You have four poles mounted with those space-age wonders and all the transformers are connected now. When?"

"Soon. Maybe we'll come back tonight after supper." He rubbed the back of his neck. "We did a run-through with the first ones we put up, and they were marginally successful. But these transformers may make the difference." His voice was tense. "It's *got* to work, Jane. I feel it. We're getting close."

"Yes, we're close." She looked out at the mist. "I feel it, too. And you deserve it,

379

MacDuff. What's more, your family needs and deserves it." She smiled faintly. "And Cira was always very protective of her family, remember?"

"You'd know that better than I. You're the expert on Cira." He wearily turned back to where Jock was working. "All I know is that we've got to get those lights working. I realize it's become something of an obsession with me, but I'll do it, Jane. There's no way on earth I'll let them beat me." He smiled faintly at her over his shoulder. "I'm glad you came today. You haven't been down here for a few days. I was afraid you'd given up on us."

"Never." She smiled back at him. "It just didn't seem the time."

"And now it does?"

She nodded as she got to her feet and followed him. "Yes," she said quietly. "Now it definitely does, MacDuff."

9:15 P.M.

Jane turned off her lantern and lay there in the dark, trying to relax. There was no use being this tense. She'd made a decision and now she had to accept that she had to —

Her cell phone rang.

Caleb.

"Lisa's fine," she said as soon as she picked up. "As long as she stays busy, she's not nearly as edgy. She's getting stronger every day and she —"

"I know all that," Caleb replied, interrupting her. "She makes sure that she tells me these days that she's a cross between Wonder Woman and Supergirl every time I talk to her. Though she really prefers Elektra, but she says Supergirl has more power. How are you?"

"What?"

"How are you? When I just called Lisa, she said that you seemed too quiet when you were at supper tonight. She didn't think you were ill and she knew her meal was fantastic and that couldn't possibly be it. You went to the north bank with the guys today, instead of painting. That might mean that you didn't want to be social with anyone at the camp. So is it something that Lisa's doing that you're not telling me about? Should I talk to her about it? Should I return?"

"Oh, for heaven's sake." She couldn't believe this. "I was quiet and suddenly your sister is doing something terrible that could cause me to spiral downward into some kind of depression?"

"It was a thought. I could tell she was worried." He paused. "And what you might think terrible wouldn't necessarily appear that way to Lisa."

"Yes, it would. She's not as callous as you, Caleb. Or she wouldn't be worried about me."

"True. But she doesn't think I'm callous at all, and most of the time she thinks I can do no wrong. So there you are." He paused. "If it wasn't her, what is it? Lisa has excellent instincts and she's gotten closer to you since you've been together."

"Sometimes overpoweringly so. No, I didn't mean that. I care about her, but I always have to keep on guard around her. She can be as disturbing as —"

"Me? She hasn't even reached the first rung. And you didn't answer my question."

And she wasn't going to do it. She was going through enough bewilderment and soul-searching without bringing Caleb into the mix. She told him a half-truth. "I've just been doing some thinking. Everything around me seems to be changing. But I've been standing still. I've been reacting instead of acting. I've been wondering if I have to change, too."

"In the present situation, I much prefer you to react."

"And I wasn't asking for your advice. You

wanted an answer and I gave it to you." She changed the subject. "How are things going with you? Did you find out anything else?"

"Well enough. Information? Palik has a lead on where the Romanos might be located. And I found out their interest in Dubai was centered on a medical center that caters to the richest and most influential patients in the country. They also wanted all the architectural drawings of the American Hospital at Dubai, plus all the personnel records of the staff."

"Why?"

"That's the next question and one I can hopefully ask the Romanos in the near future."

"Then go do it and stop worrying about Lisa . . . or what Lisa's doing to me. I promised you I'd take care of her. No sign of her following in your footsteps."

"For which you're grateful."

"Fervently." She paused. "Though lately she's been much more charming and easy to get along with when she makes the effort. But it's nothing like you."

"Almost normal?" he asked mockingly.

"Right. Good night, Caleb."

"Good night, Jane." He was laughing as he hung up.

That's all I needed, she thought with

exasperation. The knowledge that both Lisa and Caleb were watching her and trying to decipher what she was thinking and might be doing was disconcerting. They were treating her as if they were the caregivers, when that was the role she'd chosen for herself.

Calm down.

It was kind of Lisa to be concerned. It was natural that Caleb would try to dominate everything and everyone around him. She decided to just ignore both their responses and try to regain the composure she'd had before Caleb's call.

What composure?

Then just go back to trying to go to sleep . . . and the waiting.

CHAPTER 14

2:30 A.M.

Something was happening down by the campfire.

Soft conversation . . .

Was that a low bark?

Jane had been expecting it, Eve had warned her it was coming, but it still startled her. She tossed on her clothes and ran out of the tent.

Joe Quinn was silhouetted against the flames of the campfire and Eve was already beside him. She had Michael in her arms, but Joe was holding both of them close.

"They're busy. Come and talk to me so I won't feel neglected." Margaret Douglas was sitting on the ground in front of the fire and jumped to her feet and gave Jane a hug. "After all, Joe told me that you're to blame for rushing me over here with Juno. There are responsibilities involved here."

Jane held her close for a moment. It seemed like a long time since she'd seen her friend Margaret. But all she'd had to do was to tell her she was needed and she'd come.

She took a step back. "Juno?"

"She's lying over there on the bank beside the lake. She didn't really like the trip over here and wanted to get back to nature." She nodded at a large white dog, who was only a blur in the darkness. "Come meet her." She led Jane toward the dog. "She's a golden retriever but an English crème variety and has all the gentle, loving temperament you asked Eve to find." She stopped by Juno and reached down and stroked her. "You can't be with her for more than a few minutes and not realize that."

Huge dark eyes were looking up at Jane, and Juno's tail was wagging.

"Hello there," Jane said softly. She knelt and rubbed the spot between the retriever's eyes. She could see what Margaret meant. Those dark eyes were brimming with love and affection. "I hope we'll be friends. You're very beautiful, you know."

Margaret chuckled. "She knows. But she still likes the attention." She looked around her. "And I think she'll like this place."

"I'm glad you're so familiar with her likes

and dislikes," Jane said drily. "Because I'm not at all sure she's going to like the mist."

"Neither am I. We can only hope." Margaret's face lit up as she smiled. Margaret always seems to be lit from within, Jane thought. She was only twenty-one but seemed younger, and her tan skin, blue eyes, and taffy-colored streaked hair made her appear to be touched with the gold of the sun. "Hey, and from what Eve told Joe, I'm still not sure what you need." Margaret tilted her head. "I don't think you do, either. But Juno is my best hope. I was at Summer Island and I had my choice of dogs, but you wanted sensitive, and Juno does therapy work in hospitals." She added soberly, "And she lost the little girl who owned and loved her in an accident a few years ago. She's very loving, Jane."

"Love is good. You're right: I don't know what I want or need. I'm operating purely on instinct. I'm betting on a wild card and just have to hope it pays off." Jane gave Juno a final pat, stood up, and walked back to Joe. "Thanks for bringing Margaret so quickly, Joe. I know after all this time maybe I shouldn't feel this sense of urgency, but I do. It just seemed important that we do this *now.*"

"The urgency isn't any more bizarre than

the idea itself," Joe said drily. "But who am I to argue? The entire thing with Cira is bizarre." He kissed her forehead. "But you're the one who will have to convince MacDuff that using dogs is better than transformers. He spent a small fortune on those Australian lights."

"I don't think they'll work," she said flatly. "That's not the way Cira wants it. I realized that when I had that dream about her last night. I believe she was telling me how it was and how she wanted it to be. Or maybe just the only way it could be."

"What's going on here?" MacDuff had come out of his tent. He was half-dressed, but his shirt was open and his dark hair ruffled. "Hello, Quinn, why the hell are you here? Eve said that you weren't coming for another week or —"

"A change of plans." Joe pushed Jane gently toward MacDuff. "Orchestrated by Jane and Cira. I've brought you someone you should meet. This is Margaret Douglas, MacDuff. But I believe it's over to you, Jane."

Jane drew a deep breath and then strode up the hill to stand before MacDuff with fists clenched. "I don't think the lights are going to work. I think you have to try another way."

"Really?" he said coolly. "You didn't mention anything about that opinion yesterday afternoon. What brought this on?"

"Cira." She went on quickly, "I'd had a dream about her the night before."

"Indeed?"

"And I didn't want to mention it to you until I had everything in place. You're so far along with that light system, and you can be very hard to convince."

"You're saying I'm hardheaded?"

"You know you are. Look, you were always so sure that those dreams I had about Cira meant something. I was the skeptical one. But there was something about what I saw that night that made me — I have to believe that maybe this one — we should at least try it, MacDuff." She briefly told him the details of the dream, attempting not to leave out anything. "Don't you see? It just seemed like the answer. The mist was just as bad during Cira's time, but she found a way. Marcus's dog, Galo, was able to get through the fog and find his way to the cave. I don't know how. It could have been pure instinct. But he did it."

"According to this latest dream?" MacDuff's tone was faintly quizzical. "I know I've encouraged you to think that Cira led us here. Hell, I've used those dreams of yours to get my own way and keep you searching. That's why I'd like to believe you. But we're too close, Jane. In this instance, I prefer to base my faith on my lights rather than on Cira's hound."

"Marcus's dog," Jane said, correcting him. "And you've tried half a dozen different light systems to break through that mist over these last years. None of them has worked. And this might be just another one."

"And it might not."

"MacDuff, you know how Jane fights believing in anything that's connected with Cira," Eve said. "You tried to persuade her for years before you got her to come on your treasure hunt." She took a step forward. "Cira may have been a guiding force in Jane's life, but Jane's a realist. Since the night she had that first dream when she was a teenager, she questioned everything. She didn't want any explanations that weren't based on pure fact." She met his eyes. "But she didn't question this dream. She had enough faith to get me to call Joe and ask him to bring our friend Margaret Douglas and her dog, Juno. They're here now." She smiled and gestured to Margaret. "You've always liked experiments, MacDuff. Let's see what happens."

MacDuff was frowning and didn't answer.

Eve had been very persuasive, but no one was more stubborn than MacDuff when he got his mind set on something. Jane had been afraid that stubbornness would set in when she had talked to him yesterday. She could see that he had invested so much time and effort in the idea of making those blasted light systems work that he was reluctant to give them up.

Okay, she'd have to find a way that he wouldn't have to do that.

"Look, you said that light system was ready to test out. Let's still do it. If it works, you can forget all about anything but your space-age technology." She made a face. "And I'll have to go down on my knees to beg Margaret for forgiveness for dragging her here."

He raised a brow. "And so you should. But I perceive an *if* somewhere in that entirely reasonable suggestion."

"We might as well take Margaret and her dog, Juno, with us when you're testing, and see if an alternate solution might work if the tech world fails us again."

MacDuff chuckled. "Like turning loose a dog that has no knowledge of the Highlands or the north bank? And certainly should have no homing instinct that would be triggered to take her to Marcus's cave?"

She met his eyes. "Yes."

"It's the stuff of madness, Jane."

"Perhaps. But then why do I feel it's the right way to go?"

He didn't speak for a moment, and she thought she'd lost him.

Then a reckless smile lit his face. "How can I resist? It's too mad a challenge not to accept it. After all, I am a Highlander. Let's get going, Jane."

She blinked. "Now? In the middle of the night?"

He glanced at Margaret. "Unless this lass hasn't the stamina to go for a trek through the mist. Why not?"

Jane was sure she could think of a dozen practical reasons. But she'd been the one to make the offer, and if it had aroused that innate streak of recklessness in MacDuff, she'd be foolish to make excuses that might cause him to have second thoughts.

She turned to Margaret. "What do you say? Are you too tired?"

Margaret smiled. "Tired? It's why I came. It's a great adventure." She met MacDuff's eyes. "Of course, the laird may need his rest. He's not as young as Juno and I are."

"Ouch." MacDuff turned on his heel. "I'll go dress, wake Jock, and meet you here in fifteen minutes." He disappeared into his tent.

Jane turned back to Margaret. "You're sure? It can wait, Margaret."

"But you don't want to wait." Her gaze went to MacDuff's tent. "And neither does he. I think the wait has gone on too long." She smiled. "Go finish getting dressed, Jane. Or we'll be leaving without you." She turned to Eve and Joe. "Are you coming along? Or are you going to keep the home fires burning?"

Joe and Eve exchanged a long look and then Joe said, "We'll stay here. Cara, Lisa, and my son have to be protected, and I'd prefer to do that than to go off on a Cira treasure hunt." His arm tightened around Eve. "Eve and I have always been aware Cira's been Jane's special beacon." His gaze shifted to Jane. "Go and find her. You know we'll take care of everything here."

She gave him a quick hug. "Thanks, Joe."

She flew up the hill toward her tent.

But she stopped when she was only halfway there.

Lisa.

She stared at Lisa's tent, which was just a short distance from her own. It was a wonder that Lisa hadn't awakened when Jane had. But then, Jane had been on the alert for an arrival.

Should she wake Lisa now and let her go with them? She knew there was no question Lisa would come. The mist had fascinated her since she'd arrived here.

"Decisions?" Eve was coming up the hill toward her. "Lisa? You're hesitating. That usually means it's no clear choice."

"She'd want to go."

"And?"

"Are you just letting me talk this out?"

"Of course." Eve smiled. "Then I can't be blamed for steering you in the wrong direction."

"I'd never blame you."

"And?" she repeated.

"It might be a rough night and hard on her."

"True."

"But she'd still stay with us and never let us know. I'd have to watch her."

Eve was silent.

Jane met her eyes. "I don't want to have to concentrate on anything but what I have to do tonight."

"Cira?"

"Cira." She smiled. "So I think I'll let her make the decision. I'll go to my tent and finish dressing and then go down to the campfire. If Lisa hears me and comes out and asks what's happening, then I'll tell her."

"Fate?"

"Yes and the fact that I told Lisa earlier that I wouldn't let her interfere with what I knew had to be done where Cira was concerned." She turned back and started climbing the hill. "But I could use a little help with explanations if I end up leaving her behind. . . ."

"This is completely weird," Margaret said as she walked beside Jane through the mist. "These flashlight beams hardly do any good at all. I can barely see MacDuff and Jock up ahead."

"Then you can see the problem. We haven't even reached the curve of the north bank. Once we pass that pile of boulders, the mist thickens and becomes almost impenetrable to light."

"Why?"

"Who knows? The phenomenon has been studied by several universities, including Oxford, and there are theories but no answers. MacDuff wouldn't let them tear apart his lands to try to find them." She shrugged. "And maybe they wouldn't have found the answers anyway." She gazed at Margaret. "I know it's eerie. Does it make you nervous?"

"No, I grew up in the woods, remember? I like it." She glanced at Juno, who was trotting a few feet away. "So does Juno. She seems . . . comfortable."

"And what does that mean?"

Margaret chuckled. "Just what I said. Juno and I are friends and I'm not going to intrude on her. I've told her what you want from her. I've also told her that if she can't give it, I'll understand."

"That's all I can ask." Jane looked at the shimmer of white that was Juno in the fog. "You know, when I first met you and that vet you worked for on Summer Island told me that you could communicate with animals, I thought she was crazy. Well, that is, I would have if she hadn't been so professional about it."

"Put a professional mask on anything and it seems to conceal any bullshit?" Margaret chuckled. "Admit it: You believed it because you wanted to believe I could diagnose what was wrong with your dog, Toby, when no one else could. You wanted to believe it so that I could find a way to save your dog's life."

"And you did. Toby lived." And Jane was still passionately grateful to her. Toby was now in a special program on Summer Island that increased the longevity and strength of dogs, and the last time Jane had visited he was wonderfully well and happy. "And here I am asking you for another favor, and telling you that I need you."

"No, you need Juno. I'm just along for the ride . . . and to find out what's out there."

"Which may not be up to us, if MacDuff's lights work. He and Jock will be exploring that bank the minute they can see it." She tried to smile. "And that will be good for MacDuff, too. It will just confuse me. I don't think that's the way Cira wants it."

"We'll find out, won't we?" Margaret said. "And the worst thing that will happen is that Juno will get a long walk to stretch her legs after that trip across the ocean."

"If she doesn't fall in the lake running down these banks."

"She swims well. And I'd jump in to help her."

Jane smiled. "Because she's your friend. Just like you jumped in to help me."

"Something like that. But you offered me an adventure to sweeten the pot. There are so many mysteries in life and nature, and it's not often we get the chance to explore one as interesting as this." She squinted, trying to peer through the mist. "Are those the boulders you spoke about just ahead?"

■ ■ ■ ■

"It will be just a few minutes." Jock smiled at Jane and Margaret. "Sit down on those rocks and get as comfortable as you can. We were almost ready before we left here yesterday. It's just the control switch." He disappeared back into the mist.

"You're right," Margaret said as she slowly stroked Juno's head. "The mist is much worse . . . or better here. I can see how any search team would be paralyzed. You feel totally isolated and disoriented."

"Does it bother you?"

"No, and it doesn't bother you, either, does it?"

Jane shook her head. "I've never felt a threat here. I feel . . . at home." She glanced at Juno. "How about her?"

"She's alert . . . a little tense. She's not frightened." She paused. "She's waiting for something."

"So are we," Jane said wryly. "And I wish MacDuff and Jock would just —"

"Ready." MacDuff appeared out of the mist, his eyes shining and eager. He was carrying a large utilitarian-looking switch. "Jock, attach that last transformer," he called before he turned back to Jane and

Margaret. "It's going to work." He reached over and ruffled the hair on Juno's head. "Sorry a fine lass like you won't get your chance to prove yourself, but that's life." He turned to Jane, his excitement almost tangible. "Four poles and the power of those new lights will cause the entire area to light up like a fireworks display on your Fourth of July. Only these fireworks will stay on until we turn them off."

"Last transformer connected." Jock had appeared out of the mist. "Press your magic switch, MacDuff."

"Jane?" MacDuff was holding out the switch to her. "You've been in this from the beginning. I won't leave you out."

She shook her head. "Your treasure. Your family. Good luck, MacDuff."

He smiled. "Thank you. And you won't call down a Cira hex on me?"

"Never."

"Then here goes." He drew a deep breath and pressed the switch.

And the lights came on!

MacDuff gave a shout. "*Yes.* Jock, do you *see* them?"

"Aye." Jock's gaze was fixed on MacDuff's exuberant expression. "You did it, MacDuff."

"Fourth of July, MacDuff," Jane said

gently. "Congratulations."

He jerked her to her feet and whirled her in a circle. "Now let's go take a look down that bank. Now that we can make out some of the topography and the —" He stopped, frowning.

Juno was on her feet, whimpering.

Jane glanced at her in puzzlement. The dog's dark eyes were bright with eagerness, not fear, and her tail was wagging.

"Afraid not, Juno," Jane told her. "It appears that this is as far as we go tonight."

"Maybe not." Margaret's gaze was on Juno, too. "She's not waiting anymore."

And Jock was muttering curses under his breath, his gaze on the four poles with their brilliant lights.

Which were no longer brilliant.

The lights appeared to be dimming, slowly losing their power.

"No!" MacDuff's face was tense with strain. "Come on. We have to fix it. There must be something wrong with the connection, Jock."

Jock had already moved deeper into the mist, which was less obscuring than before but fast becoming worse. MacDuff was with him in seconds, and Jane and Margaret watched them working frantically at the connections fixed to the poles.

And Juno was still whimpering.

Jane shook her head in bewilderment. "What's happening here, Margaret?"

"With those lights? How should I know?" She gazed at Juno. "With her? She wants me to give her permission to go. She says it's time." She met Jane's eyes. "It's your call."

Or was it Cira's?

Jane watched MacDuff and Jock moving quickly in the mist. "MacDuff is the only one who has the right to tell me that." She stood up and smiled faintly. "Cira would agree. I'm sure anyone who challenged the head of the family in her day wouldn't have lived long." Then she was striding into the mist toward the two men.

"What's wrong?" she asked as she reached them. "Can you fix it?"

"We don't *know* what's wrong," Jock said tersely. "There's nothing wrong with the lights, transformers, or the connections." He glanced up at the light on the pole. "And the lights aren't going completely out as some of the other light systems did. You can see the lights are still burning. They're just not at full power."

"It could be that the lights had too much power and the heat interacted with the condensation from the mist once it was turned on," MacDuff said in frustration. "At any rate, those lights aren't going to give illumination for more than a distance of two or three feet from each pole until we figure out a solution."

"We'll do it, MacDuff," Jock said. "It will just take a little longer."

"It *should* have worked."

"Aye, but think how you'll be able to rub that Australian bloke's nose in the fact that it didn't. We'll just make a few improvements and show him how the Scots do it better."

Warmth, friendship, healing.

MacDuff was responding, albeit reluctantly. "We can do it. But who knows how long it will take. God, I'm tired of struggling with those damn lights." He was silent a moment and then whirled to face Jane. "No 'I told you so'?"

"It could have worked. I'm sorry for your sake that it didn't."

"But you still think you're right about using the dog."

"I don't know, MacDuff. I believe I might be." She paused. "Margaret's retriever, Juno, wants permission to go hunting. I won't let Margaret let her do it unless you're okay with it."

He stared at her for a moment and then

waved his hand impatiently. "Go ahead. A deal is a deal. Try not to fall in the lake."

She didn't move. "Margaret said that she'd jump in the lake to rescue Juno. She made no promises about me. So I think the two of you should come along. Forget about starting to fix those lights now." She took a step closer, her gaze glittering with the excitement suddenly zinging through her. "I really think you should be with us tonight."

"Do you?" MacDuff's gaze was fixed on her face. "Aye, I can see you do." His face was suddenly lit with that reckless smile again. "Well, who am I to argue? I apparently have nothing better to do at the moment." He turned to Jock. "Come on, we have to protect Jane and my property from that fierce, marauding Juno."

Mist.

Thicker than Jane had ever seen it.

She could hear Juno barking ahead of her in the distance.

The retriever sounded far away and probably was, because their pace had been so painstakingly slow since they had left the boulders.

They were having to travel slowly and single file because the path was narrow and the lake only feet away.

She could feel her heart beating hard, her palms damp, as she traveled blindly through the mist.

"It's okay, Jane," Margaret called from behind her. "I wanted to give Juno free rein since she seemed to know where she was going, but I'll have her start to come back and lead us. This path is too dangerous without a guide."

"Tell me about it." She steadied her voice. "Isn't Juno having any trouble?"

"No. She's fine." She paused. "As I said, she knows where she's going."

"Do you?"

"No, I'm getting little wisps of what Juno knows, but I can't put it together. It doesn't make sense to me." She was silent a moment. "Okay, Juno will be coming back and forth now. We'll be able to move faster."

A few minutes later, the barking was closer and Jane could see the gleam of Juno's white coat in the darkness. Then the retriever turned and started back in the direction she had come, but not going too fast for them not to catch glimpses of her in the mist.

It was still difficult, but not nearly as bad as before.

So familiar . . . this perilous narrow path where Cira had walked.

Galo leading Cira and Antonio to her son . . .

Not a pure white retriever, but a pale tan hound. But the love was the same, and so was the service rendered.

Darkness.

Mist.

A dog barking, warning, protecting, leading them . . .

Where?

She rounded a curve in the path.

Juno was sitting on the path in front of her. She was seven or eight feet away, but Jane could make her out in the mist.

She was not moving, but whimpering that excited, joyous sound deep in her throat.

"You did well, Juno." Margaret had come even with Jane and was looking down at the retriever. "Here?"

Juno ran to the huge boulder to the north of the path and sat down in front of it. As Marcus's dog, Galo, had done as he had waited for Cira and Antonio.

"Here," Margaret repeated. She turned to Jane. "She's done her job. It's up to you now." She smiled. "Are you ready?"

All the dreams.

All the years.

All the wondering why.

All the reaching out but never finding.

"I'm ready." She turned to MacDuff and Jock as they came toward them down the path. "Just in time. That big boulder rolls back, but I don't have the strength. It takes muscle." She smiled. "Antonio did it by himself, but the centuries and dampness probably made it bury itself deeper in the earth. It might take two."

MacDuff was standing stiff, frozen, his eyes on the huge boulder. "My God." Then he shook his head to clear it. "It's just a rock. Probably nothing behind it."

"There's something behind it," Jane said. "There *is*, MacDuff. I know you're scared to think it's true. So am I. But I know there's something there." She swallowed. "So flex those muscles and prove me right. Okay?"

Jock stepped forward. "Come on, MacDuff. I could probably do it alone, like Antonio, but then I'd have to rub it in for the rest of your life. You wouldn't like that. Hop to it."

MacDuff stood looking at the boulder. "You think I'd allow that to happen?" He came forward and braced himself beside Jock. "On the count of three."

It took five counts of three to even budge the deeply embedded rock and then seven more before they managed to roll the boulder to one side.

Jane went slowly forward to stand beside them, staring into the darkness.

"Now I'm truly terrified," MacDuff murmured.

"Me, too."

Afraid of being disappointed, of losing that extraordinary feeling of eternity and continuity that Cira had given her.

A whimpering, a brushing against Jane's legs, and then Juno pushed past them and ran into the darkness.

Jane drew a deep breath. "It appears that Juno isn't scared." She lifted her flashlight. "I suggest we follow her example." She stepped inside the cave. "Juno, where are you?"

A low whimper.

"She's over there against the far wall," Margaret said as she came to stand beside Jane. "Something about a *Galo.*"

"Galo?" Jane leveled the beam of her flashlight across the cave.

Then she forgot everything else as she saw the ledge built into the cave wall. She was transfixed, in shock. On the ledge was a ruin of bronze and granite and beautifully carved wood. A ruin, but the size was right, and so was Jane's memory of it.

Cira looking down at the carved casket with

tears in her eyes. "And now I believe we'd better go take him into that mist . . ."

"Marcus," she whispered. "This is where they laid him to rest."

MacDuff's beam pierced the darkness next to where Jane's light was pointing. "It's hard to tell what —"

"It's him," she said. "You can verify it to your heart's content later, but it's Marcus." Her beam moved down to where Juno was huddled on the floor beside another, smaller heap of bronze and wood. "And I'd bet that's the coffin where they placed Galo, Marcus's dog, when he died." She could feel the tears sting her eyes. "So they'd always be together." She moved her beam around the cave, which was not clean and neat as it had been in her dream. Fallen rocks, wet earth, even the walls of the cave seemed to have shifted from what she remembered. "And Cira's treasure should be in that wall over there, MacDuff. Go and see if it's in a cavity behind those rocks jammed against the wall."

"I can look later." His beam was still on Marcus's casket.

"No, look now. I have to be sure. Cira wouldn't have gone to all this trouble if she hadn't wanted you to find that treasure." She smiled. "She knows you'll give her son all due respect. After all, she set him to watch over it. Now go see how well she preserved her fortune for you and the family."

MacDuff hesitated and then slowly crossed the cave to the rock she'd indicated. "If you're sure she won't throw a thunderbolt at me."

"No guarantees. She always hated to be predictable. You'll have to take your chances."

She stood and watched as MacDuff and Jock began to try to pry the boulder away from the cavity in the wall.

I've brought them here, Cira. It will make your family safe for a long time to come. Are you pleased? Is this what it was all about?

Cira's bronze treasure chest was in bad shape but, incredibly, still intact. Its enclosure in the cave wall must have helped to keep it tight and dry. The coins inside it were in various degrees of discoloration, but there appeared to be hundreds, possibly thousands of them almost overflowing the chest.

"Cira's gold," MacDuff whispered as he lifted a handful of coins from the chest and let them flow through his fingers. "Do you know that sometimes I doubted that it ever existed."

"You knew it did," Jane said. "You searched and nagged and made everyone miserable, because you knew it was out here somewhere."

"I guess I did." MacDuff looked at her and smiled. "And evidently I wasn't the only one nagging. I had someone on my side helping out."

"Cira's always been very demanding." She gazed at the huge heap of coins. "They appear to be in decent shape and the gold coins might not even be the most valuable. History and rarity count more in today's market. It will probably take a number of experts and a good amount of time to do the appraisals. What's your next step, MacDuff?"

"The safest, best-protected bank in Edinburgh. Which in my opinion is the Royal Bank of Scotland. Then arranging for all the appraisals to take place in a secure room at that fine establishment."

She smiled. "What a canny Scot you are, MacDuff."

"But first we've got to get it out of here and on its way to that bank," Jock said. "And I'm not toting all of this treasure in my backpack. Too many trips. We'll go back to the poles and get the utility wagon."

Antonio unloading the treasure from a crude wooden wagon and carrying it into the cave.

"I think that's a great idea." She turned to Margaret. "But that's a round-trip to the boulders where the poles are set up. Then another trip when we load the treasure to take it back to camp. Will Juno have any trouble leading us all that way?"

Margaret shook her head. "Not if I stay with her and remind her that it's important she concentrate on the lead and not what she's leaving behind here. She wants to stay. She . . . likes it here."

Jane glanced at Juno, who was lying with her head on her paws. She could see that comfort, the serenity. "Then will you do that, please? I'd like to get this task finished."

Margaret nodded. "I told you back at the camp that I knew you all thought it time for this to be finished." She turned to MacDuff. "Let's go. We'll make much better time now that Juno is staying with us and not having to search ahead."

"At your command." He gave a mock bow. "We're literally at your disposal, or we'd never get out of here."

"Power." She grinned. "How I love the power." She glanced at Jane. "Do you want to go first? Or do you want me to go ahead with Juno?"

"You go ahead." She looked at MacDuff. "I'm going to stay here until you get back with the utility wagon."

His brows rose in surprise. "Why? I wouldn't think you'd want to stay here by yourself. Even the finest tombs are seldom pleasant."

"It's Marcus's final resting place. Cira left it sealed and secure for him. I'm not going to leave it alone and unprotected even for a short time. Once you get back and take the treasure, we'll seal it again and won't touch it until we decide how to restore it." She added, "Does that sound all right with you?"

"Very much all right," he said softly. He turned and headed for the cave entrance. "Let's go, Jock. We'll be back soon, Jane."

"I know you will."

She watched them striding down the path until they disappeared into the mist. And after that, there was still the sound of them moving through the brush and Juno's occasional barking.

And then there was nothing but the darkness and the sound of the waters of the lake lapping against the shore. As it had been for all the centuries this little boy had been here with his friend Galo, who now shared his resting place.

412

She turned back and went inside the cave. She stared at the ruins on the ledge for a moment and then slid down the wall beside the entrance and leaned her head back against the stone.

"Here we are, Marcus," she whispered. "I know Cira is taking care of you, and you don't really need me. But I think she'd like the idea of my being here right now. In a way, she kind of raised me, too." She closed her eyes. "Are you there, Cira? You gave me something in that last dream. I'm not good with faith, and I was having trouble coming to terms with what comes afterward. Did you know that I'd lost the man I loved? You probably did. It was hard coming back, but I had to do it. Just as you did. But you were given something in this place, and you passed it on to me. I want to thank you." She opened her eyes and said unsteadily, "Now, unless you have any other gifts to give, we'll just stay here and listen to the wind and the lake and be together. . . ."

The dawn was starting to break when they came out of the mist and started to walk down the bank toward the camp.

Jane could see Eve, Lisa, Joe, and Cara sitting around the campfire. But it was Lisa who jumped to her feet and ran down to

413

meet them.

"Eve said you called and told her you'd found the treasure." Lisa turned to Margaret. "You must be Margaret Douglas. I envy you. I didn't care anything about the treasure, but conquering that mist intrigued me." She made a face. "Actually, I was a little put out that Jane left me behind, but then Eve explained that you have some kind of special qualifications."

"That's true," Jane said. "And I don't think that it's a skill you could pick up as readily as you do most other things. This is Lisa Ridondo, Margaret." She looked back over her shoulder at Jock and MacDuff, who were several yards behind them, bringing the utility wagon. "Could I talk you into making breakfast, Lisa? Nothing fancy. But it's been a long night, and we're all pretty drained. We could use a little sustenance."

Lisa was gazing at her face. "I can see that. But you look . . . at peace. You found what you wanted, Jane?"

Jane nodded. "I found what I wanted."

She smiled. "Then I'm glad, and I forgive you for not letting me be there when it happened." Her eyes were twinkling. "Though I'm hoping that guilt for depriving me of something I wanted will push you toward giving me the next thing on my list."

"Don't count on it," Jane said drily.

"I never do. I just work toward it, and most of the time it comes." She turned. "And what do you mean, 'nothing fancy'? It's a celebration, and at least that part of it will be mine. Now I'll run back and start a splendid breakfast that will show everyone what a great team player I am."

Jane watched her streak down the bank. "And it will be a splendid breakfast. She's a fantastic cook, Margaret. Though we may be too tired to eat it." She looked at Juno, who was staying close to Margaret. "Even Juno looks as though she needs some rest."

"She's fine," Margaret said. "She got what she wanted, too, Jane. She did what was asked of her and it made her happy." She smiled. "Me, too. It was a very special night."

She did what was asked of her.

Was that also why Jane was feeling this sense of peace? She had done what Cira had needed her to do, and had received gifts in return that she still didn't fully understand. But one of them was this knowledge that she was more complete and serene for doing it. "Yes, very special." She turned to face Margaret. "And you're special, too." Jane said. "You know that there are no words to thank you."

"Sure. That's why you don't try," Margaret said. "And now we'll just have a good time relaxing and setting up Eve's wedding and being together. Joe said he was going to try to have everyone else here by next week."

"That sounds like a plan." Jane paused. "After we make sure that Cira's treasure is safely stored in that bank MacDuff was talking about. I'm the one who insisted on going after that treasure right away because I thought Cira wanted MacDuff to have it. I want to make certain it's safe."

"Isn't that MacDuff's responsibility?"

"Yes. But we could have left it in Marcus's tomb and made arrangements to transport it later. I wanted that tomb resealed, so no one else would know about it and there'd be no chance of theft or violation. That meant moving that treasure, so it wouldn't be a lure for anyone." She jerked her head back at MacDuff and Jock. "That's why we might have a billion dollars' worth of coins in that wagon back there." Her lips tightened grimly. "So I'd say it's my responsibility, too."

"And that means that Eve and I will have to do wedding plans on our own until you get MacDuff's treasure safely settled?"

"It shouldn't take more than a day. Jock isn't going to let MacDuff take a deep breath until he safeguards that treasure. He's very protective of him."

"I've noticed." Margaret shrugged. "Oh well, I'll bring in Cara and Lisa to help until you're free. All their vim, vigor, and youth will be a big help."

"You're only twenty-one yourself, Margaret."

"But I have an old soul." She grinned. "Ask Juno."

CHAPTER 15

Lisa's breakfast was just as splendid as Jane had promised: eggs Benedict, pancakes, special cinnamon pastries, sausages, and a spicy potato casserole that was as delicious as it was unusual. After breakfast, Margaret and Juno went to the tent Margaret had been given to get some sleep, and Lisa and Cara took Michael for a walk down to the lake. Jane suspected that had been Cara's doing, a way to give Jock, MacDuff, and Jane privacy and allow them to stay at the campfire drinking coffee and talking with Eve and Joe. She had noticed that Cara's influence on Lisa was very subtle, but she usually managed to get her way. Amazing, when Lisa was older and clearly so willful and determined.

"You're very quiet." Eve glanced at Jane. "Need to get some sleep?"

"Probably. But the coffee will help." She looked at MacDuff. "And I have an idea you're going to be dashing out of here soon, and I want to be ready. What did you and Jock decide when you were lugging that utility wagon down the trail? When are we going to Edinburgh?"

MacDuff shook his head. "Go get some sleep, Jane. There's no need for you to go with us."

"The hell there's not. I've been along on practically every step of the journey since I first started having dreams of Cira. On some of those steps, I've actually made the decisions." She stared him in the eye. "I have to be there to wrap up this part of it."

"She's right, you know," Eve said quietly. "Don't cheat her, MacDuff."

He grimaced. "Aye, she's right. But she's also exhausted, and I'm feeling wildly grateful that she's given me the prize I've been trying to win all these years. I thought I'd try to be gallant."

"Bullshit," Jane said. "Just tell me when we're leaving for Edinburgh."

"Two hours should do it. We all need to clean up, or they won't even let us into that bank. After that, we have to pack Cira's chest in a durable box that won't fall apart during transport." He smiled. "Then we'll be on our way."

"What about security?"

"You, MacDuff, and I will take Cira's chest in the Toyota," Jock said. "I've set up another car, a Range Rover, to follow us, driven by our man Angus Macauley, who will have three other guards in the car. None of the guards know that we've found Cira's treasure, nor will anyone at the bank until we're actually inside their doors. MacDuff will call the vice president of the bank when we're twenty minutes away and request an immediate escort for an important transaction." He made a face. "That should be no problem. MacDuff has all those bigwig types on his speed dial."

"Satisfied?" MacDuff asked.

Jane nodded. "Very smart. Very discreet."

"So can we do it without you?"

"Not a chance."

MacDuff sighed. "So be it."

"That's the first time I've heard you use either that philosophic tone or words. It's not at all like you." Jane got to her feet. "It's probably the last time I'll be quite so demanding, MacDuff. We're almost at the end of this particular road."

"We are?" He tilted his head. "I hadn't thought of it like that. I'll miss you, Jane."

She would miss him, too. As well as the journey, the puzzle, the search. Don't think of it right now, she told herself. They still had a little more distance to travel on Cira's path. She started up the hill toward her tent. "I'll see you in two hours. Don't you dare leave without me."

Dubai
11:05 A.M.

"I have to talk to you, Caleb," Palik said curtly. "I'm in the lobby of your hotel. Do you want me to come to you or do you want to come down?"

"You can't tell me what you need on the phone?"

"I could, but I'm not going to do it. I want to see your face when I talk to you. Though God knows if I'll be able to tell anything from that, either."

Palik was clearly upset, and Caleb didn't like it. It took a good deal for him to lose his cool. "I'll come down. Meet me in the bar."

"Fine. I could use a drink."

Not good, Caleb thought. Palik never used drugs and seldom drank. In his line of work, he regarded lack of control as hazardous.

And his expression was not encouraging when Caleb walked into the bar and dropped down on the red leather banquette across from him. It reflected he was both nervous and angry.

"What's the problem?"

"I'm not sure. You tell me." He stared Caleb in the eye. "I've been straight with you. I know you don't trust anyone, but that's how I operate. I don't lie to you." He paused. "And you don't lie to me. That way, I can cover my ass for what's coming."

"You think I lied to you?"

"I don't know. Maybe. I'm hoping you didn't, because I definitely don't want to get on your bad side. But if you did, I'm here to tell you that I can't work for you any longer."

Caleb's gaze narrowed on Palik's face. "I can't recall lying to you, though it would be a lie if I said I wasn't capable of doing it if it was to my advantage. In what instance am I supposed to have lied to you?"

Palik didn't speak, his hand clenching on the glass in front of him.

"Palik, I'm beginning to get impatient."

"You said that you were through with Said Ben Kemal. That you had all the information you needed from him."

Caleb nodded. "Yes, I did. So?"

"Did you decide you needed something more from him? Or were you annoyed at what he was doing to that kid?"

"No. Yes. And both issues were resolved. Why?"

"Because Ben Kemal was found in his apartment this morning gutted and with his throat cut."

Caleb went still. "It couldn't have happened to a more worthy victim. I take it that no one knows who committed the happy act?"

Palik shook his head. "The police think it might be a mob hit."

"But you thought it might be me."

"It occurred to me. You're very clever. You could have made it look like anything you wanted."

Caleb grimaced. "But gutting and slitting a throat? I'm surprised you'd think I'd be so crude. Why would I when I have other ways to make someone's death look totally natural?"

"You didn't do it?"

"I didn't do it."

Palik let out a relieved breath. "I had to be sure. My business is based on contacts, and if it got around that I'd set up Said Ben Kemal for a hit, everyone would run for the hills when they saw me coming."

"No retirement palace in Morocco?" Caleb asked absently. His mind was moving quickly, trying to put the new piece into the puzzle. "Why do the police think it was a mob hit?"

"The gutting and slit throat isn't enough?" He shrugged. "He was also missing his tongue. Mob retribution usually calls for a statement to indicate a snitch."

Caleb stiffened. "And it didn't occur to you that the only one who had received information from Ben Kemal lately was me? Which meant that someone found out that he'd told me everything he knew. It's logical that person could be Santara or one of his men who was royally pissed off that Ben Kemal had talked. It's the kind of example Santara would set." He lowered his voice to lethal softness. "Just who did you tell about my little trip to see Ben Kemal?"

"No one," Palik said flatly. "I'm a professional. I don't make mistakes like that, Caleb. Maybe it was Ben Kemal himself."

"Not possible. I gave him orders not to talk, and he wouldn't disobey them." That post suggestion he'd given him would have made it too excruciatingly painful, Caleb knew.

"Well, it wasn't *me.*"

Caleb was inclined to believe him. That kind of indiscretion was unlikely in Palik. He was too sharp, and as he'd said, he was a professional. So Caleb either had to believe it had been a payoff or that Palik was innocent.

Yet there had to have been a leak.

"I swear it," Palik said. "Not from anyone I dealt with and not from me. Find someone else to blame. Look in your own backyard."

That was what Caleb was trying to do. His mind was going over every possibility, every person who had access to the information. There had to be some someone who —

"What about that kid, Ahmed, you sent out of the apartment that night?" Palik offered. "Though my latest report on him is that he's scared shitless and is just trying to dig a deep hole for himself. I made sure no one knew where he was."

"The boy didn't know what was happening. Even if someone got to him, he wouldn't know that I was after information from Ben Kemal. As you say, it was a statement, and he —"

He stopped, his entire body electrified as a thought occurred to him.

Look in your own backyard.

Holy shit!

He reached for his phone.

"I can't believe everything's going so smoothly," Jane murmured to Jock as she watched MacDuff and Nigel Tambry, the bank vice president, disappear into the vault area accompanied by two security guards. "Hey, you did good, Jock."

"Told you so." He smiled. "And only MacDuff and that vice president will know what's in that box until it's locked in a special compartment in the vault. Even then it will be on a need-to-know basis. See, you should have trusted me."

"I did trust you. I just felt I had to put a period to Cira's gold, and the only way I could do it was to see it disappear into that vault." She reached out and took his hand. "Understand?"

He nodded. "It's been a long journey for you. But I have to tell you how grateful I am that you took MacDuff along." He squeezed her hand. "We owe you a great debt, Jane."

"Bullshit. We've all been in this together from the beginning." She gave a mock sigh of relief. "And now there's a small chance that we may be able to live normal lives

426

again. I might even be able to finish that painting of Michael."

"It's a wonderful painting."

"He's a wonderful subject. And I think that Eve's going to —"

Her phone rang and she glanced down at the ID.

"Caleb." She accessed the call. "I hope you haven't been talking to Lisa again. That was pure nonsense that —"

"Who's there with you, Jane?"

"What? Right now? Jock."

"That's good. Who else is there at the camp? MacDuff?"

"Yes. But we're not at the camp. We're in Edinburgh."

Caleb cursed, his voice low and vehement. "What the hell are you doing in Edinburgh?"

"We're at the Royal Bank of Scotland, making a deposit." She could feel her chest tightening. Caleb was never this upset without reason. "What's going on, Caleb?"

"What's going on is that I thought you were all safe at the camp at Loch Gaelkar, where the situation could be controlled. Instead, you're all running around the damn country."

"Lisa's not here. She's fine, Caleb. It's not as if we left her alone or unprotected at the camp. We took only four of the guards with us to Edinburgh, and Jock said that he'd left enough there at the camp to assure security. Besides, Joe stayed behind, and you know he'd never let anything happen to Eve or Michael."

"No, he wouldn't. I still don't like that you're all away from camp."

"We won't be as soon as we get this business finished. Are you going to tell me why?"

"Said Ben Kemal's throat was slit and his tongue ripped out. Someone didn't like that he'd talked to me. I'm assuming that someone was sent by Santara."

Shock. "That seems . . . reasonable," she said after she had recovered. "And how does this impact our leaving the lake for half a day?"

"No one should have known I talked to him. Not Palik. And I guarantee Ben Kemal wouldn't have told anyone."

"Well, someone evidently knew."

"Yes." He paused. "You, Jane."

"What? Are you crazy? I'm supposed to have told Santara that you —"

"No, but you're the only one I told Ben Kemal's name to and that I was going to pay him a visit."

She felt as if she'd been kicked in the stomach. "What are you saying?"

"I'm saying that your phone has been tapped. Maybe Lisa's, too. And since I doubt that anyone could have had access to your phones, I'd bet that Santara is right on top of you at that camp with special wireless extender instruments."

"You have to be wrong." His every word was destroying that precious sense of security she'd had during these last days. "There's been no sign of him. As far as anyone knows, he hasn't even located Lisa since we escaped."

"Oh, I think he knows exactly where you are. He's been stalking, waiting for his chance. He probably realized that the security at the camp is pretty well impregnable, so he's trying to find a way to get around it. That's why he's tapping your phone."

"You think he's that close?"

"Maybe not near enough for his presence to be detected, but he's probably imported a lot of high-tech equipment and technicians to be able to scan your phones from a safe distance. But they'd only be able to do it within range of their equipment. If you're in Edinburgh, I'd think this call is safe."

The idea that Santara might be listening was chilling. She still couldn't comprehend how it could happen. "But we're so careful.

There's not been even a hint of danger, Caleb."

"Not careful enough to avoid a tap. And killing Said Ben Kemal wasn't a discreet move on Santara's part. He had to know it was a risk that he'd tip his hand. Maybe he's getting impatient and ready to make a move."

The thought sent a bolt of panic through her. All the people she loved were at that camp. "Are you sure, Caleb?"

"It's the only answer. I wanted to warn you. I'm on my way to my plane right now. I should be in Scotland in about five hours." He added grimly, "And then I'm going hunting."

Five hours seemed a long time to her right now. She was only about an hour and thirty minutes away from the lake. "I'm going to go back to the camp right now. I promise Lisa will be okay. I'll see you when you get there." She pressed the disconnect.

"What the hell is wrong?" Jock asked, his gaze on her face. "You're white as a sheet."

"Lisa. Caleb says that he thinks Santara is close enough to the camp to tap my phone. Could he be right?"

He thought about it. Then he nodded slowly. "We were really careful, but Santara is good, and his background and contacts could make the difference. If Caleb says that it's true, then we'd have to bank that it is."

"That's what I was afraid you'd say." She turned toward the front entrance. "I'm going back to the lake. I'll ride back in the Range Rover with Macauley and his men. Come as soon as you can."

"Wait, Jane. It should only be another fifteen minutes or so. Communications might have been breached, but I swear no one can get past the security at the lake."

"No. I can't wait." Her voice was shaking. "I'm going now. Eve and Joe and Michael . . . Everyone is there. And I promised I'd take care of Lisa. I promised. . . . I have to be there with them. Caleb said he was going hunting, but what good will that do if Santara decides to move before —"

"Then I'll leave MacDuff and go with you."

"No, finish up here. It's not as if there's a direct threat. I'm just scared. Go and hurry MacDuff along and then go straight back to the lake. I'll call Joe and warn him to be on the alert once I get on the road with Macauley." She didn't wait for an answer, but ran out the glass doors of the front entrance and started down the street, where Macauley was waiting in the Range Rover.

No direct threat, she reminded herself.

Once Joe was warned, he'd be able to keep everyone safe. But it was Jane's job, her responsibility. Eve had come to be with Jane on that special day she was planning.

And she had promised Lisa, and Caleb, that she'd take care of her.

No direct threat.

Yet her stride unconsciously quickened as she moved toward the Range Rover.

She called Joe as soon as Macauley had reached the highway leading to Glasgow.

He listened intently and then said quietly, "Stop worrying, Jane. I can almost feel the waves of angst. We're all grown-ups and we don't need you to take care of us. We make our own decisions."

"Michael's not a grown-up, and what about —" She stopped and drew a deep breath. "Okay, I'll calm down. Caleb just hit me where it hurt."

"He has excellent aim that way, but he probably didn't mean to strike to the heart. He has concerns of his own in this." He added, "But I'll be glad to be one of his hunting party when he gets here."

He was so calm that she was beginning to settle down. "Is everything okay there now?"

"Fine. And as soon as I get off the phone with you, I'll go check on everyone in camp

432

and then have a conference with MacDuff's security team. By that time, you should be here and can see for yourself."

She felt a sudden rush of love for him. "I don't need to see for myself. I just need you to tell me that all the people I love are going to be okay, including you."

He chuckled. "Then you've got it. Now come home and we'll talk about how to keep them that way. I think right now you're so on edge from lack of sleep that you're overreacting. Possible?"

"Maybe." She paused. "I love you, Joe."

"Likewise," he said softly. "See you soon, Jane." He hung up.

He could be right, she thought as she put her phone away. She'd gone without sleep, and when they'd found Cira's treasure, she'd lost an essential motivation that had driven her life. Maybe her reaction to Caleb's call *had* been extreme.

But so had his reaction been, for God's sake. He was probably flying back to Scotland even as she'd been talking to Joe. There was no doubt he'd been worried. And why not? He'd almost lost Lisa a short time ago. He wasn't about to risk that again if he —

Macauley was muttering a curse, his eye on the rearview mirror.

"Bastard. Get off my tail."

She glanced at the side-view mirror. Macauley had a right to be pissed off. That yellow Hummer was only a couple yards behind them. She hadn't been aware of anything when she'd been talking to Joe, but now she realized that Macauley had seemed tense and irritated for quite a while. "I agree. What an ass. Can you pull off and let the driver get ahead of us?"

He shook his head. "Ditches on both sides. Maybe in the next ten miles or so."

But the yellow Hummer was speeding up.

The next minute, it hit the bumper of the Range Rover!

It spun sideways and Macauley was barely able to keep it on the road. "I'm going to kill him," he said through his teeth. "I'll beat the —"

The Hummer hit them again, harder.

The Range Rover spun again, this time toward the ditch.

And the Hummer was now right beside them, ramming them in the side.

Once.

Twice!

That driver has to be crazy, Jane thought as she lurched hard against the control panel. What was he doing?

And then she saw what he was doing. Because she saw who was doing it.

Santara.

Santara was driving that Hummer.

And he was smiling at her.

And then he swung his steering wheel forty degrees to the right and rammed their Range Rover at full force.

It was already on two wheels, and the additional blow sent it barreling toward the ditch.

Macauley was cursing, trying to right the car.

Too late. It's going to be too late, Jane thought as she watched in horror, realizing what was going to happen.

The Range Rover skidded off the road at high speed, turned over in midair, and landed on its roof in the ditch.

Pain!

Darkness . . .

Jock saw the fire devouring the Range Rover as he turned a corner on the highway. "My God."

"Macauley?" MacDuff asked.

"And Jane," Jock said jerkily. "Jane was riding with him." There were two police cars and a fire truck pulled over behind the wreck of the Range Rover. He sped up and screeched to a stop behind them. He jumped out of the Toyota and brushed aside the uniformed policeman who was trying to keep him from running toward the wreck. "Keep them out of my way, MacDuff. I've got to see if I can get anyone out of that inferno."

"You won't. Don't even try, sir." A young policeman, covered with mud and soot, had come out of the ditch. "The driver was pinned by the air bag and was pretty bruised and broken up. But he made it out of the car and we found him trying to crawl up to the road. He's in the ambulance over there. We're trying to put out the fire now, but I'm afraid that it really doesn't matter if —" He abruptly broke off. "Are you family?"

"Why doesn't it matter?" MacDuff demanded. "Finish what you were going to say, dammit."

"Maybe you should talk to my superior. He's over there with the EMTs and two witnesses who were in a car right behind the Range Rover."

"Why?" Jock took a step closer to him. *"Now."*

The policeman took a hasty step back. "We got a look at the other three victims through the window before the tank blew. All three men were deceased. It appeared that they'd been shot in the head at close range." He saw Jock's expression and said,

"They *were* family? I'm sorry for your loss. I shouldn't be the one talking to you. Lieutenant Parren is interviewing witnesses over there. You'd better go see him." He turned and almost ran back to the police car.

"Shot at close range in the head," MacDuff said. "Execution-style?"

"Santara." Jock was gazing at the blazing vehicle. "They *were* family. How long did they work for you?"

"Since I was in the Royal Marines. I know all their families," MacDuff said. "Three men. Not a woman. Jane wasn't in that car when it blew."

"But that doesn't mean that Santara won't make an example of her later, when he has more time. I don't think there's any doubt she was the target." Jock turned on his heel and headed toward the EMTs' truck. "Let's go and see if we can get any information from those witnesses. I don't want to have to go back to camp and tell Joe and Eve that Jane's been taken until we know every-thing we can possibly know."

"I must have talked to Jane only minutes before it happened," Joe said to Jock. He added bitterly, "She was worried about us. I told her I'd take care of everyone. I didn't

437

take care of her, did I?"

"Because no one thought that Jane would be a target. She was always afraid for Lisa." Eve moved closer to Joe. In this nightmare, she wanted to feel his warmth. "It doesn't make sense." And men who acted without reason terrified her. She had seen too many deaths committed by impulse and revenge on the innocent. "What did the witnesses say, Jock?"

"Not much. Only that they saw a yellow Hummer drive the Range Rover off the road. It turned over and the driver of the Hummer got out with two other men and ran down the ditch and opened the passenger-side door. Then they heard shots and saw a woman being carried up the ditch and thrown into the Hummer. A few moments later, the gas tank of the Range Rover caught fire."

Eve's fingers dug into Joe's arm. "Carried?"

"She seemed limp, probably unconscious."

"She was in a car turned upside down," Eve said jerkily. "She could have a concussion or spinal damage or heaven knows what other injury." She remembered another word Jock had used. "And *thrown*? You don't throw people when they're hurt or injured; that's for trash or garbage." That wasn't for her Jane. She was suddenly being bombarded by memories of Jane at ten years old; Jane sitting on the floor with Michael, sketching; Jane looking out at the mist as if she were trying to see Cira in the shifting clouds.

Joe's arm slid around her waist. "Jane's tough," he said gently. "We'll get her back and she'll be fine."

She nodded jerkily. She had to believe that or she wouldn't be able to function right now. And she had to function; they had to find out the answers. "Why? If Santara has been stalking Lisa, why take Jane? And why now? Does it have anything to do with Cira's treasure?"

"That might be logical," MacDuff said. "But it's almost certain that Santara knew nothing about it. Only the people in this camp knew we'd found it." He grimaced. "And it was a surprise to all of us . . . except perhaps Jane. Not even the guards knew what we were taking to the bank today. No, he must have had another agenda. And Jane was a target of opportunity."

"Jane?" Lisa had suddenly appeared behind them. Her gaze flew from one to the other. "Target? What's wrong with Jane?" Her eyes narrowed on Eve's face. "You're scared. You *tell* me what's wrong with her."

Eve should have known that Lisa would have seen them talking, noticed Jane was not with MacDuff and Jock, and instantly gone on the offensive. What could she say? She had an idea that beneath that tough facade Lisa kept so firmly in place she had a deep affection for Jane. Which was confirmed by the fierceness of this response when Lisa suspected Jane was in trouble.

"*Tell* me." Lisa's eyes were blazing. "I should have gone with her. I shouldn't have relied on anyone else. I just didn't think that Jane was — And, if she was, I thought you all would be able to —"

"Easy." Eve took her arm and drew her a few yards away. "Yes, there's a problem." An understatement, she thought bitterly. But Lisa didn't need to get any more upset than she was right now. Yet there wasn't any way to avoid the truth, so she told her quickly what had happened. "MacDuff doesn't think it has anything to do with Cira's treasure. We're not sure yet why she was taken."

"Aren't you?" She moistened her lips. "Does Seth know what happened?"

"Not yet. As I said, he told Jane he was on his way here now." Her lips twisted. "He was going hunting for Santara. We'll tell him when he gets here."

"No, you won't. I'll call him and tell him now. He needs to know."

"You're upset. It could probably wait. What can he do while flying a plane? It will be only a few more hours, Lisa."

"A few hours might make a difference with Santara. I don't know. I'm not smart enough about things like that. But I'm not going to take a chance. Seth will know." She looked at Eve. "Are you afraid I'll get all hysterical and upset him and make you cope? I won't do that. I'll just tell him and get off the phone. But he has to know." Her voice was suddenly filled with passion. "Do you think I want to do it? I *hate* having to tell him, because they may have found a way to get him after all."

Eve frowned. "What do you mean?"

"Of course it's not about the treasure. It's about Seth." She reached for her phone. "It's always been about Seth."

"Wake up!"

Jane's cheek stung and her neck jerked backward with the force of the blow.

"Open your eyes. She wants you awake."

Pain.

Not only because of the slap.

Her head was throbbing, Jane realized dazedly.

441

She slowly opened her eyes.

Santara.

He smiled down at her. "That's better. Teresa doesn't trust me. Can you imagine that she'd believe I'd not take care of you in just the manner she ordered? She wants me to keep you awake to be sure that concussion doesn't cause you to slip into a coma. She has plans for you and wants to make sure you're healthy and able to perform."

Vibration.

And that low familiar hum of sound.

A plane.

She was on a plane. . . .

"You're not saying anything. The queen bitch said I had to make sure that you were coherent. Talk to me."

"We're — on a plane. Where are you — taking me?"

"That was clear enough. Should I answer?" He pretended to think about it. "Why not? We're on our way to the land of sun and money, where Queen Teresa wishes to receive you and deal with you herself."

"That's no answer."

His hand lashed out and struck her cheek again, hard. "Be polite. I'm sick to death of dealing with you female vipers who think you can tell me what to do."

She was dizzy and had to hold on to

442

consciousness.

"No, you're this big man who has to prove himself by torturing — a young girl. I'm surprised you didn't go after Lisa again."

"You're slurring a little. I guess I'd better not hit you again. Disappointing."

"Where are you taking me?"

"Dubai. You didn't recognize my description?"

"And you were talking about Teresa Romano?"

"See, perfectly coherent."

She was trying to fight the dizziness and clear her mind. The car . . . She had been in the Range Rover . . . "Macauley. What happened to Macauley?"

"Who?"

"The driver. Macauley."

"He may be alive. His air bag went off and I couldn't get to him. I didn't have time to fight that damn air bag." He smiled. "But his three friends were right there and available to us. It didn't take any time at all to dispose of them."

"You killed them?"

"It seemed the thing to do. It made a statement. I believe in statements."

Caleb had said something like that. . . .

"Said Ben Kemal."

He nodded. "I don't know how Caleb got

him to talk, but he had to be punished for it. I would have enjoyed being there to do it myself, but unfortunately I had to delegate. I was busy keeping my eye on the lake."

"Do you know — why you're taking me — to Dubai?"

Silence. "Why should I tell you?"

She studied his face. "You don't know. She's just using you as an errand boy and doesn't confide in you."

"Bullshit. I'm just done with asking her questions. I'll do what she wants and then let her pay what *I* want." He added roughly, "And I'm done with answering your questions. You're not going to go into any coma unless I decide to put you in one. So just shut up." His smile was malicious. "Every now and then I'll come back and check and give you a reminder that will leave a bruise or two and show Teresa that I always do what she wants me to do." He got to his feet. "I missed that after you and Caleb took Lisa away from me. Do you know it wasn't only Caleb I was angry with that night? You were right there with him, another bitch to humiliate me in front of my men. Actually, I'm very glad that Dubai is still a good distance away."

She watched him stroll back down the aisle toward the cockpit.

Vicious. Totally vicious and without conscience. She had known that he was both those things, but this was firsthand experience with him. He liked the pain and terror he could dispense. He wanted her to be afraid.

Statements. That was an example of his basic philosophy of terror. She had to remember that, in case she could use it later.

Though it was hard to remember anything with her head whirling like a windmill. Perhaps it would be safe to close her eyes for just a moment and rest.

Macauley. Was he still alive? She had always liked and respected him. Neither he nor his men would have been hurt if she'd not made the choice to have him take her back to the lake.

But then MacDuff and Jock might have been the victims. There was no good decision when it came to a murderer like Santara. Unless the decision was for her to crawl into a hole and cower there while they trampled over everything good and clean in the world. How could she do that?

It was impossible. So the only solution was to fight, and she would do that. As soon as she could shake off this pain and dizziness. Until then, she would lie here and recover and try to figure out why Teresa

Romano had decided it was worth her while to choose her as Santara's target.

And why she had decided to come forward out of the darkness of the shadows to deal with Jane herself.

CHAPTER 16

"She was unconscious?" Caleb asked tersely as he strode down the slope toward Eve. "Jane was still out when they put her in the car?"

"As far as we know. We have to rely on a secondhand report from witnesses." Eve shivered. "And the word they used was *thrown.* I can't get it out of my head. She has to have been hurt in that wreck. No one was caring what kind of additional damage they were doing to her."

"But she was alive, or Santara wouldn't have bothered to take her," he said. "And they won't let her die as long as they believe she has any value to them." He met her eyes and the glittering ferocity in his own was overpowering in its intensity. "She's not going to die, Eve. I won't *have* it."

She took a deep breath. She had seen Caleb in a rage before, but never like this. He was electrified, every muscle alive and supple, casting out a sheer aura of power. "I hope you're right. No, I have to believe you're right. And then we have to figure out what Santara wants and how to get her back."

"Money is the usual answer," MacDuff said as he came toward them. "And you know that I'll be willing to meet any ransom request. I have a sizable fortune of my own, and once we're able to process Cira's treasure, I'll be able to augment —"

"What the hell are you talking about?" Caleb asked. "Cira's treasure?"

"We found it. That's what we were depositing in Edinburgh," MacDuff said. "Lisa didn't tell you?"

Caleb's lips twisted. "She said two sentences. She probably didn't consider the treasure important in the scheme of things. I'm not sure that I do."

MacDuff shrugged. "The search of a decade, and it's not important? That puts things in perspective."

"We don't think Santara knew about the treasure," Eve said. "Another agenda?"

"Or the same one." He paused. "With new bait."

Eve stiffened. "Lisa said it was all about you. Is that true?"

"It could be. Probably. I'll have to make

sure." He turned to MacDuff. "And I don't think that you're going to be contacted for ransom."

"But you might be." Eve's gaze was searching Caleb's face. "Money? Or something else?"

"Whatever it is, I'll pay it." He was silent an instant. "If I think it will do any good."

Eve felt a chill. "And I'm supposed to let you make that decision? This is Jane, Caleb. One false step and she might die."

"Do you think I don't know that?" His voice was rough, his face tight. "I told you that I wouldn't let that happen." He said to MacDuff, "I don't think that Santara would bring her back to this area after he had her, but I have to make certain. I'm going hunting tonight and I'll verify."

MacDuff nodded. "Jock is already setting up security for the camp while we go take a look in the hills." He grimaced. "Verification that he slipped through our fingers? Not the hunt that we hoped for."

"We're here and we have to be certain," Caleb said grimly. "Before we take that next step that Eve is so worried about."

"And you're not?" Eve asked. "You're about to explode, Caleb. You'd just better not explode where Jane could be hit by the shrapnel."

He didn't answer. He asked instead, "Where's Lisa?"

"Over there by the fire. Though she looks like she's frozen there. She hasn't said a word since she talked with you on the phone."

Caleb turned and started toward the campfire. "I'll be ready to leave in fifteen minutes, MacDuff."

Lisa watched Seth cross the grass to where she was sitting by the fire. She didn't want to look at his face, because she knew what she would see there. She forced herself to do it anyway.

It was exactly what she'd expected.

"You have to go after her," she said jerkily. "I knew it. The minute I heard about it, I knew that you wouldn't be able to help yourself. They've got you, haven't they?"

"Yes." He sat down beside her and stared into the fire. "But only to the extent that I'm being forced to play their game. The results are always up in the air in any game."

"It's my fault. I thought they'd go after me again. I didn't think it through. Jane was so protective of me, and I just accepted it." She added bitterly, "Why not? I'm always the important one, aren't I? At least to myself. I shouldn't have let her go to Edinburgh without me, Seth. I should have been there for her."

"You're not to blame. I thought you'd be the target, too."

"Of course I'm to blame. Just because I was the one they took before, it didn't mean they wouldn't go in another direction. Santara probably thought I was guarded too well." She shook her head. "I guess they were smart to choose Jane. Your link with her is so strong. . . . But I didn't think that anyone but me realized that. How did Santara know? Did he just take a chance?"

"I don't believe he has the option of taking chances. I'd say that the order came directly from Teresa Romano." His lips tightened. "And I found out a long time ago that Teresa can be very clever about things concerning me. I just didn't think she'd bother to probe that deep."

Her gaze flew to his face. "You did? You've never mentioned that about her."

"It wasn't necessary. She was doing what I needed her to do for you, and that was all that was important." He added, "Or what I thought was all that was important. Evidently, she evolved and decided to use you to get to me." He glanced at her. "I'm sorry that I made that mistake. I thought you'd be safe."

"Do you think I care if you made mistakes? Everyone makes mistakes. Even me." She reached out and grasped his arm. "The only mistake I won't forgive is if you leave me again." She added unsteadily, "And I won't forgive you if you get killed, Seth. So that can't happen."

He turned his arm and took her hand. "I'll keep that in mind. But right now I have to worry about Jane, don't I?"

"I'd like to say no." Her hand tightened on his. "I told Jane once that you were the only one I cared about. I wish that was still true. It's easier like that."

"Yes, but it's changed, hasn't it? I could see that before I left. I heard it in your voice whenever I phoned you."

She was silent. "She can't die, Seth," she whispered. "And Santara can't do the things to her that he did to me."

"He won't, Lisa. I promise."

"How can you promise? She's already been hurt. Eve doesn't even know how badly."

"But that's the end of it. I'll find a way to get to her and keep her safe." He got to his feet. "I have to go check out the hills, which will probably yield nothing of value. But it's something to do until Teresa makes her next move."

"Teresa? Not Santara?"

"No, I have an idea that it will definitely be Teresa's game from now on."

"And you don't think that any move will be here at the lake?"

He shook his head. "Everything seems to be centered in Dubai. Whatever Teresa wants to happen, she has plans to do it in Dubai. Probably somewhere in or near the American Hospital." He leaned down and gently brushed his lips across her brow. "None of this was your fault. If there was a mistake, it was one I made years ago. But I'll make it right, Lisa." He turned and strode away to where MacDuff, Joe Quinn, and Jock were waiting.

Lisa gazed after him, her hands clenched into fists as she watched him disappear from sight. Yes, he'd make it right. He'd always made everything right for her. But no one had ever taken the trouble to make anything right for him. He'd never been permitted to make mistakes as a child. She could remember instant, almost savage punishment for any tiny infraction and Seth lifting his chin and just accepting it. She hadn't realized until later how hard that must have been for him when he had known what he could do and how swiftly he could stop those cruelties.

And tonight he was shouldering all responsibility and blame again and would face it as he always had.

Alone.

"Nothing?" Eve asked Joe as he came into the tent.

He shook his head. "We found the remains of a few campfires on that third mountain. It looked as if Santara and his men had been moving around to keep from being spotted." He looked down at the sleeping Michael. "But they were never close enough to be a danger to anyone here."

She nodded. "Jane said we had an armed camp."

"I wish to hell she'd stayed in it," he said harshly. "Who would believe that —" He broke off. "But it happened. Now we have to get her back."

"How? Interpol?"

"Any way that doesn't get her killed. Lisa said that she was sure Santara was going to kill her before she escaped. We can't count on anything better for Jane if they think she's a danger to them." He paused. "Caleb is asking us to back off until he can get a fix on how to do it. How the hell can I do that?"

"I don't know." She pulled him down and into her arms. "How can you? Tell me.

Convince me that it's the wrong thing to do." She held him close. She could *feel* his pain. "Or is it the smart thing to do?"

He didn't speak for a moment. "Yes. That's the worst thing about it. Caleb thinks all this centers around him."

"So does Lisa."

"And it very well might be true. Everything points to it. I don't see any way out. But I'd have to let Caleb go off and control every — It's Jane."

"I know," she whispered. It was a horrible decision for him and for her. To stand on the sidelines when they wanted only to plunge into the battle. "And we have to do whatever is best for her, Joe."

"And who the hell knows what that is?" He was silent, stiff, fighting the battle. Then he muttered a curse and got to his feet. "Okay, he wins."

She got up and followed him to the tent entrance. "I don't think anybody wins this one, Joe," she said wearily. "It doesn't feel like it." She watched him go down the hill and stop before Caleb, who was sitting there drinking a cup of coffee before the fire.

"Okay, I'll back off," Joe told him. "You have a clear shot at trying to locate her and setting up a rescue. But the minute you do, you get in touch and bring me into it.

Agreed?"

"No choice," Caleb said. "I knew that's as much as I'd be able to get from you."

"And you'll keep me informed, dammit."

He nodded. "I'll let you know how she is as soon as I can. I know Eve's worried."

"See that you do." Joe didn't move, staring down into Caleb's eyes. "And if you do the wrong thing, if you get her killed, I'll hunt you down and break your neck." He turned and strode back up the hill to the tent. "Done," he told Eve as he took her back into his arms. "He said earlier that he thought he'd be contacted soon. I hope to hell he's right."

Caleb turned back to the fire as Joe left him. It had gone as he'd expected. Joe Quinn was smart and always managed to overcome personal feelings if they got in the way of what was best for any situation. But it had been more difficult than usual, since it concerned Jane.

Caleb didn't know if he could have made that choice.

He was on fire right now.

And he didn't think he'd hidden it very well. Eve had said he was ready to explode and she had come close. He was burning with rage and panic and the multitude of searing, complex emotions that were always there when he thought about Jane.

So don't think about her, he decided. He had to be calm and cool when the call came.

And it would come soon. He'd delved into everything that he knew and had experienced, and unless there had been a greater change than he thought, the call would be coming within the next hour or so.

So he would sit here and wait and wouldn't think about Jane.

Instead, he'd think about the most painful ways to kill Santara.

The call came forty-five minutes later.

He smiled grimly as he saw the ID. He could feel the rush of adrenaline sending the blood zinging through his body.

And so the hunt begins. . . .

He pressed the access button. "Hello, Teresa. You've kept me waiting. But that was always one of your strategies. However, I imagine it was just as disturbing for you as it was for me this time. You've probably been salivating for the chance to display how clever you are."

Silence. Then she laughed. "As it happens, you're right, Caleb. I was just sitting here thinking about you, wondering what you were doing. What blind alleys you were running down while trying to find her."

"I didn't waste my time. A cursory check at Loch Gaelkar and then I sat down to wait for your call. Do you have Jane yet?"

"She just arrived. However, she won't be of use to you, Caleb."

He kept his tone indifferent. "She's alive?"

"Yes. A wrenched neck and concussion. But I made sure that Santara kept her awake on the flight. I believe the danger of coma is over now. But I had him give her a sedative just before he got here. Naturally, she's rather tense, and that's bad for her right now. I wanted her to be at her best when you saw her. She's quite beautiful, isn't she?"

"Anyone could see that." He paused. "Just as anyone could see how beautiful you are, Teresa."

"Yes, I am. But I've had to have a few nips and tucks lately. Very annoying. Particularly when I look at Jane MacGuire. But maturity always triumphs over youth in the end."

"Does it?"

"Always," she said softly. "Look at the situation. Your Jane is lying unconscious in my guest room, totally helpless. I can do anything I want with her, Caleb." She chuckled. "Or look at Lisa. I was in charge of her for years. And when I realized she'd be useful, I had Santara teach her a few of the lessons I'd wanted her to learn ever since I became her guardian. Arrogant little bitch. All that youth did nothing to help her, either, Caleb." The laughter vanished. "But you helped Lisa escape, didn't you? I knew you would come if she called you; that's why I took her. I *needed* you. But Santara was a fool and let you take her away from me. It wasn't supposed to work that way. So I had to make a correction."

"Jane MacGuire is the correction?"

"Yes, I thought you'd appreciate my brilliance in choosing her. You always admired that quality in me. No one else bothered to look for it."

"You missed the boat this time, Teresa. I'll grant that you were smart to take Lisa. You knew how I felt about family. But Jane doesn't mean anything to me."

"Oh, I think she does," Teresa said softly. "Years ago, after your parents sent you away to Scotland, I filed you away as a possible asset and forgot about you. When I needed someone to draw you into the web, I chose Lisa." She sighed. "But that was extremely difficult to manage. I knew I couldn't do too much to Lisa, because it would make you too angry. She was your little sister and there was all that protective business you'd demonstrated after Maria had been killed. I was walking on eggs. Jane MacGuire will be much easier."

"Indeed? Why?"

"Because you fuck her," she said simply.

"Wrong."

"No, after you took Lisa, I got an in-depth report on your activities over the last several years. Well, as in-depth as possible considering what a secretive bastard you've always been. But you've never hidden what a sexual animal you are, Caleb. You've gone to bed with many, many women, but you never form relationships. One-night stands." She added softly, "Except with Jane MacGuire. You kept returning to her, Caleb. You were together in half a dozen countries, and wherever she is, you're eventually there, too. Is she that good?"

"Coincidence. We have mutual objectives at times."

"I don't think so. That's why I felt I'd been given a gift when I saw her name on every page of the report I had on you."

"Would you believe we're friends?"

She laughed. "You? Have you forgotten I know you, Caleb? And I've seen her."

"I didn't think that you'd accept that. Nevertheless, you're wrong, Teresa. And why would you think you could use her for a weapon, even if you were right? Someone I fuck wouldn't have the same impact as Lisa."

"Not usually. But you're very intense, sometimes almost obsessive. Jane MacGuire might fall into that category. If she does, then you wouldn't want to give up your toy if you could help it." She added, "Especially when just performing a small service for me would permit you to keep her."

"I don't permit myself to be used. Have you forgotten that?"

"I haven't forgotten anything about you. Have you forgotten that I don't let anything stand in my way when I want something?" Her voice became honey-smooth. "Friends? I don't believe she'd feel very friendly toward you if I turned Santara loose on her when she's feeling so poorly. I didn't let him rape Lisa, even though that might have been effective, because I knew that would disturb you."

"Yes, it would have."

"But the gloves are off now, Caleb. I have to have this service performed in the next forty-eight hours. I'll do anything I have to do to MacGuire to ensure your cooperation. If you don't tell me right now that you're willing to deal with me, I'll send in Santara and any other of his men with whom he wishes to share. You know I don't bluff, Caleb."

"I also know you're capable of any deceit."

"Of course."

He was silent. She would do it. Find the safest way out. "You *are* clever, Teresa. You're right: I do find her . . . very satisfying. As a toy, she's superb. I don't like the idea of her being damaged."

She laughed. "I *knew* it. Much better choice than Lisa."

"But you know that we could take care of this in another way. I'm prepared to be very generous if you want to go the ransom route."

"Tempting. However, regrettably, though my present arrangement is fantastic monetarily, it has a downside. I was forced to ask my new partners to fund my advance preparations. Now they've told me that if I don't fulfill my obligations, they will be displeased enough to take a contract out on me. I don't intend to have to give up the splendid life I've planned in order to go into hiding."

"And I have no intention of backing myself into a corner for any woman. What are you asking me to do?"

"What you're so good at doing. What your dear mother was so afraid you'd do. What else?"

"Exactly what I assumed. You want someone killed in a way that would not be able to be detected. Who's the target?"

"You haven't found that out yet? I thought you might have stumbled across it. You did find out about the American Hospital in Dubai from Said Ben Kemal."

"Who?"

"That's enough information for now. I have to be sure that she's enough to keep you under control. So you'll come here and we'll have a few discussions and renew our acquaintance."

"Come where?"

"Dubai. You'll be picked up at the airport and brought to me." She chuckled. "And to Jane MacGuire. She should be better by that time. If I'm feeling generous, I might let you have a welcome present as a deposit before you actually give me what I want. I'm sure you've missed her while you've been flying around trying to find Santara."

"And you."

"That goes without saying. I knew you'd realize I was behind it almost from the beginning. We do know each other so well. Good night, Caleb. You'll have my phone number now. Let me know when you arrive." She hung up.

Keep cool. Keep calm. Now that the need

for pretense was over, the rage was beginning to drown out everything else. Rage and fear. Teresa always knew how to push the right buttons and she'd found one in Jane.

And she would push it and push it until it was broken or she had what she wanted. She would have no compunction about breaking Jane. She was totally without any sense of right and wrong. The perfect sociopath, he'd discovered during their time together. Whatever served to advance an agenda was what she did with speed and consummate skill.

But she couldn't be permitted to trample over Jane.

Control. It had always been the battle that had defined their struggle for power.

Teresa had started it, and he would finish it.

He got to his feet and strode up the hill to his tent. He changed, threw clothes into a bag, and exited the tent.

"I'm going with you." Lisa was standing a few yards away. She was dressed in black pants and shirt and had her backpack. "You've heard, haven't you? I saw you talking on the phone down there." Her lips were tight. "You're not going to leave me again, Seth."

"The hell I'm not." He didn't need this

right now. "I'm going to have enough problems. If you want to help Jane, you'll stay here, out of my way."

"Jane's alive?" she asked shakily.

He wasn't going to lie. "I don't have proof. I think it's true."

"Then we'll go get her."

"It's not going to be that easy."

"You have to trade something? I knew that was going to happen. What?"

"I've no idea yet. Whatever it is, it's going to be difficult, or she wouldn't want me."

"She? Teresa?"

He nodded. "As she put it, 'the gloves are off.' "

"She said she'd hurt Jane?"

"Yes. But I won't let that happen."

She shook her head. "*We* won't let that happen. I'm going with you."

"No." He had to reason with her. She was as scared about Jane as he was right now. "Look, if you come and we're captured, Teresa will have two weapons she can use against me. That's what you said you didn't want."

"I wouldn't be captured." She met his eyes. "You showed me how to keep that from happening. I won't let them use me against you. All I'd have to do is kill them."

"All you'd have to do," he repeated.

"Simplistic. You made a promise."

"It didn't include stuff like this." She took a step closer, her eyes pleading. "I wouldn't do it unless I had to. You're going to Dubai? I wouldn't even have to be with you. For heaven's sake, some women there run around in robes and veils. No one would even know who I was. I wouldn't get in your way. I'd just be there to do what you needed me to do."

"It's not a good idea, Lisa."

"Then make it a good idea." She suddenly wasn't pleading any longer. "When that bastard Santara was torturing me, I held out. I kept my word. But I swore nothing like that was ever going to happen to me or anyone I cared about again. I want to do whatever you want, but I won't let them hurt you or Jane." She stared him in the eye. "So I'm going to Dubai whether you like or not, Seth. You're going to find me something of value to do that will help Jane and hopefully cause Santara to have a fatal accident. Make it *work,* dammit."

He stared at her in frustration and something else, which might have been pride.

He shrugged. "Whatever. Listen, you'll do what I say. No arguments. Not ever." He went past her down the hill. "And I'll make it work."

"You really have to wake up now, Jane. I've let you sleep as long as I can because I needed you fit and ready. But we're running out of time." It was a woman's voice, smooth, deep, and musical. "And I really don't want to use Santara's methods on you. So do open your eyes."

Easier said than done, Jane thought groggily. Her head felt stuffed with cotton.

Santara . . .

It was all rushing back to her. She wanted to push it away and go back to the darkness.

Santara . . .

There was no going back.

Force it. Face it.

She slowly opened her lids.

"There we are." The woman sitting in the peacock blue brocade chair opposite the couch where Jane was lying was smiling at her. "I knew you must be a smart woman. Caleb doesn't tolerate stupidity for very long." She handed her a delicate china cup. "Coffee. Very strong. Do you need me to help you hold it?"

"No." Though her hand was shaking, every instinct was telling her she mustn't show that weakness. "I'm fine." She took a sip. Hot. Black. Bracing. She took another sip, her gaze fixed on the woman who must be Teresa Romano. She was dressed in a long black skirt and fringed overshirt that managed to make her look both exotic and flawlessly elegant. She was far more beautiful than in that photo Caleb had shown her. Glowing skin, glittering blue eyes, long lashes, and her blond hair, coiled in a chignon, was a faultless frame for those perfect features.

"You're not fine, you know." Teresa Romano was smiling at her. "You're in a terrible predicament, if you'll remember. But if you cooperate, you may come out of it alive. It appears you can be valuable to me. I suppose you've guessed I'm Teresa Romano?"

Keep her talking. Keep drinking the coffee. Stronger. She had to get stronger. "Yes. And you're the one who put me in this predicament. You must be desperate. You couldn't get hold of Lisa, so you grabbed me instead?"

Teresa's smile lost a little of its wattage. " 'Desperate'? I'm never desperate. Poor choice of words. As it happens, I'm much happier with you than I was with Lisa. All she could offer was to reach out to Caleb's protectiveness. You'll appeal to more basic appetites, and we both know how basic Caleb can be."

"Do we?" She took another sip of coffee. She was getting steadier. "You went to a great deal of trouble to find someone you thought would make Caleb perform for you. Would you care to tell me what you need from him?"

" 'Perform'?" She threw back her head and laughed. "Now that's a fitting word. No one's better at performance than Caleb." She leaned back in the chair. "Oh, I intend to tell you what I need from him, Jane. I want you to be able to know what's going to save your life so that you'll be infinitely persuasive with him. No matter how much you please him, Caleb can be very difficult to manage."

"No one manages Caleb. But I'm curious to hear what you think you can make him do. He said something about the American Hospital."

She nodded. "Yes, he's guessed that he'll be required to do a little blood adjustment, but I refused to tell him anything until I had him here in Dubai. I've no objection to sharing it with you, because you're not going anywhere." She smiled. "And when Caleb sees that I really do have you and you're

469

not 'damaged,' he won't go anywhere, either."

"Who is it?"

"Tarik El Haroun."

"Why?"

"Because he may be the most important man in Dubai outside of the royal family, who are the sole rulers of the country." She tilted her head contemplatively. "No, he has more power than some of the members of the royal family. Money is everything, isn't it, Jane?"

"I've never found that to be true. He's some kind of oil sheik?"

"No, oil provides only about seven percent of the wealth of Dubai. It's such a magnificently rich city. I knew as soon as I started giving dinner parties for Gino's clients from here that it was my kind of place. Then when Haroun was pointed out to me at a gala, I started to keep my eye on him." She smiled. "Because eighty-six percent of the wealth of Dubai is tied up in real estate. And Haroun owns or controls most of it. He has a distant connection to the royal family, but he's such a fantastic businessman, that has little to do with it. But he's made Dubai flourish, and that's made the royal family very happy." She paused. "Except for one or two members who would prefer that his power and influence just go away."

"And you've promised them that you'll see that it does," Jane said slowly. "With no way to detect that it was murder."

She nodded. "It's been an exciting project for me to develop from the moment I found out that Gino had been fool enough to send us close to bankruptcy." She leaned forward, and for an instant her beautiful face turned ugly. "Do you know how I felt when I learned that bastard had ruined everything that I'd worked to achieve in the last twenty years? I should have kept a closer eye on him, but I thought even he couldn't get rid of that much money on his whores and drugs." Then her expression cleared and was once more serene. "But it will be fine once I'm able to get Haroun out of the way. I've negotiated an amount that will make me as wealthy as I've always dreamed of being. Far richer than the life Gino could ever provide me."

"And what's Caleb's part in this?"

"Tarik El Haroun is having a heart procedure done two days from now. Only stents inserted, so no problem is expected." She added softly, "But heart operations can always be iffy if not performed correctly, or even if they are. Of course Haroun has the

471

best surgeons and staff available, absolutely above reproach. And, since the royal family regard him as something of a national treasure, they're providing security to protect him while he's in the hospital. So if anything were to go wrong, it would cause an uproar that would shake everyone at the hospital and the political hierarchy. An autopsy, investigations — everyone would be suspect. But in the end it will be found that his death was due to a ruptured artery not caused by poison, medicine, or the surgeon who performed the operation." She smiled. "And that Allah just wanted to take his good servant off to paradise."

"And how is Caleb supposed to get close enough to that 'good servant' to send him packing to Allah?"

"That's up to him. I remember Caleb as being so very clever, and I'll provide him with detailed maps of the hospital and any personnel records he might need."

"He won't do it."

"For your sake, I hope you're wrong. I believe you are."

"Because you think if you threaten me that he'll soften and do whatever you want?" She shook her head. "Soften? The only chance you had of Caleb softening toward anyone on this earth was when you kidnapped Lisa. When Santara lost her, it blew that for you."

"I never mention softening." Her smile deepened. "Quite the opposite. I agree Lisa is an anomaly in Caleb's life. I've always found him to be both ruthless and manipulative. He doesn't allow anyone that close. But closeness isn't necessary to influence him. He's a sexual animal and he evidently has developed an obsession for you. I have reports that he constantly seeks you out."

"Coincidence."

She laughed. "That's what he said. But he eventually told me himself that he finds you pleasing and wouldn't want you damaged."

Jane felt a ripple of shock. "You've talked to him?"

She nodded. "He's on his way here. I thought it time I put plans in motion."

"If they include me, you're going to be disappointed. You're completely wrong about Caleb's attitude toward me."

"I won't be disappointed. I'll just make adjustments if I need to do that." She was gazing at Jane critically. "But he might be disappointed if you look like that when he gets here. Dreadful. Finish that coffee and get into the shower. I'll get you something to wear that doesn't make you look like you've been upside down in a vehicle."

"Which I was."

"And I was thinking about leaving you in this condition, but it would be counterproductive. My entire plan for you is based on the fact that you don't arouse Caleb's sympathy, but another emotion entirely." She got to her feet. "So you will be presented to him in as pleasant packaging as possible, something that reflects what he will be missing if he makes me dispense with his toy. And my generosity in allowing him to keep you." She looked back at Jane as she reached the door. "You will shower and take care of doing that, or I'll send Santara in to assist you. You won't like that, but he would."

"I'll do it myself." Jane put down her coffee cup. "Because I'm filthy and not because I'm complying with your orders. I dealt with Santara on the plane. I'm not afraid of him."

"You should be. He went easy on Lisa. Because I told him he had to." Her gaze narrowed on Jane. "But you're annoying me. And you're beautiful, but I can't see why Caleb's obsessed with you. You're nothing like —" She turned away. "I might have to observe him closer when he gets here."

"And you'll find out you're totally wrong," Jane said. "You formed all those wild, unsubstantiated assumptions because you were frantic to —"

"I don't like the word *frantic* any more than I do *desperate,*" Teresa said. "You're digging a deep hole, Jane."

I probably am, Jane thought. She was still bleary and disoriented, and everything that Teresa had thrown at her in the past few minutes had bewildered and frightened her. "I'm just trying to tell you that you're mistaken. And I don't understand why you think you know Caleb well enough to jump to those conclusions."

Teresa's brows lifted. "Why, who would know him better, Jane? After all, we were lovers."

The door shut behind her.

Jane was frozen, staring at that door.

Lovers. That possibility had not occurred to her. Caleb had never given a hint there was a sexual relationship between them.

But then, she never knew anything about Caleb except what he wanted her to know.

So why was she so shocked? She felt almost ill at the thought of them to-gether. . . .

She couldn't let it affect her like this. She was weak and unable to process it right now. She needed to give herself time and a little space. She slowly got to her feet and headed for the bathroom. Her muscles felt sore, but she could move with more litheness than she had thought possible. A hot shower would help, and then she would try to clear her mind of the picture that Teresa Romano had insinuated there. She didn't know if that was possible.

Lovers . . .

CHAPTER 17

"He's in the driveway." Teresa came into the bedroom. "I thought I'd meet him there, but I changed my mind. I told Santara to bring him directly here." Her gaze went over Jane in the cream-colored flowing silk pants and matching blouse. "You'll do very well. Elegant, but sexy."

"I'm surprised you didn't put me in a harem outfit," Jane said sarcastically. "Or something you'd picked up from a local bordello."

"Oh, I would have if I hadn't thought it would turn him off. Caleb is much more subtle."

"As you said, who'd know better?"

"Exactly," Teresa replied. "You're being more aggressive than when I left."

Jane met her eyes. "I had to recover some-time."

"Don't be too aggressive. I'll be patient only so long." She tilted her head. "I think I

477

hear him." She threw open the door. "Caleb, how good it is to see you." She stepped aside for him to enter. "Particularly at this time and place. I see you've rushed to our Jane's side." She smiled. "But then I knew you would."

"So you told me," Caleb said as he entered the room. "You never lacked confidence, Teresa." His gaze went to Jane. "I'm sorry that you became involved in this. Are you all right?"

She nodded. "Stiff neck. Headache. How is Macauley? Santara didn't know or wouldn't tell me."

"Broken ribs and arm. He'll live."

Jane felt a rush of relief. She hadn't realized how worried she'd been about Macauley. It was good to know he'd survived that death and carnage. "I'm glad."

"So was MacDuff. Santara didn't leave him much to be grateful for. You know about the other three men?"

"Yes. Terrible."

"Enough," Teresa said impatiently. "That's not why I brought you here, Caleb. You have a job to do. I promised to tell you who your target is going to be."

"Tarik El Haroun," he said. "On the flight down here, I checked pending surgeries within that forty-eight-hour window you gave me from the list that Ben Kemal got for you and Santara." His lips twisted. "Haroun's the big fish. You wouldn't have wasted your time on anyone else."

"No, I wouldn't have. But you know how it annoys me to be thought predictable."

They knew each other so well, Jane realized, looking at them. No affection. No desire. But their familiarity was very clear.

Caleb smiled. "I could hardly trust you to tell me the truth. I had to find out for myself. You didn't tell me because you weren't sure that I wouldn't betray you because I don't like to be controlled. You couldn't be certain that Jane would be a strong enough draw."

She smiled back at him. "But here you are. So I must have been right."

He looked at Jane. "Perhaps. Give me your offer."

"She lives. You live. Tarik El Haroun dies. I get on a plane for Moscow, which has no extradition policy, that same day." She smiled. "Just in case you're not as skilled as I believe you are. Though the stories I heard about how you eliminated all those cult members who killed your sister did impress me."

"You're not mentioning Gino. I take it that he's no longer included in your plans."

She shrugged. "I won't have him dragging behind me. He's been annoying me lately. I've put up with him for too long. What do you expect?"

"Nothing less." His gaze returned to Jane. "I could take her with me now. I guarantee that you wouldn't be able to stop me."

"Of course, as I said, I delight in all those bizarre stories about you. But one of Santara's men who are guarding the house would stop her. You must have noticed how many men are patrolling the estate. I gave orders that if she escapes, they do not take her alive. She's to be shot on sight."

Caleb shook his head. "Now that would be truly unfortunate."

Jane had had enough. "It's truly unfortunate that you're talking about me as if I weren't here. Are you going to let me speak?"

Caleb smiled. "Not unless you have something to offer her that I can't. I don't believe that's the case." He turned back to Teresa. "I don't care anything about this Haroun. I don't see why I should let him rob me of something I want."

"I thought you'd feel that way." Her tone was almost purring.

"Then you were right. I'll need to come and go as I please until the operation. I have free access to the woman whenever I want. No damage is done to her. After I take care of Haroun, you deliver her to me immediately. Agreed?"

"It sounds reasonable," she said warily.

"And you don't try to cheat me," Caleb said softly. "I'm going to a good deal of trouble to have her, Teresa. I won't be forgiving or forgetting."

"How suspicious you are."

"And I don't have reason?"

She shrugged dismissively. "That was a long time ago."

"Precisely. And in the end, you learned a lot about me, didn't you? It would be wise of you to remember what I taught you."

To Jane's surprise, Teresa's cheeks suddenly flushed and she looked away from him. But then she raised her chin and stared at him defiantly. "As I recall, I was the teacher. That's all I remember."

"But then, you always did prefer to delude yourself." He changed the subject. "Now get out of here and let me have an hour or so with Jane. I can see how upset she is about all this, and I'll need some time to make it right. You might send some food after I leave her. Have you fed her?"

"No." She paused, taken aback. "You're being very — I wasn't expecting —"

"You don't tell me how to treat her." He was staring her in the eye. "We made a deal. I own her. She belongs to me. I treat her as I please. Do you understand?"

Teresa nodded, still frowning. "It's not what I expected. Do what you wish."

"Oh, I will. In any way I wish. But it's my way. You don't call the shots . . . ever." He opened the door for her. "I'll need a car to take me back to Dubai in about an hour. I'm staying at the Grand Hyatt. I'll study the hospital plans tonight and I'll pay a visit to the hospital tomorrow to plan the best place to have access to Haroun. I don't need to be within touching distance during the operation, but I need to be close."

"You'll need a security badge. I'll arrange to —"

"No, I'll call an associate and have him deliver one to the hotel tomorrow morning. My job. My way."

Teresa hesitated. "You were always an arrogant bastard." She shrugged. "Why should I care? I'll make sure you're watched every minute. And Santara has an orderly, Asad, at the hospital who will make certain that you've done what you promise." She glanced at Jane. "And I do have my ace in the hole, don't I? I'll want regular reports, Caleb." She swept out of the room.

"You *own* me?" Jane's voice was danger-ously low. "What the hell are you —"

"Hush." He took a tiny black box out of his pocket. "Give me a minute." He moved around the room before nodding. "No electronic devices. I'm surprised. Teresa has always had a passion for cameras." He came back to her and dropped down in the peacock chair Teresa had formerly occupied. "Now go ahead and let it loose. I could see it building up all the while Teresa and I were talking."

"I felt like a piece of meat in a butcher shop," she said through her teeth. "You ask why it should bother me?"

"As far as Teresa is concerned, that's what you are. She thinks she's found the way to buy what she wants from me. And you're too intelligent not to realize that's the way I have to go to get you out of here. You had to have picked up on that even before I got here."

"Yes," she admitted reluctantly. "She was all ready to serve me up on a silver platter. I was ready to choke her."

"I'm glad you refrained." His eyes were searching her face. "You don't look as if you could take her down at the present mo-ment." He leaned forward and gently pushed back her hair and probed the muscles of her neck. "Hurt?"

She flinched. "A little. More stiff than anything else."

He touched her cheek. "Bruise. From the wreck?"

She shook her head. "Santara's gentle way of making sure I stayed awake. Teresa evidently thought I wouldn't be as appetizing in a coma."

"Santara . . ." His hand dropped away. "The list keeps getting longer and longer." He leaned back in the chair. "No other injuries?"

"No." She was silent. "I could have died in that car crash. Santara was . . . reckless. He didn't care. I think he's a little crazy, Caleb."

"Probably. Don't worry about him. I'll take care of it."

Her lips twisted. "Just like you're taking care of Teresa Romano? But you don't know him as well as you do her, do you?"

His gaze was suddenly narrowed on her face. "What do you mean?"

"You were lovers."

He was silent. "Is that what she told you?"

"Is it the truth?"

"What do you think?"

She moistened her lips. "I think you know

each other very well. There's an . . . inti-macy."

"Yes."

She was beginning to wish she hadn't said anything. It had tumbled out. "It's none of my business." But she couldn't leave it alone. "I just don't see how you could — She's a terrible woman. Look what she did to Lisa. She was responsible for everything Santara did and —"

"I'm not going to make excuses," he said, interrupting her. "Everything you say is true. She was a mistake. The only thing that wasn't the truth is that we were lovers. It was a much . . . darker relationship."

"I don't want to hear about it. I said it wasn't my business."

"Oh, no, too late." He was smiling reck-lessly. "You asked the question. You can't go hide away when I answer it. The word *lovers* requires a certain emotion that was never there. Teresa never knew the meaning of the word; I knew it but had never experi-enced it. So when she decided to seduce me, I cooperated fully, but I admit to hav-ing been confused and uncertain about the nuances."

"*She* seduced you? You'll forgive me if I don't believe you. Seduction is your role in life."

"One has to start somewhere." He asked mockingly, "You're thinking that our association was fairly recent? No, it was a long time ago."

"How long ago?"

"I was quite young. Fourteen or fifteen, if I recall."

"What?" She stared at him, stunned. "You're joking."

"No joke. I was intensely serious at the time. But I understand one is always serious with the first one. Yet since I'm by nature intense, I contend it struck me harder than most. I was isolated and very much alone and told constantly what a demon I was. It was refreshing to have someone who apparently wanted to be close to me in spite of my many faults." He tilted his head. "And, of course, she was beautiful, an older, experienced woman, and sex was probably more of a factor than anything else. As I said, I was very confused at the beginning. However, I can assure you that we were not lovers."

Was there something deeper hidden beneath that mockery? It was always hard to tell with Caleb. "She seduced a teenage boy? You said the Romanos were good friends with your parents. Why would she take the chance of their finding out?"

He chuckled. "I'd like to tell you that she found me totally irresistible and couldn't help herself. But you wouldn't believe me, would you?"

She might believe him. She could imagine that stormy, beautiful young boy who possessed all the passion and magnetism he did now. "I think she's totally calculating and would have a reason for everything she did."

"Exactly. This was no exception. Though she *did* enjoy me, Jane."

"Why did she take the chance?" she repeated.

"She's attracted to power. She pretended the same repulsion as my parents to my potential when she was with them, but she thought she might be able to use me in the future. She thought I was vulnerable and sex would seal the deal. So we had an interesting summer, until she realized that I wasn't exactly what she thought I'd be."

"What do you mean?"

"She had me pretty dizzy for a little while, but I wasn't a fool. I could see the manipulation and the deceit." He shrugged. "I'd had experience in that all my life. I wasn't about to let her control me, as she wanted to do. Of course, the sex made it very tolerable until I figured out what to do about it."

"I can see how it would," she said drily.

"Why not? I deserved it. And I was angry with her. Though, actually, in retrospect, I realize I should have been grateful. I hadn't had the opportunity to develop that Persuasion talent because of my limited opportunities up to that time. But I decided that there couldn't be anything that Teresa would fear or hate worse than lack of control." He smiled, reminiscing. "It took me four weeks. The experiments were fascinating and I enjoyed every one of them. But Teresa, not so much. She didn't like the idea that she no longer dominated but instead felt she *had* to come to me, to do anything I wanted. She could see what direction we were going, that her control was slipping away. I could feel her fear. . . ." He leaned back in his chair. "It was enough. I gave her a push to end it."

"What push?"

"I mentioned how much I was enjoying her and how upset I'd be if my parents sent me away to my uncle, as they'd threatened to do. The next week, my mother told me that I was going to Scotland. Evidently, Teresa had casually said she'd noticed that I was getting completely out of hand and suggested it might be better for me and for the family if I were sent away."

"You manipulated that move to Scotland yourself," she murmured wonderingly. "What a devious man you are, Caleb."

"Yes. I've never denied it. But principally a survivor, and being devious is one of the apparatuses that make that possible." He tilted his head. "And is this particular story of lies and manipulation filling you with your usual disgust at me again?"

She gazed at him in disbelief. "Are you crazy? Do you think I can't see what that bitch was trying to do to you?" Her anger was growing with every word. "You were just a kid. Maybe around Cara's age. Helpless to make —"

"I was never helpless, Jane."

He wouldn't admit it if he had been, Jane thought. "You could have been, for all she knew. She didn't *care.* She was a grown woman and you were only a boy. She took advantage of the fact that — I'd like to strangle her. She's worse than Santara and it's —"

"Shh." He took her hand and lifted it to his lips. "I pride myself on never being an 'only' anything. Yet I find I'm touched that you want to fight my dragons for me. But most of them were slain a long time ago."

"Not her." His touch was disturbing her, as usual, and she pulled her hand away.

"She's still here and trying to use you. She's been in your life a long time. I'm surprised you let her take over guardianship of Lisa."

"I had no choice unless I wanted to kill Teresa or go back to the game I'd already won over her. She and Gino wanted the executor fee for managing the estate. I looked the situation over and decided if I kept an eye on the situation that Lisa and Maria could have a decent life. Teresa had no desire to go up against me again and she would treat them well." His lips thinned. "I didn't count on her life being turned upside down and desperation giving her the impetus to go back to square one as far as I was concerned. She went on the attack."

"But not toward you. She went after Lisa." Jane was trying to piece together what she'd seen and heard. "It was a very roundabout way to get to you." She met his eyes. "And you were setting rules before she left here today. And she let you do it."

"I told you: That last four weeks was about control. She lost and it frightened her. I thought there might be a few threads of memory remaining. It will allow me certain allowances as long as she doesn't feel too threatened." He added quietly, "But there will be resentment and it won't prevent her from killing you if she decides it's necessary. So I'd appreciate it if you'd make things easier for me and not antagonize her."

"Heaven forbid I cause you a problem by not keeping my mouth shut when she treats me like your whore."

"It *would* be a problem. Because now that the deal's been struck, that's exactly what you are in her eyes. She's very proud of herself that she's found a way to force me to do what she needs. It was perfectly reasonable that she thought sex was the way to go. It worked for her at the start of that summer and she got to know me very well. It was natural she'd think I wasn't interested in anything else."

"I can't argue with that statement," she said drily. "And I'm supposed to pretend I'm not interested in anything else, either? Well, it's not natural for me, Caleb."

He smiled. "We could work on it."

"Not likely."

His smile faded. "Teresa thinks I have a sexual obsession with you that's been going on for years. It's what's giving her a sense of power and the belief that I'll do anything to maintain the relationship. She's not going to believe that I'd tolerate your not being equally involved after this length of time. She'll remember those four weeks when I took over control in my relationship with her. If she decides she doesn't have that power, it's going to strike a note that could be dangerous."

" 'Tolerate'?"

"Wrong word. But you get the concept."

After her time with Teresa Romano, Jane wasn't stupid enough not to realize Caleb's theory had merit. The woman had to believe she was superior in every way, and the path that Caleb was walking was very dangerous. "Will you be able to save Haroun?"

"Possibly."

Her gaze flew to his face. "But you're not sure."

"How could I be? I haven't looked the situation over yet."

That was too vague for her. "But you'll try?"

"I'll try," he said. "But I told Teresa the truth. I don't care anything about Haroun. If it comes to a choice between you and him, he'll die, Jane."

"No! It doesn't work that way, Caleb."

"For me, it does," he said simply. "I said I'd try. Take it or leave it. He won't have any chance at all if I have to take another path."

"I'm just supposed to accept that a man might have to die so that I can live?"

His lips tightened. "I won't let you die, Jane."

"He might have people who don't want him to die, either. Does he?"

He didn't answer.

"I don't even know anything about him." She met his eyes. "But you do, don't you? He's not just a name to you. You probably know everything about him. After all, he's the target."

"Not everything."

"Enough," she said jerkily. "Tell me about him."

"I don't think that's a good idea."

"I don't care what you think. He's no target to me. He's a man who could die to keep me alive. *Tell* me."

He hesitated. Then he called up a photo on his phone and handed it to her. It was a strong face, bearded, with a faint scar beneath his left eye. The man was smiling and those dark eyes were full of intelligence. "Tarik El Haroun. Age forty-eight. Born into a middle-class family here in Dubai. Muslim. But he had a principally Western upbringing from the time he was a teenager. Attended Yale University and then came home to Dubai and started to build his empire. During the last twenty years, he's increased the economy of Dubai enormously. Fair business practices. Extremely charitable. Has one wife, Fatima. Married fifteen years. No children."

"Caleb," she whispered. She couldn't take her eyes from that photo.

"I told you that I didn't want to tell you about him," he said quietly. "I can't promise you, Jane."

She gazed at him in frustration. "Then find a way that *I* can help him. He's an innocent man."

"Innocent . . . I doubt if that's an accurate description for any of us. Innocence is generally lost before one reaches puberty." His lips twisted. "But you're going to be difficult about this. I can see it. It's not as if I'm not going to have enough trouble with Lisa. No, you *cannot* help him. But I'll redouble my efforts to get him out of this alive. Will that —"

"Lisa?" She had caught that one sentence and it had terrified her. "What about Lisa?"

"She's here in Dubai."

"What?"

"She was struck with guilt and various other emotions and insisted I bring her along."

"And you did it?" She gazed at him in horror. "You're an *idiot.*"

"That may be true. But I had no recourse.

It was bring her or have her come by herself. I dropped her off at the border and had Palik pick her up and take her to the hotel."

"And what if Santara gets his hands on her again? I worked so hard to keep this from happening. She was *safe,* Caleb."

"And you were not. To use that word that offended you so much, Lisa would not tolerate it. She appears to have a fondness for you that totally baffles me."

She could feel the tears sting her eyes. "You should have stopped her. It was a mistake."

"As you can see, I do make them on occasion. But all I can do is the best I'm able. She would have come after you on her own, Jane."

She could see that happening, but it didn't make her feel any better. "We have to keep her safe. I won't forgive myself if anything happens to her."

Caleb was shaking his head. "Everyone has to be kept safe? Haroun, Lisa. Where do you figure in this, Jane?"

"Maybe behind you," she said shakily. "I won't lose you either, Caleb."

His smile vanished. "How generous of you to include me. An unexpected honor."

"Be quiet." She blinked back the tears.

"You came here to try to save me. Okay, I don't like the way you're doing it. But you could *die,* dammit. And I'm not supposed to care whether you do?"

"Oh, I approve. Because I'm certain that I'll do something soon that will nullify all my good deeds in your eyes."

"Probably." She swallowed hard. "As long as it's not something that will get someone killed. Don't do that, Caleb."

"I'll be very selective." He frowned. "I don't like to see you this upset. It bothers me." He got to his feet. "And now I'd better get back to Lisa at the hotel and make certain she's not being troublesome for Palik. She promised she'd do as I told her, but she might have had her fingers crossed."

"She was very good when she was with me at the lake. She did exactly what I asked her to do. My only complaint was that she did too much."

"I rest my case."

"When will you be back?"

"Tomorrow afternoon. Try to rest. I don't think Teresa will bother you."

"As long as I don't antagonize her?"

"That's right. We have to make sure that she's happy and content with herself." His eyes were suddenly glittering with mischief. "Which reminds me that you don't look at all like a femme fatale I can't keep my hands off. I think we have to correct that image."

Her eyes widened. "Not necessary."

"Oh yes." He fell to his knees in front of her. "I'm sure Teresa will be in to see you after I leave. We have to keep the image intact, don't we?" He was swiftly unbuttoning her blouse. "Just a tiny bit of foreplay that will make you look the part. There's no one who looks more beautifully sensual than you do after you've been touched."

He was so close, she could catch the clean scent of him. She could feel that electric magnetism that always surrounded him. His hands were moving deftly and her bra was suddenly gone. "Bullshit." She could barely force the words out for the heat that was tingling through her. "You're taking advantage —" She inhaled sharply as his hands cupped her bare breasts. "Not fair, Caleb."

His fingers were tugging at her nipples. "But you're so grateful to me, remember? This is only part of my doing my duty. Think of it like that." His breath was hot on her nipple and then he was nibbling, sucking, biting.

She cried out and her back arched as she lunged upward.

"Shh, just a little more." His mouth enveloped her and he shook his head, making her feel both pressure and force.

One minute.

Two minutes.

She was only aware of sensation, suction, movement, hunger. . . .

He was leaving her, she realized. She instinctively reached out for him.

"No." He held her down and rubbed his cheeks back and forth on her breasts. "You'd just be angry with me later." He got to his feet. "You'll be annoyed with me anyway, but not too bad." He stood looking down at her. "Beautiful," he said softly. "Shining. Glowing. Mine." He turned and headed for the door. "I'll see you tomorrow, Jane."

She lay there unable to move as the door closed behind him.

Damn him.

She slowly sat up, put on her bra, and started buttoning up her blouse. Her hands were shaking. *She* was shaking. She had been upset and emotional before it had erupted into this sexual chaos. Now all she could think about was sex. Was that Caleb's intention? she thought suddenly. Who knew what he was thinking. At least her nerves didn't feel as shredded as before. And anger and exasperation had replaced the tears.

"You satisfied him?" Teresa was standing

in the doorway, gazing at her. "Yes, I can see you did. You're practically melting." She came forward. "You're a fool, you know. He'll always be too much for you. I can't understand what it is he sees in you."

Don't antagonize her, Jane thought, remembering what Caleb had said. "Yet here I am and you brought me here. You could let me go."

"That's not an option. I'm just telling you that if you live through this, you should leave him."

"So that he won't get what he wants?" she asked softly. "It's killing you that you have to deal with someone who has so much power over you. I don't think you would have done it if you'd seen any other way."

"As I said, you're a fool. You don't know anything. He has no power. Only what I choose to give him. I'm the one who was always in control." Her eyes were blazing, her hands clenched. "From the beginning, he was only a tool for me to use. I used him well and then I threw him away."

"Did you?"

"I said it, didn't I?"

Yes, she had, and the picture Jane was seeing was sending the rage searing through her. Teresa's view might be completely skewed, but her intentions were not. She had wanted to use a boy, twist his psyche, when he had already been mistreated in the most horrendous and painful ways possible. The fact that boy had been Caleb made it even more terrible in Jane's eyes. At the moment, she couldn't separate that boy from the Caleb she had known all these years. She wanted to *hurt* this woman as she had hurt that young boy.

Teresa took another step forward. Her voice was taunting. "Why aren't you saying anything?"

To hell with it. "There's nothing to say." Jane lifted her chin and glared at her. "Because you're so terribly obvious, Teresa. He wasn't the tool, and you know it. You went up against something you didn't know how to handle. And all through the years it's been the same. It's been gnawing at you, so you tried to ignore him. But you can't do it, can you? You still don't know who he is or how you can handle him. And it's driving you crazy that you think I might."

"That's a joke."

"Maybe. But I don't think so. Because it doesn't change the one fact that you're broadcasting loud and clear." She'd already said too much and she'd say more if she didn't get out of here. Sorry, Caleb. She got to her feet and headed for the bathroom.

"And what is that?" Teresa asked through set teeth.

Jane couldn't resist it. She struck out one more time in the way that could hurt Teresa the most. "Why, that you're sick with jealousy, Teresa." She went into the bathroom and slammed the door. She leaned against it, breathing hard. Precisely what Caleb had warned her against. His fault. She hadn't been able to take what he told her about the life he'd led all those years ago.

No, her fault. She'd reacted with the same heat and recklessness she'd previously warned Lisa of showing with Santara. But Jane had maturity and she should have been able to control herself. Now, by holding up a mirror to Teresa Romano, she had earned her hatred.

But the hatred is only for me. Caleb will be able to take care of himself, she told herself. If there were going to be repercussions, she'd be the one to suffer them.

And then she'd only be back to where she'd been in the beginning — facing her own responsibility for getting herself out of this nightmare and not relying on Caleb or Lisa or anyone else.

She went to the sink and splashed water on her face. If she stayed here for a few minutes, the probability was that Teresa would have left the room when she came back out. That vengeful anger would still exist, but who knew if it wouldn't have been there anyway. The queen bee must have no rivals, even if she'd arranged and manipulated to use Jane.

She decided to spend the evening resting and healing and then go out on the balcony and try to see where Santara's men who had been ordered to shoot her on sight were located. And worry about what Caleb could do to keep Lisa from making the same reckless mistakes as she had just made.

Grand Hyatt Hotel
Dubai

"How is she?" Lisa ran out of the bedroom the minute she heard Caleb's key in the lock. "Was Teresa telling you the truth?"

"About Jane? Yes. She'll be fine by tomorrow." He was looking around the suite. "Are you alone? Where's Palik?"

"Here." Palik was coming out of the kitchenette. "Your sister was asking too many questions and not accepting no for an answer, so I decided to make myself a drink to get away from her."

"I told him that you'd tell me anyway. It

was just about the hospital and this Haroun," she said impatiently. "I thought maybe I could do something about seeing Haroun and finding out more about him." She added quickly, "If that's what you want."

"Big if," he said drily. "What's Lisa doing in this suite, Palik? I told you not to put her anywhere near me. I'm being watched."

"She's in the penthouse, above this floor. But it can be reached by the same service elevator. She insisted that she had to be close to you." He made a face. "She's a pain in the ass, Caleb. I didn't sign on for this."

"Yes, you did. Keeping her alive is the most important job you have."

"No," Lisa said quietly. "Keeping *you* alive is his most important job. I'm not the one running around dodging Santara, and playing Teresa's games. So that's his job and mine, too. I'll be a pain in the ass until this is over. I'll just be *your* pain in the ass and I'll never be stupid." Then she was smiling sweetly at Palik. "And I'll do everything you tell me as long as it makes sense. You were treating me like a kid. Okay?"

"Maybe." He shrugged. "Do you want me to order room service, Caleb?"

"No," Lisa answered for him. "Not until I go back upstairs. He won't want anyone to know that he had a visitor in the suite. You could make some coffee." She made a face. "But not that thick black stuff. I've never been able to take it."

He stared at her for a moment. "It's a fine brew once you get used to it. What does a kid know?" He disappeared back into the kitchen.

"Treat him gently," Caleb said. "He's smart and useful, Lisa. Did he check the suite for bugs?"

"Yes, right away." She smiled. "Even the terrace and hall. That impressed me. I'll see that we get along, Seth. We had a rough beginning because I was so afraid for you when you left me. It made me . . . a little aggressive. When are you going to tell me what's happening?"

"Right away." He brushed his lips across her cheek. "I have to call Joe Quinn. Come out on the terrace and you can sit with me and calm down a little."

"I'm fine now."

"No, your blood is still pounding too hard and your pulse is —"

"Okay. Okay." She followed him out on the covered terrace and dropped down in an orange-and-beige chair. "I'm *almost* fine now. Why didn't you call Joe in the car coming here?"

"The car was bugged. I have to expect that wherever I go now. Teresa will want to know that I'm not doing anything that isn't in accordance with our agreement. I had to wait until I was in a place I could trust was safe."

"But you're not safe anywhere now," she whispered. "You told me that Teresa is the one we had to worry about, but it's hard for me to take it in. All those years when she was my guardian, I never realized that she was anything but a spoiled woman who only wanted to use me to increase her social status. I was impatient with her, even a little contemptuous, but I never thought she was any kind of threat."

"And she might not have been if she hadn't felt threatened herself. I thought you'd probably reach your majority and walk away from her with no bad effects." He shrugged as he took out his phone. "It didn't happen. So now we have to make the adjustment." He punched in Joe's number. "I'll put it on speaker so that I won't have to brief you afterward."

"Brief me? That sounds like a military operation." She grinned. "And you said 'we.' Are you starting to accept me?"

"I wouldn't have let you come if I hadn't accepted that you had to be used," he said soberly. "And because I may not be able to

505

protect you, we have to find ways to keep everyone alive." He made a rueful face. "Jane gave me a list of everyone who has to be saved from Teresa Romano and Santara." Joe Quinn was picking up the phone and Caleb spoke into it. "Caleb. I was just with Jane. She's not badly injured. A wrenched neck and bruises. Probably a mild concussion, but it's not too serious and shouldn't even give her a headache past today."

"Thank God." Quinn was silent. "But you gave me the present report. What do we have to worry about in the future?"

"Enough. I have to do a job for Teresa Romano, and if I screw it up or don't perform it to her satisfaction, then she'll probably be delighted to kill us both."

"Then do it right, dammit."

"Oh, I will, but Jane's put a roadblock in my plans and is insisting that I don't commit a murder to get her away from Teresa."

"Murder?"

Caleb briefly filled him in on the Haroun operation. Then he added quietly, "You knew what Teresa would ask me, Quinn."

"Yes. I had an idea."

"And you're reluctant, but like me, you feel Jane is the first priority."

"Yes." Another silence. "How can we get

around it?"

"Tricky sidestepping. And you on hand to snatch Jane away at the crucial moment. The operation is to take place day after tomorrow. I need you here before that. Okay?"

"Of course it's okay," he said roughly. "I'm on my way. Tell me where and when I can help."

"I'll know details after I look over the hospital tomorrow." He added, "And be prepared to grab Lisa, as well." He met Lisa's indignant glare across the room. "At that point, her part in the operation will be over and she'll just be in the way."

"I don't know why you let her go anyway. Eve and Cara were upset as hell when they read that note you left."

"What could I do?" Caleb asked mockingly. "I needed help. You and Eve are so besotted with the idea of family helping family. Lisa is family."

"Bullshit," Joe said. "She blackmailed you?"

"Yes." He smiled at Lisa. "But I'm becoming accustomed to the idea. I'm just putty in her hands. I'll call you tomorrow, Quinn." He ended that call.

Lisa made a rude sound. " 'Putty'?"

"Yes." He got to his feet. "Now come in

and have that coffee."

Lisa stood up. "I'm not leaving you. Joe can take care of Jane after we get her away from them. I stay with you."

"We'll see how it works out. You came to help Jane. First duty." He said softly, "You can't have it all your own way. Promise me. First duty."

She was frowning. She was silent.

"Promise me."

"I promise," she said grudgingly. "First duty."

"Good. Now come and have coffee and I'll tell you what you have to do tomorrow. You'll get to put on that hideous black robe and veil and scout all of the women's wellness section of the hospital. I'll expect a full report on where every door and closet is located."

"You could do it yourself." She was smiling at the thought. "Those outfits are so smothering and cumbersome, you can't really tell if they're worn by a man or woman. I'd like to see you in one."

"I imagine you would. You'd probably take photos. But as Eve would say, family is everything, and I'm going to make certain that I let you do your part. . . ."

CHAPTER 18

"You're looking better." Caleb's gaze was narrowed on Jane's face. "A little color and you're more rested." As he spoke, he was walking around the bedroom, checking for bugs. "Teresa seemed a bit short when I arrived. Is there a reason?"

"You know there is," Jane said tersely. "You're checking for bugs again. I've been in here most of the time. They wouldn't have had time to install anything new."

"I don't believe in 'most.' " He put away the device. "And even if you were here, there are bugs that can be put in air ducts from outside a room. Teresa likes her gadgets." He sat down. "But you're still clear. Now tell me why she's angry?"

"I said the wrong thing. What does it matter?"

509

"It matters. You must have said exactly the thing that would piss her off. What was it?"

"I'm not going to tell you. It's over and I just have to deal with the fallout." She met his eyes. "Me. Not you. You're still her golden boy."

"Never that. Perhaps her favorite demon."

"Then just keep her from sending you back to hell." She grimaced. "And if there's a problem, just stay out of it and give me a chance to make a run for it."

"I intend to go along with the last instruction on your list." His lips tightened. "I wish you'd done what I asked. She's not as confident as she pretends and she's likely to strike out to prove herself. You may become her target of choice."

"I never intended to try to annoy her. I just did it. She said something I found I couldn't bear." She shrugged. "I regret it, but I'm not sorry."

He was silent. "If it's something that hurt you that much, I'm not sorry, either." He smiled. "We'll just have to find a way to keep her from arranging to cut your throat."

"I'd appreciate that." She drew a deep breath. "What's happening? Did you go to the hospital this morning?"

He nodded. "The best place for me to be

stationed is the stairwell outside the fourth-floor operating room. I'll be close enough to where the operation is going on to be able to control it, and it's a good escape route to the elevator on the third floor. If there's too much commotion going on, there's a linen closet on the third floor where I can stay until it's safe for me to leave the hospital. There are bound to be guards all over the place both before and after, but I can get around them."

"How, for God's sake?"

"I'll manage," he said. "And there will be a lot of turmoil if Haroun doesn't make it."

She stiffened. "But he's going to make it. You said that you'd try to make sure of it."

"Yes, I did. And I will. But I've never gone back on the main priority, Jane."

"*Please,* Caleb."

"I'll do what I can," he said, then added, "But even Quinn agrees that one has to weigh every decision."

"Leave Joe out of this."

"I can't because I've already arranged for him to be here in Dubai to whisk you out of the country. Quinn won't be left out of that without doing me bodily harm." He held up his hand as she started to speak. "I've just told Teresa that I want you driven to the parking garage adjoining the hospital at nine in the morning. I've told her that I want to look you over and make certain that they've not done anything else to harm you before I go through with the kill. Haroun's operation is at ten. She'll expect word before ten-thirty that he's died on the table. When she gets word I've done my part in her plan, she's to release you immediately, let you get out of the car to walk down to the exit ramp to the street, where Palik will pick you up."

"And you think she'll do it?"

He was silent. "She might, but after seeing her this morning, I wouldn't get my hopes up. But you'll at least be away from this house and Teresa and Santara's men. You'll be safe enough in that parking garage because Teresa won't want any incidents to raise red flags while they're investigating Haroun's death."

"A body tucked in the trunk wouldn't raise a red flag, would it?" she asked wryly.

"It would if there was a search. Teresa won't allow anything to spoil her big score. Even if she doesn't order your release, she won't have you killed until she thinks she's found a safe place to do it. I'll have Quinn and Palik watching that parking garage from the building across the street, and the minute they see you exit, they'll be on your tail."

"Well then, I have nothing to worry about, do I?" she asked flippantly. "I'm glad that I have someone so cool and collected in control. You're always able to —"

"Control?" His hands were suddenly grasping her arms. "I'm getting tired of having that word thrown at me." His dark eyes were glittering in his taut face. "I'm not at all collected and certainly not cool at the moment. I *hate* this."

She inhaled sharply as she looked at him. Darkness. Fire. Desperation. She'd seen the first two many times before, but she'd never seen desperation. And she knew she was responsible for it.

"I was joking because I was scared," she said unsteadily. "And I used that description because it sometimes defines you. You know that, Caleb. And, right now, I appreciate cool and collected."

He was staring into her eyes and she couldn't tell what he was thinking. His grasp tightened and then his hands dropped from her shoulders. "Then that's what you'll get." He turned away. "But none of this will take place until they get word that Haroun is dead. You'll be safe until after that happens." She couldn't see his face, but the muscles of his spine appeared taut, knotted. "And I can't be the one to be there for you then. It will all go down too fast. Then it will be up to Quinn and Lisa to get you away from them. And it might mean that even if they can save you from Teresa and Santara, they may have to make a run for the airport and get you out of the country. Dubai might not be safe for you."

"You're talking about Haroun dying," she said harshly. "Or you being arrested and the police searching for accomplices."

"I'm talking about possibilities." He turned to face her and his smile was mocking, as usual. "In my cool and collected way. That's how it's going to go down."

"But it's not cut in stone," she said desperately. "You're still trying to find a way so that it won't happen."

He nodded. "As I said, there's a possibility. I'm very, very good. There's always a chance."

She gazed at him in despair. "And if that chance doesn't work, Haroun will die and you might get shot in that damn stairwell and Teresa will be overjoyed and fly off to Russia with her loot."

He nodded. "But you'll have your chance to be free and alive. I'm trusting Quinn to make sure of it." He stood up. "That's the only thing you can count on, Jane." He reached out and touched her cheek with gossamer gentleness. "I'll see you tomorrow."

"Caleb, don't you —"

"Shh, trust me. I know it's hard for you, but I might be able to pull it off." He headed for the door. "Tomorrow . . ."

Grand Hyatt Hotel
Tuesday, 2:30 P.M.

"What the hell are we supposed to do, Caleb?" Joe asked as he strode into Lisa's penthouse suite with Palik trailing several steps behind. "I don't like any of the things you told me over the phone when I was coming here from the airport. Is there any way that we can just go to Teresa Romano's house and stage a raid and get Jane out? I talked to Palik and he said he could supply enough men."

"We could do it. I've already set it up as a backup plan," Caleb said. "Hell, I'd love to do it. But Jane probably wouldn't survive it. Santara isn't wonderfully bright, but he's cunning, and his first instinct is to kill any hostage rather than give the person up. And Teresa wouldn't put any barriers in his way if she thought she was going to lose what she's fighting for. Jane's managed to make an enemy of her."

"Shit."

"Seth said that getting her away from the parking garage would be easier," Lisa said. "Though I like your way better, too, Joe."

"I'm sure you do," Caleb said. "Explosions and gunfire and direct assault. What's not to like? Except that Jane would end up dead."

"Don't say that. She's *not* going to die," Lisa said. She drew a deep breath. "Okay, whatever you think will work."

"Quinn?"

Joe looked at him without speaking for a moment. "And do you think that we can make it work, Caleb?"

"It can work. It will depend on a lot of different elements and some luck." He met Joe's eyes. "But it's no slam dunk. She could still die." He added harshly, "And I won't even be able to reach out and help her. It will all be in your court, Quinn."

Joe was gazing at his face. "And that's going to kill you," he said softly.

"Who, me? I'm completely cool and collected about all this. Ask Jane. As I said, it's in your court."

Joe's lips twisted. "Well, if that's the case, I'm going to spend the evening gathering information and making certain we'll be able to spot Jane and keep track of her when they take her into that parking garage. I'll set up video cameras in that office building across the street where we're staking out the garage to catch every entrance and exit. I'm also going to keep on working on that backup strategy." He turned to Palik. "I want to know how many men I can count on if Caleb's plan comes crashing down on us. Come and talk to me about numbers."

"Not now," Caleb said as he headed for the door. "I'm going to need him for the next few hours. You can have him later."

Palik made a face as he followed Caleb out into the hall. "I'd be flattered to be so popular if I didn't think it might cause me to end up in an alley with my throat cut."

"So much for the ball being in my court," Joe said wryly to Lisa as the door closed behind them. "I was afraid of this when I knew I was coming here."

"Seth is used to being on his own. This is hard for him."

"And you think that it's not hard for me?" His lips tightened. "This is Jane. Eve and I consider her our child. We love her. I've got to get her back and I feel as if my hands are tied."

"So do I," Lisa said quietly. "It was

because of me that Jane even became involved with Santara and Teresa, and I'm having to fight to get Seth to let me help her. In spite of what he says, he's not going to let me do anything that has any real risk." She met his eyes. "And I don't think you will either, Joe."

What can I say? Joe thought. She's sitting here looking young and vulnerable and full of life. She's already gone through a hellish experience and now she wants to dive into another one? "I wouldn't have brought you here, Lisa."

"Yes, you would have." She smiled. "I would have found a way to persuade you, Joe."

He shook his head. "You're too young. You have no experience. I'd feel guilty as hell asking you to do something that could get you killed."

"So you won't do it. I knew that would be your reaction. But I thought that I should tell you a few things that might make you feel better if I override you." She held up three fingers. "I'm in excellent physical shape now, though I'm having to build up my endurance again. I can swim like a fish. I know how to shoot a pistol, but I'm much better with a rifle, since I took part in the Olympic biathlon ski and shoot tryouts at my school in Switzerland." She smiled. "Not great qualifications if I were applying to be a SEAL, like you were, but adequate for emergency situations."

He grinned. "I'm sure you'd be more than adequate."

"But you'd still hesitate when it came right down to it." She shrugged. "I do have other . . . skills. But I'm not going to be able to convince you, so I won't go into them." She got to her feet. "So suppose I get you a cup of coffee and then we can talk about those video cameras that you're going to need to set up. I'm very good with cameras. I took a photography course before I went on last year's field trip to Venice."

"Why does that not surprise me? No hard feelings?"

"A little. I want this, Joe." She looked over her shoulder at him. "But you *care* about me. You *care* about Jane. I . . . like that. I think Jane must be very lucky."

She disappeared into the kitchen.

JW Marriott Marquis Hotel
Dubai
Tuesday, 5:40 P.M.

"There he is," Palik murmured as he met Caleb's gaze in the rearview mirror from

519

where he was sitting in the driver's seat of the silver Maserati Quattroporte. "Why do I feel this is going to be a total disaster?"

"Because you're a natural pessimist." Caleb watched Tarik El Haroun stride from the entrance of the tallest hotel in the world, make his way across the impressive tiles, pass the fountain, and come in their direction. "It will be fine. We have Haroun's car, and you're in the appropriate chauffeur's uniform. The doorman will open the car door for Haroun. Haroun will get in and you'll take off."

"He's supposed to get in *after* he sees you're in the backseat?" Palik asked skeptically.

"Yes. Since the windows are blacked out, it will take him a few seconds to adjust his eyes. But he's going to feel suddenly faint and he'll only think of getting out of the sun and sitting down."

"He's one of the most important men in Dubai. The royal family considers him a national asset. And you're just going to scoop him up?" Palik was shaking his head. "It's got to fail."

"No, it won't," he murmured. "I can't afford that."

The doorman was rushing forward toward Haroun with a broad smile. Haroun smiled and tipped him as the man opened the rear door of the Maserati.

Then Haroun's smile faded as he gasped and dropped onto the backseat.

"Go!" Caleb said.

Palik pressed the accelerator and the car jumped forward. In seconds, they were out of the driveway and speeding down the street.

Haroun was crumpled back in the seat, his hand clutching his chest. He was gasping with pain as he suddenly focused on Caleb on the seat beside him. "Who . . . are you? Never mind. I think I'm having a heart attack. Get me to a hospital."

"No, you're not. You'll be better soon. I released the pressure," Caleb said. "I had to do something to distract you, and this seemed the most efficient way. You're extremely difficult to approach, Haroun, and I needed a few hours alone with you."

Haroun's breathing was beginning to ease. "Who . . . are you?" he asked again. He shook his head to clear it. "Is this a kidnapping? Did you bribe someone to put something in my coffee at that luncheon to cause this damn pain?"

"No, to both questions."

"Terrorists?" His gaze flew to Palik. "Where's my chauffeur, Hakim? If you've hurt him, I'll have every police officer in Dubai on your trail."

"Only a minor wound," Caleb said. "He's very loyal and he put up a good fight. You must use him as a bodyguard as well as a chauffeur. He wouldn't give up, so I had to put him out for a while."

"How badly is he hurt?"

"He'll be fine." He smiled faintly. "But Jane would be impressed you're so concerned over an employee. I sincerely hope that I'm going to be able to work with you."

"That won't happen," Haroun bit out the words. "And who is this Jane, another accomplice?"

"No, perhaps your savior. You certainly need one. It depends entirely on you."

Haroun began to curse.

"It's definitely going to be a disaster," Palik said gloomily.

"He doesn't believe you'll be cooperative, Haroun," Caleb said. "I hope he's wrong."

"I don't cooperate with criminals. What do you want from me?"

"I'll explain it all to you. We're going to take you to a small house near the bazaar and I'll give you explanations and a small demonstration that will show you what I can do and don't want to do. Then we'll talk about cooperation."

"All your threats won't intimidate me. This world is full of bullies, and if I give in to them, then they'll be the ones who will turn out ruling it. I don't want to live in a world like that."

"A fine philosophy, if a little hazardous." Caleb smiled. "I'm trying to avoid threats and appeal to your good sense instead. Though I can't deny the threat exists, I want to be on your side."

"Then pull over and let me go."

"Two hours. Just give me two hours. I'll tell you my story and you'll learn that you have more enemies than you dream exist. And then you'll live to go home to your wife tonight."

"I'll give you nothing. Your driver is right. This move will bring you nothing but disaster."

Strength. Stubbornness. Idealism. This was going to be even more difficult than Caleb had thought. His talent for persuasiveness could usually change perceptions and sway opinions, but Haroun was going to be a massive challenge in a situation like this. "I won't accept that from either of you. She wants you to stay alive." He stared Haroun in the eye and said softly, "So I'm no longer asking. You'll definitely give me my two hours, Haroun."

■ ■ ■ ■

Haroun lived on the outskirts of Dubai in a beautiful two-story home with three fountains cascading down a rock wall. Palik pulled up at least a hundred yards from the front gate.

Caleb got out and went around the car to open Haroun's door. "As promised." He stepped aside as Haroun got out of the car. "Have a good evening. Tell your wife I'm sorry I made you late for dinner."

Haroun stood there, staring at him. "You're a formidable man, Caleb. In more ways than one."

"It was only a little bit of pain. I had to show you that you were vulnerable. If not tomorrow, then another day, another place. It would be so easy for me. But I don't want it to be me. So if you'll do as I want, I'll promise that it won't be and that I'll give you fringe benefits."

"And I'm supposed to believe you?"

"You *do* believe me." He smiled. "I got that far. I'm not certain I overcame that streak of bullheadedness. That could still tip the scales against me."

"How can I possibly trust you? You haven't even given me any names."

"I gave you mine. I don't mind the risk, but I'm not going to let your version of a SWAT team barge in and get Jane killed."

"You know I could cancel the surgery tomorrow."

"Yes, and that would put me in a corner. You don't want to do that."

"I can make certain that I have enough protection so that you couldn't get close to me while the operation takes place."

"That's a possibility."

"Or I could alert the guards at the hospital that you're a threat and they'd hunt you down and blow your head off."

"Also a solution."

"And you're still going to let me go into the house?"

He nodded. "At some point, I have to trust who and what I am." He turned and got into the passenger seat next to Palik. "But I have to warn you, no matter how this plays out, if it puts Jane into more danger because she wanted you to stay alive, then you're a dead man." He motioned for Palik to go. "Think long and hard, Haroun. I hope you make the right choice."

"It's time to go, Jane," Teresa said as she threw open the bedroom door. She was wearing an elegant white suit and long pearls; a Vuitton leather carry-on was sitting on the floor beside her. Her blue eyes were sparkling and she was flushed, glowing with satisfaction. "It's a new start for me. Today I erase all the failures of the past. Now you'll see how well I can handle Caleb." She smiled maliciously. "In spite of everything he says about being in control, he's dangling like a puppet on my strings." She looked over her shoulder at Santara. "Take her. You have your orders. You've already taken care of that other small matter?"

"No problem."

"Good. Then when you call and tell me that Haroun is dead, I'll transfer the final fee into your Cayman account. When you meet me at the airport, I'll give you cash for these additional little jobs."

"It had better be the correct amount, or I'll be following you to Moscow." His gaze shifted to Jane and he moved forward to cuff her wrists in front of her. "Here we are again. I've missed you."

She ignored him and turned to Teresa.

"You're still going through with it? It's crazy, you know. Nothing's happened to make you change your mind?"

"What could do that? Haroun is being prepped for the operation now. Of course, it appears that the guards have been doubled and the hospital is under alert, but we expected that to happen. Haroun is such an important man. I talked to Caleb earlier and he said it won't affect the job, though it will make it more difficult." She smiled again. "He wanted me to assure you that he needed to take care of Haroun to make you as safe as he'd promised you'd be. And that it would be done." Her smile deepened as she stared into Jane's eyes. "So that's what I'm doing. Just obeying him one last time. Good-bye, Jane. It's been interesting." Teresa turned and swept out of the room.

Jane felt a cold chill as she stared after her.

Hatred.

Teresa was going to kill her.

That was as clear to Jane as if she'd put it into words instead of that farewell that had dripped of self-satisfaction and malice.

"Come along. We don't want to be late," Santara said as he pushed her toward the door. "The queen bitch won't be pleased if I don't let this Caleb get his final glimpse of you so that he'll complete the kill."

And it will be after that glimpse that Santara will kill me, Jane thought. When the word came that Haroun had died on the operating table, he would take care of that one more task before he got his money.

Haroun. She felt suddenly sick. Caleb had told her he would try, but he'd made no promise. He'd only promised her she'd have her chance to live.

And Teresa was going to make sure that she would not.

And what about Caleb? Security had been doubled. After Haroun died, there would be craziness and Caleb would be in the thick of it.

After Haroun died.

Don't think about it, she told herself. All she could do was pray for him now. And pray for Caleb's soul for making that terrible choice.

Then try not to let Teresa win by allowing the woman to kill her. Santara didn't realize that she suspected that Teresa was going to betray the deal she'd made with Caleb and kill her. There might be a way that she could use that.

Two of Santara's men were digging behind the shrubbery in the garden.

She stopped short as she and Santara

reached the Mercedes, and her gaze fixed on the black tarp-wrapped bundle lying on the ground beside the men shoveling.

Santara smiled as he waved at a giant bald-headed man who was overseeing the burial. "Just a little bonus job that Teresa authorized. Evidently she thought that the money she received for Haroun was enough for one but not for two."

"Gino Romano," Jane said dully, her eyes on that tarp. "She's tying up loose ends."

He opened the passenger door and pushed her inside. "He was useless to her. He was a weak link. I could see it coming."

Jane hadn't seen it coming. She hadn't even seen Teresa Romano's husband since she'd been brought here. He'd clearly stayed in the background and let his wife handle everything, as he'd done all through the years.

And she'd handled her husband's own death with the same efficiency as everything else that she'd wanted to put behind her.

Now you'll see how well I can handle Caleb.

Jane stiffened in shock as the words Teresa'd spoken before she left came blasting back to her.

It's a new start for me.

Today I erase all the failures of the past.

And Caleb had been a major failure for Teresa.

So that would mean Jane would not be the only one scheduled to die today.

American Hospital, Dubai
10:10 A.M.

"Where is that bastard?" Santara muttered as he drove up and around the ramps of the third-floor parking garage. His gaze searched behind the multitude of cars parked on either side of the row. "He was supposed to be here when I got here. It's after ten and he should have already done the job."

"Maybe he thought he had something more important to do than keep to your schedule," Jane said. But she was looking for Caleb, too. She needed to see him. The world was spinning and it all seemed that it was in a purely downward spiral. "Or maybe he changed his mind and went directly to the fourth-floor operating room."

"I thought he'd end up there anyway," Santara said sourly. "That bitch Teresa tried to sell me a bill of goods about how he can do some kind of blood voodoo, but I know better. That's all bullshit. He's probably try-ing to sneak something into the anesthesia.

That's what I'd do." He scowled. "And I'd do it better than Caleb. She should have given the job to me."

"You appear to be very busy," she said drily. "So she had to rely on someone who obviously doesn't have your intellect or skill."

"Sarcasm?" He shot her a look. "Did I tell you how happy I am that we're able to be together today? It's going to be — There he is!" The brakes screeched as he stomped down on them as Caleb walked out of the line of cars parked on the left side of the row. "Caleb!" He pulled into a parking space and stuck his head out the window. "Get over here. Where the hell have you been? You're damn late."

"I'll ignore your rudeness. As it happens, I was making sure the third-floor linen closet was unlocked. I'm going to need to use it after poor Haroun breathes his last breath."

"He should have breathed it ten minutes ago. Teresa wants the job done. You wanted to see Jane MacGuire? Here she is. Not a mark on her."

"I see she is here." He came over to Jane's window. "But she still has a mark or two from your previous encounter with her. I want to make sure that Teresa's been keeping to the terms of our agreement. She was a trifle irritated with Jane yesterday. Roll down the window, Jane."

"That would be difficult." She held up her cuffed wrists. "Santara seems to be afraid of what I'll do to him."

"Roll down her window, Santara."

Santara rolled down the passenger-side window.

"Now take those cuffs off her. She's uncomfortable."

Santara pressed his gun against her side. "The hell I will."

"He *is* afraid of you, Jane. How amusing." Caleb's smile faded. "But somehow I'm not amused. I don't like to see Jane that helpless except with me. Take off the cuffs and give them to me. Or I'll stand here until you do. I guarantee Teresa will be getting very nervous when that operation upstairs goes on and on with no finality. As you remarked, I'm already running a little past her desired schedule for Haroun and should have been up there ten minutes ago to take care of him."

Santara glared at him. "I have an orderly on the payroll who's working that fourth floor today. The minute Asad Kadir knows that Haroun is dead, he'll call me. If he doesn't call me, you won't have to worry about this bitch feeling helpless because of a pair of handcuffs. You've got Teresa snowed, but I know you're a phony."

"Do you?" Caleb crossed his arms over his chest. "If I had time, we'd discuss it. Or maybe we do, because I'm not moving until you do what I want."

Santara cursed, reached for Jane's cuffs, unlocked them, and threw the cuffs at Caleb.

He caught them and dropped them in his jacket pocket. "Now sit still, Jane, and let me see if they've done any damage." He moved her head back and forth, examining her face and head for bruises. Then his hands were lifting her hair and gently moving her neck back and forth. "This strain seems better."

She suddenly stiffened as she felt something cold slip down the back of her shirt.

"Did that hurt?" Caleb asked. "I remember that twist was the worst of the injuries."

She swallowed. "Just a little."

Caleb glanced at Santara. "I was very irritated with you about that car wreck."

"Tough. Get the hell out of here."

Caleb took his hands away and stepped back. "It will be extremely tough if you cause me to have any more problems with her treatment. I'm sure Teresa has discussed it with you."

"Get going, Caleb," Jane said suddenly. "Get out of here and do what you have to do. You don't want to annoy any of these people right now. Teresa said this was the day for erasing all the failures of the past. I'm sure Santara agrees with her." She met his eyes. "You may not be afraid of what he'll do right now, but I am."

Caleb was silent and then he nodded and smiled. "Just playing with him a little. If it's bothering you, I'll stop it and head upstairs to do my job." He turned and headed for the stairwell. "Later, Jane . . ."

She knew that he had gotten and translated the warning she had tried to give him. That's all she could do right now.

" 'Later'?" Santara repeated. "That son of a bitch." He looked at Jane. "You're smarter than he is. You should be afraid." He looked at his watch. "And if I haven't heard from Asad in five minutes, then I may cause considerably more damage to that twisted neck."

She moved carefully, shifting only a little as she tried to identify the object Caleb had slipped down the back of her shirt by the feel of it against the flesh of her back.

Cold. Metallic. Slender. Perhaps four or five inches.

A dagger? Too small.

She shifted again.

Not totally made of metal.

Glass or plastic on the top.

A hypodermic needle.

She inhaled sharply. And Caleb would have made sure that the fluid in that hypodermic would be fast-acting and effective.

But how to get it out while Santara was only inches from her with that gun ready?

Carefully. Very carefully.

Caleb was on the phone to Joe Quinn as he took the stairs two at a time back to the fourth floor. "Santara is on the third floor of the parking garage; he's driving a black Mercedes. And he's parked in space thirty-two." He paused, trying to gather his thoughts and subdue the fear. "You may have to be ready to go get Jane and not wait. Get up there where you can see what's going on. Jane tried to let me know that things could be changing, that I may be a target. She said I should be worried *now.* But if I am a target, Santara would have to dispose of her before he'd be free to try to take me out. I didn't think he'd risk that in the parking garage. It doesn't make sense."

Joe was cursing. "How much time do we have?"

"Not long. Maybe five minutes. The minute Santara hears that Haroun is dead, he'll start the cleanup. I managed to slip Jane a hypodermic with curare, a poison. But she may not get a chance to use it. Dammit, I want her *away* from him."

Joe muttered a curse. "Then don't let him get the word that Haroun is dead."

"I *can't* stop it. It's too late. And it won't make a difference. He'll still want to cover his own ass if he thinks that the job's gone bust. If the wait's too long, he'll think I failed. He's leaning in that direction anyway. Let me know when you get up on the third-floor level, where you can see what's going on." He hung up.

Keep calm. Pretend this is just another hunt. Not that Jane was sitting next to Santara with a gun in her ribs. And he had been so damn *close* to him. But even if he'd struck at the arteries of Santana's heart, he might have pulled that trigger before the blood surge did its work.

Count on Joe Quinn.

And pray.

Asad Kadir. Concentrate on the orderly. He'd already zeroed in on Kadir's location in preparation for the move. He was working near the nurses' station, a few doors down from the operating room. Now he only had to locate him.

And keep his mind off Jane's expression that last minute, when he'd turned his back and walked away from her.

"You're shifting around quite a bit." Santara was gazing maliciously down at Jane. "Nervous?"

"Why shouldn't I be?" In the last five minutes, she'd managed to get the hypodermic from her back to the shoulder of her right sleeve, but it would take more active maneuvering to get it down her arm to her hand. "You've not been very encouraging about my chances to get out of this. You're entirely too happy I'm here with you."

He nodded. "I'm very transparent. Of course, I'd be happier if I was to be allowed free rein with you, but the queen bitch is too selfish. You must have managed to annoy her even more than you did me."

"Maybe." She stiffened. "But what do you mean? She's too selfish?"

"She wants the pleasure all for herself."

Jane said drily, "I gather you're not talking about the pleasure of releasing me herself?"

He chuckled. "I think you put two and two together this morning. Teresa has a horror of leaving witnesses. We agree about that."

She had realized that she was going to be a victim, but she'd thought that Teresa would have shunned doing the kill herself. But it seemed that the woman was transforming, developing more fangs and poison as she evolved.

She had the hypodermic down past her shoulder. Just five or six minutes more . . . "I hoped I was wrong."

"Oh no. And I wanted you to realize what she had in store for you even though she told me not to tell you." He smiled. "Did I tell you how I hate her telling me what to do? Someday I may pay her a visit in that palace she's going to build outside Moscow. When she least expects it." He checked his wristwatch. "Asad should have called. I may still be able to toy with you a little and blame it on Caleb. After all, I have to keep —" His phone rang. "Too bad. Want to hear the good news?" He put the call on speaker as he answered. "What's the word, Asad?"

"Dead. Five minutes ago," Asad Kadir said, his voice shaking. "I can't talk long. The soldiers and police are running all over the place, shouting questions and accusations. They're threatening to put the chief surgeon under arrest. Everything's crazy up here."

"How crazy? Did you see Haroun's body?"

"Just for a second. Blood all over his chest. Flatline." His voice was suddenly panicky. "I've got to get out of here. I didn't count on its being like this. I'll contact you later for my money," he said before disconnecting.

Santara turned to Jane. "Success. But I still think Caleb did something with the anesthesia."

Blood all over his chest.

Flatline.

She felt sick herself.

"You're not overjoyed? Teresa will be." He took out his phone and punched in her number. "It's done. Asad just confirmed the death, Teresa. Yes, he's certain. I'll be there as soon as I finish here. That check had better be ready." He glanced at Jane. "Yes, I know what I'm to do. I'm not the fool you treat me like." He hit the disconnect button and smiled. "But I think Asad is correct about ending this quickly. Teresa certainly agrees." He pressed a button on the phone and spoke into the receiver, "You can have her now, Ganlad."

She stiffened, her gaze on his face. "What is this?"

He unlocked her car door again. "This is good-bye. Though I may see you again if we cross paths before I get my money." He got out of the car as the giant bald-headed man she had seen in the garden of Teresa's house came toward him. "This is Victor Ganlad. Perhaps you remember seeing him at Teresa's?" He exchanged car keys with the man. "I have something to do here, but Ganlad followed us and parked down on the second level to wait until I was ready for him. He'll be glad to take over for me and drive you to Teresa's waiting arms."

Caleb, she thought in panic. Santara was going after Caleb. Her hand instinctively flew to the door handle.

"Oops, forgot something." Santara leaned back into the car and his fingers dug into the carotid artery in her neck. "I wouldn't want Ganlad to have any trouble. I might not get my money. Good night, Jane."

Darkness.

CHAPTER 19

The linen closet on the third floor was only marginally safer than the fourth floor, which was in total chaos right now, Caleb realized as he ran down the stairwell from the fourth floor. But the focus would be on that operating room for at least an hour or so. The lack of proof of murder would stop any in-depth floor-to-floor search until someone high in authority took the reins and ordered it.

It didn't matter; he had to be there anyway. Santara had to be taken down. And he didn't have the faintest doubt that Santara would show up in that linen closet, where he thought Caleb would be hiding, within the next few minutes.

His phone vibrated as he reached the third floor.

Quinn.

"She's not *here*," Quinn said. "No Mercedes. No Santara."

Caleb froze. "What?"

"Dammit, you heard me. But I ran across the street and checked the videos of the outgoing cars for the last fifteen minutes. A black Mercedes left the garage five minutes ago. We must have just missed it while we were running up the ramps to get to the third floor. But it wasn't driven by Santara. It was a heavyset man, bald-headed. No sign of a passenger."

"Switched drivers."

"That's what I figured."

No sign of a passenger.

The words had almost paralyzed Caleb. Think.

She could have been slumped over or on the floor in the backseat. She had to be in that car.

"Then Santara might still be here and targeting me," he said. "I'll have to get my hands on him to find out what's happening with Jane. Where are you?"

"In our car, driving up one street and down another, trying to catch sight of the Mercedes." Quinn muttered a curse. "Damn poor chance."

"I'll call you." Caleb pressed the disconnect.

Spotting that Mercedes was not a matter of a poor chance; it would be almost impossible. Think. Okay, the switch in drivers was unexpected, but it didn't mean that Santara was assigning someone else to kill Jane. Caleb knew Santara would prefer to do it himself. So she might still be safe.

Or she might not.

Assume that Jane's first guess was right and Santara had been assigned to kill him.

Go back to square one. And that square was centered on the third-floor linen closet.

He'd give Santara another five minutes before he started going down a blind alley like Quinn was doing now.

Caleb slipped into the linen closet with no problem. All the nurses and other personnel were watching the intercom videos to see what was happening upstairs. It was dim, almost dark, in the deep closet, almost thirty feet long, but he didn't turn on the light. He could make out shelves piled high with sheets and linens, and mops and brooms shoved against the wall. He went to the very back of the closet to wait.

He could feel his heart pounding.

Had he guessed wrong? Was he wasting precious time?

Come on, you son of a bitch.

Let me get at you and rip your heart out.

Three minutes.

Don't think about him not coming.

Think about your strategy when he gets here.

Santara wouldn't use a gun — too much noise. His orders were to not cause anyone to suspect Haroun's death was anything but natural. It was an indication of how much Teresa wanted to rid herself of him that she'd ordered Santara to do the kill at all. So it would probably be a knife. Swift. Silent. Efficient.

Not efficient enough.

He heard the door open quietly.

Yes.

In the dimness he could still make out Santara's sandy hair and spare build as he warily entered the closet.

"Back here, Santara," he called softly. "She must have paid you well to take a chance like this. How are you planning to get rid of my body?"

"A laundry hamper to the basement and then the incinerator." He moved forward cautiously. "It's all set up. Even a bribe in place with the janitor to get rid of the ashes. No one's going to pay any attention to the basement with what's going on up on the fourth floor. She did pay well, but I would have done it for much less. I keep remembering San Leandro and all the things I had to do because that bitch Teresa was so sure

544

that I couldn't be trusted to take you out."

"And you're so sure you can?" He chuckled. "Why do you think she changed her mind? She's willing to take a chance you'll kill me because she wants it so badly. But if you don't, she'll get rid of an expensive hit man who could also be a witness. Did you consider that?"

"No, because I *will* kill you. And I'll take her money and then plan a few surprises for her. So all her plans won't be worth shit."

"How did you get rid of Jane? Who took her?"

"You know about that?" He chuckled. "Worried? I wish I could see your face. Teresa thought she might matter to you."

"Who took her?" he repeated.

"Victor Ganlad, an errand boy suitable for deliveries. Teresa wasn't finished with her." He was moving forward. "Are you ready? Do you know how good I am? Better than some slick con man who has a few tricks and a couple sticks of C-4 explosives. Just tell me one thing. I was right, wasn't I? About you altering that anesthetic?"

"Why don't you come a little closer and find out?"

"Oh, I'm coming." Santara was only a few yards away. The knife in his hand was gleaming in the dimness.

He suddenly dodged to the left and went for the jugular!

But Caleb was no longer there. He'd dropped to the floor and rolled forward, ramming into Santara's knees.

Santara's legs buckled, but he recovered immediately and his knife was plunging down at Caleb even as he fell.

Caleb grabbed his wrist, avoided the blade, and was suddenly on top of Santara. He'd have only seconds, but it should be enough.

One second.

Two seconds.

The arteries in Santara's right wrist exploded!

Caleb's hand covered Santara's mouth to smother his scream. "You wanted an answer," he whispered. "Do you think you have it now?"

Santara was cursing, his eyes on the blood pouring from his wrist.

"I've not compromised all the veins and arteries. I can still stop the blood so that you won't bleed out," Caleb said. "But you'll have to give me answers very quickly, or it will be too late."

Santara was still frantically trying to reach for the knife he'd dropped. Caleb pushed it aside. "You're very stubborn. You'd rather kill me than live? And you might live if you tell me what I need to know. Then who knows if you'll get another chance to slit my throat. You said Jane was being delivered to Teresa Romano. Where is Teresa now? She mentioned an airport but we've checked out Dubai International. No reservations. No sign of commercial or private rentals of any sort. Where is she? Where did you send Jane MacGuire?"

"Stop this damn blood." Santara was panting, his eyes wild as he watched the blood begin to pool on the floor. "I'll kill you if you don't."

"You're not thinking clearly. Killing me isn't an option right now. Tell me what I need to know."

"Stop the blood, you freak!"

"Where is she?"

"Stop it and I'll show you. I'll take you there. I'm supposed to meet her there anyway. She'll be expecting me."

Jane said she thought Santara was crazy, Caleb thought, and the evidence was right here before him. Santara was going to risk bleeding out, and Caleb couldn't afford to let that happen.

"She'll kill her, you know," Santara said. "She's usually so cool, but she wants Jane MacGuire dead. I think it has something to do with you." He gasped. "Stop the blood."

Caleb knew it had everything to do with him. He made the decision. "Shut up. Shallow breaths. Give me a couple minutes."

"I'm feeling weaker. You're not doing —"

"Shut *up*."

It took more than a couple minutes. Santara had let it go on too long. But the blood finally stopped and Caleb grabbed a hand towel from one of the shelves and wrapped it around Santara's forearm. "Let's go."

"I'm too weak right now."

"You'll be weaker if I open those arteries again." He jerked Santara to his feet. "You'll take me to Teresa *now*. You'll tell me everything I need to know about where she is and what I'll have to face to get to her. And you'll do everything I tell you to do to help me get Jane away from her."

"What if she's dead?" Santana asked. "That won't be my fault. Teresa wanted all the ends wrapped up. She even had me kill Gino Romano."

"Believe me, if Jane is dead, I'll consider it your fault." He was pushing him toward the door. "And the fault of anyone else who even touched her or said a foul word to her. Bleeding out will be nothing compared to what you'll all go through before you die if you don't get me there in time to help her."

"Jane's being taken to a small private airport in the desert, near Mleiha," Caleb said as soon as Joe picked up. "That's the airport where Teresa is taking her flight to Moscow. She had Santara arrange with a few of his drug-running friends to set up a discreet disappearance for her. She's occupying one of the dealer's houses, which is in walking distance of the airport, while she's waiting for the plane."

"Jane's alive?" Joe said. "Thank God."

"And she's going to stay that way. I'm on my way there now," Caleb said grimly. "Though we've got to move fast. Teresa is going to be tying up loose ends, and one of them is Jane. We may have a little time. She delights in taking time with her cat and mouse games, and I can't see her not doing that with Jane. But her plane is supposed to arrive to pick her up at one."

"And Jane won't be with her when she leaves," Joe said. "How long is it going to take us to get there?"

"Forty minutes. But Santara says that Teresa had him set up protection for her until she boarded the plane. Six men, including Ganlad, who will be delivering Jane to her. It will be hard to get near her."

"Shit. Positions?"

"I'll have them for you by the time you get there. Santara is having trouble remembering. He says it's my fault because he's so dizzy. I'll nudge him a little." He paused. "But I can't risk Jane's still being alone with Teresa when any attack begins. End of game."

"So what do you do?"

"Insert another piece into the game to keep it going. I'll call you again when I'm closer to Mleiha," he replied, and ended the call.

"She's alive," Lisa whispered. "I was so scared, Joe."

"Me, too." Joe hung up and turned to Palik in the backseat. "Do you know anyone in Mleiha that we can hire on this short notice?"

"Can I work miracles?" Palik asked. "Maybe one or two. But I'll lose credibility with anyone I bring in to —"

"*Do* it," Lisa said fiercely. "I'm the one you don't want to lose credibility with, Palik." She met his eyes. "We're not going to lose her. Do you understand?"

Palik nodded slowly. "I understand that you're more like your brother than I thought." He averted his gaze and reached for his phone. "Two. I can't promise more

550

than two."

Lisa whirled on Joe. "You're not going to have enough people. You're not Superman. What are you going to do? Tie me up in the backseat so that I'm safe and won't get hurt? Take a chance that Jane will live through what's going on in that house if one of Santara's men rush in because we don't stop him? Well, I won't take that chance." Her eyes were blazing in her white face. "Dammit, give me a gun and tell me what to do. How many times do I have to tell you? I can *help,* Joe."

He stared at her for a long minute. Then he reached down and took the gun from his leg holster and handed it to her. "Stay close and obey orders," he said curtly. "I don't think Jane would forgive me if I got you killed."

Mleiha, United Arab Emirates
Wednesday, 12:40 P.M.

The first face that Jane saw when she opened her eyes was Teresa Romano's. She was smiling as she gestured for Ganlad to put Jane down on a low scarlet paisley couch a few yards away. "Ah, now that's timely. I didn't want to waste a moment." She waved a hand at Ganlad. "You may go.

551

I won't need you."

"Santara said that there might be extra money in this for me," Ganlad said.

"Then you can discuss it with him when he gets here. Get out."

He hesitated and then turned and left the house.

"Fool." She went to the parquet desk and picked up a sleek pearl-handled gun from the top drawer. "He should know I can take care of the rest myself." Her smile widened. "Would you like a glass of wine, Jane? I believe that the tradition is a last meal or something like that, but I have no servants here and I —"

"You're very satisfied with yourself." Jane lifted her hand and rubbed her neck. It was sore and she was a little dizzy, but she had to function. She was not going to let herself be killed by this bitch. Teresa had taken too much from everyone she had touched over the years. She had to be stopped before she —

Oh dear God. Caleb.

The last thing she remembered was Santara's leaving her to go after Caleb. Was that why Teresa was being so smug? "Caleb?"

"I'm sure that Santara told you that I'd ordered our mutual friend be taken out."

She stiffened. "And he did it?"

"I haven't had a report back yet, but I'm sure Santara —"

"Then he might not have been able to do it." She had to believe that. Caleb had been warned, and that might be all that was needed. "And you might not ever have a report from Santara again. You were afraid to put him up against Caleb when he had Lisa."

"Surprise could be everything. It was time for Caleb to go. Sometimes fate takes a hand, and this could be that time. I deserve it." Her gaze was moving hungrily over Jane's face, trying to extract every bit of emotion. "You'll miss your lover? Oh yes, I can see it. But I told you that you'd never be enough for him. And you won't miss him for long. I promise you'll join him soon."

Block the panic and the pain. "Santara didn't call you."

Her lips tightened. "He will, or he'll show up here, as we agreed. He won't let me get on that plane without my giving him his money for the kill."

The kill.

Caleb.

She wouldn't be able to maintain control if she let Teresa keep digging, probing, using Caleb to hurt her.

Change the subject, but keep Teresa talking until her mind was clearer and she had a plan. "That's a very elegant pistol. Do you even know how to shoot it?"

"Close range," Teresa said. "I admit that I didn't bother to learn much more. It was far easier to hire someone to do it. But you're the daughter of a detective. I suppose you know far more."

Jane glanced quickly around the room, looking for a way out. Elegant furnishings that all had an Arabic flavor. French doors that appeared to lead to a terrace. Another carved door at the other end of the room. "Yes, Joe taught me, and I'm pretty good."

"But here we are, and all that coaching isn't going to help you one bit. All I do is come a few steps closer and I can hit the center of your forehead with no problem at all." Her smile was triumphant. "I win, Jane. I always win."

"Then why did you feel that you had to bring me here and brag about it?" Had the hypodermic been found when she was unconscious? She lifted her hand to rub her temple and felt the thin cold metal right above her elbow. One shake would bring it down to her palm. If she could get close enough to Teresa to use it. "Are you feeling insecure? Are you trying to rid yourself of everyone who you feel threatens you because you know you're not smart enough to deal with them?"

Teresa's smile lost only a little of its brightness. "Insecure? Do you realize what I've done? I've gotten the best of everyone. I'm going to live the life of an empress."

"In Russia. You always wanted to be the queen of society and have everyone bow down to you. But how are you going to get anyone in social circles there to recognize you as anything but a criminal who just happens to have money?" She slowly sat up on the couch and swung her legs to the floor. No sudden movements to startle or threaten her. "They'll find out about you and you'll be a very lonely empress, Teresa."

"You lie." Her eyes were blazing. "No one will find out. You can buy anything with enough money."

"That's true. I'm sure that the people who cared about Haroun's death will pay an extraordinary amount of money to find out how he died. When they do, they won't bother with extradition; they'll send assassins . . . like Santara."

"But I might decide to hire Santara to protect me from them." Her lips curled venomously. "He's been very accommodating."

"If he's still alive now. You're not sure of

anything."

"I'm sure that you'll be dead in about twenty minutes. Think about that, Jane. When that plane touches down, you'll no longer be able to —" Her phone rang and she glanced down at the ID and a smile lit her face. "Oh, Santara's still very much alive." She answered the phone. "Tell me you didn't fail me, Santara." She listened and her smile widened. "By all means. I told you I'd have the money waiting for you. Five minutes." She hung up and turned back to Jane. "You look a little sick. I told you surprise could be everything. No more Caleb. I knew when I first saw him as a young boy that he was only someone I could use and then toss away. And I did it, didn't I? I rather like the idea of him ending up as a pile of ashes that I could scatter into the wind."

Jane felt sick, too. No more Caleb. Hold on. Don't give up. It might still not be true.

But there was less chance of that now. And if it was true, then she couldn't let either one of these monsters walk away from what they'd done. "Santara could be lying to you."

"He isn't. I tell you: I won. Caleb is nothing. He was always nothing. I just didn't realize it. It was all my imagination that made me believe that he could make me do what he wanted me to do." Her head lifted. "I hear Santara's car." She moved quickly toward the front door. "You'll see."

"Will I?" Jane got to her feet and turned toward the door. She mustn't appear to be a threat. But she *was* a threat now. One shake of her arm and the hypodermic would be in her palm. Teresa was going to be occupied with Santara, and this could be the moment.

Teresa threw open the door. "Come in and show this bitch proof, Santara. Give me details. I told her that —" She frowned. "You look terrible. You're white as a sheet."

"How do you expect me to look?" He strode into the house. "You're the one who sent me after that freak." He nodded at his bandaged arm. "He almost killed me before I took him out."

Jane went still. Teresa might not be aware of what that wound meant, but Jane was. If Caleb had gotten that close to Santara, then there was no way that he should be alive.

Unless Caleb wanted him to be.

Distraction. Caleb had sent him in as a distraction so that he could make his move.

But Teresa still had a gun, and when Caleb made that move, he could die.

No!

"You heard her." Jane moved to where Santara was standing next to Teresa. "I didn't believe her. Details. Convince me."

Wait for the moment.

"I don't have to tell you anything, bitch." He didn't look at her. "Give me my money, Teresa."

"Maybe." Her gaze was narrowed on his face. "Or maybe not. You're one more end to tie up, Santara. I was going to wait until right before I got on the plane, but this will —"

Now!

Jane dived forward and tackled Teresa just as she raised her gun and pointed it at Santara.

Teresa fell backward, but not before she pressed the trigger. The gun went off!

Jane felt the bullet graze her temple as she frantically shook down the hypodermic into her palm.

Teresa was cursing, her lips curled viciously as she pushed Jane over and then took aim again. "Do you think you can beat me? I don't let anyone beat me. You're just some little whore Caleb took to screw. And I took you both down. And now I'll put a bullet in —"

Jane plunged the hypodermic into the hollow of Teresa's shoulder and pressed the plunger even as she dodged sidewise to avoid that second bullet.

"What did you —" Teresa was gazing in horror down at the hypodermic sticking out of her shoulder as the gun dropped nervously from her hand. "What did — you do to me?"

"I have no idea." Jane was breathing hard as she stared down at her. "It's a gift from Caleb. But I hope it's fatal."

"It is." Caleb was standing by the open French doors. "Curare, one of my favorite South American remedies. But you couldn't wait a few more minutes, Jane? I send Santara inside and then all hell explodes in here. I gave Quinn the signal to take out her guards and I was supposed to dispose of Teresa, but you did it instead." He crossed the room and pulled Jane to her feet. "Okay?"

She nodded jerkily, still looking down at Teresa. The woman's eyes were open, but she was fighting for breath. "I had to be sure. She had — that gun. She could have shot you."

"Kill — you." Teresa was gasping, her eyes on Caleb. "Kill you all. I'll win. I always win."

"Not today." Jane dropped to her knees beside Teresa, staring into her eyes. "Not ever again," she said fiercely. "And you never won anything from Caleb. Don't think you did. He never let you take anything from him. You only gave him the weapons to kill you."

"No!" Her eyes were wide with horror. "I won't die. You can't do that to me. It's not supposed to be this way. I'll never let it —"

Her face froze with disbelief, and then her mouth fell open in a silent scream.

She was dead.

Her eyes were still staring in horror up at the ceiling.

Over, Jane thought as she gazed down at her. All the death and destruction caused by this woman is over.

Caleb was suddenly tense. "Stop right there, Santara."

Not over.

Santara was standing by the French doors, a gun in his hand — the gun Teresa had dropped when Jane had stuck the hypodermic in her shoulder.

"Stop, hell." His eyes were glittering in his pale, strained face. "You stay away from me, Caleb. Don't you touch me, you freak. I have money in Cayman, and there's a plane landing now that can take me out of here." He swung the gun to cover Jane. "You take one step and I'll put a bullet in her. I want to do it anyway. In fact, I may come back and do it later." He turned toward the open French doors. Then he suddenly whirled back and fired directly at Caleb.

But Caleb had already dropped to the floor, jerking Jane with him.

Santara didn't stay to risk another shot, but dashed out of the house.

"Son of a *bitch.*" Caleb was up and after him in a heartbeat. Jane was on his heels.

Santara was on the runway, close to the jet, and waving at the pilot to lower the steps.

The steps swung down just as Santara reached them.

But someone reached Santara before he could start to climb them.

Dark hair flying, dark shirt and pants, slender body taut and lithe as she launched herself in a tackle at Santara.

Lisa.

Jane gazed in horror as Santara's gun lifted, pointed at Lisa's head as she covered him with her body, her hands flat on his chest.

But he wasn't pressing the trigger; he was screaming, his spine arching in horrible pain. He was thrashing back and forth, his eyes on Lisa's face.

Then he was still, frozen rigid with pain

even in death.

Jane stopped short on the runway, stunned.

Then she saw Caleb beside Lisa, lifting her gently off Santara's body. He held her for a brief moment and then set her on her feet.

The sight shattered Jane's shock and she ran over to her. "Dear God, Lisa." She didn't know what else to say as she stared at her. The shock she was feeling was nothing to the frozen expression she saw on Lisa's face.

"He was going to get away," Lisa said dully. "I couldn't let him get away, could I?"

"No." Jane took her into her arms. "You couldn't do that."

"And he hurt people." Her body was stiff against Jane's. "He liked to hurt people. He hurt *you*, Jane."

"Let's get you back to the house to sit down."

"Not now." She moistened her lips and pushed Jane away. "I have to see if Joe needs me. There were still a couple of Santara's men we hadn't found. They might have run away, but we have to be sure. Joe says you always have to be sure." She brushed her hair away from her face with a shaking hand. "I shouldn't have left him. But I saw Santara and I had to come."

"I think Joe can do without you," Jane said gently.

"He shouldn't have to do without me. I promised him I'd obey orders." She turned and started back up the hill. Her back was rigid, as if she would crumple if she didn't keep it very straight. "I'm fine. I can help. . . ."

Jane whirled on Caleb. "Why did you just stand there? Why didn't you say something to her? You saw what she did and what it did to her."

"There wasn't anything to say. Not now." His gaze followed Lisa. "And she's right to go help Joe. It will help her, too. Hunter instinct. . . ."

"She's not a hunter. She's a nineteen-year-old girl."

He shrugged. "We'll see." He took Jane's arm. "And now we'll go and see if we can also help Joe and do something to make these bodies go away before we have diplomatic problems with Dubai."

She was immediately brought back to a horrible reality. "And get you out of Dubai before they find out about you and Haroun. I can't let you take the blame. It wasn't your fault. It's mine. You did it for me."

"Nothing I do is any fault but my own." He smiled faintly. "But I knew you'd feel like that. I can manage to shoulder almost any guilt, but I find I can't permit you to do it." He paused. "So we're fortunate that Haroun made it through that operation with flying colors."

She stopped, her gaze flying to his face. "What?"

"I told you I'd do my best." He grimaced. "And Haroun required my best. He was a very hard sell, since I couldn't give him names or any info regarding you. But he eventually allowed me to persuade him under certain conditions."

"Persuade."

"Oh, I used that, too. But he was more interested in getting the names of the moneymen in the royal family who had funded his assassination. I had to make a few promises to get him to arrange to fake his death."

She was dazed, trying to make sense of it. "But Asad Kadir, that orderly who reported to Santara that he'd seen Haroun's body?"

"Staged. And the rest was pure Persuasion to make his panic appear authentic to Santara." He grimaced. "Much easier than Haroun. The bastard even had me on a time limit. He agreed to give me only five hours before the rumors that he'd died on the operating table had to be refuted. He was afraid the stock market would plunge at the news and hurt Dubai's economy."

"But he's alive." The relief was overwhelming. "Dear God, Caleb. He's *alive.*"

He nodded. "More alive than most people I've met. He's fairly exceptional. I was glad it worked out."

"And you couldn't tell me, dammit?" Then she shook her head. "No, I know you couldn't. It would have been a risk you couldn't take if I hadn't thought he was dead, too."

"Judgment call," he said quietly. "Not one I wanted to make."

"I know. I know. I'd probably have done the same." She swallowed to ease the tightness in her throat. It was hard to think, hard to absorb everything that had happened in the last twenty-four hours. Death and pain and violence, and yet a good man who might have died had survived.

And people she loved had also survived.

So think of the good things that made life worth living.

She whirled on Caleb. "Do one more thing for me."

"What?"

"Call Haroun and tell him to pull some

strings and get us out of here as soon as possible. I don't care if you reason or blackmail or even use that damn Persuasion. Make it happen." She turned and started back up the hill. "Just get me back to Loch Gaelkar to be with Eve."

CHAPTER 20

Dubai International Airport

The strings that Haroun had pulled had been both efficient and magically speedy, Jane thought eight hours later as Joe drew up at the terminal in front of Caleb's Gulfstream.

"I'll run up and file the flight plan," Caleb said as he jumped out of the car and headed toward the jet. "I'll contact you later, Quinn. If there's any trouble, call me and I'll try to straighten it out with Haroun."

"I don't believe I'll require your help," Joe called after him drily. "Just get Lisa and Jane back to Gaelkar safely and leave all the diplomacy and legal stuff to me. At least no one is going to hire a hit man to take me out. I'm not too sure about your prospects."

Caleb gave him a wave and disappeared into the plane.

"How long will you have to stay here,

Joe?" Jane asked as she and Lisa got out of the car. "I thought we were almost finished."

"We are," Joe said. "The local police just want reports filled out and all the details explained. We tried to blur what had been going on, but explanations will come better from me, since I'm a cop, too. With any luck, I should be only eight or nine hours behind you. I called Jock and asked him to pick you up in Edinburgh when Caleb flies in." He turned to Lisa and said quietly, "You did very well. You can play on my team anytime."

"Thank you." She smiled faintly. "Told you so. Good-bye, Joe." She moved toward the steps. "I'll see you at Gaelkar."

Joe was frowning as he watched her climb the steps. "She's too quiet. She's been like a zombie since we left Mleiha. I don't like it."

Neither did Jane. But she hadn't had time to think about a way to get through to Lisa during the past hours. "I'll work on it." She turned and went into his arms and held him tightly. "I want you back at Gaelkar, Joe. I want us all together, with no exotic bazaars or burning sands or people wanting to shoot each other. You know I'm going to have to answer to Eve if I show up without you."

"Eight or nine hours," he repeated gently.

She stepped back and gave him a quick

kiss on his cheek. "See to it." She turned and ran up the steps and into the plane.

Lisa was sitting on the white leather couch in the main cabin and was staring out the window. She glanced at Jane as she came through the door. "Seth came out of the cockpit and said that he'd been given permission to take off and that we should just relax and try to rest."

"Good for him." Jane was gazing worriedly at her pale face and taut shoulders. "Did he happen to tell you how we're going to do that? Because I haven't got a clue right now."

"Seth said it would be the best thing to do." She looked out the window again. "It's a long flight."

"It's going to seem even longer if you don't tell me what's wrong." She hadn't meant to jump right into jarring Lisa out of this icy lethargy, but she couldn't *stand* it. Lisa was always brimming with vitality and passion. The sight of her like this made Jane ache to reach out to her. "What's wrong with you? How can I help?"

"You can't." Lisa forced a smile. "I'm fine. Everything is fine. Seth is alive. You're alive. What could be better?"

"You tell me," Jane said grimly. "You look as if you're going to shatter in a million pieces if you move the wrong way. Stop pretending and let me do something for you. Talk to me."

"I . . . can't." She moistened her lips. "I want to do it. I think I care about you more than I do anybody but Seth. You'd try, but you couldn't — I'm sorry, Jane."

Jane could see that. There was desperation mixed in that fragile balance that was Lisa at this moment. Whatever was bottled up inside her, she wasn't going to be able to release right now.

But that didn't mean that she couldn't give Lisa the knowledge that she was here for her.

"Scoot over." She grabbed a fur coverlet from one of the chairs and sat down on the couch beside Lisa. "You don't have to say anything." She pulled her close and tucked the throw over both of them. "Try to nap. If you can't do that, just relax. That will make Caleb happy, and that's always the number-one game plan with you."

Lisa was still stiff. "What are you doing?"

"Isn't it obvious? When I was a kid, I wasn't easy for Eve. I'd grown up on the streets and in a dozen foster homes. Independent. Stubborn. Afraid to let even her get too close. But sometimes when things went really wrong for me, we'd curl up together on the porch swing, and that helped. So shut up, relax, and let me pass what I learned on to you."

Lisa's back was straight, unyielding, but she gingerly laid her head on Jane's shoulder. "I'm not a kid."

"I know. Neither you nor Caleb really had the chance to be. So make up for lost time." She was gently stroking back the hair from Lisa's temple. "Hey, use me. And I'll use you. It was a bad day for me, too."

"I know." Lisa was gradually relaxing against Jane. "A day you would never have had if I hadn't come into your life," she whispered. "I *hated* it. And I knew I couldn't ever let Santara hurt you. . . ."

Edinburgh Airport

Jane opened the cockpit door the moment Caleb turned off the engine after taxiing to the hangar.

"Go back there and be with Lisa," she said curtly. "She needs you. And don't tell me to wait or that it's not the time. You *make* it the time." She dropped down in the copilot's seat. "I'll wait here for you. I did my best and it was a good best. But nothing's going to help until you tell her how to handle this."

571

Caleb's gaze was on her face. "I knew there would be a problem. Did she talk to you?"

"Lisa? I tried to get her to talk, but she wouldn't do it." She met his eyes. "But I figured it out pretty quickly. She wouldn't talk to me because she knew I couldn't understand. No one could understand but you." She paused. "That was the first time she'd used her blood talent to kill anyone. She's probably filled with all kinds of confusion and emotions. Even if Santara deserved to die, killing is a terrible thing. To kill as Lisa did must be traumatic."

"She's known it was coming for most of her life," Caleb said. "She was welcoming it when she thought it would protect me." He nodded. "But, yes, the first time isn't easy to accept." He got to his feet. "I'll take care of it."

"How do you take care of something like that?"

He smiled. "I talk to her about choices and forgiving herself and then I listen and let it all come out." He shrugged. "And maybe I tell her about what I went through my first few times. It might help her."

It was indicative of Caleb's feeling for Lisa that he was willing to reveal that vulnerability. "It might help her more if you can convince her not to do it again."

He turned and opened the cockpit door. "That's included under choices." He closed the door behind him.

She leaned back in the seat and tried to relax. It might be a long conversation, because Caleb would take his time and not cheat Lisa of one bit of the attention she needed from him.

Choices.

So much of her life since she had met Caleb had been connected with choices. Good choices. Bad choices. Sometimes no choice at all because it was safer. She had made a lot of those decisions over the years.

And Caleb had made choices, too. One of those choices had been to come after her and save her life when he knew that it could mean losing his own.

And there had been other choices that had saved both her and Eve and Michael. Easier to sidestep those choices and ignore them because the emotional impact would have been too great to ignore otherwise.

But after today, it was time to look at all those choices and make a few more of her own. . . .

"Better?" Jane asked quietly as she walked down the airplane steps with Lisa after

Jock's car drew up in front of the hangar.

Lisa nodded. "Much better."

Jane smiled. "I should have known that Caleb would be able to 'fix what ailed' you as they say in Atlanta."

"What a peculiar saying." Lisa smiled faintly. "And Seth told me to fix myself and he'd always be around with a Band-Aid. I told him that you'd already given me one."

"Not nearly as effective, I'm certain."

Lisa stopped as they reached the bottom of the steps. "No, but healing, very healing." She gave Jane an awkward hug. "It made me feel . . . wanted."

"And you are." Her arms tightened around Lisa and then she took a step back. "Go on. Eve's going to want to know everything that happened. Joe has already talked to her, but the main thing she's going to want to know is that he's safe. Make sure you tell her that this final cleanup he's doing isn't dangerous."

Lisa frowned. "You're not coming with me?"

Jane shook her head. "I have a few things I need to talk to Caleb about. Tell Jock I'll wait until Joe flies in and return to Gaelkar with him."

Lisa nodded. "Whatever." She moved toward Jock's car. "Seth didn't mention you weren't going with me." She smiled mischievously at Jane over her shoulder. "But I was talking all about me, wasn't I? He probably couldn't get a word in edgewise. I can never imagine anything more interesting than what I'm going through." She picked up her pace as she saw Jock wave to her. "See you later, Jane."

Jane lifted her hand and watched Lisa get into the car. Lisa was always making flip comments about herself and her own self-absorption, but she had tried to protect Jane today at the risk of her own life. So how did that relate? She was probably as complicated in her way as her brother.

What was she thinking? No one was as complicated as Caleb. She turned and went back up the steps of the plane.

Caleb was waiting for her at the top of the steps with a cup of coffee in his hand. "Hello." He handed her the cup. "I thought you'd be back. You were far too quiet when I came back after talking to Lisa. But then Jock called and said he was coming onto the airport grounds, and I knew you wouldn't be happy until you knew for sure that Lisa was going to be all right."

She took a drink of the coffee. "You're right. I had to know." She smiled. "So I had to ask her. That's why I went down to the tarmac with her. It was far more reassuring coming from her than it would have been from you."

He went still. "Then why did you come back?"

"Unfinished business." She set her cup down on the table beside the door. "We have so much unfinished business, Caleb." She moistened her lips. "And I'm going to choose to finish it tonight, if you're willing." She began to unbutton her blouse. "Choices, Caleb. How many times have you told me that I was afraid of you, that otherwise I'd —"

"What is this?" He was very still, his eyes on her fingers moving on the buttons. "Why now? What are you doing?"

"You didn't let me finish." She shrugged, her fingers dropping away from the open shirt. "I *was* afraid of you. I always felt too much whenever I was around you. You played all those mind games with me and I never knew where I was at." She met his eyes. "Or where you were going to take me. I still don't. But I'm choosing to take a chance on you."

"Why?"

"Because you *mean* something to me. I don't know what it is yet, but I get angry when I think of what you went through all those years ago. I'm mad at myself that I might have treated you like that, too, because you made me feel —"

"Don't be foolish. You never treated me like them," he said harshly. "You don't know anything about what I —"

"No, I don't. And I probably won't ever know. But I know I'll never judge you because of fear or ignorance again."

"No, you'd rather melt all over me with that crappy sympathy," he said through set teeth. "I told you I didn't want or need it. I've never needed it. My terms, Jane. Always, my terms. So get the hell out of here."

"Why? Because you'll only come after me again." She took a step toward him. "Or I'll come after you. Because it's not finished."

"No. But then it will be on my terms. It won't be because you think I saved your damn life and —"

"Which you did."

"Or because you listened to all that crap from Lisa about how we grew up."

"Not crap. But in the end, the main effect of that was that it held up a mirror to me."

His lips twisted. "And judging by the fact that you're taking off your clothes, you're letting that mirror reflect a person dripping with pity who's trying to save me from myself with sex." He added mockingly, "Not that I don't approve of the means. It's my very favorite. It's just in this case, I resent the implication that I —"

"Shut up." Her hands clenched into fists at her sides. "Don't you know how hard this is for me? I'm trying to be honest with you because I believe it's the only chance we have. But truth makes me incredibly vulnerable with someone like you." She moistened her lips. "But there's really no one like you, is there? You developed that Persuasion as a protective device, but you became too good at it. For heaven's sake, when you were only a kid, you found a way to dominate Teresa Romano. The only way she thought she could regain control was to kill you."

"Extreme example, Jane."

"Is it? It's one of the things I have to learn about you. I want to learn, Caleb. I don't think you want me to be anyone but who I am, but I could be wrong." She stared him in the eye. "Am I?"

He was silent. "God no," he finally said roughly. "I have more than enough to deal with in you as you are."

"Then deal with me." She shrugged out of her shirt and let it drop to the floor. "But no hallucinations about rose gardens or Cira and her Antonio or any of the other tricks you can pull out of your hat. All very fascinating and addictive." She was walking toward him. "But I want it to be honest, Caleb. Please. No Persuasion."

He let her come within a foot of him before he spoke. "You made the choice. This may not be what you want from me. Too bad. I'm not going to let you go."

She took another step. "Honesty is all I want from you, Caleb."

He gazed at her for an instant and then slowly nodded. "No hallucinations, no game playing." He was smiling at her. "This time. But I'm not going to be able to hold off forever. I want you addicted." He was shrugging out of his clothes. "I want you to wake in the middle of the night burning. I want you to reach out for me in the dark and feel empty if I'm not there. I want you to look at me across a room and feel your stomach clench because you want to take me inside you." He was quickly stripping off her clothes. "Too long, Jane. We've waited too long."

Yes, we have, she thought dazedly. And she couldn't wait any longer. She could feel the warmth his naked body was emitting. She tried to step closer to him.

"No." He was lifting her, sliding her legs around his hips. "Let me. . . ." He was sitting down on the couch, positioning her, while his lips moved across her breasts, biting and licking.

She inhaled sharply as he took her nipple in his teeth and shook it. More. She needed more. She tried to move closer.

"No."

"Don't tell me no. I *need* it. Don't try to control me."

He stopped and then chuckled. "Control can be good in this position." He looked her in the eyes. "But have it your way."

He was suddenly inside her.

But still moving excruciatingly slowly, filling her, teasing her.

She couldn't breathe. She was dizzy, shaking.

Then she was burning, throbbing, her skin flushed, her whole body racked with sensation.

"I could go on like this." His voice was suddenly thick, tense. "But it will kill me."

"That can't happen." Her nails dug into his shoulders. "I won't — allow it."

"Thank God." He lifted her and then plunged deep.

She cried out.

Wildness.

Fullness.

Deeper.

She heard him muttering in her ear, but

she couldn't make out the words.

Fast.

Fierce.

Lifting.

Moving.

Strong. He was so strong. . . .

He was looking down at her, his face flushed, his lips beautifully sensual. "I . . . need —" He broke off. "Don't look now, but that control you were so afraid of is about to . . . shatter." His head lowered until their lips were only a breath apart. "With your permission . . ."

She couldn't answer. She lunged upward, taking his mouth, taking anything and everything he was offering.

Madness.

Wildness.

Deeper.

She was gasping.

Sensuality.

Darkness.

Flame.

Caleb!

She desperately held on to him as wave after wave of pleasure rocked through her. She kept her eyes closed because opening them might mean it was over.

Darkness.

The feel of his body against her.

The sound of his heart beneath her ear.

But he was leaving her. . . .

Then she felt herself being shifted to lie on the leather couch and the fur throw being draped over her body. "I don't want that throw." She opened her eyes and saw him sitting on the couch beside her. "Poor substitute, Caleb."

"I'm glad you think so. I'd be disappointed if you didn't." He was smiling down at her. "But I thought it was wise to give you a break. You're still very tentative about me. And I don't know if I can obey your rules next time." He bent down and kissed her breast. "But I did pretty well, didn't I?"

"You could say that." Even now she could feel her breasts tighten and start to tingle as he touched them. "I think. I was a little dizzy and not noticing much. But it felt as if you were being honest with me. That was what was important."

He sighed. "Then I have to admit I wasn't entirely honest." His dark eyes were dancing with mischief. "No heavy stuff. No hallucinations or changing perceptions. I just cleared the way so that you'd feel everything more intensely."

"Caleb."

His smile faded. "Opportunity was knocking. I wanted to make sure you enjoyed it.

582

Because there wasn't any way I was going to let you walk away from me afterward."

She stared at him with exasperation and trepidation. "Listen to you. That's exactly why I've been so wary of you since that first day I met you. I'll walk away if I please, Caleb. But I don't want to do it. That's what I was trying to tell you."

He was silent. "And I listened, but I know there will come a time when you'll want to walk away. You can't really trust me, can you? Why should you be different from anyone else?" He smiled mockingly. "So I'll take what I can get and make certain you enjoy the giving."

She wanted to reach out with tenderness and pull him close. But he wouldn't accept that from her because he didn't believe it had anything to do with him.

"You're thinking too much." He lifted the fur throw off her and tossed it aside. "That's always bad for me. We probably have six hours before Quinn shows up in Edinburgh. Suppose I try to eliminate the thought process until he walks through that door?" His lips slid down from her breasts to her belly . . . and then lower, rubbing back and forth against her softness. "Let's start here. . . ."

■ ■ ■ ■

"When Quinn just called, he said he'd be another thirty minutes." Caleb was still naked as he lay on the couch, watching her dress. "We could do a lot in thirty minutes. Trust me."

"Oh, I trust you." She glanced at him and then looked away as she felt the stirring. "In that category, you're absolutely reliable. But I'm not going to have Joe walk in on an orgy."

"We didn't have an orgy. Next time, I'll show you orgy."

"I don't believe many people could tell the difference." She tried to keep herself from thinking about the last few hours. Erotic. Imaginative. Completely sexual. Caleb. "But evidently you're an expert, so I won't give you an argument."

"And you didn't," he said softly. "Not once. It was . . . extraordinary. Thirty minutes . . ."

"No," she said firmly. "Joe."

He grimaced. "Okay. I should stop pushing it. It's a lost cause where you're concerned. Quinn was like a father to you while you were growing up. You have all those family feelings for him."

"Yes, I do." She glanced at him. "You once said that one of the reasons you liked to be around Eve and Joe and me was that you liked to watch us together."

He nodded. "The family dynamic is a curious and wonderful thing." His tone was purely objective. "I always found it fascinating."

Because he's never had it himself, she thought. "It's more than that." She finished buttoning her blouse. "Eve and Joe's wedding is going to be scheduled for next week. You'll be there, won't you?"

"I doubt it. I have business to take care of in Dubai. I'll be leaving right after I deliver you into Quinn's hands."

She stiffened. "Dubai? You didn't mention it."

He gave a half shrug. "It doesn't involve you any longer. You'll be safe and back with Eve and Joe."

"It doesn't involve me? Everything that happened in Dubai involved me. Why are you going back?"

"I promised Haroun that if he went along with arranging to fake his death that I'd not only put down Santara and Teresa but I'd also get rid of the money people in the government who had financed them. It made it far more palatable to him to know that he wasn't going to have long-term enemies ready to stab him in the back."

"So you're going to go back and let those bastards take their shot at getting rid of you because you might be a future danger? Do you even know their names?"

"Two of them. Palik will have the other name by the time I get back to Dubai." He smiled. "You shouldn't be concerned. I'm a hunter. This will be simple enough. Not like Haroun."

"How do you know?" She could see she wasn't going to be able to talk him out of it. She tried another path. "Will you at least postpone it? Maybe Jock could go with you. And I'd like you to go to the wedding. Eve and Joe will expect you."

"No, they won't. This is your family. I don't belong with them. I'm always the outsider, and that's fine with me. It's better that I go now."

Strikeout. And she was going to be terrified all the time he was gone.

"Then will you try to wrap that damn Dubai business up soon and get back here for it?"

"I won't promise you, Jane," he said quietly. "I'm going to finish the job for Haroun." He rose to his feet with one fluid motion and moved toward the bathroom.

He stopped and looked back at her. "Do you want promises from me?"

She wanted him to be safe. But they were still too tentative and uncertain with each other for her to ask him to do anything against his will. She didn't know if she would ever be able to do that. She didn't know what those promises would mean or what she'd have to give in return. "No, I don't want you to give me promises."

He smiled and nodded. "I didn't think so. So I'll go keep my promise to Haroun. And then afterward I'll take you to my place in the Highlands and show you all my dark secrets and we'll discuss orgies." He closed the door.

She was filled with bewilderment and fear as she stared at that door.

No promises.

Outsider.

Secrets.

All the elements that had defined their relationship in the past. In spite of that erotic experience that had changed her concept of what sex could be, she couldn't tell whether or not she had made inroads in establishing a permanent foothold on this perilously rocky relationship with Caleb.

Or if she wanted to do it.

These last hours had given her a taste of

that erotic skill and sexual dominance that Caleb possessed and used so well. It had shaken her to the core.

She was backtracking, she realized. Going back to the fear and wariness that she'd sworn she'd never feel again. She would *not* do that. She'd decided she wanted him in her life and she would meet all those damn challenges he'd thrown at her.

She just didn't know how the hell she was going to do it.

EPILOGUE

Loch Gaelkar
Sunrise

Eve gazed out over the lake as the pink and gold streaked the sky and turned the mist hovering over the water to stormy amethyst.

The sight filled her with wonder along with a deep thankfulness and contentment.

"Beautiful," Joe said across the tent from where she was standing by the open entrance. But his eyes weren't on the lake. He sat up in the bedroll and held out his arms. "Can't sleep? As I recall, this wedding isn't supposed to be until sunset. Having second thoughts?"

She smiled as she went back and fell to her knees beside him. "I wouldn't dare. After all, I'm responsible for this shindig. Not that you would know it. Cara, Jane, and Lisa have completely taken over all of the arrangements. I've only been allowed to take care of Michael." She chuckled. "And what about you? I'm the one who proposed to you and then promptly sent you out to hunt and gather for the ceremony." She went into his arms and cuddled close. "If anyone should be having second thoughts, then it should be you. You've not had an easy life since you knocked on my door all those years ago."

"True. It's amazing that I put up with you," he said gruffly. "It just goes to show what an incredibly forbearing man I am that I was able to do it."

"Yes, it does," she said softly. "And I thank God every day for it."

"Hey, you're being a little more than I can handle today." He got up on one elbow and looked down at her, his brown eyes, which were so like Michael's, glittering with moisture. "I have an idea you're going to tear me apart."

"Nonsense. You're too tough." Her hand reached up to stroke his cheek. There was the faintest stubble and it was like a caress on her palm. "You can take it. I just wanted to tell you something before we go through that wedding ceremony today. You know I love you. That goes without saying."

"Well, a little 'saying' doesn't hurt."

"It's just that it's always there. It never

goes away. Every time I look at you, I think about how much I love you, Joe Quinn." She put her fingers over his lips as he started to speak. "Let me finish. When I first thought about doing this, I believed it was all about Michael and conforming to society and making life as easy for him as possible. All very good, solid reasons. But after I came here and had time to think, I realized that it was also about us. It was about remembering the past and celebrating the present and looking forward to a wonderful new future. In a way, it was Cira who taught me that, Joe."

He kissed her fingers and moved them from his lips. "Now that's remembering the past in a big way if you're hobnobbing with Cira," he said unevenly.

She smiled. "I wouldn't presume. That's Jane's territory. I've just been thinking a lot about her and her son Marcus and her Antonio. And about all her struggles and triumphs and tragedies. Her story is all about life and how we all have to face it and make the best of it." She met his eyes. "And how, occasionally, someone comes into your life who makes it so special that we have to acknowledge and celebrate the beauty of it." She lifted her head and gently kissed him. "That's what we're going to do today,

Joe." She kissed him again. "Life will never be easy for us. That's not the kind of people we are. But when it gets rough, we'll be able to look back and remember the people we love who are here and one perfect day of celebration."

"Are you done?" He was holding her close, his lips buried in her hair. "Because I'm not as tough as you think I am." She could feel the dampness on her cheek. "Am I allowed to say how much I love you and how glad I am that you came into my life and let me join this celebration?"

"Of course." She held him tight, feeling his heart beat against her. A golden moment.

Life. Love. Celebration.

"Because you're the one who makes it perfect, Joe. . . ."

Sunset

Caleb wasn't here.

Jane's gaze was roaming quickly over the guests strolling about the hillside before it was time for the ceremony. So many people from Eve's past and present. Catherine Ling having a glass of wine with Venable, Eve's old friend from the CIA who had first recruited her. Kendra Michaels talking to

Beth Avery, Eve's half sister, at the magnificent buffet table Lisa had spent hours preparing. Jock sitting beside Cara on the bank of the lake, smiling as he watched her tune her violin.

But no Seth Caleb.

What had she expected? He'd said that he might not make it. And she'd told him she didn't want him to promise her anything. She was *not* disappointed.

It just felt that way for this one solitary moment.

"It's going to be a beautiful wedding," Margaret Douglas said as she came to stand beside Jane. "But why wouldn't it be in a setting like this?" She suddenly chuckled. "Is it true that MacDuff arranged to have one of his men signal the start of the festivities by playing the bagpipes?"

"With some encouragement from Lisa," Jane said drily. "She said, 'What's the good of being in Scotland if you can't be authentic?' But she refrained from ordering them played during the entire ceremony. However, it was only because she had other plans." She looked around the hillside. "Where's Juno? I saw her earlier."

"I left her over there where Michael's playing. She didn't want to leave him." She gazed at the white retriever, lying quietly beside the small boy, watching his every move. "She thinks he might be magic."

"Don't we all?"

"But she's almost sure of it." Margaret smiled. "And why not? There's so much magic in this world that we don't even notice. It's nice to have confirmation that every now and then it shines brightly enough to light our way." She met Jane's eyes. "We were all glad it was bright enough to bring you back safely to us."

"That wasn't magic. It was people who cared and went the extra mile for me."

"And you don't think that's magic? I do." She glanced around her. "Speaking about the extra mile, I haven't seen Caleb today."

"He said he might have another commitment." She shrugged. "His loss. There are so many people here that Eve and Joe won't miss him."

"No? But I understand that he makes his presence felt." She looked out at the lake, which was beginning to glow and shimmer with the scarlet-and-gold reflection of the setting sun. "Sundown," Margaret said softly. "It's almost time. This is just the right hour for the wedding, isn't it? All that golden mist that seems to be fading and then returning, swirling, and then hiding wonderful secrets."

Secrets, Jane thought, gazing into the mists.

Cira?

Bonnie?

Trevor?

Will we ever learn all your secrets?

And do we want to know them?

Why not live life to the fullest and have wonderful secrets of our own?

Honor the past. Remember with love. Reach out for whatever is given to us every single moment.

As Eve and Joe were doing on this day.

The light was fading, only the glittering water and golden mist remained.

The bagpipes sounded. Wild. Lonely. Stirring.

And Joe and Eve were walking down the hill together, holding hands as they walked through life. They were both dressed simply, as Eve had decreed for the ceremony. Joe was in black pants and a long-sleeved white cotton shirt. Eve had chosen a rust-colored silk maxi dress that caused her red-brown hair to glow in contrast.

Wonderful. Natural. Perfect.

Jane could feel her throat tighten as she watched them approach the priest, who was waiting beside the lake.

The piper had stopped his music, replaced

by Cara playing the Rachmaninoff Eve loved. The strains of the violin floated over the hills in wild beauty that touched the heart.

Jane could see the priest's lips move, but she was only aware of Eve's and Joe's expressions, the love that went on forever, the serenity of certainty, the eagerness of looking at what lay ahead.

And they were all being permitted to share it with them. She could see the knowledge of that privilege on the expressions of the people who were gathered here. How fortunate to be here in this incredible moment. How lucky she was to have had Eve and Joe in her life. When so many other people had never known anything but bitterness and pain.

Caleb.

He should be here, she thought. Not for Eve and Joe, but because, in this moment, these friends who had come to be with them were also like members of their family. The family Caleb had never had. Gathered from all corners of the earth, from all walks of life, they had still become a family because of how they felt about one another. She desperately wanted Caleb to know that was possible. That if he reached out, he wouldn't have to be alone. She wanted to tell him, *teach* him.

Eve and Joe were now turning to face them all, laughing as they raised their joined hands.

Applause and cheers. There was a surge as everyone moved across the hill toward them.

Jane was applauding, too, and started to rush —

She stopped.

She could feel something. . . .

She turned toward the slope that led to the road.

He had come only halfway down the slope and was standing there watching, alone.

Caleb.

She could barely make him out in the darkness that was falling so rapidly. He was almost a shadow figure, standing there with legs slightly parted and that easy, jaunty set to his shoulders. If she could see his face, it would probably have that mocking smile that was so familiar.

None of it mattered. He had come.

Yet he was so alone.

And he had lessons to learn.

She smiled and reached out her hand to him.

ABOUT THE AUTHOR

Iris Johansen is the *New York Times* best-selling author of *Hide Away, Night and Day,* and *No Easy Target,* among many others. She began writing after her children left home for college, and first achieved success in the early 1980s writing category romances. In 1991, she began writing suspense historical romance novels, and in 1996 she turned to crime fiction, with which she has had great success. She lives near Atlanta, Georgia.